THAT'S ME IN THE MIDDLE

By the same author in this edition:

Three Cheers for Me
The Journals of Bartholomew Bandy Volume I

THAT'S ME IN THE MIDDLE

The Journals of Bartholomew Bandy

VOLUME TWO

REVISED EDITION

DONALD JACK

A DOUGLAS GIBSON BOOK

M&S

McClelland & Stewart trade paperback edition published 2001
First published in hardcover by Doubleday Canada Limited 1973

National Library of Canada Cataloguing in Publication Data

Jack, Donald, 1924–
That's me in the middle

(The journals of Bartholomew Bandy ; 2)
"A Douglas Gibson book".
ISBN 0-7710-4379-1

I. Title. II. Series.

PS8519.A3T42 2001   C813'.54   C2001-901127-X
PR9199.3.J33T42 2001

Portions of *"Conversation Galante,"* from *The Complete Poems and Plays: 1909–1962,*
by T.S. Eliot. Copyright © 1963, 1964 by T.S. Eliot. Reprinted by permission of
Faber & Faber Ltd.

We acknowledge the financial support of the Government of Canada through the
Book Publishing Industry Development Program for our
publishing activities. We further acknowledge the support of the
Canada Council for the Arts and the Ontario Arts Council
for our publishing program.

Printed and bound in Canada

A Douglas Gibson Book

McClelland & Stewart Ltd.
The Canadian Publishers
481 University Avenue
Toronto, Ontario
M5G 2E9
www.mcclelland.com

1   2   3   4   5   05   04   03   02   01

Contents

PART 1

Mon Commandant   1
The Auchinflints   11
Bulrushes   19
A Big Cheese   38
Seated in My Office   50
Lord Rackingham   56
All Kinds of Disgraceful Goings On   68
Me, Riding to Hounds   88
Treadwell   98
That Rotten Boy Again   106
My First Speech   117
Flight from Fallow   136
Hopelessly Lost   144
Picking Morosely at My Wings   160
Me, Hedging   169
In the Mess Again   173
In Disgrace   177

PART 2

Posing with the Forty Thieves   187
Looting and Pillaging   221
Deep in Conversation   257
Me, on My Honeymoon   267
Catching Up   283

Beside a Brook, Babbling   294
Wearing a Hunted Look   301
At the Garden Party   314
That's Me at the End   334

THAT'S ME IN THE MIDDLE

PART ONE

Mon Commandant

After lunch that Saturday, the instructors gathered in the mess to moan and complain to each other. The clouds were wet and low, and there were no training flights, but so far the commandant had refused to give the word that would have let us off for the weekend.

"Doing anything this evening, Bart?" Fielding asked. "Assuming the old grouch lets us off at all?" Fielding was a lanky, nineteen-year-old captain whom most people thought conceited.

"I was supposed to be spending the weekend with my fiancée–"

"Aye, aye."

"–and her family, in Berkshire," I said, gazing morosely out the window at the moist airfield and the mixed bag of B.E. 12s, Bristol Fighters, Armstrong-Whitworths, Sopwith Camels, and Avro 504Js that littered the airfield.

"That's several miles, Bart. Are you sure your navigation is up to it?" Fielding asked.

"Well, I can always fly low and read the road signs."

"They wouldn't have stopped training in the old days for weather like this," Potter said hoarsely. Red-faced and patriotic, he was one of the few instructors who had not flown at the front. "Two or three hours' instruction, then pack 'em off for a solo, regardless of the weather. Huns, we called them. The pupils, that is."

"Yes, you used to get rid of them pretty fast," Fielding said pointedly.

I went over and sprawled in an armchair beside Captain Treadwell. He looked at me searchingly for a moment before staring down again at his brilliantly polished boots.

"I remember the old days, too," Fielding said. "The instructors didn't give a damn about the students. They nearly broke my neck for a start."

"What a terrible loss," somebody muttered.

"Fighting, that's the main thing," Potter said. "I don't go for all this mollycoddling."

"I remember an instructor," I said, "who allowed one of his pupils, a former Lancashire comedian, to solo after only half an hour."

"Half an hour's a bit short, I must admit," Potter conceded. "He must have been a born flyer."

"Actually he had no particular aptitude for flying," I said. "It was just that the instructor had a prejudice against Lancashire comedians."

The adjutant, who was standing at the bar busily wringing pink gin out of his mustache, turned and said, "Doesn't seem to matter whether you mollycoddle them or not. Look at Mansergh."

He was talking about a charming but hopeless pupil of mine, Michael Mansergh. Michael was a splendidly patriotic Irishman who had escaped from a German prisoner-of-war camp in 1916 and made his way back to England to receive a Military Medal and a commission.

This achievement could have kept him out of the fighting for the rest of the war. Nevertheless he had transferred to the

Royal Flying Corps, where the average life expectancy was less than a month.

The trouble was he had shown no aptitude whatsoever for flying. The day before he soloed, for instance, he had stalled an Avro 504J and very nearly dropped it smack onto Southsea Pier. As I was also in the Avro I'd determined there and then to wash him out for good. Besides, he'd already had eight hours' dual instruction.

Unfortunately, on returning to Fort Grange airdrome, at Gosport, he had, purely by chance, made his first good landing, and the commandant, witnessing this, had insisted on his being put down for a solo flight the following morning.

Michael had survived his solo all right, but not a lone trip a few days later. It was supposed to be a cross-country exercise, but he had somehow strayed over the Channel. A soldier walking along the shore near Abbotsbury had seen his plane dive in and sink several miles offshore.

After the adjutant's remark there was a brief silence. Potter muttered, "Don't know why you were all so fond of that Irishman. What was so special about him? Getting a medal for escaping, I ask you. They'll be dishing them out with the porridge next," he added, looking at my row of ribbons.

"He didn't get it for escaping," Fielding said. "He got it at Mons, where he was captured."

"There you are, you see? They even give you a medal for being captured."

Treadwell stirred and prepared to speak. We waited expectantly.

I liked Treadwell. He had the complexion of a Sicilian bandit, and dark, disbelieving eyes. The way he looked at you made you feel as if your flies were wide open – and that you were aware of it.

"Another instructor I heard about," he said slowly, "allowed a student to solo even though it was obvious he was practically blind."

Everybody fell silent. Treadwell spoke so rarely that everybody listened intently whenever he did.

"The student," he said, "was so shortsighted he had to feel his way along the fuselage to find the cockpit."

"Well, I never."

"Did he survive?" somebody asked.

Treadwell considered the question carefully. He always thought carefully before answering, however trivial the query. "He fractured quite a few planes," he said at length. "But they kept him on, until the day he mistook a playing field for his airdrome and landed in the middle of a rather important cricket game. A county match. That was going too far, of course. They washed him out after that."

He thought for a moment, then added, "He knocked down the wickets, you see."

The adjutant then turned and treated us to a rather long-winded account of his first experience as a pilot. He had arrived at a training squadron in Surrey in a wicked downpour, he said, and it had continued to rain for weeks on end. "Nineteen sixteen it was. Rather a wet summer, actually." After nearly a month of complete inactivity the aircraft had begun to turn moldy in the hangars, the students were sunk in a state of dank despair, and even the instructors were becoming irritated because they couldn't fly off to binge at other messes. To make matters worse, another intake arrived prematurely, so the whole airdrome was choked with students, "all splashing around like pregnant ducks."

Finally the rain stopped and the sun came out, and the instructors rushed onto the field to see how many students they could train from scratch in one day, before the rains returned. The adjutant was one of the first to be picked.

"We taxied about for a bit, occasionally hopping into the air to make sure the Longhorn was still capable of flying with all that fungus on it," he said. "Then we did a circuit and bump. Then the instructor climbed out and said, 'Right, lad, you're all set to go solo.' And hurried off to train the next man in line."

The adjutant turned back to his gin. Potter said, "You soloed after that much training? That was very good, Adj."

"No, I didn't, as a matter of fact," the adjutant said. "Actually, as soon as the instructor disappeared, I got out of the plane and went back to the office for a cup of tea. You see, the instructor had grabbed me and rushed me to the aircraft before I had a chance to explain that I wasn't a student at all. I was just a pay officer who happened to be passing the hangar at the wrong moment."

There was quite an uproar at that, cut short abruptly as the commandant strode into the mess with a creak of bones and leather. He cast a glowering glance over our erect forms before waving us down again. He joined the adjutant at the bar.

"He's got his spurs on," Captain Cole whispered as the commandant ordered a whisky.

We all looked at the commandant's feet. He had his spurs on, all right. Everybody brightened.

The commandant was a cavalryman who had transferred to the R.F.C. soon after it became apparent that horses were not going to be much use in the trenches, except as a supplement to the field rations. But his heart, or rather his heels, were still with the Charge-of-the-Light-Brigade days and he always wore spurs when he went flying.

As he was wearing them now, it meant that he intended taking off for the weekend. Which meant that those of us who were prepared to brave the elements would be allowed to fly off for the weekend as well.

But he continued to stand at the bar and glower into his whisky without uttering a word except to bark for the whisky bottle. When the mess waiter handed it to him, he examined the label closely.

"WEE SLEEKIT COW'RIN' TIM'ROUS BEASTIE HIGHLAND CREAM," he read, then handed the bottle back despondently. "Good God," he muttered. "What a war!"

The murmur of conversation slowly revived as the commandant made no move except to stamp his foot now and then and snort through his nose.

"I'm sure he was a horse in another life," I whispered to Treadwell.

"Look who's talking," Captain Jolley said.

"Bandy!"

I started, thinking the commandant had overheard me.

"Sir?"

"Slacks and shoes again! Slacks and shoes!"

"Yes, sir," I said. Then: "How d'you mean?"

"How do I mean? I mean slacks and shoes! That's what I mean!"

He meant that I was wearing slacks and brown shoes instead of the regulation breeches and boots. Slacks and shoes were not yet officially permitted. Nevertheless, a fair number of R.F.C. officers wore them, and most C.O.'s were resigned to the new informality.

"An officer should set an example, Bandy!" he barked into his glass. "Can't have him going round looking like a traveling salesman. Breeches and boots, Bandy, breeches and boots!"

I opened my mouth to reply. Someone tugged at my sleeve and whispered, "Don't argue with him or he'll never let us off!"

So I didn't argue. Besides, I knew he was just warming up. I knew the real reason he was in such a bad temper.

Sure enough, just as we were starting to mumble among ourselves again, he turned and gave that ferocious glare of his that had been known to silence a flock of crows.

"And another thing, Bandy! Young Noakes-Brierley! You've recommended that he be washed out. That correct?"

"Yes, sir. His heart's not in flying."

"But damn it all, man – his father's an aircraft manufacturer!"

"Well, you see, sir," I said, in what Fielding, in one of his friendlier moments, had once described as my whining North American drawl, "he keeps missing 'A' Flight hangar."

"What's wrong with that?"

"By inches. The fact is, sir, he'd much rather write poetry than fly."

"Poetry? Rubbish!"

"Actually, some of it's quite good."

Trying to sound threatening – and succeeding – the commandant said, "His father, Bandy, happens to be a very good friend of mine."

"You could see for yourself, sir," I answered, placatingly and respectfully; at the same time looking at him in a manly, clear-eyed fashion to show that however perversely and illogically he might behave, I myself would remain a model of restraint, the very soul of reason. "Why don't you take him up for a few minutes?"

But this didn't seem to appeal to the commandant. Perhaps he had seen Noakes-Brierley just missing "A" Flight hangar.

I watched him cautiously but not unsympathetically. I quite liked the commandant, though I was aware that he looked on me with a certain uneasiness, as if he suspected I was some kind of imposter but couldn't decide what kind.

I had an idea he still wasn't finished with me. I was right. He said suddenly to the adjutant in a loud voice, "Well, Colin, perhaps it's just as well, what? After all, look what happened to that other pupil of his – Mansergh."

My mouth contracted to the dimensions of a wrinkled rosebud. Heartened by this response, the commandant turned back to me.

"Damned funny business that, about Mansergh," he barked.

"How d'you mean?"

"I mean it was a damn funny business!"

I looked away, still pouting.

"Falling into the sea like that," the commandant went on.

"Well, I told you he was a hopeless flyer," I muttered, running a forefinger up and down the red brocade of my armchair.

"Even a half-wit can tell the difference between land and sea. Or perhaps you're telling me Mansergh was a half-wit?"

"Certainly not." Somebody tugged at my sleeve. "He was just a hopeless flyer, that's all."

"He soloed perfectly!"

I continued to run my finger over the brocade. It had a raised pattern of red weals and welts, as if somebody had recently given the armchair a thorough flogging. "Well," I mumbled, "I still think he wasn't cut out for flying."

"Maybe you're not cut out to be an instructor, either," the commandant said meanly.

"Well, I don't care. He just wasn't ept, that's all."

"Wasn't what? Ept? *In*ept, man!"

"Exactly. He wasn't any good."

"He was!"

"Wasn't."

"He was! I saw him!"

"And I flew with him."

The commandant started to glare this way and that as if searching for some reply that might be lying about unused.

Failing to find one, he had to fall back on "Not good enough, Bandy. Not good enough; that's all I can say." He turned to face the bar again.

"I know," I said. "I kept telling you he wasn't good enough, but you wouldn't listen."

By now, all the officers were glaring at me, having given up all pretense at nonchalant conversation. Captain Jolley heaved a loud sigh, slammed himself into a seat, and, as if to emphasize the hopelessness of the situation, picked up the first volume of *War and Peace* and turned pointedly to page one.

"He was a rotten flyer," I said. Then, after another nasty pause: "Rotten."

The commandant's knuckles turned white.

"I kept telling you," I said. "But no, you wouldn't listen."

Perhaps it was just as well I couldn't see his face.

The adjutant could, though. He looked worried.

"Don't pay any attention to Bandy, sir," he said. "You know it's not good for your veins." He turned and gave me a warning look over his sodden mustache.

The commandant continued to stand like a pillar of salt for what seemed like several minutes, glaring into his glass. We were all familiar with this posture. He was busy summoning up some lightning repartee.

Finally a suppressed smirk twitched across his shopworn face. He turned confidentially to the adjutant, and in a very loud aside whispered, "A pilot who could fly fifty miles without realizing that his underwear was streaming out behind him, is in no position to criticize other people's abilities; that's all *I* can say. Mentioning no names, mind you." And he turned back to his drink and chortled into it; but a moment later couldn't resist flicking me a glance of utter triumph.

He was referring to a juvenile prank of Fielding's. A few days before, I'd been sent up to flight-test an Ak-W. While I was running up the engine, Fielding had sneaked up and tied a pair of yellowing long johns to the tail skid. By the time I arrived back over Portsmouth the underwear was ballooning most obscenely. Several people had complained to the commandant about it, including the mayor of Portsmouth and, for some reason, the R.S.P.C.A.; and also a naval officer, a friendly rival of the commandant's, who had rung up to ask if this was a new signal the R.F.C. was originating, to indicate an aircraft in distress.

"Wasn't my fault if some saboteur stuck a pair of coms on my airplane," I muttered.

When Brashman looked at me and nodded encouragingly, I went on, "Anyway, it's no worse than a certain person I could mention, who got his spurs caught in the rudder bar during a dogfight, causing him to crash-land slantwise on some Chinese coolies."

This was exactly what had happened to a certain party I could mention. He or she had caught his – or her – spurs in the rudder of a Morane Parasol and had come down smack in the middle of a Chinese labor company that was cutting timbers for the Somme battlefield.

The commandant's neck turned brick red.

"And being chased into the woods by a maddened Chinese chappie with a machete," I murmured.

The commandant gave a bellow, raised his arm, and flung his glass at the wall. It struck a colorful poster advertising Peace Bonds, and shattered into a thousand shards.

Potter ducked nervously. Captain Jolley sighed, gave me a look, then turned viciously back again to page one.

The Auchinflints

It was a flight of less than three hours from the School of Special Flying at Gosport to my fiancée's home in Berkshire; thirty-seven minutes, to be exact.

As I came spluttering and banging out of a dampish cloud and glided over Burma Park in my tastefully decorated RE.8, I caught sight of Katherine on the far side of the enormous front lawn. She was strolling across the wet grass with a couple of guests, a short man and a tall woman.

Katherine was wearing a leather coat. It was so long that the skirts were trailing on the ground. She flapped one of the sleeves at me as I sped onward toward the house at about 100 feet.

The Lewises' wee Scots maid also waved to me from the kitchen door at the back of the house, with what was either a very short scarf or a longish piece of haddock. Or possibly it was a bulrush. A malicious neighbor had given Mrs. Lewis a book for Christmas on the art of cooking bulrushes. Discovering that cattail, plantain, and sheep sorrel flourished, even in December, in the swampy pasture to the east of the house, she was instantly converted to the art, declaring, ad nauseam, that it was our bounden duty to eat weeds and thus conserve the nation's larder. In typically autocratic fashion she had imposed the new regime on the entire household, including the servants; though how she managed to reconcile her determinedly patriotic words with her equally determined purchases of black market products I don't know.

However, everybody put up with it, because they adored her and also because they guessed that the fad wouldn't last any longer than had her attacks of Confucianism and beekeeping.

I banked carefully over the tree-lined avenue that led from Burma Park to the outside world, cut power, and drifted down over the greenhouse. The biplane leveled, sank, held off a few inches above the grass, then bounced gently onto its wheels and tail skid.

In a few seconds it was rumbling along at taxi speed, leaving behind three wavy green lines in the soaking lawn in front of the Lewis family's Georgian mansion, which I had fallen in love with from the moment I first clapped eyes on it.

Come to think of it, that was almost exactly one year ago. I had crash-landed on their estate while I was learning to fly, in January 1917. Katherine, then a shy, withdrawn girl of twenty-two, had found me wandering in the woods. Thinking I was suffering from concussion – though in fact I was wearing my normal expression – she had led me up to the house to meet her father. Had I really been in a state of shock, this might not have improved matters much, as Mr. Lewis was a pretty disorientating sort of person, with the kind of mind that tended to fade out at awkward moments, like the newfangled wireless signals they were using on the Western Front.

Heaven knows how Mr. Lewis had managed to last so long at the Foreign Office, or even to get into it in the first place. The main trouble was that he was more interested in ferns – Pteridophyta was his hobby – than in writing stiff notes and persuading excitable foreigners to pull themselves together and start behaving sensibly, like Englishmen.

When I finally met her, Mrs. Lewis was even more of a shock. Some years older than her husband, she was an autocratic dragon of a woman whose conversation was like an artillery barrage. If you didn't get your head down right away, you were likely to be demolished by her first salvo. Only last week in London she had reduced a posh dinner party to a shambles, with her subversive intervention. I had loved her from the moment she first hit me with her knitting needles.

But initially it was the house itself that had impressed me most. The first Georgian house I'd seen, it stood on a grassy plateau in an estate of several hundred acres; it had held me spellbound from the moment I first came out of the woods and gazed upon its graceful chimneys and its long, white, superbly proportioned façade softly tinted by the amber sunlight. With every subsequent visit my feelings for Burma Park had kept pace with my growing affection for its occupants; an unfamiliar sensation, for affection had been considered rather a sissy sentiment at my home in the Ottawa Valley.

Two minutes after landing, the RE.8 was bedded down under the trees near the west corner of the house, the engine clicking its teeth noisily as it cooled.

Having arrived, I proceeded to pack my bags for the journey.

I'd just finished transferring my best uniform to the valise when Katherine came up. She draped the half-empty sleeves of her leather coat over my shoulders, and stood on tiptoe to give me a kiss.

"I couldn't find my coat so I put this one on," she explained, when I asked her why she was trying to disguise herself as a seal. "It's Robert's old flying coat. He's got one of those new, electric sidcots." Robert was her brother, who had miraculously survived one and a half years of the air war and was at present flying with a Home Defence squadron in Essex.

The two guests with Katherine strolled up just then. One of them was Edith Auchinflint. She was still wearing her moral expression. I'd warily jousted with her the previous weekend at a London dinner party given by the Air Minister. The man with her looked rather dramatic in a dark cloak over a strangely cut gray suit.

Mrs. Auchinflint stopped dead when she saw my pink and yellow aircraft.

"My," she said after a slight pause. "Colorful, isn't it?"

Mrs. Auchinflint (pronounced Afflunt, for some peculiar English reason) was a tall, bony woman with a mass of dark hair mantling her topknot. She had a thin, hungry face and a pair of sarcastic brown eyes.

At the moment, however, she was looking at me with an expression of amusement. It was the first time I'd seen her smile, and I was surprised how youthful it made her. I'd taken her to be over forty, but at the moment she didn't seem to be a day over thirty-nine.

"How very original of you to arrive this way, Mr. Bandy," she said, as Katherine took my arm and hugged it to her. "Are you allowed to go wherever you like in that gaily colored craft?"

I admitted I could, within reason.

"How very convenient," she murmured, her eyes straying to her companion, who was walking slowly around the Harry Tate. "By the way, this is Donald Andreyevitch Rodominov, a Russian friend of Mr. Lewis'."

"How d'you do?" I said heartily. "Donald, that's a fine old Russian name."

Rodominov, a short, crude-looking man with a heavy face, paid no attention, but continued to inspect the aircraft from all angles. He stopped and looked up at the enormous exhaust scoops above the engine, and frowned. Admittedly they looked like factory smokestacks, or possibly a couple of old drainpipes that some apprentice designer had welded onto the engine in a fit of aesthetic incompetence; but that was no reason, I thought defensively, for him to look at them quite so critically.

"He was given that name by his Scottish nanny," Mrs. Auchinflint explained, drawing her brown fur coat around her lisle shanks. "Perhaps she was homesick for Scotland. His parents didn't mind, apparently."

Rodominov was now peering into the rear cockpit. He spoke for the first time.

"You have your drawers in here," he said.

I nodded. Mrs. Auchinflint frowned, hesitated for a moment, then went over and looked in as well, and saw it was true. I had my drawers in the rear cockpit.

This was one of the advantages of owning a two-seater. Most of the air staff at Fort Grange airdrome had been provided with single-seat Camels for joyriding, attending binges at other messes, and for flying home to their loved ones – and occasionally their wives. But there hadn't been a spare Camel for me when I arrived at Gosport, and I'd had to make do with an RE.8 observation machine.

I'd been flying Sopwith Camels myself on the Western Front for several months, and at first I'd thoroughly despised the lumbering, sway-backed Harry Tate, with its smokestack and generally winded appearance. I'd always considered the RE.8 a machine fit only for transporting elderly staff officers from their rear headquarters to destinations even farther behind the lines.

But after a few days I'd begun to appreciate its phlegmatic performance. Its steadiness in the air was a pleasing contrast to the alarming gyrations of my students. And when I realized the full possibilities of the rear cockpit I was completely converted. It was a perfect place for packing my smalls whilst visiting my fiancée. So I'd had one of the riggers build a small chest of drawers into it. This, incidentally, improved the plane's center of gravity no end. By the time a Camel became available I wouldn't have parted with the dear old Harry Tate even for one of the new Snipes.

Rodominov listened attentively as I told him all this. Halfway through my recital he turned to stare at me. As I talked I found myself peeling off my flying helmet and flapping it about. The

Russian made me nervous for some reason, perhaps because of the intensity of his gaze.

He continued to stare unblinkingly at me. But I wasn't to be intimidated. I picked up my valise in a decisive sort of way. Then I put it down again.

Without preamble he began to ask me all kinds of questions about the RE.8, concerning its speed, range, and capacity. His voice was a surprise. I'd expected something as deep and murky as a Siberian forest, but it was light, almost peevish in tone, as if nothing ever quite came up to his expectations – including the speed, range, and capacity of the RE.8.

His interrogation ended as abruptly as it had begun. He turned away restlessly and started to cough. He took out a lady's handkerchief and spat at it.

For a moment I thought he was some kind of misogynist. But then I recognized, from my four years' training as an undistinguished medical student, the symptoms of T.B.

"Come on; it's freezing," Katherine said, tugging at my arm. "Let's go inside."

Rodominov trailed increasingly far behind as the rest of us made our way up the grassy plateau on which the house stood. "Who is he?" I whispered as we approached the front door. "Looks like a trainee anarchist to me."

"He's a prince, actually," Katherine said. "He's with the Russian Embassy."

"Assuming there still *is* an Imperial Russian Embassy," Mrs. Auchinflint said in a schoolmistressy voice. "I can't quite see the Communists continuing to supply it with funds, can you, Katherine?"

"No, I suppose not," Katherine said vaguely, recollecting that there had been some kind of revolution in Russia recently.

"Did you say he was a prince?"

"Yes."

"You mean like the Prince of Wales?"

"Hardly," Mrs. Auchinflint broke in with an indulgent smile. "His title is, or was, fairly common in Russia. He's a *knyaz* by Imperial decree rather than by descent. He prefers not to use his title, by the way."

"What do we call him – Comrade?"

"For heaven's sake, don't do that," Mrs. Auchinflint said quickly. Then: "Oh, I see. But I wouldn't joke about the Bolsheviks if I were you. Not after what they did to his family."

As we crossed the entrance hall her husband, Major Auchinflint, emerged from the drawing room on the left.

"Where've you been?" he asked sharply. "You were supposed to be playing bridge." The way he was looking at his wife suggested he was about to tear off her buttons and badges and drum her out of the regiment forthwith.

"I thought your friend was talking to Mr. Lewis."

"They finished half an hour ago. I've been looking all over for you."

"I'm sorry, dear," Mrs. Auchinflint said, neutralizing his acid tones with the alkali of her indifference. "We just went out for a short walk, that's all."

Auchinflint (who was also pronounced Afflunt) was a major in the Royal Artillery, attached to the War Office for special duties of an unspecified nature. He was already developing the War House rump. This, in combination with a small head and a prominent beak, gave him the appearance of a bad-tempered ostrich.

He regarded his wife irritably for a moment before turning to Katherine. He smiled briefly at her, then nodded at me.

"It's you," he said, cleverly disguising his ecstasy at meeting me again.

He grimaced at his boots for a moment; then, in a series of jerks, cranked his head up until he was staring though the fanlight above the front door.

"I, yah," he began; then cleared his throat and started again. "I understand you've been up to Bland House again," he said abruptly.

Bland House was the London residence of the Secretary of State for Air, Lord Rackingham. That was where I'd first met Major Auchinflint, and when Lord Rackingham had taken me into his study for a casual chat after dinner, the major had been consumed with curiosity to know why I was being thus favored.

Possibly he had also been a bit jealous, as he had been hoeing and cultivating that particular garden himself, in the hope that some influential crop might result.

And now he had heard that Lord Rackingham had invited me back the following Wednesday for another cozy discussion about the Flying Corps.

Auchinflint seemed to be reading some special significance into this. He didn't seem to realize it was just another of Lord Rackingham's unconventional impulses. Since his appointment as Air Minister, Rackingham had been seeking out the views of some quite insignificant members of the Flying Corps, instead of relying exclusively on his senior advisers. He had got into this bad habit during his years with one of the country's great newspapers. As a result, he was said to be causing a great deal of friction at the Ministry.

"M'yes," I said. "We did have another little chat."

"What about?"

"Oh . . . Flying Corps organization," I whined airily, and gestured in a lordly fashion, to give him the impression that

I'd been setting the Minister straight on a few points of government policy.

In fact, Lord Rackingham had done nearly all the talking, while I'd spent most of the time fidgeting about in his senile armchair.

Bulrushes

Half an hour later I was safely ensconced in Katherine's sitting room, having washed and brushed up, and changed into my best regimental tunic. Mrs. Lewis had given Katherine permission to serve afternoon tea in her rooms upstairs.

I was feeling only slightly peckish that afternoon, so contented myself with just three tomato sandwiches, two tea cakes, and one hunk of birthday cake. Katherine had celebrated her twenty-third birthday ten days before.

After all, I didn't want to spoil my appetite.

But then I remembered we were still in the Bulrush Period. So I hurriedly polished off the sponge cake and the gingerbread cookies; and, on an afterthought, ate the last piece of bread and butter as well.

"Are you sure you wouldn't like me to fetch you the loaf?" Katherine inquired. "And some cheese?"

"Oh, no," I said, sighing contentedly and stretching my legs toward the fire that glowed hotly in the grate. "I mustn't be a guts. Unless – what kind of cheese is it?"

Katherine picked up the poker and weighed it thoughtfully for a moment before leaning over to give the coals a couple of whacks. She hunched her shoulders together, with her hands on her knees and said happily, "This is lovely and cozy, isn't it?"

"Sure is."

"Just you and me, and a lot of empty plates."

She raised her eyes to mine. The very slight squint in those lovely dark eyes of hers made her look enticingly erotic.

But of course it would have been ungentlemanly to do anything about it. After all, we were practically in her bedroom.

No. I was no more capable of behaving dishonorably than of being irrational or disrespectful. My religious training had seen to that. I had been brought up to respect a woman's virtue – a bit more than they seemed to respect it themselves, as a matter of fact.

"Who's coming to dinner, by the way?" I asked, wrenching my gaze off her ankles.

"The Honorable Hyphenated and his wife. Rody. Some M.P. or other. The Auchinflints," she said, in that abrupt way of hers. "Mrs. Cary . . ." She hesitated; then, with a mischievous smile: "General Perris."

"Oh, gosh. Not him *and* Auchinflint?"

"'Fraid so."

"After the way he treated your father, I'm surprised they're still on speaking terms."

"They barely are. But Papa has fresh instructions from the permanent under-secretary. General Sir Hubert Perris has to be Firmly Spoken To."

Her father, who had been given the thankless task of dealing with Irish affairs, had been attempting for some weeks to persuade Perris to behave a little more tactfully as Commander-in-Chief in Ireland. Perris, apparently, was a Protestant Ulster supporter and had little sympathy for the aspirations of the southern Irish.

I looked up as a sudden thought struck me. "Does he know about the Bulrush Regime?"

"No."

We began to titter and giggle.

"He doesn't know he'll be expected to eat . . .?"

"Nobody else does, either. The only guests who know are the Maitlands – and they're not coming. They telephoned last night and babbled some excuse or other. Mother was very annoyed."

After a bit more spluttering and sniggering: "I wouldn't be surprised," she said, "if Papa's done it on purpose."

"Yes. . . . He has a mean streak in him, all right," I said, suddenly morose. I was thinking of the Fallow Speech.

The headmaster of Fallow, a posh public school in Chester, had recently bullied me into agreeing to address the school on their next speech day. The Fallow Speech was traditionally delivered by a war hero, but none had been available for March. So Mr. Lewis had persuaded the headmaster to invite me – though Lewis must have known that no good was likely to come of it. Apart from anything else, I'd never delivered a speech in my life.

There was a sudden movement opposite. Katherine had leaned back on the sofa and put her arms behind her head.

"Bart?"

"Yes?"

"We won't be disturbed for several hours, you know," she said, looking innocently at the ceiling. She started to whistle tunelessly.

I wished she wouldn't do that – put her hands behind her head, I mean. She didn't realize it, but this had the effect of tightening her clothing and outlining her form rather.

I cleared my throat and moistened my index finger and dabbed it daintily around the Crown Derby to pick up a few crumbs. "How's, um, how's the hospital?" I asked.

She lowered her arms hopelessly. "Packed full of wounded," she said.

She was now doing part-time work as a nursing assistant at a hospital near Maidenhead. She had resisted war work for many months, after meeting a chap called Bertie Russell, a mathematics teacher and defender of conshies. However, pressure from practically everybody in the county (except her own family) had finally driven her into war work.

"I had to carry somebody's leg out of the O.R. the other day," she said. "Matron found me weeping over it in the corridor, and she said if I had to go around dripping tears like that, I should save it for the floor, which needed washing. So she made me scrub the corridor.

"I scrubbed 960 square feet of it," she said wryly. "I worked it out."

"I guess they don't like you upsetting the patients."

"I'm cheerful, usually. I get on very well with the soldiers. They're so lovely, I almost hate to see them leave."

"With you around they probably don't want to."

She looked at me with a strange expression. I was somewhat shaken when I realized that it was one of gratitude.

It suddenly occurred to me that though I often felt it, I didn't often show her much affection. It wasn't the custom to show affection in my own family. I suppose I'd never really developed the habit.

I thought it was about time I made amends, so I said, "*I'd* sure hate to leave you if I, yum, was in hospital."

With that over with, I seized the fire tongs and stuck them up the chimney, dislodging so much soot in the process it nearly put the fire out.

Katherine got up and went past the open door to her bedroom and stood at the window, looking out intently.

After a moment I went over to see what she was staring at. Her rooms overlooked the stables. In the yard below, the groom was walking one of the horses. I glanced at Katherine's intent profile, then out the window again, but it still didn't seem a particularly stimulating scene to me, especially when the groom suddenly cleared his throat and spat a great whirling bolus of phlegm past the horse's rump.

As I stood slightly behind her I couldn't help being aware of her chest, delectably rounded under her white blouse. I tried to avoid noticing these things usually, as there didn't seem much point to them – it. I mean, there was no point getting all excited for nothing, was there?

I had to keep reminding myself that women's breasts were there for a purpose, and were not meant to be goggled at.

But somehow that argument was never entirely convincing. I sometimes felt very resentful at Nature, the way She had designed the female breast so provocatively, as if the intention was to lure men to their doom rather than to provide the off-spring with an instant lunch counter. Why the devil couldn't nature have made them square, or bottle-shaped, or something? There'd have been no problem, then. But that blasted curvilinear geometry of theirs, it stirred you up something chronic.

I put my arm round her waist from behind and kissed her rather clumsily on the side of the neck. As I did so my hand shifted slightly, so that my wrist was resting against her left breast. I was dying to raise it a bit higher – my hand, I mean – but she would have been shocked, I was sure. She was tense enough as it was. Her face was unusually hot. Perhaps she had been sitting too close to the fire.

"Fine weather we're having, isn't it?" I croaked, and coughed into her earhole.

She twitched and leaned against me. This was embarrassing. I was now in no condition to be leaned against. I tried to curve my spine outward to avoid any contact between her and my pelvis. But she moved closer again, so I had to crank my spine still farther back, until I must have looked as if I were about to set off on a mad tango with a partner who preferred to dance backward.

"Maybe we – you should lie down after that little snack of yours," she whispered.

"Good idea," I croaked. Letting go of her, I scuttled crabwise to the door and clawed it open.

"Where are you going?"

"Why, to lie down," I said. "Or maybe go for a long walk in the freezing cold," I said, and hurried out. I sped along the corridor to dash cold water at myself in that ancient bathroom of theirs, the one with the huge bathtub with the whacking great canopy at one end – the one with all the knobs marked HOT, COLD, DOUCHE, SPRAY, WAVE, SHOWER, FOUNTAIN, WATERFALL, SPRINKLER, and so forth. The purpose of these controls was to fling water at you from all directions out of numerous ghastly wounds, slits, and gashes in the sides and top of the canopy, but hardly any of them worked any more, especially since the plumbers had been at them. The plumber and his mate had been beating diligently at the galvanized nipples for a solid week, but had utterly failed to trace the course of the water through all those convoluted pipes, bushings, elbows, crossed tees, and extension couplings, and had succeeded only in dislodging a family of field mice and rerouting the used bath water back into the tub though the old gas fixture in the ceiling.

"Damn good job the war came along when it did; that's all I can say," General Perris said. "Just in time to put paid to that Irish Home Rule Bill. What?"

He was leaning against the grand piano in the long drawing room, obviously pleased to be dominating the conversation.

It wasn't much of an achievement. The rest of the guests were too hungry to put much energy into chit-chat. By 1918 the food shortage had become severe, and a free dinner from a member of the privileged class was an event of importance.

Little did they know.

Besides the general, Rodominov, the Auchinflints, and a Conservative Member of Parliament, the guests included the Honorable Hyphenated and his unnecessarily healthy-looking wife. The Honorable Hyphenated was about twenty and had a silly, high-pitched laugh. He was an assistant censor with Military Intelligence. As for his wife, the last time I'd met her she'd talked about nothing but food. She was still talking about it, though admittedly she was beginning to falter as the odor from the kitchen seeped into the drawing room. But she probably thought it was just the cook boiling old underwear in a caldron.

"Quite right, Sir Hubert," Major Auchinflint said ingratiatingly. "Though if they hadn't suspended Home Rule," he went on, "Ulster would have done something about it soon enough."

"Quite right, Auchinflint. By force if necessary. As they did in '12." Sir Hubert rolled his ill-fitting eyes toward the major. "You were one of them, weren't you? The whatyoucallems?"

"Yes, sir. The Ulster Volunteers. We threatened rebellion if the government went through with Home Rule."

"Dashed well think so," Sir Hubert grumbled, addressing the major but obviously aiming his remarks at Mr. Lewis. It looked as if Mr. Lewis hadn't quite succeeded in turning the general into a Hibernophile. "Luckily His Majesty saw the light, and put a stop to that infamous measure. What?"

"Quite."

"What?"

"Quite," Auchinflint repeated.

Lewis murmured, "Nobody's denying that Ireland should remain within the British Empire, Sir Hubert. Even the Irish Parliamentary Party–"

"We'll hold onto Ireland," Sir Hubert interrupted, "for three reasons: the Tory Party, Ulster, and the fact that the mass of British opinion won't tolerate any weakening of our sovereignty over the worthless Irish."

The Honorable Hyphenated called out, "That's certainly true, Sir Hubert. My chief was saying only the other day that any interference in our sovereignty in Ireland was unthinkable. Unthinkable – that's the very word he used." He gazed around, as if inviting us all to celebrate his chief's vocabulary with fireworks and a Lancashire clog dance.

"Those Sin Feigners who started the Easter Rebellion," Sir Hubert said loudly, "I'd have executed every man jack of them, 'stead of just the principals. What? What?"

He was referring to the rebellion in Dublin in 1916. I was still in Canada at the time, and well remembered the stir it caused in Beamington when we heard (some time after it was all over) that Irish nationalists had proclaimed a provisional government and Irish independence and had proceeded to occupy the General Post Office and a biscuit factory or two. They had apparently been taking pot shots at the British for a week before they were bombarded into submission. My father, the Reverend Mr. Bandy, was, I suppose, fairly typical in his outrage at the Irish treachery. "After all England has done for them," he growled, and preached a sermon the following Sunday on the ingratitude of the Irish. However, it's possible that his sermon was inspired not so much by the Easter Rising as by the conduct of his part-time gardener, Kevin O'Keefe, who had won first prize in a lottery after borrowing the ticket money from father, and who had not only failed to share the proceeds but had celebrated by getting drunk and being sick on father's gaiters.

"Executed every man jack of 'em," the general repeated, glaring at Lewis, daring him to reprieve the worthless Irish.

"And look what the government did last July," Auchinflint said. "Let all the remaining rebels out of prison after only a year, allowing 'em to continue their treasonous activities."

"The reason we let them go," Mr. Lewis said, plainly wishing to drop the discussion but unable to let the general get away with his oversimplifications, "is . . . well, with the leaders in prison in England, there was some danger of the Irish Revolutionary Brotherhood taking over the Sinn Fein. The danger still exists, in fact. The I.R.B. are becoming more active every day. The men we held were relatively moderate–"

"Moderate?" Sir Hubert had been trying to ignore the Foreign Office lackey, but this was too much. "Moderate? The men who shot down hundreds of our soldiers in cold blood?"

"As it is," Mr. Lewis persisted, perspiring, "we may have been too late. They elected De Valera as president a few weeks ago – an I.R.B. member."

The general grunted disdainfully and turned his faded eyes in the direction of Mrs. Cary. She was seated on the piano bench, listening with respectful attention.

As he leaned forward, the general's face began to convulse alarmingly, and his chin, already unpronounced, seemed to merge completely with his fluctuating gullet.

For a dreadful moment I thought he was going to vomit into the grand piano. As a music lover of note – several notes, in fact – I made a sudden move to slam the top down before he could ruin all the little felt hammers. I realized just in time that it wasn't nausea on his face at all. It was just an indulgent smile.

"What do you think, Angela, my dear?" he asked.

Mrs. Cary smiled warmly at the general. "Oh, I agree, Sir Hubert," she said. "I agree completely."

As the general smirked contentedly, she cast a charmingly apologetic smile at Mr. Lewis as if to say, "What else can I say?"

Mrs. Cary, whom I had met once or twice before, was the widow of an Indian Army major who had been captured at Kut al-Amarah in 1916. I understood that her husband had refused to believe his own patrols when they informed him that the Turks were just beyond the next sand dune. He had subsequently died in captivity.

Katherine had already warned me twice that Mrs. Cary was a social climber and was not to be trusted. She looked all right to me, though. She was a handsome woman in her thirties, with a smooth round face that she had protected remarkably well from the Eastern sun, and beautiful yellow hair drawn back in a bun. In fact she looked so inviting it occurred to me that Katherine had told me a little fib so I wouldn't get too pally with the widow. In contrast to Mrs. Auchinflint, who looked as if she would find sex rather a bore, Mrs. Cary gave you the impression that she took quite a practical interest in it. She was certainly quick enough to notice the way my eyes kept fluttering to her prominent bust and perching on it unsteadily.

Otherwise she ignored me almost completely. So maybe Katherine was right. After all, I was merely a no-account captain.

The guests were assembled in the drawing room, or Long Room as the Lewises called it. They had different names for everything here, and you weren't really one of the gang until you could use the names with aplomb. The drawing room was the Long Room, the reception room on the other side of the hall was the Small Room because it was only thirty feet wide, the open field in the woods to the east (the East Woods)

was the Wood Pasture, and the lawn in front of the house was
The Field; and while the Lewises usually referred to the house
as Burma Park, you weren't really in with the locals, xeno-
phobes to a man, unless you dismissed Burma entirely and
called it simply The Park.

"Ah, Bartholomew," Mrs. Lewis said as she came sailing into
the Long Room shortly before dinner, wearing several hair
combs, a queenly gown, and a severe smile. "You are here."

"I trust," I said in the courtly manner that Mrs. Lewis often
inspired in me, "that you are in good health, Mrs. Lewis."

"Then your trust is misplaced, Bartholomew," she said, her
voice booming like a sunset gun. "My rheumatism has been
giving me the very devil since that trip in Robert's unreliable
motorcar. And I was so looking forward to the Meet."

"The meat? You've given up vegetarianism, have you?"

"The Meet, Bartholomew. Of the *hounds*, man. I subscribe
to Auchinflint's hounds."

"Oh, I see," I said, taking a sherry from the tray proffered
by Burgess before remembering that I'd given up drinking. I
offered the glass to Mr. Lewis, but he already had one.

"How are you, sir?"

"Fine, thank you, Bartholomew," he said, passing a hand
self-consciously over his scantily clad pate. "I've managed to
get the library sorted out after your last visit."

"Oh, good," I said.

He was referring to my previous visit here, when, Katherine
being away at the hospital, I had volunteered to help him cat-
alogue his library. It was in a state of chaos by the time we
finished, but our efforts were not entirely wasted, as we had
come across some very interesting books that Lewis claimed
to have inherited from his father. These included a first edition
of *How to Carve Fertility Symbols*, and a *de luxe* quarto volume
filled with water colors in the Chinese style illustrating such

loving attitudes as *flexio gallinacea*, *inversio palligrada*, *saltus subversum*, and other erotic games and return matches between greasy Mongols with faces like pig-tailed macaques, and wanton, delicate flower maidens.

We had been absolutely disgusted. But by the time we had this volume classified it was midnight, and time for our cocoa. So the rest of the books, law reports, Dictionaries of National Biography, and works by such enduring writers as William Vaughan Moody, Mrs. Henry Wood, Dinah Mulock, and Mrs. Humphry Ward had to remain where they were, banked up around the great tiled fireplace that the wee Scots maid was forbidden to light because a couple of tits had their nest in the chimney and Mrs. Lewis didn't want to give them a bad cough.

I stood chatting to Mr. Lewis for a few minutes. Nearby, Mrs. Cary was talking to Rodominov.

"I understand you're selling all the paintings you brought from Russia, Prince Rodominov," she was saying, looking at him with a keen smile.

Rodominov glanced at her, then looked away, shrugging.

"I was just asking," she went on, "because I might be interested in purchasing an item or two." When he again failed to respond: "I believe you've sold a few things to my good friend General Pusey, haven't you?"

"Couple of ikons," he muttered, lifting a plant pot and looking under it as if searching for edible insects.

There was an uncomfortable silence until Mr. Lewis changed the subject. I'd no idea what topic was being avoided, until he explained later that like the rest of the Imperial Russian Embassy staff, Rodominov, who was a second secretary, had not been paid for three months and was in financial straits. Lewis thought that Mrs. Gary had been trying to find out just how difficult things were for him.

"In fact," Mr. Lewis said later, "he's having to give up his Bloomsbury flat – or Bloomersbury, as he calls it – and is selling everything he has. We're seeing what we can do – I knew his mother, she's living in Paris now – but he's not an easy man to help."

The Conservative M.P., a man with startled eyes, dinky rosebud lips, and a large portentous belly, thrust his way into Katherine's group, breathing heavily as if he'd just moved several weighty amendments. He took Katherine's hand, patted it, and treated her to an indulgent smile.

"Well, well," he said loudly. "I hear you're engaged at last, Katherine. We wondered when you were going to get married."

"Yes. This is my fiancé," Katherine said, trying to move away from the M.P.'s stomach, which was so large it seemed to scale down the eighty-foot room to the size of a mop cupboard.

"I'm so sorry; I didn't realize you hadn't met," Mr. Lewis said quickly. "Allow me to introduce . . . uh . . ."

He stared at me fixedly, his face taking on a look of rising panic.

There was an agonized pause. Mr. Lewis had obviously forgotten my name. His mind, he once confessed, invariably went a complete blank a split second before a name was mentioned, and even when it was repeated he had difficulty in retaining it. As a result he was terrified of having to perform introductions; but his memory was such that he also frequently forgot to avoid performing them.

Without giving anyone a chance to help him, he rushed on in panic. "And, uh, Captain," he babbled, "I'd like you to meet, tum . . ." And he whirled toward the M.P., obviously hoping to take his memory by surprise. "And this is, un . . . Mr. . . . ."

There was another ghastly silence. Sweat burst from his dome. He went rigid. He had forgotten the M.P.'s name as well.

"Bandy!" I shouted.

The M.P. started back. There was a crunching sound as he trod on Rodominov's foot. The Russian went rigid as well, and turned the color of wet, glistening dough. "Hoots," he said. "Hoots . . ." Then, catching his breath again, he glared at the M.P. ferociously. "*Succinsin!* You crush foot!"

He limped to a settee and fell into it, stretching his neck in a peculiar fashion and hissing. "*Na vsiakovo mudretza dovolno prostoti!*" he said, or words to that effect, and embraced his instep and rocked it back and forth in his arms. "Damn fool!" he exclaimed.

The M.P. stared at him for several seconds in a disorientated sort of way, his little, rosebud lips falling about slackly. "Who the . . . who the devil does he think he's talking to?" he asked in well-modulated, almost reasonable tones. He gave a short, incredulous laugh and stared around at everybody as if genuinely anxious for an answer.

Rodominov shut his eyes and leaned back, panting. The M.P.'s face slowly froze.

"I'm so sorry. It was my fault," Mr. Lewis muttered wretchedly.

Actually it was *my* fault, but I wasn't going to remind anyone of the fact. I had determined to be on my very best behavior that weekend.

"But what do you expect of member of War Committee," Rodominov hissed, glaring at the M.P. with a detestation that seemed out of all proportion to the injury.

I learned later, however, that the two of them had already had an acrimonious argument about the war. The Tory M.P., who represented a Cheshire riding, was a member of the Unionist War Committee, a group of back-benchers who, in response to a growing though still hesitant and fearful tide of criticism of the military leadership, had set themselves up as its defenders in parliament and the country at large. He was

being entertained at Burma Park not because Mr. Lewis had
any sympathy with his views but as a favor to Lewis' superior
at the Foreign Office.

Apparently Rodominov had little sympathy with the M.P.'s
views either, and had not been backward in putting forward
his own opinions.

Katherine, seeing that her mother was enjoying the spectacle
of two grown men glaring and hissing at each other like greylag
geese and had obviously no intention of intervening, hurried
over to Rodominov and whispered, "It was an accident, Rody.
He didn't mean to."

"Was not accident! That is typical of way he walk over
peoples! Is bloathèd, flat-foot reactionary!"

By now the Tory was quivering all over with wrath. "How
dare you speak to me that way, you – damned *foreigner!*" he
spluttered, his face bulging with rage. "By God – you come
over here from that benighted country of yours – throwing
wild parties – debauching our women–! A damned parasite,
that's what you are, sir! Oh, yes, I've heard all about you,
'Prince' Rodominov!"

"And I have heard about you and that committee of jackals
– I hear you talk about nothing but crush subwersives regardless of cost–" Rodominov jumped up, wincing as he put his
weight on his hurt foot. The pain enraged him further. He
started to speak rapidly in a high-pitched, choking voice.
"You know how to deal with them, do you?" he shouted,
apparently taking up a former argument. "With clubs and
bullets, perhaps – the way we try to deal with peasants of
Russia. Oh, yes!"

Mr. Lewis tried to get between the bristling combatants,
but they side-stepped him until they had a clear, uninterrupted
view of each other's hateful faces again. Rodominov's eyes were
glittering like broken vodka bottles.

"To run them down with cavalry – to beat them, starve them, shoot them, until snow is red! That is the way to lead people, oh, yes!" He was jerking his hands around wildly. Mrs. Auchinflint hurriedly moved a tray of glasses out of the way and started to say something in a soothing voice, but Rodominov was shouting again. "You want to encourage revolutionary, tyrants – Bolsheviki! That's the way, oh, hoots mon, that is right way!" He flung out his arms. "As for me, I drink, I gamble, I lie, I cheat – I fornicate like rettlesnake whenever I have opportunity–" Mrs. Cary gasped, and looked at him with increased interest. "But that is nothing, nothing!" the prince cried. Then he started to cough. He dragged out his ladies' handkerchief and held it to his face.

I guess he meant that immorality ought to be of minor concern compared with the unprofitable effects of knouting peasants and intellectuals and people; but judging by the expressions around him he had not succeeded in making his point. Realizing this, he tried to enlarge on his argument, but little emerged except for an incoherent splutter that enraged him still further. He broke into an uproar of Russian in which the hated Bolsheviks seemed to feature prominently.

His extraordinary outburst ended as suddenly as it had begun. He sat down with a bump, and the feverish excitement died from his eyes like doused campfires.

As for the Member of Parliament, he was too busy bursting a number of small blood vessels to respond further. He was dissuaded only with difficulty from storming out of the house there and then.

Finally Mrs. Lewis lost patience with him.

"Don't be so childish, Arthur," she said sharply, with such contempt that Arthur immediately subsided into a grumbling heap. "You know how excitable Russians are. Read Dostoievsky, man!

"Besides," she added, as the rest of us crept silently into the dining room (known as The Dining Room), "you must have heard far worse speeches in that miserable talking-shop of yours in Westminster."

All in all, it wasn't one of the Lewises' more successful dinner parties. Our host was too preoccupied with blaming himself to ease the tension; Rodominov had fallen into a sulk; the Honorable Hyphenated and his wife were too frightened by the sight of the food to utter a word; and the M.P. was too busy glaring at the Russian, as if mentally seeing him off to Vladivostok in a condemned Staten Island ferry.

Only Mrs. Lewis made any real effort to distract the company – but I think they'd rather she hadn't.

"There is a rich harvest of delectable foods to be gathered whilst roaming through field and stream," she warbled, and attempted to prove it by dishing up a four-course meal composed almost entirely of weeds, beginning with a sheep sorrel soup that put everybody off before they'd even tasted it, because of the sluggish bubbling sounds it was making. It looked like boiled swamp. It was an unprintable color.

I was most aware of Mrs. Cary's reactions to the meal, because she was seated opposite me. When she received her soup she looked around with the kind of smile that suggested she thought we were all conspiring to play some practical joke on her, and that the joke was neither literally nor figuratively in very good taste.

When she saw Mr. Lewis begin, albeit resignedly, to actually *eat* the stuff, she looked back at her own soup, and her eyes widened as if she were seeing a miniature version of the

Frankenstein monster clambering out of it, coughing and
retching.

If the soup looked unappetizing, it was nothing to the
boiled cattail that followed. By then it was becoming a visible
effort for anybody except our hostess to swallow a mouthful.
But Mrs. Lewis continued to extol the virtues of wild bulrushes and similar vegetation as if she were talking about
French truffles.

Then came the sweet-and-sour plantain and the lamb's-
quarters fritters, which bore a striking resemblance to rotting
algae. It was at this point that the guest nearest the slime-
covered chafing dishes, the Honorable Hyphenated, abruptly
abandoned his sodden pods and hurried out. He didn't reappear until the port was circulating, and he was still looking
decidedly pale.

He was, of course, never invited back to The Park.

As for Katherine, the crafty devil managed to use the dis-
traction caused by his exit to empty her pods into her new
handbag. It quite ruined the lining, she confessed later, but
she'd had nowhere else to put them, as her father was already
using the nearest plant pot for that purpose.

As for me, I'd have made any sacrifice for Mrs. Lewis. It
wasn't hard. All I had to do was remember the food I'd eaten
in the trenches: the eternal tasteless bully beef, the burgoo, the
heavily chlorinated water, and the biscuits that the rats liked
to use for filing down their teeth.

Besides, it was worth it just to see the general's expression
as, with cleverly simulated appetite, I started to fork great
mouthfuls of the stuff into my mouth. This time there could
be no misinterpreting his heaving gullet.

The irony was that, aside from Mrs. Lewis, the only person
who was prepared to eat the lot was the only one who didn't

have to, as an urgent telephone call came for me in the middle of dinner. It was from Gosport. I was to report back as soon as possible.

Some sort of emergency, they said.

As soon as I got back to the airdrome the following morning, I was summoned to the office. I found the adjutant standing at the window, gazing fixedly into the past.

Without a word he handed me a couple of signals. I peered at them suspiciously.

The first announced that Bandy, B.W., was detached from Training Division and was to report to the Hotel Cecil in London at 10 A.M. next day, for special duties.

For an awful moment I thought they were making me a cook.

The other signal stubbornly repeated what I thought was a misprint in the first. It stated that Acting Tempy. Captain Bandy, B.W., was gazetted Acting Tempy. Lieutenant-Colonel, effective immediately.

Lieutenant-Colonel. Not captain any more. Not even major. Lieutenant-Colonel.

Lieutenant-Colonel Bandy, D.S.O., M.C., Chevalier of the Legion of Honor, Croix de Guerre, Order of St. Michael (2nd Class).

"Well, I never," I said.

I fumbled for a chair and sat down. Then I got up again and asked if the commandant was available. But apparently he wasn't available just at the moment. He was lying down on his bunk, the adjutant said, and staring sightlessly at the ceiling. Apparently he had suffered some sort of seizure.

Overwork, I supposed. After all, there was a good deal of responsibility involved in running a training squadron, keeping the instructors in their places, maintaining discipline among the riggers and fitters, making sure the eggs were hard-boiled, et cetera. I expect that was why he was feeling a bit poorly, I said to the adjutant, who, now that I looked at him more closely, wasn't looking too well himself.

A Big Cheese

Every day for three days, morning and afternoon, I reported at the Hotel Cecil, in the Strand, trying unsuccessfully to get an appointment to see Lord Rackingham. For he was the person responsible for my sudden elevation. The bleak looks I received from his numerous enemies at the Ministry and the comments I was meant to overhear made *that* perfectly clear.

In the meantime I strutted around town in a brand-new, off-the-rack uniform, with blood-red tabs and lovely new pips and crowns, not to mention the wings, ribbons, and wound stripes. I received so many salutes from the lower orders I had to purchase a jar of Sloan's Liniment to ease my weary arm.

But I didn't mind. It was all in the cause of good Army discipline.

My initial astonishment at my good fortune soon faded into a feeling of bland contentment. Whatever the promotion was for, I felt I'd thoroughly deserved it. From my new gold-braided perspective I realized that my contribution to the war effort had been far more significant than I had imagined.

I began to cultivate an aloof detachment that seemed to suit my Gothic countenance, and to develop a commanding presence in keeping with my station, which worked so well that the junior warts also developed a tendency to hide in the cloakroom whenever I turned up at the Army and Navy Club with my new, silver-tipped swagger stick. I began to look up everybody I'd ever met, however briefly, to show them that the Army was still capable of appreciating intelligence, initiative, and devotion to duty, and of rewarding outstanding merit.

Like the time I visited a battalion mess just outside London to see a friend of mine called . . . I've forgotten his name, but I remember he had a boil on his neck.

Everybody stood to attention when I entered the mess. I pretended I'd forgotten something and went out. Then I came back, and they all went rigid again. I was tempted to return a third time, but they foiled me by remaining on their feet, wearing insouciant expressions; so, trying out a brand-new expression modeled on Treadwell's, with a dash of General Perris' bulbous stare thrown in, I inquired after my good friend. I just happened to be in the neighborhood, I said, swishing my stick lazily, and thought I'd look him up.

Unfortunately he had just been cashiered for exposing himself in Wandsworth – a suburb of London, I believe. Quickly pointing out that the fellow was merely a fleeting acquaintance, I withdrew in a hurry. Still, on the whole it was fairly satisfying.

The same afternoon, I marched along to the City of Westminster Infirmary to impress another acquaintance, a trainee pilot by the name of Pearson, who'd been in some kind of accident.

I remembered his name all right, though he had recently changed it. On transferring to the R.F.C. he had given his real name, Lester Pearson; but his C.O., another Canadian, said he certainly wasn't having any of *his* pilots named Lester. So he'd put him down as Mike. Thus Mike Pearson he had become.

I sauntered casually into the ward he shared with two other officers. They were all swathed in bandages. "Don't get up," I said. "This is an informal visit."

As I approached, Pearson peered out of his bed of pain and spluttered, "Bandy? For heaven's sake. . . . You'll get into trouble, impersonating an officer that way."

"Impersonating? How d'you mean?"

"They can't possibly have made *you* a colonel."

"Yes, they have," I said, preening. "They've seen the light at last."

"Seen it? They must have been blinded by it! You mean you really are a colonel?"

"Course."

"Coarse?" he cried. "It's pothitively obscene!"

He tried to sit up, uttered a moan, and sank back again. "God," he lisped brokenly, "it's true after all. This really is a war to end all wars. After seeing you, nobody'll have the heart to fight on."

Pearson and I had attended the same university, but as we'd been in different colleges – Pearson had been taking modern history at Victoria College, I'd been studying medicine – we hadn't met until the day we both took part in some O.T.C. maneuvers in the Don Valley, near Toronto.

It was supposed to be a gentlemanly training exercise in infantry tactics, but because of the intense rivalry between colleges, it had rapidly degenerated into a vicious brawl. Among other incidents, a group of divinity scholars had thrown a mechanical engineer off a cliff. In retaliation, the engineering and medical students had banded together to make a bayonet charge against Victoria College's unoffend-ing C Company, which was cowering in a ditch, and had been restrained only by the classical threats of their company commander, Dean Vincent Massey. But not before Cadet

Pearson had flung a small boulder at one of his assailants.

He'd wandered over to the casualty station later on to see if he'd fractured my skull, and subsequently a friendship had developed as far as was possible between a third-year medical and a first-year Arts student.

"M'yes, well, pull yourself together, Young Pearson," I said (he was at least three years younger than I), "and tell me what all this is about?" I gestured around at all the broken limbs. "Been in a plane crash, have you?"

"Hit by a London omnibus," he mumbled.

"You what?"

"I was hit by a bus!" he shouted.

"Hit by a *bus?*"

"Yes! You know – one of those large things on wheels that travel about the streets, carrying the common people," he said sarcastically. "But perhaps you don't care to know about such plebeian things, now you've reached the heights?"

"Now, now, no need to be that way," I said, "just because I've got on and you haven't."

The other two officers in the ward sat up to get a better look at me.

"And pray how," I went on, tapping my breeches authoritatively with my silver-chased swagger stick, "did you come to be hit by this common omnibus?"

"Oh, go away."

"I beg your pudding?"

"Go away, *sir.*"

"That's better," I said, and after some further sympathetic prompting, persuaded him to relate the incident. One evening last December he had been dining out in London, he said, and the air-raid rattles had sounded midway between the parsley soup and the Aberdeen herring. He had insisted on returning to the airdrome at Hendon in case he was needed.

On the way back, several bombs had fallen near the road and the bus driver had heaved everybody out and switched off his lights. Lester (or Mike) had darted behind the stationary omnibus to cross the road, to be promptly clobbered by another bus that was *far* from stationary.

"Some time afterwards," Mike (or Lester) said, "I came to and found myself lying on a sort of pushcart being trundled along the Edgware Road by a couple of London bobbies. To make matters worse, somebody in the crowd saw my shoulder flash and I heard him say, 'Another drunken Canadian officer.'"

"You allowed yourself to be trundled along in a *pushcart?* That's letting the side down a bit, don't you think?"

"I was in no condition to protest!" he said angrily. Then he winced, and went on more cautiously, "The damnable thing was I was in town in the first place only because I'd been shaken up in a training accident, and they'd given me a couple of days' leave to recover. Some recovery."

He glared at my red tabs. "And now this," he said. "You of all people turning up as a brass hat. It's going to give me a relapse, I'm sure of it."

I frowned at his insubordinate expression. When this failed to do any good, I turned to the other damaged officers and said with an indulgent smile, "I really don't know what's happened to this formerly obedient student of Plautus and Terence. He used to be the very soul of tact, and respect for his elders and betters."

The other two officers stared back, wearing rather stupid expressions.

"I've been hounded once too often by doltish brass hats like you!" Lester cried. "Mucked about from the moment I left Canada in the bilge of a ship that was ready for the knacker's yard even before the Boer War. Being forced to march back

and forth across the Egyptian desert with full pack, as a pun-
ishment for refusing to line up naked and be hosed down like
a pig or a jailbird, instead of being allowed to bathe in a civilized manner. Being given tropical uniform to fight in the
freezing Balkans. Seeing my pals killed unnecessarily, or dying
of blackwater fever in badly organized hospitals. And . . ." And
he went on in this extravagant vein for some time, recounting
his experiences with a wealth of indiscreet detail, then going
on to comment imprudently, tactlessly, and slanderously on
the parentage, intelligence, and qualifications of several of our
most respected military leaders. I was quite shocked.

"By gosh," he ended, "if they fail by some incredible fluke
to kill me off before this war ends, I swear I'll go into politics,
or Foreign Affairs, to try and ensure that diplomacy never
again deteriorates to the point where war becomes not merely
a logical consequence but an enormous relief."

"You? A diplomat?" I laughed lightly. "My dear Lester." I
smiled. "With those intemperate sentiments of yours and that
wild way of expressing them–"

"I wasn't wild before *you* came in!"

"–we'd be at war again in a month. No, if I'm any judge of
character, Pearson, you're the very last person on earth to go
into either politics or diplomacy."

I patted him paternally on the shoulder, and after placing his
present on the side table – it was a picture of me – turned to go.
"Take my word for it, you'll be far better off teaching history
than attempting to make it. Give up that mad dream, Pearson.
Just do your duty, lad, and leave the conduct of affairs to–" I
flicked a few motes off the pip and crown on my starboard sleeve
"–to people with the right qualities, who know what they're
about," I said, and, saluting the gaping officers nonchalantly
with my swagger stick, departed, my gracious exit somewhat
spoiled when I stepped into a bedpan that some darned fool had

left near the door, and clunked off, looking as if I were wearing a new style of cast, or an outsized porcelain moccasin.

As for the Lewises, they refused to believe me when I cabled the good news, until two of them turned up at the Spartan Hotel, where I had taken up residence on a handsome living-out allowance. They were hoping, no doubt, to expose my delusions of grandeur.

"I heard Rackingham was doing some pretty unorthodox things at the Ministry," Lewis murmured. "But this . . ."

For some reason, Katherine seemed displeased at the way I was coming up in the world. "You might at least have bought a pair of breeches that fitted," she said. "You look as if you're taking part in a sack race."

A week before, I would have been keenly displeased at such a jibe, but I was now impervious. "Don't worry, my dear," I said in a kindly fashion. "When I have a moment I'll have them taken in."

"Good idea," she snapped. "Have them taken in at the nearest Salvation Army."

"But what exactly do you *do?*" Lewis asked for the third time.

"Oh, this and that," I replied airily. "Affairs of state. You know."

"I mean, what's your position?"

Finally I had to admit that the Minister had been too busy to see me so far, so I didn't actually know what my new title was to be. "But it's bound to be some responsible post," I said with an offhand gesture that sent Katherine's hackles springing to attention. "Probably in Air Equipment or Supply."

"Well, congratulations anyway," Mr. Lewis said.

"Thank you, Lewis," I said.

"By the way," I went on, regarding myself offhandedly in the mirror, "what did Mrs. Lewis say when she heard?"

"She was most impressed, Bartholomew," Mr. Lewis murmured, turning away to pick lint off his striped trousers.

"Was she?"

"She laughed so much," Katherine said meanly, "she fell into a Japanese quince and had to be helped up to bed."

However, they weren't long in telling everybody the good news, for a couple of days later I received an invitation to take tea with Mrs. Cary.

She lived in a nicely proportioned semidetached house in Hampstead, with its name, DARIEN, carved into the stone gateposts. Like so many London houses, however, the interior did not quite live up to the façade. The window sills were rotting because of excessive condensation, the hall hadn't been painted since the War of Jenkins' Ear, and the living room floor sloped so markedly I had to tilt myself slightly, to keep the view vertical, as it were.

Not that I wouldn't have minded having the view horizontal. Mrs. Cary really was an exquisitely preserved woman, the narrowness of her waist emphasizing the forthright contours of her breasts, if emphasis were needed. Only a slight creak now and then confirmed the presence of stout corsets on those peaks in Darien.

After inquiring politely about the Lewises, and revealing (as she praised Katherine to the skies) that she disliked the girl almost as much as Katherine detested her, Mrs. Cary sat beside me on the sofa and proceeded to probe me in various subtle ways, in an attempt to find out what sort of unspeakable service I had rendered Lord Rackingham to have caused him to favor me so spectacularly. It had taken her own husband, Gerald, thirty years of spit, polish, and duplicity to reach the rank I had surpassed in twenty-four months.

"I just made a splendid impression on him, that's all," I said.

Mrs. Cary nodded disbelievingly. After a moment she said, "Gerald was much older than me, of course. But such a wonderful man. So virile, you know."

"Oh, good," I said, shifting slightly under her steady gaze.

"If you only knew how I miss him," she said, with a heavy sigh.

My heart began to thump like billy-oh. And was it accidental when she leaned against me to rearrange the fancy cookies on the cake stand?

"We used to play a lovely game called Rapies," she said, putting her hand on my knee to help her straighten up again.

"Rapies?" I faltered.

"I'd dress up in some old clothes, and he'd run after me and tear them all off." As she sat back again, her fingers ran a few inches along either side of my thigh. "There's such a lot to be said for a hot climate, don't you think?"

I was incapable of thinking anything. With constricted throat and calorific brow, I swallowed, crossed my legs, and put another four spoonfuls of sugar in the tea.

Luckily her mother came in just then. I'd already been introduced to her in the kitchen, where she had been stuffing herself with pastries and cider. She was wearing binoculars and a mustache, and she had a voice like my old sergeant-major at Niagara. ("What are you, Mr. Bandy, what are you? A clumsy f— hofficer, that's what you are!").

Mrs. Cary looked displeased at the interruption. "We're talking, Mother," she said.

The old lady paid no attention, but snatched up an *ersatz* cream bun in passing, and waddled to the window.

"Mother is just visiting me from her place in the country," Mrs. Cary said with a restrained smile, as Mother stared out the window, gutsing. "She's just up to town for the shopping."

"Oh, yes?"

Mrs. Cary idly picked up a cookie in the shape of a female in crinolines and nibbled the head daintily. "She doesn't stay here, of course," she murmured. "I'm all alone, you know."

"Oh, yes?"

Mrs. Cary turned and started to order her mother out of the room, firmly but pleasantly; but the old lady was now busily commenting on the passing show.

"Coppers round 'ere don't seem to 'ave much to do," she rumbled, wiping her breath off the window. "Look at 'em, flirting with them foreign nursemaids."

"Mother, dear. If you don't mind—"

"Not like where we come from, eh, Angie? Coppers got plenty to do round our old neighborhood, eh? – chasing all the pickpockets, and carting the drunks 'ome."

There was a crunching sound. Mrs. Cary carefully laid the remains of her cookie on the plate.

"Ooh, look – there's Miss Turnbull's great black bitch taking Miss Turnbull for a walk," her mother continued.

"Mother."

"That's the first time she's been out since she got her nightie caught on the stepladder and 'ung there, showing 'er mole to all and sundry," Mother said, resting her massive backside on an oriental elephant that stood trumpeting in the window bay.

Mrs. Cary smiled at me in a helpless, feminine sort of way, then darted a venomous glance at her aged parent.

Meanwhile the old lady was fumbling among her sagging breasts – there seemed to be three of them – and took up the binoculars. As soon as she'd gotten them focused: "Cor," she said urgently. "Look at that!"

I started up, before recollecting myself and sinking back again. Mrs. Cary's complexion, which she had preserved remarkably well against the Indian sun, was evidently not proof against her mother. Her cheeks were bright pink.

"It's that boy what lives opposite," the old lady went on censoriously. "Well. I'm sure *that's* not going to do no good to Mr. Moody's evergreens."

"Mother, I'm talking to the Colonel," Mrs. Cary said. But Mother refused to budge from her reviewing stand, and finally Mrs. Cary leaned over and murmured, "You must come again when we can talk in private, Bartholomew. Or perhaps I could call on you, sometime."

"I'm staying at the Spartan Hotel," I said, meaning that I didn't have a place of my own where I could entertain. But Mrs. Cary responded by squeezing my hand, almost as if we'd made an assignation.

The only friend entirely indifferent to my promotion was Rodominov. At Burma Park he had muttered something about my visiting him when I was next in Bloomersbury, so I went along to his flat as much to renew his acquaintance as to show off my insignia. I was intrigued by Rodominov, in spite of his surly manner.

As we sat sipping tea in his living room, there was a muffled thumping from the adjoining room.

"Is nothing," he said. "Just the bailiffs."

"Oh, I see."

"I have decided to move," he said, tapping another glass of tea from a magnificent copper samovar, which had doubtless been presented to his family by Ivan the Terrible or Catherine the Great or somebody. "Bloomersbury is – pfff." He gestured defiantly. "I have decided to live in Balaam."

"Balaam – that's Arabia, isn't it?"

"Is suburb of London."

"A suburb of . . .? Oh – Balham."

There was a longish silence. The thumping went on. A bailiff looked in, then closed the door again.

"That's a beautiful samovar," I said, tugging at and smoothing my sleeve in case my new badges got wrinkled.

"Picked it up for forty bob in Portobello Road."

He noticed my badges at last. He touched my sleeve. "You have only two peeps now," he observed.

"Two peeps?"

"Before, you had three peeps."

"Oh. Ah, no. Actually–"

"Is no need to be ashamed. I also have been demoted."

"I'm not ashamed. I–"

"You have money?"

"Money? Yes, certainly. 'Specially now that I'm a col–"

"You want to buy a picture, Bandy?"

"What?"

"I have picture," he said, turning his heavy face toward the fireplace. Above it was an oil painting in a big, florid frame. "Was given to my mother when she marry." He got up and looked closely at the artist's signature in the lower right-hand corner. "Henri Matisse. French painter. I let you have it for five hundred pounds."

I squinted at the painting. It showed a woman in an armchair in a very tastelessly decorated room, all done in gaudy, kindergarten colors. It looked a terrible daub to me.

"I couldn't possibly afford that," I said.

"Three hundred."

"I'm saving up for a Stutz Roadster," I said. "Look, I even have the advertisement on me." I read it out to him enthusiastically.

" 'Raise the dust! Terrify your girl! Infuriate farmers with one of the great sporting–' "

"Hoots mon, you take it for two hundred. I need money, Bandy. *Pazhalsta*. Before bailiffs come into room."

"But I'm a senior officer – I can't stagger through the streets carrying a dashed great painting. It's not done."

"Hundred and fifty – and I throw in samovar. Quick. Fly now – pay later."

As I lurched out just ahead of the bailiffs, carrying the heavy painting and the even heavier samovar, I felt thoroughly resentful at my own weakness in accepting a picture I didn't like by an artist I'd never heard of.

A hundred and fifty quid. It was practically my life savings.

Seated in My Office

It was Wednesday before I finally caught up with Lord Rackingham – literally, for he was pounding along the hotel corridor with his private secretary when I caught sight of him. I chased after him. The subsequent interview was conducted at about seven miles an hour through the turmoil of the Hotel Cecil, with frustrated admirals looking out of their bedrooms and calling imploringly to the Minister, like gold-braided harlots.

"Quite right, Sprain," Lord R. was saying to his private secretary as I caught up. "I don't intend to let things slide. New broom and all that." An anxious-looking sea dog plucked importunately at his sleeve as he went past. "Not now, not now," the Minister said irritably. "Yes, there are going to be drastic changes, Sprain, as soon as I find out what everybody is up to. Above all, there's going to be efficiency. In a leading article I once referred to you people in the Civil Service as models of efficient inefficiency. After only a short time here I begin to understand what I meant."

"How do you mean, sir?"

"Oh, just general things I've noticed. For instance, nobody's been bringing me cups of tea in the afternoon. It's a small thing, of course, but a major example of what I was–"

"But we don't have tea in the afternoon, Minister."

"No tea in the afternoon? But I always have tea in the afternoon. We had tea every afternoon at the newspaper."

"Oh."

"*And* cream buns. See to it, Sprain."

"I'll see what I can do, Minister. Oh, by the way," Sir Aubrey said, gesturing toward me as I scuttled alongside, "this gentleman is the one I reminded you about this morning – Colonel Bandy."

"Not now, not now," Lord R. said, trying to wave me aside.

"But what am I supposed to do, sir?" I said, as we panted up yet another flight of stairs. "I mean, what are my duties?"

"Tchk," he said irritably as he hesitated at a junction of corridors. "Haven't you talked to Sprain yet?"

"He doesn't know either, sir."

The Minister glared at me. "Well . . . well, come and see me tomorrow at ten. We'll discuss it then," he snapped, and marched off.

"But . . . but . . ."

But by then he was out of sight. When I tried to retrace my steps I got lost for the third time that week. The hotel had more than a thousand rooms, and almost as many staircases, it seemed. When I asked a naval captain which was the best way out, he growled, "The best way out is to resign! That's what I'm thinking of doing," he said, and slammed the door of his converted mop cupboard.

The lobby of the hotel was nearly as crowded and disorganized as the rest of the building. There were never fewer than fifty Army, Navy, and Flying Corps officers hanging around there, waiting for something to happen. They usually started to muster into impenetrable cliques of from two to eight every morning at nine-thirty. As the day dragged on, the scene began to resemble a badly run dance club, with pairs of angry commodores pacing through the Dashing White Sergeant, and circles of majors and such sullenly advancing and retreating in suspicious Eightsome Reels. Only the civil servants seemed to know what they were doing, as they threaded their way purposefully through the military toward the tea wagon.

As I was pushing my way through the mob the following morning, there was a sudden gasp, and a lieutenant seized my arm.

"Bandy!"

"Milestone!"

Dick Milestone, who had been in my squadron in France, had been posted to Home Establishment at about the same time I'd been sent to Gosport. Two months away from the front had worked wonders with his health and appearance. When he left he had been twitching with exhaustion and nervous tension. Now he was positively bursting with dissipation, as befitted a soldier on the home front.

We embraced, and a flood of exclamatory insults followed before I recollected my dignity.

"But, good God, what's all this?" he cried, seizing my sleeve and staring at it. "What kind of farce is this?"

"Whatjamean, farce? They've recognized my talents, that's all."

"Talents? You?" He gave a high-pitched cackle of laughter and fell against his companion, a lieutenant with an observer's badge on his breast. The observer smiled uncertainly.

"This frozen-faced imposter was a flight commander in my squadron only a few weeks ago," Milestone told his friend.

He looked back at me dazedly. "Jesus. . . . They'll never believe it when I tell them. Even *I* don't believe it, and I'm looking at it. . . . Come on, Bart–" He stopped, and his face lit up in relief. "Amateur theatricals! That's it, isn't it? You're in a play about intrepid birdmen!" He shook my arm. "Come on, let's have it!"

I looked at my watch and said in an offhand sort of way, "Sorry, old bean. Have to rush. Pow-wow with the Minister, you know. Ten o'clock."

"Garn!" Milestone said. Then: "All right: I'm coming with you!" He looked at me challengingly.

"Very well," I said, moving off. "Come this way, Lieutenant. Excuse me, Brigadier."

"I'll show you up, you mummer," Milestone said, a little less certainly. "You've got away with a hell of a lot in this army, but this is too much. I'm calling your bluff."

"Good morning, Sir Aubrey," I said as we entered the private secretary's office. "Lord R. free, is he?"

"Ah, good morning, Colonel," Sprain said, rising. "Exactly on time, I see," he went on, looking a bit embarrassed about it for some reason.

Milestone, who had grown more and more subdued the deeper we penetrated into the labyrinth, was now looking quite apprehensive, as if some cataclysm were about to be announced.

"Oh, by the way, this is a minor acquaintance of mine, Richard Milestone," I said to Sprain, gesturing offhandedly in the pilot's direction.

"How do you do, Mr. Milestone," Sir Aubrey said with that reserved Civil Service charm of his. "Not related to Mr. Milestone, are you, by any chance?"

A damn silly question, I thought; until Sir Aubrey added, "the surgeon?"

"He's my father," Milestone said, looking as if he were in need of his father's services.

It was now my turn to stare at Milestone, as Sprain went on to say that he had been at Eton with Mr. Milestone, and that they still saw each other occasionally.

Soon the two of them were chatting away as if Milestone were the favored visitor and I were there merely to read the meter.

Finally I interrupted somewhat peevishly to remind the secretary about my appointment with Lord R.

But that wasn't any good either. The Minister was out again. He had been called to 10 Downing Street for his weekly dressing-down.

"But he asked me to explain the situation," the private secretary said, looking as if he were still no nearer to understanding what the situation was.

"I'll see you later, then," Milestone said dazedly. "Where are you staying?"

"I have a suite at the Spartan," I said.

"A sweetie at the Spartan? Good God, is there no end to it . . .?"

"A *suite*," I said irritably. Well, it was practically a suite – there was a very large cupboard off the bedroom.

After Milestone had felt his way out, the private secretary seated himself at his desk and, placing his fingers together, said, "Apparently, what the Minister has in mind for you, Colonel, is a liaison job between him and his Chief of Staff."

"Ah."

"Though I must admit I can't quite see why he needs an intermediary. However . . ."

"Do I have a title?" I asked hopefully. "And an office?"

"Well . . . He did refer to you once as his military secretary, as distinct from . . . myself, I suppose. So perhaps that's what we should call you. As for an office . . ." He hesitated and pulled out a drawer; then closed it again. "There's only the one room available, I'm afraid. It's the, the room next to his." He inclined his well-groomed head toward the far side of the minister's chambers.

An office right next door to the Minister. This was even better than I'd expected.

"Splendid," I said.

"Well, it's . . . actually it's. . . . Of course you understand that this used to be a hotel and we must all make do with what we can . . . make do with," Sir Aubrey said. He cleared his throat a couple of times and fiddled with a paper knife in the shape of an African witch doctor.

"Of course. Naturally I don't expect a room as imposing as the Minister's," I said, looking around somewhat disdainfully at the private secretary's own cramped quarters, with its single, rather grimy window. I tactfully refrained from adding that it could hardly fail to be superior to *this*.

And in fact it *was* larger, and brighter, as I found when Sir Aubrey led me along the corridor and pushed open the door on which were the initials of the former occupant, W.C. I was rather taken aback, though, to see that my office was tiled instead of plastered, and that there seemed an awful lot of pipes around.

Still, it did have good cupboard space – six or seven of them – and an impressive number of filing cabinets; though for some

strange reason they were separated from each other by strange
white-porcelain projections.

It was only when I looked into one of the cupboards and saw
the fitting that was squatting inside it that I realized where I was.

I had been installed in a Gentleman's Convenience.

Lord Rackingham

Though it occurred to me that Lord Rackingham had
installed me at the Ministry principally as a sort of shock
absorber between him and his staff, I can't say I tried too hard
to understand how I had come to be one of his *protégés*. As with
women, Providence, and jokes in *Punch*, the logic of our
leaders seemed best left unanalyzed if moral confusion and
ultimate madness were to be avoided.

It was, of course, perfectly in character for him to disregard
the military conventions by raising me two steps in the military hierarchy. He was contemptuous of a system in which
dunderheads could climb the ladder of success as readily as
men of talent. Discovering that he couldn't batter the organization head on, he tried to sneak around it by promoting every
likely lad in sight.

But this opened up yet another area of discord between him
and his staff, particularly his Chief of Air Staff, who was
already in a wax about the excessive numbers of able-bodied
officers who were being favored with administrative jobs
instead of being sent where they were most needed – to the
squadrons. So if my purpose was to take some of the advisory

pressure off Lord R., the effect was the opposite: the pressure increased from the moment I first padded into the C.A.S.'s office, wreathed in coy smiles.

I had met the C.A.S. once before, when he came to visit us at Gosport, and had made a notable impression on him when I put the case for distributing more egg timers among the cookhouse staffs of the various front-line squadrons.

Consequently I was looking forward to meeting him again, to find out how he'd got on. But at the sight of my face and insignia, he promptly recoiled into the wainscoting, cracking one of the panels rather badly.

Then, forgetting he wasn't on speaking terms with the Minister, he stormed off along the corridor to complain. He bellowed at the Minister so intemperately, in fact, that colonels and commodores came out of their offices in droves to listen in, with mean smiles on their faces.

Unfortunately for the C.A.S., he had recently dismissed another of the Minister's favorites, a major whom Lord R. had raised not just two steps, but three – to the rank of brigadier – and had sent to Mason's Yard as the new Director of Training. Still smarting over this defeat, Lord R. dug in his heels and refused to part with me, and, short of resigning, there was nothing the chief of staff could do about it.

He made his feelings plain enough, though, the next time he saw me. "Just keep out of my way, that's all," he shouted, as I looked at him with a hurt expression. "I don't want to see you or hear another word from you, do you hear?" Then added, somewhat illogically and to the mystification of his office staff, "And if you so much as breathe a word about egg timers, I'll have you shot! *Shot!*"

Though he remained firm in this instance, Lord R. soon revealed that under normal circumstances he possessed remarkable reserves of vacillation, which he brought into action whenever he failed to browbeat his officers into taking the wrong course. As a result, no one ever knew what was expected of him, and vital decisions were constantly being deferred until the Minister was forced to make up his mind, if only to clear the way for further confusions.

As the days went by and hostile cliques of R.F.C. officers and quarterdeck types multiplied, Lord R. retreated still deeper into his shell of indecision. Soon only the most persistent rapping on his carapace would bring his heavy head into the open again; and even then he only listened to what he wanted to hear.

But he had his faults, too. He wasn't above sowing discord among his enemies by sending them memos that were supposed to clear up misunderstandings but were really designed to increase the muddle, in order to make his own administrative efforts seem, by comparison, supremely well organized.

He seemed happiest with summaries, policy papers, charts, and balance sheets, and by the middle of February had abandoned almost all personal contact with the various naval and military advisers who were struggling to get the Royal Flying Corps and the Royal Naval Air Service decently married before their infant, the Royal Air Force, was born on April Fool's Day.

The result was that when he was finally cornered into making decisions, they were usually the wrong ones. In February, for instance, he ordered a new monoplane into production on the strength of its low cost and other theoretical criteria, in spite of a test pilot's report that it was barely capable of getting off the ground. He looked at the figures and dismissed the test pilot as a pessimist. "A monoplane has one wing instead of the usual two, hasn't it, Bandy? There you are, then. We'll be able to save 50 per cent right there. As for needing a strong wind to get it off the ground, that's no problem. It's been extremely windy on every airdrome *I*'ve ever visited."

It was only when the C.A.S. challenged him in a strongly worded letter that his lack of self-confidence reasserted itself, and to save face he sent me along to Martlesham Heath for a personal report.

I arrived at the testing squadron in the Minister's Daimler, and was received with gratifying ceremony. As I climbed into the cockpit of the monoplane, I informed the C.O. that I'd have time only to test the rate of climb, speed at various altitudes, general handling capabilities, and optimum ceiling, as I was due at 10 Downing Street later that afternoon.

Half an hour later I trundled back to the experimental hangar, having managed to get the plane only two and a half feet off the ground, and that only because I ran over a runway flare.

"Seems a bit underpowered to me," I informed the C.O. Then I hurried off to collect Lord R.'s umbrella from 10 Downing Street, where he had left it after the previous night's bout of Welsh nagging.

Another time, the Minister received a request from the First Lord of the Admiralty for an allocation of aircraft to combat the critical submarine menace. He asked me for an inventory of stock, and when I reported that we had four thousand engines and about the same number of airframes in reserve, he offered the lot to the Admiralty, before it was pointed out in a rather rude memo from the C.A.S. that the four thousand engines didn't necessarily match the four thousand airframes, and in fact there weren't even four hundred spare aircraft available, let alone four thousand, and even if there were, the Navy certainly couldn't have them.

"It's all your fault," the Minister shouted at me. "You should have told me!"

"I gave you what you asked for, Minister," I replied stoutly. "An inventory of–"

"You should have known what I had in mind! You should have listened properly! You never listen to me – nobody listens to me!"

"I do, too."

"All right, what did I just say?"

"I never listen to you."

"You see? You admit it!"

He could be pretty difficult sometimes. On other occasions, however, he treated me almost like a son, albeit one that hadn't quite lived up to his expectations.

"You're the only Army person I can talk to," he said gloomily one morning as he finished misfiling some state papers. "I suppose it's because you haven't any dignity."

"I beg your pardon?"

"Well, you know what I mean." He gestured despondently. "Half the time they look at me as if I'm talking arrant nonsense, even before I open my mouth. They seem to think nobody but a military man has the right to run this damn war. Well, they haven't done spectacularly well themselves, have they?"

He opened a black dispatch box and stared into it as if it were filled to the brim with summonses for indecent assault. "Even the few among them who realize how badly things are going refuse to admit it publicly. If only one, just *one* of them . . ." He looked at me heavy-eyed. "Did you know that Lloyd George has been trying to get rid of the C-in-C for several weeks now?"

"Is that right, sir?"

"But that man still has too much support from the public and the newspapers."

"Lloyd George has?"

"*Haig*, man. Even most of the P.M.'s own supporters are behind Haig, in spite of the mess he's made of things."

I raised my eyebrows. It was only a few weeks since Lord R. (and therefore his newspaper) had been among Sir Douglas

Haig's shrillest supporters. I wondered if the P.M. had been exercising his wily Welsh malevolence on Lord R. Or – the unworthy thought suddenly occurred to me – had Lloyd George given Lord R. his present job in return for the support of his newspaper?

"You're giving the speech at Fallow this year, aren't you, Bandy?" he asked suddenly.

"I'm supposed to, Minister. Third Wednesday in March. But I won't be able to go, of course."

"Why not?"

"Well, you can't spare me."

"Course I can."

"No, no, you can't, sir. You know I'm indispensable."

"Nonsense."

"But, sir, who'll bring you cups of tea – *and* cream buns? Who'll tidy your desk, who'll deliver all your memos? Who'll–"

"It's only for a day, man. I'll manage."

"But, but."

"That's settled, then," Lord R. said, looking at me in a rank-pulling sort of way. "I want you to go."

He regarded me speculatively as I plucked sulkily at my wings. "You know, of course," he went on evenly, "that one or two national newspapers will be covering the event."

I looked up sharply. *Now* what was he up to?

"Well, we'll talk about that later," he said, lowering the heavy lids of his eyes and toying with a stick of sealing wax. He was fond of sealing wax and used it all the time. In the bottom left drawer of his desk was a full-face photograph of his Chief of Air Staff. Whenever he received a particularly rude memo from that quarter, Lord R. would take out the C.A.S.'s picture and drop hot, sizzling blobs of red wax onto it.

"In the meantime," he said, "what have you found out about the reserves?"

"Ah, yes," I said. "The reserves."

Late last year the prime minister had persuaded Haig to agree to withdraw several units from the line as a strategic reserve in case of a German offensive. Such an offensive seemed likely, now that the fighting on the Russian front had ended, giving Ludendorff scores of extra divisions to play with.

Lord R. had asked me to find out which units Haig was allocating to the reserve.

I pursed my lips judiciously, raised my eyebrows portentously, and gave him a level look – which wasn't easy, as he had provided me with an exceptionally low chair.

"As a matter of fact," I said, "I haven't found out anything yet."

"Indeed?" He looked at me coldly. "You realize, of course, that it's nearly a week since I asked for that information?"

"Well, the generals won't tell me a thing."

"*Make* them tell you! What d'you think I made you a colonel for!" He rapped the desk sharply with the sealing wax. "Get on with it, Bandy! I want that information by the second week of March. Do you understand?"

But it wasn't that easy. Records of military movements weren't open to just any old Tom, Dick, or Bandy. I'd already spent three days in the cavernous halls of the War Office, being shunted from one office to another by people who didn't seem to have the faintest idea what I was talking about. I was beginning to wonder if the Army had actually gotten around to keeping records yet.

Make them tell me, indeed. How was I supposed to do that when he had told me not to say who the information was for? Such an order canceled out any authority I might have had for asking questions.

Really.

The task was made all the more difficult because the only person I knew at the War House was Major Auchinflint, and he was no more forthcoming than anyone else when I finally cornered him in his office that afternoon in the Military Operations section upstairs. He went into a defensive twitter the moment I mentioned the Reserve of Maneuver.

"I couldn't possibly tell you that," he said.

"You don't know any more than anyone else does, eh?"

His ostrichlike head twitched, and he flushed in annoyance. "The D.M.O.'s the only person who could authorize that sort of information," he said sharply, closing the file he'd been working on and slipping it under his desk blotter.

"Who's that?"

"Pusey, of course."

"I'll go see him, then."

"He's away at the moment," Auchinflint said. He sounded glad that Pusey was away at the moment. His lip curled as he regarded my red tabs.

"Where?"

"G.H.Q."

For a moment I considered following up at G.H.Q. But I could hardly travel all that way, by land, sea, and/or air, to mention to the Director of Military Operations that I just happened to be passing and was wondering if he felt like giving out any confidential information today. He would almost certainly tell his pal Haig that somebody was snooping on him. I had the impression that Lord Rackingham wanted me to be a bit more subtle than that.

"Who wants this information, anyway?" Auchinflint asked, sounding terribly casual as he stared into a red fire bucket filled with sand.

"Me," I said.

"But on whose behalf?"

"Oh, you know," I said, gesturing in the direction of the Hotel Cecil. "When is Pusey due back?"

"I've no idea," Auchinflint said, twitching again as he stared into the bucket. I wondered if he was contemplating burying his head in it.

Instead, he started tidying a heap of Army forms, tapping the edges together with his thin, restless fingers. "Now, if you don't mind, *Colonel*," he said with a sneer, "I'm rather busy at the moment."

On my way downstairs I was so busy dismembering Auchinflint with a blunt meat cleaver, that I descended one floor too many and found myself in a dingy basement passage lined with steel shelves. The shelves were buckling at the knees under their load of Army forms and stationery and bundles of dusty files bound in red tape.

I was about to go up again when I heard voices coming from a room farther along the passage. "Switchboard," a voice said cautiously. Then: "Very good, sir," and a clicking sound.

I looked thoughtfully at the open door. Then, straightening my cap and whipping my stick smartly under my oxter, I marched in.

Along one distempered wall stood several telephone switch-board units. Two private soldiers, wearing headsets with curved mouthpieces, were busy filling holes with brass plugs. A corporal was lounging at a small desk at the far end of the room, smoking a cigarette the size of an earwig.

He sprang up as I strode in, hiding his fag-end hurriedly behind a bunch of nicotine-stained fingers.

"Look here, General Farthing-Prebble has been waiting in the entrance hall for fifteen blaaasted minutes for Major Auchinflint," I said, looking fierce as anything. "Call him again, Corporal, and tell him he's got just one – repeat – *one* minute to get down there. D'you understand?"

"Major Auchinflint, sir? Yes, sir. I'm very sorry, sir. I–"

"Yes, well, get on with it," I said, and about-turned smartly and goose-stepped out, glaring at the startled privates in passing.

The second I was out of sight I raced back upstairs, taking them three at a time, and hurried along the first-floor corridor, hoping the empty office a few yards along from Auchinflint's room was still unoccupied.

It was. I tiptoed in and stood behind the door, trying not to pant too loudly.

Not more than ten seconds later, Auchinflint went scuttling past the half-open door, straightening his tie, smoothing his hair, and twitching like mad.

I nipped back into his office. The file that he had closed so furtively while he was talking to me was still under the blotter on his desk.

I slipped it out, starting guiltily as the word SECRET appeared. It was stamped twice on the cover in black letters.

Accompanying the file was a ruled buff envelope on which were the words R.Sup.Ops.(SICC) and a lot of numbers and half a column of people's initials.

R! Reserve! Just as I'd suspected. Pausing only to stop breathing until some feet had loped past in the corridor outside, I flicked open the file and began to skim through it.

The first dozen or so items in the file made no sense at all. But at last there was a coherent bit, a summary on War Office stationery headed *Naval-Military Conference: Baltic Theatre*.

It was agreed that the purpose of the proposed intervention in Russia (Baltic) would be:
1. To support the Baltic States in their resistance to Bolshevik aggression.
2. To neutralize the Bolshevik fleet.
3. To–

I thought I'd better not read any more. It had obviously nothing whatsoever to do with strategic reserves.

Still, Auchinflint was more helpful than he knew, because I suddenly remembered that Mrs. Cary had mentioned a General Pusey. As she seemed to cultivate senior officers quite assiduously, maybe she could help.

So I telephoned her first thing next morning from my office; which showed how desperate I was. Telephones scared me. My worst nightmare was the one in which I had been demoted to telephone operator on a large London exchange staffed entirely by deaf-mutes.

"Hello, hello," I bawled, as soon as I'd got the telephone cord unwound from one of the pipes in my office. "Is that Mrs. Cary?"

There was a ringing Cockney curse at the other end, followed by a metallic crash. A moment later a voice said cautiously, "Angela Cary here. Who is this, please?"

"Bandy! Colonel Bandy!" I said. "You remember we met–"

"Yes, I remember. I wonder if you'd mind not speaking quite so loudly, Colonel. I'm not in Poona, you know."

"No. Right. Ah – how's your mother?"

"A little deaf at the moment, but otherwise. . . . What can I do for you, Bartholomew?"

After rambling on nervously for a bit, I finally got around to explaining that I needed some information that only General Pusey of the War Office seemed to be in possession of. I wanted to find out what Army units were being allocated to the Western Front reserve, but I couldn't go to him cold, and as I had understood her to say that Pusey was a friend of hers, I–

"Yes, I know Marmaduke quite well, as a matter of fact."

"No, no," I said. "It's Pusey I want to see, not Marmaduke."

"As I was saying, Bart, I know Sir Marmaduke Pusey quite well–"

"Oh, I see. Good."

"But I don't think I can help you there, Bart."

"Oh! Oh, well! Goodbye."

"Wait. You are in a rush, aren't you? I was going to say that it's not the kind of thing I ought to know about, surely? Wouldn't it be highly confidential, that sort of information?"

"Yes, I guess it would. Well, I'd better hang up now."

"Wait. I didn't say definitely I couldn't find out for you, Bartholomew. Marmaduke will do anything for me if I – put it to him in the right way. But the trouble is, I don't know you all that well, do I?"

"No, that's true."

"Of course, if I *did* know you better . . ."

"What? Could you speak up, Mrs. Cary. I can hardly hear you."

"It's because I'm holding the instrument at arm's length, Bartholomew."

"I see. What were you saying?"

"I was saying that if I could get to know you better . . . perhaps we could discuss it?"

"Yes, that's a good idea."

"You could call round, or – No, better still, I could call on you sometime when you're free."

"Yes, that's a good idea," I said, wondering if I'd said this before.

"It just so happens that I'm free today, as a matter of fact," Mrs. Cary said, laughing a trifle breathlessly.

"Oh, are you?"

"It's a pity Mother wasn't out when you called the other day," she said, laughing again.

"Sure is," I said enthusiastically, not quite grasping this abrupt change of subject.

"It might've been very interesting, I thought."

"Yes, very."

"Anyway, as I was saying, I am free today. I can't come too early, I have another engagement, but – I could call round at, say, ten o'clock?"

"Fine," I said. "Well, goodbye."

When I looked at my watch, though, I saw it was already nine-fifteen. I wondered how she thought she was going to fulfill an engagement and get all the way from Hampstead to the Strand in forty-five minutes.

Apparently she couldn't. In fact she hadn't even arrived by lunchtime, and when I called back, there was no answer.

Well, perhaps it was just as well. I hadn't exactly relished the thought of ushering her into a converted gentleman's convenience. It might have given her the wrong impression, somehow.

All Kinds of Disgraceful Goings On

"Energy, resourcefulness, and initiative aren't the least bit of use in this business," I complained to Katherine and Milestone that evening, in the dining room of the Spartan Hotel. "Goldarn it, if the Secretary of State for Air, with all the resources of the Cabinet and War Committee at his disposal, can't drag the information out of the brass, how does he expect me to?"

"It shouldn't be so difficult," Katherine said airily. "After all, you're one of the brass now, aren't you?"

"So, surely all you have to do is drag the information out of yourself," Milestone chipped in.

"Unless, of course, he's not on speaking terms with himself."

"Yes, he has been a bit unspeakable, lately."

They both sniggered childishly, and when I started to lash my thigh crossly with my silver-tipped stick, they giggled and snuffled all the more. They had been ganging up on me ever since we had entered the huge dining room of the hotel twenty minutes before.

Recovering, Milestone looked around at the densely packed tables, among which whey-faced waiters were dispiritedly circulating.

"The colonel doesn't seem to have much pull here either, does he?" he said to Katherine. "Everybody's getting served but us."

"Darling," Katherine said. "Why don't you start lashing your haunches again with your nice new stick? Maybe that will attract some attention."

"No," Milestone said decisively. "They'll think he's a horse, and all they'll bring is a bag of oats."

This set them off again, and several diners looked across and smiled at the happy couple. Even one or two waiters glanced over for a second or two before turning away again.

I gazed around as if I weren't with them. They looked at my face and almost went into hysterics.

Fortunately the disgraceful noise they were making was almost drowned by the racket in the dining room. The air pulsated with the clash of cutlery and conversation. In the distance an orchestra of retired seaside landladies was playing a catchy prelude and fugue in either D or E minor, or both.

Finally tiring of making an exhibition of himself, Milestone, looking suspiciously respectful and naive, said, "Perhaps we'd better order dinner in your suite, Colonel."

"In his *what?*" Katherine said.

"His suite."

"His suite? He doesn't have a suite."

"That's funny. He gave me to understand he'd practically a whole floor to himself."

"He has the whole floor to himself all right, but just in one room."

"One room?"

"Yes. And a bathroom you have to use a shoehorn to get into."

"That's funny. He distinctly gave me the impression he had several rooms."

"Well, there is a large cupboard, of course."

They both turned and looked at me, straight-faced. I picked up an embossed fish fork and studied it woodenly. Like the rest of the hotel's cutlery, it was stout enough to have served as an entrenching tool. I breathed on it and polished it with a napkin.

"By the way," Milestone said, turning back to Katherine, "has he invited you up to his office at the Air Ministry yet?"

"Listen," I said quickly, "listen to the music. Isn't it swell music?"

"No, he hasn't, Richard."

"I've never been up there either, Katherine. He always insists I meet him in the lobby."

"Same here. One almost gets the impression he's hiding something."

"Gee, that's a swell tune," I said, twitching my head two or three times toward the orchestra.

"You don't suppose he doesn't really have an office?" Katherine suggested, wide-eyed.

"I say, maybe that's it! Maybe he sits all day on the roof, watching out for Zeppelins and things."

"Or feeding the carrier pigeons?"

Luckily a waiter came up at that moment. I buried my nose in the menu.

The waiter stood stolidly by, a stub of pencil poised patiently over his grubby pad.

I became aware that Katherine was staring at the waiter. I looked up.

"Roast beef is special," Rodominov said. "But is finished. You should have ordered before."

"Rodominov!" I ejaculated. "For heaven's sake, what are you doing here?"

"Waiting."

"No, I mean–" I gestured at his mildewed tails. "What is this? A rehearsal for *The Lower Depths?*"

Katherine frowned as if I'd been tactless. She held out her hand. "How nice to see you again, Mr. Rodominov," she said.

She was obviously trying to put him at his ease. But Rodominov didn't seem the least self-conscious at having come down in the world so drastically. He leaned over and kissed her hand, his fair hair flopping over his broad brow.

The diners nearby continued to stare as the bulky Russian, who seemed about to burst from his narrow-shouldered outfit, stood chatting to Katherine, with his foot on my chair.

"I have room in Balaam now," he said.

"Yes, so Bart was telling me."

"Peoples downstairs always getting dronk, leavink on gas – without putting match to it. Voof! Twice this week I have been blown out of bed. Is wery interesting place."

The people at the adjoining table also seemed to find it interesting. They had stopped eating and were all leaning sideways, eavesdropping shamelessly.

"Also, overhead is railway treck. When train comes over, makes wery frightening noise. Lyittle old voman next door come running into my room in nightie gown, for drink of gin, to calm shattered nerves."

"It sounds quite a lively place."

"Och, aye. Lots bedbugs and mice."

"Surely the Embassy can do something to help its own people," Katherine said. She turned to Milestone. "Rody was with the Russian Embassy."

"Things must be very difficult," Milestone said politely.

"Everybody in same boot. Some are trying to get back to Rossia, others hoping to leave here, go to United Stets. As for me," Rodominov said tonelessly, "maybe I join White Russians, kill Bolsheviks."

"But look here," I said, "you oughtn't to be here, Rody. Waiting at table, I mean. Not with *your* disease."

The people at the next table slowly straightened and stared into the next century.

"Really, Bart," Katherine said.

"Well, it's not very hygienic, is it?"

"Hotel peoples don't seem to mind if I have consumption," Rodominov said, as the people at the adjoining table signaled for their waiter.

Finally Rodominov became aware that the headwaiter was looking at him. He removed his foot from my chair. "Well, don't just sit there," he muttered. "Order somethink."

"What is there to eat?"

"Hoots, you leave it to me. I bring everythink is worth eating."

He must have done quite a bit of bullying in the kitchen, for the meal he served was the most ample I'd ever had at the Spartan. I reflected gloomily that even to get a good dinner nowadays you had to have personal contacts.

"That's the first time I've ever been served pork chops by a prince," Milestone said, tipping the last of the port into Katherine's glass. He had already given her most of the rosé. Her face was quite flushed.

"I feel so sorry for Rody," she said. "He's lost everything, you know. Not just his estates, but his family as well."

"Your father said Rodominov's mother was in Paris," I said snottily.

"She's the only survivor, though," Katherine said. She turned to Milestone. "Did you know that Rody's father was a Cossack general? No, of course you didn't. Well, he was.

"It's quite a story, as a matter of fact," she went on excitedly. "You know, in some of those Russian aristocrat families, when a boy reaches sixteen his parents arrange a match between him and a likely-looking girl."

"A marriage, you mean?"

"Not exactly," she said, a shade self-consciously. "It's a temporary liaison with a healthy peasant girl, until it's time for the boy to marry somebody more suitable. Some of the old Russian families consider it essential for the boy's health, you see."

"Wish my family'd had a custom like that," Milestone said, stroking her hand and glancing at me mischievously.

"Yes," Katherine said, preoccupied with her story. "Anyway, that's the arrangement General Rodominov made for the prince, and Rody had a son when he was barely sixteen."

"Lovely grub."

"Well," she went on, "no one ever bothered to find out what happened to Rodominov's child. Until a few weeks ago, during the October Revolution, which, as you know, happened in November."

We waited. But she was determined we should ask what happened next, so we did so.

"Well," she whispered, her eyes alight with pleasure at the idea that life could sometimes be almost as interesting as fiction, "On the day the Bolshies stormed the Winter Palace in St. Petersburg, or Petrograd, or whatever it's called, and brought

down the provisional government, General Rodominov's
orderly came to him and told him who he was."

"Who the general was?"

"No! Who *he* was, the orderly. He told the general that he,
the orderly, was Prince Rodominov's son.

"And then," Katherine whispered, "he shot the general."

She gazed at us, thrilled. "In the name of the revolution, of
course," she added.

As Milestone had to get back to his squadron for a night-flying
exercise, he left shortly afterward. We saw him off into the
chill night air, then went inside again, silent and thoughtful.

The hotel lobby was crowded with the usual mob: office
workers, war profiteers and their wives, air raid wardens with
their rattles, young subalterns trying to look married as they
sauntered to the elevators with thin, casual flappers; and
a couple of doughboys, who veered toward Katherine the
moment she appeared, smiles wreathing their smooth, uncom-
plicated faces – until they saw this huffy-looking colonel take
her arm possessively. Whereupon they continued past as if it
was one of the theater posters that had attracted their attention (*Love in a Cottage*, with Marie Löhr). They were the first
American servicemen I'd seen in London.

The moment Milestone had weaved off into the murk, a
constraint descended on Katherine and me. As we stood in the
middle of the lobby's threadbare Axminster, I glanced at her
averted face. Her long eyelashes were lowered, concealing
her dark, loving eyes.

As I looked at her, a strange sensation overwhelmed me.
Holding my breath, I sank slowly into a well of contempla-
tion, introspection, and soul-searching. I thought about my
conduct over the past weeks – my haughtiness, my superior
attitude, my overweening self-esteem, pride, and engorged

dignity. And I couldn't help feeling that it was all her fault.

Well, she had been behaving with increasing chilliness ever since my elevation, almost as if she disapproved of people getting on in the world and hobnobbing with lords, generals, admirals, administrative civil servants, and other toffs. I mean, I might have understood it if she herself had come from an underprivileged background and was afraid of being out-classed; but her family was accepted in the most exclusive drawing rooms in the land.

I don't know. It was almost as if she considered it a crime to leave one's sordid acquaintances behind and become a gentleman.

"What's happening to us, Katherine?" I asked. "You've changed, you know."

She looked at me in utter astonishment. Her glorious dark eyes seemed to expand to the size of brandy balls.

"I really don't know what's gotten into you," I said.

"Into *me?*"

"You act as if I were some kind of pincushion, for you to stick pins into."

"Not so much a pincushion," she said haughtily, "as a balloon."

"Exactly. Er, no, a pincushion. You hardly ever talk to me properly nowadays."

"You want me to call you 'sir' – is that it?"

"Course not," I said. "Don't be ridiculous, Katherine. Whoever heard of a girl calling her fiancé 'sir.' No, 'Colonel' is quite good enough."

Katherine sighed and raised her eyes to a plaster nymph that was sheltering embarrassedly in a niche above the hotel desk.

"No, but I mean, what kind of start is this for a marriage?"

She looked down at the threadbare carpet and said some-thing inaudible.

"Pardon me?"

"I sometimes wonder if it's really my home and family you want to marry into, rather than me."

"Course not."

"Course not what?"

"I love you just as much as your stately home."

For some reason her head drooped even lower.

"You see," I said. "You're still not chatting nicely."

"You haven't been chatting very nicely yourself tonight."

I twirled my swagger stick. "You and Milestone were, though," I remarked.

"Why shouldn't I chat to him? I thought he was very nice."

"I could see you thought that."

"What does that mean?"

"I could see you thought he was very nice, that's all," I said. Then, as she continued to look at me unblinkingly: "Letting him hold your hand and everything."

"Oh, don't be so silly, Bart."

"Um not."

"Yes, you are. You're being childish."

"I yam not," I said, lashing my thigh again, and wincing at the blow.

We fell silent. Nearby an enthusiastic young man was talking to a girl in a fluffy dress.

"I say!" the girl was saying. Her eyes were sparkling with excitement and trepidation. He seemed to be leading her toward the elevator.

"Oh, come on."

"Shocking."

"Why not?"

"No, really."

"Pretty please?"

"We shouldn't."

"Rather."

"Priceless."

"Frightfully."

"Mumsy?"

"Won't mind. Does it herself."

"All right – let's!" the girl said; and they hid behind a potted plant and lit a couple of cigarettes.

"Well, I suppose I might as well go to bed," Katherine said.

When she was in town she usually stayed with her Aunt Clotilda in Kensington, but on this occasion had elected to put up at the Spartan – apparently without mentioning the change of plan to her parents. She had a room on the same floor as I did.

She looked so dismal as she ascended in the open-cage elevator that my heart melted like a lump of lard in a hot skillet. I was just about to follow her and apologize for being such a grouch when somebody tapped me on the shoulder blade.

"You have room in hotel?" Rodominov asked. He was still in his waiter's garb.

"Yes."

"I want to ask favor of you, Bandy."

"Wot?"

"I want your room for couple of hours."

"Eh? You want my room? Why?"

"I have voman friend."

I looked at him disapprovingly. But for some reason it seemed to encourage him. "My room in Balaam is too noisy," he said. "Trains run over roof all night."

"Couldn't you get another room here?" I asked testily.

"She has tried. All rooms full up. She is desperate, Bandy. She has decided is last time we will see each other." A stave of wrinkles lined his brow. "What was it she said . . .?"

"We can't go on like this?"

"That is right! How did you know?"

"And what am I supposed to do in the meantime?" I asked petulantly.

"Go for valk. Is good exercise."

"But it's freezing out there."

"Please, Bandy." He brought his crude, heavy face dangerously close and said tonelessly, "Is not for me, is for her, Bandy."

"Oh, well, that makes all the difference," I said. But my sarcasm was as wasted as my disapproval.

"She has fallen in love with me. She has saved up lifetime of passion. Is spending it all on me. She is magnificent, Bandy, wild. I have never known such desperation, such passion. Is experience I will never forget. Thank God is nearly all over."

I clicked my tongue and glared at the plaster nymph as if it were all her fault. I barely managed to restrain myself from lashing my thigh again.

"Oh, all right," I said. "Give me five minutes to collect my coat, scarf, gloves, balaclava, earmuffs, two or three extra pullovers, and an umbrella, and I'll walk around in the filthy, freezing cold, if that's what you want."

I went upstairs in a thoroughly bad temper. As I stood in the bathroom brushing my teeth (in case that was the reason Katherine was being so distant), I was still seething at my own weakness, wondering why I had put myself out for Rodominov in this fashion. As if I hadn't done enough for him already, buying that rotten French painting of his. I'd had to carry it – and the samovar – half a mile before I found a taxicab. And a lot of grubby children had trailed behind me, all making rude Cockney remarks.

It wouldn't have been so bad if it had been a respectable picture, a nice landscape of trees and sheep and a few clouds and things. But no, it had to look like the third prize in an art contest for handicapped orangutans. And for that, and a samovar that made very poor tea, I had spent almost every penny I'd saved over the past six months.

I snorted in disgust.

However, there was no point in crying over spilled paint; and by the time his discreet tap sounded on the bedroom door I had resigned myself to a long, cold walk – probably in the pouring rain.

"Come in; it's not locked," I shouted.

I suppose, really, I had agreed to Rodominov's request because I couldn't help admiring his indifference to his own misfortune. I suppose that's what it was. And also because he somehow gave you the feeling that making sacrifices for him would turn out to be a rewarding experience.

"Come in," I shouted impatiently, when he tapped at the door again.

All the same, I thought, as I finished drying my hands, it was the last time I was going to help him. From now on he would have to make his own way in the world.

It had been arranged that Rodominov would come up to my room in about five minutes, and his woman friend would follow a few minutes after that, as soon as I was out of the way. But the fool must have fouled up the arrangements, for when I went into the bedroom in my shirt sleeves I found Mrs. Cary's bosom there, accompanied by Mrs. Cary.

"What . . . what . . ." I said. Then: "Good Lord, don't tell me *you*'re his lover?"

"Who?"

"You."

"Whose lover?" Mrs. Cary asked. "Which one are you talking – I mean, what d'you mean?"

"Aren't you Rodominov's . . ."

"Rodominov's? Certainly not. I think he's a dreadful man. Why should you think I was?"

"Oh, I don't know," I said, somewhat bewilderedly. "But – what're you doing? I mean, how did you . . .?"

"I came up the stairs," she said. "I didn't want to be seen in the lift."

She looked at me. Her eyes were like twin beds.

"I've just come from the most boring dinner party," she said breathlessly. "I had the most awful time getting away. I was so agitated everyone must have thought I'd had too much to drink."

It was certainly true that her face was flushed and her breathing decidedly unsteady. But, then, so was mine and I'd had absolutely nothing to drink. Well, two or three glasses of wine and port, which didn't really count.

"That's why I'm a few minutes late for our appointment."

The appointment! But – a few minutes? She was twelve hours late.

Or – had she meant ten o'clock at *night*?

Good Lord.

"Well. . .?" she asked, looking at me brilliant-eyed. "Why are you staring like that?"

"No, no . . ."

"I feel quite flustered. I'm not usually in the habit of visiting strange men's rooms. I mean, men's strange rooms. No, I don't mean that, either, but I don't see why I shouldn't."

"Shouldn't what?"

"After all, we're both still free, and . . . times are changing, aren't they?" She came close. "You really are big, aren't you. And young." She put a somewhat shaky hand on my bare forearm. My sleeves were still rolled up, as if for a fight. "Most of the men I know are so old. Oh, Bart."

"What? What?"

"You look better out of uniform," she said, staring up my nostrils, which were fluttering a bit wildly by now. "Well?" she whispered, her breath arriving in short pants. "Do we have to have our little chat standing up? Or should we get into something more comfortable?" She glanced at the bed.

"What, what?" I said.

"I do believe you're nervous." She gave a breathless laugh. "General Pusey will be back tomorrow, by the way. I might be able to find out from him then. About your reserves."

"What? I don't have any reserves."

"I'll let him take me–"

"Take you?"

"–to the Music Hall. He likes that sort of thing. I'll ask him afterwards. . . ." She put a hot hand on my chest. "Your heart's beating away."

"It's only just started up again," I said, gulping in great mouthfuls of her scent. It was so powerful I began to feel faint. I swayed against her, wide-eyed.

"You're passionate. . . . Oh, how wonderful. . . . I feel weak. . . ." She started for the bathroom. "Just give me a minute."

But Rodominov was due any time. "I don't have a minute!" I cried.

"You can't wait? Oh, darling. All right – *half* a minute, then!"

"No, no!"

There was a tap at the door. Mrs. Cary froze and stared at me, her eyes as wide as the double bed that lay spread-eagled under that sensuous French painting.

I gestured wildly for her to continue into the bathroom. She needed no urging. She had gone quite pale.

I opened the bedroom door. "Look," I said into the corridor. "Something's come up" (which was true). "Could you come back in a couple of days – minutes? I–"

Rodominov's friend stood there. Two red spots started to burn fiercely on her cheeks. She stepped back and clutched tightly at her crocodile handbag as if it were trying to wriggle back into the nearest primeval swamp.

"You were supposed to be going out for a walk," Mrs. Auchinflint whispered accusingly.

"I was – delayed. . . ."

Voices sounded down the corridor. Her knuckles whitened as she clung to the crocodile. She pushed past into the room.

"I can't stand out there. Somebody might see me."

In the room she turned away, whispering angrily, "Well? Are you going to keep the door open so everyone can look in?"

I closed it nervelessly.

"I gave you an extra ten minutes to get out. It really is inconsiderate of you, Mr. Bandy." Still with her back turned, she went on, "I suppose you wanted to see who it was? Well, now you know. I hope you're satisfied. So please be good enough to get out of your room. Or perhaps you'd prefer to stay and watch? So that's the sort of person you are, a Peeping Tom. I'm very disappointed in you, Mr. Bandy."

"I . . . I . . . aye, aye."

She turned and looked at me icily. "It's disgusting," she said. "What would Katherine say if she caught you in here? I've a good mind to tell her the sort of person you are."

There was another tap at the door. I reached for it limply. She seized my arm. "You're not expecting anyone else, are you?"

The tapping was repeated. A voice murmured, "Bart?"

"Oh, gosh," I said. It was Katherine.

The doorknob started to turn. I got my foot against the door just in time. Mrs. Auchinflint started for the bathroom.

"No, no," I hissed, "not in there! The cupboard, the cupboard!"

I pointed to the big cupboard. The bedroom door pushed impatiently against my foot. Mrs. Auchinflint, her lean, chilly face pinched and tatty-looking, hurried into the cupboard and

closed the door. "Come in," I called out jovially, wiping the
sweat from my brow and tugging at the door, against my own
foot. "It's stuck," I called out; then removed my foot.
Katherine half fell into the room. "It was stuck a bit," I said.
Then I saw that Katherine was in her dressing gown and
nightdress. "Oh, Good God," I said.

Katherine walked past me stiffly and stood in the middle of
the room, looking around. "So that's it," she said abruptly.

"It's not my fault, I didn't invite her," I began, thinking that
somehow she'd already sensed the presence of two other
women in my bedroom. But then I saw she was looking at the
painting above the bed.

"I like it," she said.

"You do?"

"Yes. It's . . . rather decorative, I think."

"It is?"

She took a deep breath and said stiffly, "I just came in to say
I'm sorry if I was rather mean to you in the dining room. I
suppose it was really my fault. It's just that you've been – just
a little puffed up lately."

"No, it was my fault; well, good night, Katherine!" I cried,
going up to her, intending to seize her arm and rush her back
into the corridor.

She put her arms round me and laid her hot face against my
even hotter shirt. "I couldn't bear to go to bed without seeing
you again and . . . you're not still annoyed at me, are you?"

"No, no, not at all," I said, taking a deep, shuddery breath
and looking in a frightened sort of way at the cupboard
door – and the bathroom door as well.

"Promise you're not still angry at me."

"No, no, not at all."

"You weren't jealous of Milestone, were you?"

"No, no, not at all."

"It wasn't that, was it?"

"No, no, not at all."

"It's just that you've been so distant."

"No, no, not in the least."

She let go and looked up at me. "You're still being distant," she said.

"Shhh!" I said, seizing her face and burying it against my sticky shirt, to muffle her. The other two women must be hearing her every word.

She took the gesture as one of affection, and clung to me. "I love you," she whispered. Then: "I don't think I'll go back to my own room."

"What? Why on earth not?" I said loudly. Then added for my own benefit, "Shhh!"

"It's so lonely. I don't like the color of the walls."

"Oh, but, but I'm sure they're a lovely color."

"No, they're not, they're terra-cotta. Like a mausoleum."

"Yes, but as you see, mine aren't much better – lime green and marzipan. Surely you don't prefer lime green and marzipan, do you? Of course not. Well, night-night, Mrs. Auch – Ange – Katherine," I said, now fully in command of the situation. I took her arm and was just leading her to the door when there was another knock – loud and insistent, this time.

"Who could that be?"

"God knows. Kaiser Bill?"

She started for the bathroom. "No, no, not there!" She started for the cupboard. "No, no, not in there either!" I grabbed her arm and almost flung her into the narrow bay behind the curtains. "Stay there! Don't breathe!"

She needed no urging.

Rodominov came in. He was wearing a cloak over his tails.

"Rodominov!" I said loudly, to prove it wasn't another woman. "Well, well, this is an unexpected pleasure!"

He stared at me lumpily for a moment, then looked around. "Where is she–"

I clapped a hand over his mouth so that the last word came out as 'sheep.' "Sheep?" I cried. "I don't have any sheep in here," I called out, laughing a trifle shrilly at the very idea of there being a sheep in my bedroom.

He wrenched my hand off his mouth and glared, affronted. I pointed frantically to the bathroom door and mimed the outline of a woman. But he thought I was showing him where his inamorata was, and started toward the bathroom.

He had almost reached it when there came yet another rapping at the door. Rodominov stopped and frowned. There was only one thing to do. I seized his arm, opened the cupboard door and thrust him inside.

As he saw Mrs. Auchinflint's pallid form within, he opened his mouth. I shut the door hurriedly, and then, pausing only to blow cooling air down my shirt, opened the bedroom door for the – what? – seventh time? Simultaneously, with lightning speed, I was deciding on a course of action. But first I had to work out what the situation was on which to base my lightning decision.

As I was doing so, Major Auchinflint came hesitantly into the room, jerking his head about in that dreaded ostrich way of his.

He looked so agitated I thought he already knew his wife was in my bathroom. No – cupboard! His wife was in the cupboard! I had to remember that!

"Sorry to bother you at this time of night, uh . . . Colonel," he muttered distastefully.

"What?" I said, wishing by now that Mrs. Cary wasn't a widow so that *her* husband could walk in as well, and resolve the problem, or render it so complicated that nobody would ever be able to make sense of it.

"I've, ah," Auchinflint was saying, "I've, ah, been in touch with the D.M.O. . . ."

"What?" I said, thinking that even if I managed to prevent each one of them from knowing that the others were there, I still had to surmount the problem of how to get rid of them – and in what order? Mrs. Cary first or last? Or Katherine? Or the two in the cupboard? Or – maybe it would be best if *I* left first?

I became aware that Auchinflint was waiting expectantly.

"Sorry, what . . . what was it again, Major?"

"I said I must know who this information is for."

"What information?"

"About the reserves, man! I mean, sir. Is it for Lord Rackingham?"

"Good heavens, what on earth gives you that idea?" I said, looking around in a distraught way.

"Then, who?"

"Oh, just the ministry in major, General," I said. Careful, I thought. I was beginning to talk with an English accent, a sure sign of panic. "Co-ordination and all that," I babbled. "Enable the Air Force to, to, to, to – co-ordinate. So to speak." I hoped he couldn't tell I was just making it all up on the spur of the moment.

"The information is not just for the Air Minister?"

"Why on earth would the Air Minister want to know about Army reserves?" I said. I took several deep breaths, then: "Well, if that's all you wanted, Major . . .?"

I opened the bedroom door for him invitingly. An elderly maid promptly entered. She made straight for the cupboard. "Excuse me, sir," she said with a quick curtsy. "I'll do your bed, sir, soon as I've put fresh towels in the bathroom," she said, and opened the cupboard.

As she did so the curtains moved. Auchinflint twitched his head in that direction just as Rodominov, with remarkable presence of mind, snatched an armful of sheets and blankets off the cupboard shelf and thrust them on the maid.

The maid backed out again slowly, clutching an unnecessarily large supply of sheets and blankets and staring into the cupboard. Rodominov hurriedly closed the door a split second before Auchinflint twitched his head back in that direction.

Meanwhile, still staring at the cupboard, the maid backed slowly into the bathroom. About two seconds later she came hurrying out of there as well. As she went past she cast me a strange sort of look, obviously taking pains not to turn her back on me. She disappeared backward into the corridor, still clutching the sheets and blankets.

Auchinflint started toward the curtains. I stood in his way.

"By the way," he said. "My wife–"

"What about her?" I shouted. "It's nothing to do with me, I only live here!"

"What?" His head twitched; his watery eyes blinked rapidly. "I just wanted to confirm her invitation to come fox hunting this weekend . . ."

"Fox hunting?" I shouted, wondering if this was some kind of foul innuendo. Well, I was getting pretty disoriented by then.

"Is something the matter, Colonel?"

"Course not!"

He opened the door and stood for a moment massaging the doorknob. "As for that other matter – I can assure the D.M.O. that you're not requesting this information on behalf of the Air Minister or any member of the cabinet, can I?"

I took a couple of deep breaths, and tried valiantly to concentrate. "Does that mean he's authorized you to give me the

information?" I asked, clearing a frog or two from my throat.
"If I answer that?"

"Well . . . no, not exactly, sir."

"Well . . ." I held my head for a second. "In that case I don't
know why we're discussing it. Do you?"

Auchinflint compressed his lips and looked at me hatefully.
After a brief, charged silence, he turned on his heel and went
out, leaving the door open. I sat on the bed and thought about
it for a minute or two. Then I went over and closed the door
and started toward the curtain, whispering hoarsely, "You can
come out now."

Katherine came out. Unfortunately, so did Rodominov.

And Mrs. Auchinflint.

And Mrs. Cary.

But all that was like a tiff at a quilting bee compared with the
ordeal that followed.

Me, Riding to Hounds

The rendezvous for the hunt that weekend was at a red-tiled
country pub fifteen miles from Burma Park. It was called
The Dingle, presumably because it lay drunkenly in a quaint
Berkshire dingle, or dell.

Robert, who was home for the weekend, insisted on setting
out for the hunt at the abominable hour of 7 A.M. With
Katherine and the groom some distance in the lead, we
clopped sedately along one of Britain's main roads. It was just

wide enough for two horses to pass, or three-quarters of a car.

"Had a tiff with Katherine, have you?" Robert asked.

"Yes. She can be very unreasonable, sometimes."

We arrived in plenty of time to stable the horses. When we led them out of the stables again, at ten to eleven, the scene was transformed. An hour ago the dirt yard behind the pub had been deserted except for a solitary hedgehog busily chewing away the foundations of the hostelry. Now there were at least fifty riders milling around, not counting the hunt servants. They were all shouting jocularly at one another, or stamping about in an effort to bestir their middle-class blood.

To my surprise, fewer than a third of them wore the traditional red coat. The rest sported khaki, black, or earth-brown coats, in a variety of styles. The headgear was equally varied: officers' caps, blue-and-green hunting caps, and a jockey cap, hard black hats, and even one mildewed topper, worn by a vicious-looking dame in a crumpled bottle-green habit who was riding sidesaddle.

Among the mob was Captain Treadwell.

"Treadwell. Well, I'm blowed. What're you doing here?" I asked.

Treadwell, who had been gazing almost tolerantly at the turmoil around him, turned his dark, cynical eyes on me and said, "Be much more appropriate for me to ask that, wouldn't it? You're the last person I'd expect to see at a Meet."

"I promised to come, unfortunately. Also, I desperately need some War Office information for my boss. Doesn't look very hopeful, though."

"From Auchinflint?" He thought about it for a moment, then: "What sort of information?"

As I told him in some detail – I knew I could trust Treadwell – a miniature whirlwind of last year's leaves danced between the excited horses, and a few snowflakes began to fling themselves around the yard. In the far corner, Katherine, who was still not speaking to me, was being helped into the saddle by her groom.

As I finished, Robert came up. I introduced him to Treadwell, then said, "When do we start shouting yoicks, tallyho, and things like that?"

"For God's sake, don't say anything," Robert said quickly. "Just follow the hunt, that's all."

In the distance a church bell bonged in a discouraged fashion. It looked as if most of the local parishioners were going to be chasing foxes this morning instead of dropping ha'pennies in the velvet collection bag and pretending they were shillings.

The minutes cantered by as the hunters tightened girths, jested coarsely, or walked their mounts up and down in a dedicated sort of way. At eleven the church bell gave up in despair, and immediately the baying of hounds was heard. A tidal bore of jolly-looking dogs came pouring along the country road, preceded by a red-faced man holding a gracefully curved horn that gleamed richly even under the gray sky. This, presumably, was the Huntsman.

Beside him rode the Master. Auchinflint looked far more impressive in his pink coat than in his major's uniform. After chatting for a minute or two to some cronies, he raised his arm, and the hunters, about sixty of them by now, stern-looking men and a handful of substantial women, began to move off. A moment later the narrow road in front of the pub was jammed with bobbing horsemen and littered with bitches.

About half a mile away we passed Auchinflint's place, a square red-brick house with a Union Jack standing out from a twenty-foot flagpole.

Then we were in Prankster's Wood, our first destination, the dogs coursing ahead in a brown-and-white swarm.

Every now and then as we lurched through the wood, the Huntsman would utter some incomprehensible cry, and tootle his horn – warming it up, I guess, the way we pilots warmed up our guns before crossing the line.

As for Auchinflint, he rode alone, looking this way and that in an alert fashion. He obviously enjoyed his duties as Master, and to give him his due he was said to be an efficient one, with an above-average record of kills.

For several minutes the chattering squadron – some of the women's remarks struck me as being rather coarse – crackled through the wood. By then I'd lost sight of Katherine, though I could still see Robert, straight-backed and remote atop his disciplined gelding.

Just ahead of me, the lady in the top hat was holding back a branch. When it was bent almost double, she released it without making sure there was nobody behind her. The branch whipped back with a sound like a broadside at Agincourt.

By the time I'd finished plucking the barbs out of my throat, the rest of the hunt was almost out of sight and the dogs sounded as if they were in the next county.

I started to gallop after the pack along a winding path. But just as I rounded a bend I saw that the redcoats were coming – back. There seemed to be several hundred of them, and they were charging straight toward me with their thongs raised.

I thought they were going to horsewhip me. I couldn't understand what I'd done wrong. When I opened my eyes again, they were streaming past on both sides, bellowing like crazy.

By the time I'd got my black beast onto a reciprocal heading, they had disappeared again. And then, just as I was charging after them once more, at full throttle, back they came, and thundered past again, in dizzying flashes of color, still shouting at the top of their voices.

The heck with this, I thought, cowering back as they swept past like Mongol hordes. I'll just stay here and wait.

Unfortunately, this time they failed to reappear. After a while I thought I'd better get after them, to make sure they didn't get into any further trouble. But I'd delayed too long. By then the fools had gotten themselves hopelessly lost in the woods.

I cantered about for nearly twenty minutes, looking anxiously this way and that, and stopping occasionally to listen; but there was no sound now, except for the panting of my hired nag, who was starting to glance over his shoulder at me in a somewhat disillusioned way.

However, I found them at last, milling about in a clearing.

"So that's what fox hunting is like," I said to Katherine. "My, that was exciting. I guess we can all go home for lunch now, eh?"

"Why? Did you see a fox?" she asked sharply.

"No. Did you?"

"Course not."

"What was all the commotion, then?"

"What commotion?" Robert asked, irritably aware that several of his friends were listening.

"You the one who charged straight through the hunt?" one of them asked sharply.

"Me? No, sir," I said cravenly.

"It was him," a woman said. "He almost broke Taffy's leg." She glared at me. I examined my fingernails. Then I started to push back the cuticles, because they were looking a bit tattered.

A couple of minutes later I saw Taffy's owner talking to the Master and jerking her head in my direction.

But it was Katherine I was concerned about. I watched her unhappily as she hauled at the reins and moved away, her back stiff and hostile. A few weeks ago she would probably have laughed at my discomfiture. But she had been in a very bad mood ever since my promotion. And following that awkward scene in my bedroom she had become still more withdrawn, even though Mrs. Cary had explained at some length that she had come to my bedroom at ten at night merely to discuss Affairs of State.

Katherine had been very unreasonable, in fact. She had marched back to her own room without even waiting to find out what Rodominov and Mrs. Auchinflint had been doing there. I would have canceled my appearance at the hunt forthwith if I hadn't been desperate for the information I was now sure Auchinflint was able to give me.

I edged over to him now. "About that business of the Reserves," I began.

"Not now, not now," he said irritably. Then, all his resentment boiling up: "As a matter of fact, after the way you treated me in your hotel room, I'm astonished you turned up today."

"I didn't treat you any way. What d'you mean, the way I treated you?"

"And don't think I'm going to forget that little incident at the War Office, either."

"Incident? War Office?" By now, if there'd been a wall handy, I'd have had my back to it.

"You thought you were being funny, no doubt," Auchinflint said loudly. "Bringing me down to the entrance on a wild goose chase. Well, all I can say is, it was a pretty puerile trick!"

"I don't know what you're talking about," I said, horribly aware that everybody was listening, and worse, enjoying the spectacle of a colonel being slowly shredded by a major.

"Do you deny you had the switchboard inform me there was a general waiting to see me?"

"Well, I, er . . ."

"Don't bother," he said cuttingly. "I questioned the corporal in charge myself, and he described you." He looked me up and down contemptuously. "You're not hard to describe – *Colonel*."

He wrenched at the reins and moved away, leaving me sweating with embarrassment and realizing that I had undergone this morning's ordeal for absolutely nothing.

"About that business in my hotel room," I said to Katherine some time later. But she turned her back on me.

Pretty soon Auchinflint and the Huntsman decided to abandon the wood and went pottering off to another location, about a mile farther on.

As soon as we reached the next wood, the huntsmen all dismounted and started eating sandwiches and swigging from silver flasks, as if preparing to stoke up for several more hours of rustic disorder.

I looked around for Katherine again. She was in charge of our sandwiches.

She was sitting on a log, talking animatedly – flirting, in fact – with some of the younger officers. When I came up they all stopped chattering and looked at me warily, almost as if they expected me to start pulling rank on them or some such absurdity.

"No need to get up," I said to a motionless lieutenant. "Just forget I'm a colonel. After all, this is a sporting occasion, what?"

Nobody answered, though Katherine made rather a rude face at me.

The afternoon dragged on and it turned steadily colder. The hunt began to diminish in size. By four o'clock even some of the dogs were starting to slink home. I'd have joined them, too, if I'd known the way.

Then, without warning, there was an earsplitting scream from the middle of a thicket, and a moment later one of the hunt servants came charging out in a frightful froth. He hurtled past, flinging up great dollops of Berkshire gumbo.

Several others took up his cry, which sounded like, "High collar! High collar!"

Then followed another charge of the heavy brigade. I hauled the gelding's head around, and followed resignedly.

The hounds, muddy and dispirited after hours of nosing around dank shrubbery, started shouting joyfully again and poured across a stream in a brownish bedlam. Then we were out of the woods and galloping at full speed across a field.

But they were all vanishing in the wrong direction. For, as I broke into the open I caught sight of the fox, loping through a clump of trees to the left, making for a hedge.

"Hobbledehoys!" I bellowed, not quite sure of the correct terminology but determined to do my bit for British sport. Standing up in the stirrups, I pointed to the left. "Yoicks, High Collar, and Hobbledehoys!" I shrieked, and after some hesitation and confusion, the hounds turned and followed.

This time I was well to the fore, galloping joyfully after the russet form, which was now tearing across a plowed field, its tail undulating in the fading light. Just beyond the plowed field was a large house.

By the time I reached it I was well in advance of the field. At an exhilarating speed my gelding stretched itself over the back gate. As I landed in the yard on the other side, intensely relieved to have been given this opportunity to redeem myself, I was just in time to see the quarry scrambling frantically through an open casement window.

It was only then I realized it was Auchinflint's house. I was pretty surprised. I'd thought we were forty miles away.

But there was no mistaking the large flag that was flapping noisily overhead against the lowering sky.

The dogs caught up, and began to fill the yard; several of them flung themselves through the window after the fox, bawling joyfully at the top of their voices.

Soon there was a hell of a racket going on inside the house. Dogs were baying, a maid was screaming, and it sounded as if a good many dishes were being broken. Luckily, most of the pack continued to mill around in the yard, prancing about and sniffing at each other's rear ends.

At this point a dreadful doubt began to assail me. I don't know why, exactly, unless it was the fact that the fox had chosen to make for the house rather than for the cover of the trees, of which there were a goodly number in the vicinity. I didn't like it at all; it didn't feel right, somehow.

I looked back uneasily. The rest of the hunt was just appearing at the far side of the plowed field. They were spread out in a long, straggly line but were closing up fast. Even from a distance they seemed to me to be looking a bit frustrated. . . .

Suddenly I didn't fancy meeting them just at that moment.

I dug my heels into the gelding's flanks and started to gallop onward across the yard and around the side of the house. Keeping the house between myself and the others, I continued down to the road and turned right. I galloped along it for perhaps two hundred yards, then turned right again.

This took me once more into the plowed field.

By then the rest of the hunt was wheeling and rearing in the yard in a highly disorganized fashion. I came up behind them, panting innocently. But everything was all right now: I was firmly established as a straggler.

I cantered up, wearing what I trusted was a puzzled expression.

By then, the dogs had been driven out of the house with kicks and blows. Ears back and tails low, they were darting back and forth between the horses' legs, looking thoroughly ashamed of themselves, as well they might. The rest of the pack was being driven furiously back to the kennels.

As for the huntsmen, my long-distance impression was confirmed. They *were* looking a trifle frustrated. In fact, they were
cursing and swearing something dreadful.

I rode up to Auchinflint, panting excessively. "What's happening? What's going on?" I demanded authoritatively. As
he seemed incapable of answering, I turned to the others.
"What's up? Where'd you all get to? I have only just this
second arrived. What's happened?"

Somebody shouted angrily, "Some damn fool chased
Auchinflint's ginger cat into the house!"

"What ginger cat? Whose ginger cat? What's this about a
ginger cat?"

"Just told you, damn it! Somebody set the dogs on the
major's cat!"

"It's still in there," a woman said, pointing at the house,
"sitting on top of the hatrack, clawing everyone in sight."

"Oh, good heavens," I panted, dismounting. "But what on
earth possessed you all to chase a cat? Surely it's the – the fox
you should have been chasing?"

The only response was a furious bellow or two. This was
followed by a general stamping of outraged feet and a puffing
out of purple lips.

But I'd obviously gotten away with it. A few of the huntsmen – including Robert and Treadwell, I was sorry to see – were
looking at me suspiciously, but it was obvious I'd thrown them
off the scent with that clever subterfuge of mine. And I was
just chortling to myself and promising myself a nice hot bath
when I got home, instead of the usual cold shower that mother
had insisted on my taking ever since I had reached puberty,
and in general congratulating myself on having gotten out
of what might have been the year's most shaming situation,
when Mrs. Auchinflint leaned out of an upstairs window and

said something so outrageously treacherous it left me open-mouthed with astonishment.

"Cyril," she called out. "It was that one there who chased the cat into the house." And she pointed straight at me. "Colonel Bandy. It was him." And she stared down at me with a thoroughly mean expression, as if defying me – nay, challenging me, to snitch on her in return.

Needless to say, I still didn't get the information I wanted from Auchinflint. In fact, the swine didn't even invite me for dinner with the others. I had to eat with the groom at *The Dingle*, where I lost ten shillings at Shove Ha'penny and another five bob at Bat and Trap.

Treadwell

It was Monday, the eighteenth of March, and I was sitting in my office waiting for distant Big Ben to toll eleven o'clock, the hour when I would finally have to go to Lord Rackingham and admit failure over the question of the Reserve.

I had tried to see Pusey as soon as he got back from G.H.Q., but not only had I failed to meet him – I hadn't even been able to get back into the building. The commissionaires had refused to issue me any further passes, on Auchinflint's orders. Which meant that now I could penetrate no farther into the War Office than its imposing entrance hall.

To distract my attention from the coming interview with Lord R., I took out the A.F.M. file and went to work on it. I had been engaged for several days in preparing Air Force

Memorandum No. 2, concerning uniforms for the R.A.F. It had been decided some time before, that the new Air Force was to be given a distinctive uniform of its own. Lord R. had immediately demanded that its use be made obligatory as from April 1, but the C.A.S. fought against this proposal, arguing that the Air Force had more important things to do than concern itself with fancy costumes. The important thing was to get on with the war.

So, yet another battle had broken out between the Minister and his chief of staff. As usual, the C.A.S. had won, though he was forced to make one minor concession. So that was the task I was currently engaged on: incorporating this compromise, and advising the airmen that khaki should be worn as service dress until the end of the war, but that the new uniform could be worn by officers as mess kit if they so desired.

There was already a considerable variety of dress in the flying services, and the introduction of yet another uniform would certainly add to the confusion. Nevertheless, I had spoken up in support of my boss, earning in the process much displeasure from the C.A.S. and his supporters. I had done so out of loyalty, of course. And also because I had been delighted with the new design and wanted to start wearing it as soon as possible. It was sky blue, with magnificent gold-lace rings round the cuffs of the tunic to denote rank, and a very fancy flying badge.

I thought it was absolutely splendid. But the C.A.S. hadn't liked it one bit. In fact, his bellows of outrage had been heard as far away as Trafalgar Square, causing the pigeons and starlings there to rise in a terror-stricken cloud and rain bird droppings onto a parade of women police auxiliaries.

Some enemies of Lord R. claimed that the new uniform had been designed by Lily Elsie, a famous musical comedy actress, who was said to be intimately acquainted with a member of the Air Council. While it is possible that she had had a hand in all that gold embroidery, I happened to know that it was the Russians who were responsible for the gorgeous blue material to which the C.A.S. particularly objected. The czarist government had ordered it from British mills in late 1916 for their cavalry, but the revolution had occurred before the material could be delivered. The British Treasury Board, who were said to be a thrifty lot, had been wondering what to do with the stuff for some months. They had tried dying it khaki, and Navy blue, but the results had been frightful. It looked as if they were going to be stuck with a warehouseful of the stuff. Then they had had a brainwave. They had proposed that the new air force uniform be of a shade of, say, light blue, and this proposal being accepted (nobody could afford to argue with the Treasury), they had then announced that by an amazing coincidence they just happened to have a million yards of natty blue material available, and would the supply department of the Air Ministry care to purchase it at a bargain discount price?

Accordingly the Royal Air Force would be officially attired in Russian cavalry cloth as from October 1, 1919.

I inserted an extra comma into the memorandum, and then read it over again. But I couldn't concentrate. I mooned over to the window and gazed down into the Strand, warming my hands on one of the hot water pipes and mentally bracing myself for the interview. I hoped the Minister wouldn't dismiss me, but I wasn't too optimistic about my chances.

Quite apart from my failure over the Reserve, I was beginning to get the impression that Lord Rackingham wasn't entirely satisfied with my work. I couldn't quite put my finger on it, but there were little signs here and there, hints, clues, that suggested a certain disenchantment on his part. Like last Tuesday, when he had muttered despairingly, "You're not much of a help to me, are you, Bandy?" And two days later, when he had shouted, "If you can't do better than this, Bandy, I'll have to send you back to the front!"

He had Sir Reginald Niles in his office that morning, a man who, rumor had it, had been appointed to the Air Council to help Lord R. get rid of his more troublesome enemies among the senior officers by accusing them of incompetence. Which was fair enough, I supposed; most of them *were* incompetent.

But I wasn't prepared to put up with this typical piece of ministerial bullying. It was different in my case. I was just as incompetent, of course; but I hadn't asked for the job, it had been thrust upon me. So I considered this threat very unfair indeed.

In fact I was so annoyed I found myself shouting back, "There's nothing I'd like better than to be back to front! So there!"

At which all three of us looked taken aback: Sir Reginald at my impertinence, Lord R. because he had grown used to employing the front as a threat and wasn't used to people taking it as a favor, and me because my rejoinder seemed to have gone wrong somewhere.

But to give Lord R. his due, he muttered some sort of apology as soon as the Air Council member had left. "Things are rather difficult at the moment," he muttered.

I knew that, all right. He was losing the battle with the C.A.S., around whom most of the Air Ministry staff had now coalesced in their opposition to the Minister's policies, or lack of them.

By then I had come to understand the real nature of the conflict between them. Lord R. had manifestly allied himself with the Prime Minister's view that after the fiascos of the 1916 and 1917 campaigns, Field Marshal Haig simply had to go; while the C.A.S. was just as determined to support the C-in-C with every man and aircraft the Air Force could muster.

It was obvious that one of them would have to resign; and very soon, if the machinery of the new Royal Air Force was not to break down before it even started up.

As I stood there between the pipes and the filing cabinets that nestled in the porcelain urinals, gazing unhappily over the rooftops of the city, I had to admit to myself it was not entirely true that I would welcome a posting to the front. While the thought of combat didn't scare me, the truth was that I had immensely enjoyed the freedom of London on a handsome pay and living-out allowance with no mess bills to settle. I had almost equally enjoyed the glazed reactions of my friends to my rise in the hierarchy, and the impotent rage of just about everyone else.

On the other hand – the thought suddenly occurred to me – if I was posted within the next forty-eight hours, I wouldn't have to deliver that speech at Fallow.

Maybe incompetence had its compensations.

No, damn it. Lord R. wasn't likely to dismiss me as efficiently as that. I'd be here at least until Wednesday, the day of the speech.

But I wasn't going to dwell on that. The prospect no longer terrified me. Because I wasn't going. I had made up my mind to come down with some fashionable disease at eight-thirty that evening. Spanish influenza, perhaps. There was a lot of it going round just then.

The doorknob of the office rattled, and somebody came in. I thought it was my summons into the presence, but it was just another officer busily unbuttoning his flies, thinking my office was still functioning as a W.C. He backed out, muttering the usual embarrassed apologies.

I wondered if there was still time to take those initials off the door.

A minute later somebody else looked in. "End of the corridor, last door on the left," I said resignedly.

But it was Sir Aubrey Sprain. "There's a Lieutenant-Colonel Treadwell to see you, Bart," he said. "He's down in the lobby. He refuses to come up."

For a moment I thought the Minister had already replaced me with my old friend Treadwell, and that this was his way of letting me know.

But as soon as I saw the colonel I realized this must be the elder brother Treadwell had mentioned once or twice at Gosport. He was taller than Treadwell and somewhat builder, but he had the same suspicious eyes. These were now flashing around the crowded lobby, examining the swirling groups of brass hats and naval officers with marked incredulity.

I scuttled over, with sycophantic hand outstretched. He ignored it.

"I can't talk with this racket going on," he said. "Come on." And he marched in a dead straight line out of the lobby and into the street. A major-general hurriedly made way for him.

It was bitterly cold outside, but I didn't have the nerve to ask him to wait while I fetched my British warm. He wasn't wearing a coat himself. I despised the way the British went around in the filthiest cold weather with practically nothing on. They made me feel so effete, the way I was forced to trundle about in extra sweaters and mufflers and double-lined coats.

"Young Douglas asked me to get in touch with you," he said loudly, over the noise of the traffic. He was striding along with huge paces, as if to see how soon he could reach the Orkneys and Shetlands. "Did he mention me at all?"

"No, he gave me no warning, sir," I said; then made a face. That 'sir' had slipped out in spite of myself.

But Colonel Treadwell radiated a good deal more real authority than many generals I had met. Moreover, he wore a row of medal ribbons that were not of the sort to be dished out for staff work above and beyond the call of duty.

I chattered on somewhat nervously, saying that I was nevertheless happy to meet him and asking him if he'd care to join me for lunch at my club.

"Haven't time," he said brusquely. "Got to get back to France." Then, after waiting irritably for a passing omnibus to cease grinding its gears: "I'm G.S.O.1 at R.F.C. H.Q. I was at G.H.Q. conference last week with the C.I.S. and the D.M.O."

"I see."

He walked straight through a puddle. I went around it and got thoroughly splashed by his size forty boots.

"At one point Pusey made a humorous reference to this business of a general reserve," he went on, a distasteful look on his face.

I stopped. The colonel continued on without a backward glance. I had to run to catch up with him again.

"I want to know exactly why you want this information about the reserve," he went on, as if there had been no hiatus.

I opened my mouth to reply.

"Yes, I know what you've told Douglas," the colonel said harshly. "But I want the facts, not the window dressing. Rackingham wants it for petty political reasons, isn't that it?" He sounded very hostile indeed.

I hesitated. If I was frank with him he would almost certainly refuse to tell me a thing. But I had a feeling that if I wasn't frank, he wouldn't even continue the conversation.

So: "I think so," I said.

He nodded grimly. "He wants to do our Commander-in-Chief one in the eye, is that it?"

"I don't think he wants it for himself, Colonel. I guess the information is really for the P.M."

"I'd call that petty, shouldn't you? Your Minister wants to cling onto his job, which I understand he's doing very badly indeed. He hopes to keep it by toadying to Lloyd George. Correct?"

"I don't know anything about that."

"Don't you?" We had reached a street corner. He turned and looked at me cynically.

"Where do you stand in all this, Bandy?"

"Me? I'm just carrying out orders."

"Balderdash."

A policeman saw the colonel and stopped about a mile of traffic to let him cross.

"How do *you* feel about Haig?" he said suddenly.

I thought to myself, well, he's obviously not going to tell me a thing, so I've nothing to lose. So I said, "Personally, I wouldn't be unhappy to see him reduced to a grousekeeper's assistant."

The colonel grunted; then: "I see. You've been poisoned by all those politicians too, have you?" he said in a deliberately insulting way.

"No. I was at the Somme for a short time. And Ypres."

He was silent for a good three minutes after that.

We approached the Y.M.C.A. Several soldiers and sailors were loitering at the entrance. When they saw us coming, they all hurried inside for a game of ping-pong.

The colonel continued to charge along the Strand, almost sweeping the civvies into the gutter with the force of his slipstream.

Finally he said, "I used to work directly for the C.A.S. A great man. And he practically hero-worships the C-in-C. I'd be a cad to stab him in the back. Don't you agree?"

"I guess so."

"But I'm going to tell you anyway," the colonel said.

He stopped dead, looking at me fiercely, heedless of the hordes of office workers that were being forced around him and into the path of the omnibuses. "Because, after Cambrai, I also think Haig is a bloody calamity."

I stopped breathing. The colonel glanced at his watch, then raised an imperious forefinger. Five taxis drew up, shuddering and backfiring.

"Get in," he said. "You can drive with me to Victoria."

I got in.

"He's done nothing about the reserves," he said. "Even though he is expecting a massive German attack at any moment."

That Rotten Boy Again

It was getting on for four pip emma when I landed at Castle Bromwich to top up the tank of the Harry Tate and ask the way to Chester.

Declining an invitation to spend the night in the mess, I took off again in a hurry. While I had over 420 hours in the log, only three of them were for night flying – and *they'd* been flown by mistake. I didn't fancy setting down in an unknown field outside a strange city in the pitch dark, which was why I was in such a hurry.

The medieval walled city appeared just as the great orange sun was breaking into a narrow band of clear sky between the

clouds and the horizon. The RE.8 glowed as it banked over
the cathedral, the spotlight of the sun playing appreciatively
over its tasteful pink and yellow surfaces.

It was the first sun I'd been bathed in for nearly two months.
I hoped this was a good omen, but I didn't believe it was. The
sun was just trying to cheer me up on my way to the gallows.

Moving a chilled finger over the plan of the city (courtesy
of Chester Corporation), I followed the winding river to the
eastern outskirts. And there, heaven help me, lay Fallow, just
where the map showed it: a long, low, undistinguished red-
brick building with a magnificent spread of frosty playing field
leading down to the River Dee.

Obviously I had not been able to get out of the speaking
engagement. In fact, it was threatening to become a crisis, not
just in my affairs but in those of the nation.

For I had been ordered to stab the Commander-in-Chief in
the back.

As I flew over the school and gloomily inspected the playing
field to make sure I could land safely, I tried not to think about
the speech. But it was no good. I'd thought about nothing else
for two days.

When I had reported to the Minister what Treadwell's
brother had said, that Field Marshal Haig had failed to fulfill
his promise to the Prime Minister to establish a Reserve of
Maneuver and had ignored the Supreme War Council's order
to do so, Lord Rackingham's thick petulant lips had flapped
about under his mustache so joyfully I knew instantly that, far
from being grave news, it was a confirmation of what he had
hoped for and that the information was to be used exactly as
Colonel Treadwell had prophesied: for political purposes.

It was then he told me that I was to be the one to spill the
beans to the great British public that very week. At Fallow.

"No," I whimpered. "No."

That was the reason he had shown so much interest in the occasion. He had intended all along to use the speech for his own ends. He had cast me from the beginning in the role of gaff-blower.

"Place yourself unreservedly in my service," he had puffed when I first went to work for him, "and there is no knowing where you'll end up."

Well, now I knew where: with my throat cut.

When I continued to say I wouldn't do it and began to cough and feel my forehead for signs of Spanish influenza, he had taken me down in his Daimler to Walton Heath to see the Prime Minister himself.

And what could I do then? One could not argue with The Boss.

"I don't like having to go about it this way, Colonel," The Boss had said with the charming, rueful smile that had fooled much smarter men than me. "But Haig has too many supporters, both inside Parliament and out, and my attitude towards him is so well known that my word is suspect."

He shook his white mane sadly, but managed to maintain a brave smile. "You try to tell the truth and that's the result: suspicion, slander, and betrayal." He sighed deeply and forgot to hypnotize me for a moment. But then he resumed the cadenza on the old, battered, but still tuneful cello of his voice, from which he could draw, when he wished, the sweetest and most convincing melodies. "But if the first shot comes from one of Haig's own men – one, moreover, whose opinions cannot be too easily ignored because of his rank, his position, and his splendid war record . . ."

By then, I was looking very pale indeed.

"There's nothing to be alarmed about," he said with an encouraging smile. "I shall be taking up the baton so promptly that your part in the affair will be forgotten very quickly. I intend to quote extensively from your speech in the Commons the following day, Thursday, and add to it certain facts that are already in my possession; and on Friday I shall call a War Council meeting and press for, and, I have no doubt, obtain, the dismissal of Haig. And if you follow those rough notes for your speech that I have given to Rackingham, I don't think this time we'll have any difficulty in saving another half million men from being sacrificed to Haig's demented policy of attrition."

I found myself nodding, as if in a trance.

"I understand from Rackingham that you're not afraid to speak out," he murmured, putting a hand on my arm in an almost affectionate way. "And after all, it's not as if I'm asking you to betray your own feelings in this matter, is it?"

"No, I . . . I . . ."

"Of course not. And you will be doing a great service to the country, my dear boy. It's desperately urgent we get rid of Haig before all our power bleeds away into that desolation of trenches." His voice sank to a warm, caressing murmur. "And incidentally, Colonel, I will not forget this little service."

"What do you have in mind, Prime Minister?" I asked hopelessly. "A seat in the Commons? Because I sure as hell won't have much future in the Army after this."

It shows how I felt, my swearing like that. And to the Prime Minister, too.

He merely smiled and patted me on the shoulder as his surly housekeeper came in with his nightly Ovaltine. "Don't you worry about that, my boy," he said. "We'll look after you, won't we, Rackingham *bach*?"

As I passed over the school building for the second time, I closed the throttle and glided down to my doom. Underneath, a straggle of schoolboys were making their way to the pavilion after a game of rugger.

As the Harry Tate sank toward the turf they started to run. They had surrounded the biplane even before it had grunted to a stop.

I climbed out stiffly, ears ringing in the sudden silence. The boys all stared at me with shining eyes. All except for Claud.

Claud. That was all I needed: the repulsive youth I'd been feuding with whenever our paths crossed.

He was doing his best to look utterly unimpressed; and succeeding remarkably well.

I nodded to him with a tentative smile, to show that I was prepared to let bygones be bygones. I might as well have nodded to a goal post.

One of the other boys whispered to him. He shrugged.

"Yes, that's him," I heard him reply in an offhand way. He swaggered forward, looking me up and down as I flapped my helmet about in the cold air to dry it. "That wasn't much of a landing, was it?" he said, his voice cracking with boredom, but obviously enjoying his fame as the acquaintance of an intrepid aviator, however incompetent.

"Well, it's getting dark," I said defensively. "It's hard to judge height when you're rounding out and–"

"The old man's house is through there," he interrupted, jerking his thumb toward a clump of trees near the school. He glanced up at the sky in a bored way. "You'd better cut along smartly, old man. He's been waiting for you since tea and biccies."

The rest of the boys stared at me unblinkingly, waiting tensely for my reaction.

"Thank you, Claud," I said in my whining, Canadian drawl. Then, confidentially: "By the way, your coms are showing, Claud." Which was true enough. An inch or so of yellowing underwear was showing below his rugger shorts. "Hadn't you better go somewhere and pull them up?"

One or two of the boys released their breaths in a snigger. Claud looked down, his face scarlet. He started to tug at his shorts, but then desisted and clenched his fists instead, his toffee-nosed face all squeezed up into a murderous scowl.

But before he could respond, a tall, skinny teacher with a long, blue chin came up. The boys made way for him respectfully.

"Ah, you must be Bandy," he said in a deep Oxford drawl, his shapeless flannel bags flapping in the breeze. He put out a hand. "My name's Hewer, as in hewer of wood and drawer of water. English and Latin. Welcome to Fallow, Captain."

Claud muttered something. There was a suppressed titter.

Quick as lightning, Hewer turned and caught him neatly by the ear. "We all know that as the Head's offspring you're a privileged person, Claud," he said, giving Claud's ear a tweak. "So you mustn't tempt me to lay hands on you, must you? It would get me into trouble, and I'm sure you wouldn't want that." He gave the ear another tweak. "Go into the pavilion and get changed – preferably into a gentleman."

I decided I liked Hewer.

"Ah, it's you," the headmaster said as Mr. Hewer showed me into the small, cluttered hall of the residence. "I thought I heard your flying machine going over. I was expecting you for afternoon tea, of course."

"M'yes, I'm very sorry, Headmaster," I began.

"Too late now, of course . . ." he said, as if I'd missed an Olympian feast, complete with nectar and dancing girls. Then, abruptly: "Where's my wife?"

"I haven't got her, sir," I whined.

"What? Oh, here she is." A gawky-looking girl, all elbows and eager teeth, came thumping angularly down the stairs.

She looked about thirty years younger than her husband.

"She used to be a games mistress," Hewer had explained on the way over. "Claud is his first wife's child – if you can conceive of Claud having sprung from anything other than spontaneous combustion."

"Hulloa," the Head's wife said, giving a self-conscious guffaw. She jerked forward into a half bow, as if somebody had just sunk a fist into her midriff.

"My wife," the headmaster muttered, after looking closely at the girl. Then, massaging his eyes: "Mr. Bandy, Mrs. . . ." His voice trailed away in ennui.

"Call me Caelia," she said loudly. "With an *a*." Her bony hand shot out, though she was still a good ten feet away.

I was wearing a brand-new electrically heated sidcot, which was all tickly fur and enormous buttons and flaps and huge pockets filled with notebooks, pencils, spare bulbs, Pears soap, Huntley and Palmer's biscuits, Beecham's Pills, fluff, dust, and old love letters. I was further encumbered with a valise, a leather map case, a Thermos, the clock from the RE.8 (in case the boys pinched it), a helmet, a guidebook to Chester, and a pair of fur-lined gloves. The result was that as I went forward to shake her hand, I had to go through some rather peculiar contortions to keep all this stuff together, so it looked as if I were clutching suggestively at myself. And as Caelia's gait was almost equally eccentric, possibly as a result of her former occupation, the two of us must have looked for all the world like a couple of arthritic Watusis.

"She'll show you up," the headmaster said.

For a moment I thought he meant that Caelia (with an *a*) intended to expose my shortcomings without further delay. But after pursing and unpursing his lips in that dreaded fashion of his and looking disapprovingly at my oil-spattered chin, the headmaster added, "Cut along to your room and wash and brush up, Captain, and, ah, we'll see you for dinner."

I started to point out that I was a bigwig now, not a mere captain; but he interrupted.

"That is, unless you'd prefer to put up in town instead of here."

"No, this'll be all right, thank you, Headmaster."

"There's a very good hotel near the cathedral," he said hopefully.

"That's all right, sir, I wouldn't want to put you to any inconvenience. I'll stay here."

"H'm. Well . . ." He turned to Hewer and said shortly, "You're coming for dinner tonight, aren't you, Hewer?"

"Thank you very much, sir," Hewer said, "though you hadn't actually invited me."

"Oh, hadn't I?" Hewer waited eagerly. "Well – come along *after* dinner, then," the headmaster said and vanished back into the woodwork, or to be exact, into his small paneled study, where he had been indulging his hobby of writing out black-lists and slitting canes.

On my way to bed that night I was extremely careful to check the top of the bedroom door, in case Claud had thought of repeating his famous poised-bucket jape. But, give him his due, he was much too smart to repeat a trick that had already failed. He waited until I was in the bathroom along the hall before sneaking up and removing the doorknob so that I couldn't get out until the headmaster happened along about half an hour later and replaced the knob.

Cunningly, Claud had left it on the floor just outside the door, so that his father would assume I'd been unnecessarily clumsy with the hardware.

This was an assumption all too easily reinforced when he came into the bathroom and caught sight of his toilet. I had yanked a little too enthusiastically on the lavatory chain and there was only about four inches of it left, dangling impotently from the rusty tank far above our heads.

He gazed up at it, his lips pursing and unpursing, but not with any desire to kiss me.

I cleared my throat and shuffled a bit, then said, "Sorry, sir, I – seem to've broken your chain."

"Don't see how you could have done that," he said sharply.

"Well, if you look closely, sir, you can see the chain is a bit rusty in spots and . . . brittle, if you look closely, sir."

"And where is the handle?" he demanded.

"What?" I said, flustered. "Oh, the – the handle of the thingamajig, the – the . . . at the end of the chain, you mean. Yes; well, it fell down there, sir, in the fluff and dust under the – I think it rolled under the bathtub, sir. I'll get down on my hands and knees, shall I, and feel around for it if you like, soon as I've finished in–"

"Look here, Captain–"

"That's, that's Colonel, sir–"

"I hope you're not going to make a spectacle of yourself tomorrow. I have the moral well-being of the boys to consider, you know."

"How d'you mean, sir?" What on earth had morality to do with a piece of rusty chain?

"We'll say no more about it, Captain, except that I expect a good deal more decorum tomorrow than you've shown thus far."

"Sorry, sir."

"Well . . . just . . . just remember, that's all. You're not in the in the . . ." He stopped as his eyes fastened on something hanging from my left pocket. I glanced down. There was an inch of lavatory chain dribbling from the flap.

After a moment, he held out his hand. Sweating and smirking, I drew the handle out of my pocket and offered it to him.

Then, on an afterthought, I took it back and helpfully wound the remains of the chain around the handle before passing it over once more.

When he had gone I stood in the bathroom for several minutes trying to think beautiful thoughts. But all I could think of was Claud.

Though I should have known what to expect by now, I suppose. Throughout my childhood and adolescence I'd been pestered and hounded by schoolfellows, cousins, teachers, and villagers alike, whose hackles had sprung up every time I turned my great blank face upon them. I had long since resigned myself to the fact that I had the sort of countenance that brought out the worst in men, children, and dogs. Even my parents' veins used sometimes to become engorged with rage when I turned to regard them with what I thought was an expression of the utmost respect and filial devotion, but which they took to be a display of the very worst sort of dumb insolence. Mother had even attacked me with a Plumber's Friend once for no other reason than that I had looked at her just a trifle skeptically. Another time, I had made the mistake of looking in an amused way at a burly cousin of mine, whereupon he had tried to drown me in a firkin of maple syrup. And then there was–

However, it was Claud I was talking about. No, but I had begun to think the world was finally coming to terms with my face, recognizing at long last that though it might be imperturbable, aristocratic, and utterly original – the very last word in faces, in fact – there was no real harm in it.

Yet here I was, at the age of twenty-four, still being persecuted for fighting the good fight under this noble physiognomical banner with its strange device. *It just wasn't fair.*

But, by George, I would go down fighting, I resolved. I had never given in to other people's dementia, and I certainly wasn't going to knuckle under now, even if my tormenter was only twelve or thirteen. He wasn't going to rile or pother me, by God! I'd kill him first, the filthy little blackguard!

Next morning I was first down to breakfast. I tiptoed to the chafing dishes on the sideboard, and as I'd expected, one of them contained the inevitable porridge.

Whipping out the cardboard shoe box I'd found in my bedroom cupboard, I filled it to the brim, then replaced the lid. Some of the porridge began to squeeze itself out from around the lid in rather a revolting fashion, but I managed to hold the lid down. With wildly pounding heart, I scuttled back upstairs and hid the box in my valise, chuckling and slavering a bit with anticipation, like a uniformed Fagin.

Then, when I came down a second time and was tucking into the remaining kipper, I just happened to mention, apropos of absolutely nothing at all, that I'd dropped a half crown out of my bedroom window that morning.

Not more than three minutes later, Claud asked to leave the table and strolled out with heavy nonchalance. Immediately I asked permission to leave the table, too, and this request being granted, dashed upstairs and squatted at the window and looked out cautiously. And sure enough, there was Claud, busily searching the shrubbery directly below the window.

Removing the lid from the now sodden and bulging shoe box, I held it out the window at arm's length and tipped it upside down. For a moment I thought the oats had set. I gave the box a couple of good shakes. Slowly at first, and then with heart-stopping suddenness, the gray, approximately box-shaped mass sucked itself free and fell on Claud's head with a distinctly audible and decidedly nauseating smack.

He uttered a shrill cry and started to run, clawing at his collar and staring upward as if expecting to see some gigantic and intemperate bird of prey hovering overhead. Sensations of triumph fought tooth and nail in my breast with feelings of shame, as I peered over the sill.

By then, Claud had stopped twenty or so paces away, and was clawing frantically at his Dotheboys collar, trying to dig out the great gobs of lumpy porridge that had slithered down his neck.

"Well, it was his own fault," I said to myself, sniggering and giggling in a breathless way.

But already I was beginning to feel apprehensive at the thought that it was now his turn; and that Claud's next jape was not likely to be as innocent as his last one.

My First Speech

All of this, however, had the effect of taking my mind off the speech until twenty after ten that morning. But the moment I entered the entrance hall of the school with Mr. Hewer and the headmaster's wife, and smelled the typical school odors of coal fires, damp wool, rice pudding, and disinfectant, I almost melted onto the parquet floor in a heap of quivering pips and blubber.

As we turned down an appallingly long corridor, a charge of schoolboys suddenly filled the view, elbowing and shouting and banging locker doors. Again my heart attempted the high jump, and jammed itself up against my Adam's apple, where it pulsated frantically.

Just as magically, the schoolboys disappeared again into the chocolate-brown walls. As we passed a flight of stairs, there was a singing in my ears. I thought I was fainting.

"That's the school choir practicing," Hewer said, pointing down into the coal cellar.

I saw Caelia looking at me, and realized I was biting my swagger stick. I'd been wondering why my teeth were beginning to ache.

"That's a lovely stick," she said, looking at the silverwork. "Chased, isn't it?"

"Chaste?" I croaked. "I never thought of asking." Which rejoinder didn't seem to puzzle Caelia in the least.

The headmaster's study was crammed with teachers and governors, and women in long, swishing dresses and hats with feathers, berries, and veils. They were all sipping tea, eating rock cakes, and talking loudly and complacently, almost as if God were in His heaven and all were well with the world – the fools.

Apart from one or two curious glances, nobody paid much attention to me for the first few minutes, which helped to steady me a little; except that the cup and saucer that somebody had thrust into my hands seemed to have a rhythm of their own, the way they were clattering about in ragtime.

I tensed my hand to still the crockery, reminding myself for the sixth or seventh time that making a speech couldn't possibly be any worse than attacking an observation balloon and being shot at by flaming onions.

After a while, the Head caught sight of me skulking behind an aspidistra. Somehow combining an expression of censoriousness with another of acute apprehension, he introduced me to a handful of people, including the Chairman of the Board of Governors. He turned out to be the Tory M.P. I'd met at The Park, the one with the rosebud lips, indignant belly, and startled, protruding eyes.

He muttered a noncommittal greeting and almost immediately turned away to resume his conversation with another of the school governors. Perhaps I was too intimately associated with his humiliation at the hands of that Russian libertine; perhaps that was why he pretended not to recognize me.

I was also introduced to the school chaplain, who had a disturbing habit of concluding his remarks by mewing like a cat.

"That's your flying machine behind the, the pavilion, is it, mew, mew?" he said. "To be able to fly must be extraordinarily . . . mew, mew."

I caught Hewer's eye. We both looked away quickly.

Another staff member was the school's O.T.C. commander, a Captain Blankett. He wore a fiery nose, possibly to celebrate his bad cold. He stared at my pip and crown and looked puzzled. "Oh, but I thought it was a captain," he bubbled. He then hauled in his Sam Browned belly, brought his great flat feet to attention, and threw a quivering salute. "Sir," he bellowed. My teacup fell over.

"Oh, for God's sake, Blankett," Hewer muttered.

Blankett cast him a disdainful glance, then sank back again into the barrel of his body with a bubbling sound.

The headmaster turned to see what the noise was all about. One of the buttons of his waistcoat was loose. Loose buttons always disturbed me, especially ones that dangled like that. I kept an eye on it uneasily.

"About the arrangements," he said.

I immediately forgot his button. My entrails slackened. I had to stand at attention myself for a moment.

"We've allowed about half an hour for your address," he said. "That'll be after the chairman's remarks, and just before the final hymn, if that's satisfactory. 'Onward Christian Soldiers', I suppose, Chaplain?"

The chaplain was trying to warm his hands at a miserable coal fire that was smoking and hissing in the fireplace. He straightened, holding his back. "Yes, one felt that that particular hymn might be mew, mew," he said. In the fireplace a small yellow flame flickered in the midst of the slag. Hurriedly he put out his hands again, but was too late. The flame had gone out again.

"It's being held in the Lessor Hall this year, isn't it?" somebody asked.

"Yes. We thought . . . because of the demand," the Head muttered.

Well, that was something, I thought. The lesser was presumably the smaller of two halls that were available.

"I don't know why there are so many journalists," the Tory M.P. grunted peevishly, not noticing me towering above him. "There's nothing particularly noteworthy about this fellow, is there?"

His wife nudged him. Then she smiled at me, revealing a couple of canines borrowed from her Doberman pinscher.

"What's that?" the headmaster asked. "Journalists?"

"There's a lot more of them than when my nephew gave the speech," the M.P. said.

The headmaster glowered. He didn't seem to approve of newspapermen.

After a moment he turned to Hewer. "Where have you put them?" he asked.

"In the gallery, sir."

The headmaster nodded, apparently satisfied that the press had been properly removed from contact with decent people. He turned back to me.

"You'll stay for a bite after the speech, won't you, Captain?" he said.

"Yes. I guess I'll be pretty ravening by then," I said. "Ravenous, I should say."

The headmaster nodded again, having made it plain that his duties as a host were to terminate somewhere between lunch and afternoon tea. He made a face as the O.T.C. commander snuffled in his ear.

"What? Course he's a captain."

Blankett muttered again embarrassedly.

"Nonsense," the Head said sharply. "I distinctly remember his being introduced as Captain. Captain Bandy, I distinctly remember."

He took a deep breath. The matter was settled. As he exhaled I looked worriedly again at his button. It was wiggling about in a dangerous way. I reached for it and pulled, intending to hand it back, so he wouldn't lose it.

Unfortunately it was held on more securely than I'd thought. But, now committed to the concept of a loose button, I tugged harder, to have something to show for my admittedly rather distraught behavior. But the blasted button continued to hang on, dangling there defiantly, and all I succeeded in doing was to yank the headmaster's waistcoat away from his body and haul him off balance.

The loose skin of his face shook bewilderedly. "What, what on earth?" he began.

"Your button, sir," I muttered hurriedly and sweating with embarrassment. "It's loose." I made to seize his button again. But he backed away hurriedly, looking at me in a strange fashion and clutching at his button possessively, as if he actually enjoyed having loose buttons dangling all over his stomach.

Perhaps it was just as well he moved away, as next time I'd probably have grabbed his button with both hands and hauled on it with all my might, maybe even putting a foot on his chest for better purchase. He'd have probably lost all his buttons if I'd done that, not to mention his waistcoat and half the hair on his chest as well, assuming he had any.

I started to prickle and itch all over, horribly aware of the hush that had descended over the throng. By then the headmaster had put a desk between us, no mean task, as it looked a pretty heavy desk for him to lift all by himself.

"It was to save the button from getting lost," I explained to a bishop. But he backed away as well, glancing quickly at his dickey, as if fearful that I might start wrenching at *his* clothing next.

After that, I had plenty of opportunity to worry, as nobody came up to talk to me for quite a while.

At one minute to eleven we all filed, with varying degrees of self-consciousness, onto the platform: the members of the school board and their wives; the headmaster and several senior masters in their shapeless gray-flannel bags, pullovers, and off-the-peg sports jackets, and their equally grubby-looking spouses; the Bishop of Chester in his best purple; the guest of honor in his best khaki; and the school janitor, who received a cheer from the boys as he shuffled onto the platform with his dustpan to collect a French letter that some precocious lad had flung up from the body of the hall.

Thinking the acclamation was for him, the chairman and M.P. for Chester pouted his rosebud lips, and beamed and nodded as he lowered himself plumply into the best chair. The guest of honor had already collapsed into his seat, trembling uncontrollably.

For if this was the lesser hall, the larger one must have been big enough to house a Zeppelin.

"Oh, my God," I said to Mr. Hewer.

Ranged in front of us on uncountable rows of wooden chairs, sat about a hundred adults and a thousand schoolboys, every one of them staring at me fixedly as they roared like untamable beasts.

"That's the Lord Mayor of Chester down there," Mr. Hewer murmured. "The one in chains."

But I was busy staring rigidly at the ceiling, to avoid those 2,200 eyes. Numerous fancy beams, with giant holes bitten out of them, arched high overhead. Great emblems of various kinds, coats of arms and shields and things, were stuck to the walls, which receded so far back they seemed to be illustrating the laws of perspective. The windows were about sixty feet up, with cords sweeping from them like trailing aerials from observation planes. On the far side of the platform was an organ so vast, the organist seemed scaled down to the size of a crotchet. Beyond him was a mural representing the Battle of Waterloo, or possibly a School Sports Day.

"Are you all right?" Mr. Hewer asked, over the reverberating din.

"Who? Me? What? Yes."

"You've gone rather pale."

"I think all the blood's drained into my socks. They feel sticky. . . ."

"It'll be all right, once you start," Hewer murmured.

"What's worrying me is being able to start at all," I said weakly, staring at the gallery at the far end of the hall and trying not to count the newspaper representatives, who were all smiling thinly about something.

As a gavel rapped I started violently and dropped my stick, which I'd brought along for self-defense. A lingering snigger chittered around the hall. The stick rolled embarrassingly far, halfway across the stage, in fact, and under the skirts of the bishop's wife. I very nearly scrambled in after it. If I had, I'd probably never have come out.

The headmaster was at the lectern, which had been placed far forward on the platform, perilously close to the audience. He rapped again for attention. The roar of conversation died down, and a deep, ominous vibration took its place, as if the hall had suddenly turned into an ocean liner. The *Titanic*, for example.

"We will start by singing Hymn number 321," he said. "'Art Thou Weary, Heavy-Laden.'"

The organ broke into a groan, and a thousand boys arose with a noise like the Messines Ridge exploding. Whipping out their hymnbooks, they turned to Hymn number 321 with a deafening rustle. The organ moaned again, then split the heavens, and the boys began to shriek, while the governors, none of whom had hymnbooks, mouthed the words and passed my swagger stick back across the stage from hand to hand as if at a particularly unenthusiastic relay race.

Fourteen or fifteen verses later, there was a long prayer from the chaplain, his voice now miraculously transformed from a weak, feline chunner into a manly basso.

Then there was an address from the headmaster, on school affairs, to which the boys listened in cowed silence. This was followed by an inspirational talk from the sports master, which seemed to be about *mens sana in corpore sano*, or maintaining a sound mind in a sound body, though it was hard to be sure that this was the topic, as he had such a hacking cough. In the midst of one bout, there was an uproar of sympathetic wheezing and snuffling from the boys until the Head cranked himself slowly into a position that suggested he was about to do his business on the platform, and glared at the audience; whereupon their respiratory ailments were instantly cured.

As the chairman rose to speak, I caught sight of Claud slipping into his seat at the end of the tenth row. I might have wondered what he'd been up to if I'd been capable of any coherent thought whatsoever.

"My Lord Bishop," the chairman and Tory M.P. intoned, "Lord Mayor and" – with a pedantic smirk – "Admiral of the Dee, fellow members of the Board, ladies and gentlemen, and, if I may be so informal, boys . . ." He waited for his laugh. "As you know, every year at this time since the beginning of this great European conflict, this crusade against the forces of evil, there has grown up in this school the tradition of the *Sanctus Clavis Fores Aperit* Speech, where a member of His Majesty's Services who has distinguished himself on the battlefield or upon the high seas, is invited to deliver a talk of an inspirational nature, calculated to appeal to the hearts of the younger generation, to renew their faith and loyalty to their elders, and, by bringing the war home to them in all its sacrifice and heroism, ensure that this will indeed, in the words of Mr. H. G. Wells, be the war to end all wars.

"This year we have the privilege of listening to the words of a representative of one of His Majesty's Dominions from across the seas, the Dominion of Canada, a country about whose fighting men we have heard altogether far too – about whose exploits we have heard a great deal, in the newspapers." He cast a quick, resentful glance at the gallery. "And no doubt Colonel Bandy will also have a tale to tell about his contributions to the war effort.

"However, before I call upon your O.T.C. commander to introduce our guest, I should just like to say a few short words about the current controversy between the political and the military arms of the government, a subject that I know is of consuming interest to you all. . . ."

His words may have been short, but his speech was certainly long enough, as he launched into the usual intemperate condemnation of the politicians, among them Lloyd George, Jan Smuts, Max Aitken, Winston Churchill, and George Smethurst, apparently a local councillor who had shot at the M.P.'s bull terrier after it had pissed all over his wife's cauliflowers.

He was interrupted several times by applause from the platform, as well as from the hall. There seemed to be no doubt where everybody stood as they sat there: foursquare behind the generals, the jingoists, the Conservative newspapers, and the Unionist War Committee, of which the chairman had the honor to be chairman.

All of which convinced me utterly that I'd better not be too critical about the shortcomings of the military.

As the chairman continued to detail the treachery of the politicians, and as the applause grew in enthusiasm, I began to realize that Haig wasn't such a bad chap after all. After all, he knew far better than anyone else what was going on. And who was I to say otherwise?

Of course, the casualties had been heavy, but perhaps that was the only way to wear down the enemy and achieve ultimate victory. Really, when you thought about it, the generals hadn't done too badly, really. They had gained a good few miles, after all, in the last few years. . . .

As the chairman continued to give the politicians six of the best, it occurred to me that people such as the Secretary of State and the Prime Minister – what did *they* know of the real situation? Only the commanders at General Headquarters could possibly know what the real situation was. After all, look at all the beautifully detailed maps they had to work with.

And what if Haig *had* done nothing about creating a strategic reserve? The Germans hadn't launched a major attack since 1915. What made Lloyd George and his minions so sure they'd attack now? Haig wasn't a fool, by any means. He was a genuinely decent chap, with a mother and everything. Why, the Sovereign himself – or Himself – was said to be a devoted admirer of his. I mean, what *right* had people like Rackingham to criticize a man like that? Rackingham, let's face it, was little better than a clerk. Why should I put my neck on the block for somebody who hadn't even been able to organize the R.A.F. in an efficient manner? I mean, why *should* I?

The more I listened to the cheers and applause as the chairman continued to give the frocks what for, the more I found myself agreeing with my old friend the King that Haig was a jolly decent fellow who was doing his level best and that the politicians ought to leave him alone and stick to their own business – voting themselves pay raises, and stuff like that.

And besides, who could replace Haig? With the possible exception of old Plumer and his excellent chief of staff, there wasn't a single general who had provided any evidence that he had an equal, let alone a superior, organizational ability. And with the possible exception of one or two of the Tank Corps people, there was no other general who had shown the slightest sign of originality, or even of sympathy with the men who had to carry out his desperate orders. Even the Flying Corps, which should have been entirely uninfluenced by outmoded traditions and concepts, had destroyed young pilots at a prodigious rate, in accordance with Trenchard's aggressive policy, which seemed designed to destroy posterity in the name of posterity.

The truth was, I was being used. Well, if the P.M. needed somebody to open his latest devious campaign, then let Rackingham do it, instead of foisting the job on a helpless colonel, the swine.

Thus, by the time the chairman had concluded his speech with an exhortation to his youthful audience to pass the baton of civilization on to posterity (ignoring the two boys in the fourteenth row who were trying to stab each other with nail scissors), I had quite made up my mind to give everybody only what they obviously wanted to hear: a thundering good account of the heroism and gallantry of the conflict, and my personal part in it, leavened with a few inspiring anecdotes about the comradeship of the trenches and the glories and chivalry of air combat. I owed nothing to Rackingham. If he wanted to stab the military leadership in the back, let him do it himself.

I felt a lot better after that, and as the chairman sat down to thunderous applause, I had almost stopped trembling, and the stifling lump in my throat had shrunk to the dimensions of a mere pomegranate.

I stuffed my hand resolutely into my pocket and screwed up the notes Rackingham has passed on from the Prime Minister. He knew what he could do with his pieces of paper.

There was a rumbling pause. Then Captain Blankett marched to the lectern, and waited complacently for the noise to die down. Behind him, the chairman was having his hand shaken enthusiastically by the bishop and everybody else within reach.

"The honor has fallen on me," Blankett said hoarsely, standing rigidly at attention, "of introducing this year's guest, Lieutenant-Colonel Bartholomew Bandy. Colonel Bandy, who has the distinction of being the youngest colonel in the British Army–"

"Hear! Hear!" a governor said, waking up with a start.

"–is, as you can see, a pilot in the Royal Flying Corps, and as such is not to be sneezed at." He sneezed. Everybody giggled. "For he has put paid – or carboneesay as I believe the froggies call it – to thirty-one Hun aircraft in air combat – a 'doubtable achievement, I might add, atchoo! achieved in only about six months at the front. For this he was personally decorated by His Majesty, King George the 'choo!"

At this there was a stir among the audience. But it was just one of the schoolboys who had been dueling with nail scissors being led out, bleeding.

"Before transferring to the Flying Corps, Colonel Bandy was an infantry officer in the trenches, and as such took part in the glorious battles on the Somme, and at Wipers. Which reminds me." And he took out his handkerchief and wiped his nose and wiggled it comically. He grinned delightedly as the boys howled with merriment. "Good old Blanks!" one of them shouted.

"At the present time, Colonel Bandy is with the Air Ministry in London, helping to form the new Royal Air Force. I am sure he will have lots of good stories to tell about his exploits on the Western Front, and if they're half as good as the one he told me just now, I know we're all in for a jolly good time."

And he proceeded to tell my best anecdote, about the time I accidentally rammed a German scout plane and, minus undercarriage, crash-landed on my former battalion commander.

"And now," he said, turning to me beaming, "I call upon Colonel Bartholomew Bandy, D.S.O., M.C., to deliver the *Sanctus Clavis Fores Aperit* Speech for 1918. Colonel Bandy."

He patted me proudly on the back as I hobbled on nerveless legs to the lectern.

The applause soon died down, and there was an expectant hush. I cleared my throat several times, sounding like a wounded buffalo. Then I started digging around my trouser pocket for the piece of paper on which I had put down some telling points – not the piece Lord R. had given me, another piece. Drawing it out, I cupped it in my hand and squinted down at the first telling point. "Final Reminder" I read. "If our invoice is not settled within thirty days" – No, that was the wrong side. I turned it over. But I couldn't read my writing.

The silence lengthened. Black spots hung before my terrified gaze, like fruit flies around an overripe pumpkin.

"Ladies an' genulmen, boys and gu– er – boys," I began, very loudly indeed. The mayor jumped, and his gold chain clanked.

Then my mind went a complete blank. I stared blindly at the audience. They stared back, beginning to shift about uncomfortably. Without realizing it, I took a step forward, past the lectern and toward the lip of the platform, as if closer proximity to the audience would somehow give me inspiration. (Or perhaps I was subconsciously hoping to fall over the edge and break a leg, so I'd be carried out on a stretcher before the full extent of my ineptitude could be unfurled and flaunted before their stupefied gaze.) In fact the mayor and his wife began to look thoroughly uneasy as I drew closer.

The ghastly silence continued. But, God, I had to say something. Anything. I coughed again. An echoing titter teetered on one of the beams overhead, then fell to its death with a choking cry.

"Ladies and genul – I've said that. Captain, uh . . ." Oh, my God. I couldn't remember the name of the man who'd introduced me. Gentle Jesus, meek and mild. Sheet? Pillow? Bolster? Eiderdown? Blanket! Blankett, that was it! "Captain Blankett has been very kind and, uh, generous, uh, about, uh, my career in the, uh, Army, but, uh, I should really set the, uh, matter straight – the record, that is, straight. Most of it's been a matter of luck. It's, uh, 'mazing how much luck has to do with being, uh, lucky. . . ." I bellowed another cough.

This time the snigger passed over the whole audience like wind over a field of hard spring wheat. For a moment I thought of wrenching out my pistol right there and then and firing a bullet toward my molars. But then, courage, I thought. Besides, I didn't have a pistol with me.

Now moisture was pattering down onto the lectern. I gaped up, thinking there was a hole in the roof. But it was just perspiration.

"Like," I went on, "the time I shot down one of them Gotha bombers. I was given this here ribbon here by the French, for that. But I didn't really shoot it down, see. What happened, pards, was, well, it was like this, see." Oh, God, what was I doing now? Sounding like a Canadian trying to imitate an Englishman imitating an American.

I passed a bunch of limp, trembling fingers over my heated brow. And it didn't help matters in the least when I saw Claud grinning at me maliciously from the tenth row.

"What happened was, I was trying to shoot it down, but couldn't get close enough because the Gotha was bristling with machine guns. Some of them even fired downwards from the belly–" I smirked embarrassedly at the ladies behind me, "if you'll pardon the expression – of the, the, the, the, the aircraft, you see, which struck me as being, uh, very unfair, and– So I withdrew from the belly to the, the, the, the nearest cloud to think things over, see. And I had just decided to go home for a stiff drink – I used to take an occasional stiff drink in those days. And," I added under my breath, "I wish I had one right now."

I started as a murmur of laughter billowed onto the platform. I must have spoken louder than I'd intended.

"And I was flying alongside the cloud," I went on, strangely heartened by the response, "when I caught sight of my shadow against the cloud. What had attracted my attention was that there were two of me. Or, rather, two aircraft shadows.

"Well, this didn't seem right, somehow. I knew I was flying only one aircraft. So I thought things over for a while, and after massaging my eyes a bit to make sure my vision hadn't become impaired by all those stiff drinks, I took another look. And there were still two shadows on the cloud.

"So I gave it some more thought, nibbling at a chocolate bar as is my wont whilst on patrol, and being suddenly smitten with an idea, I glanced behind. And as I'd expected, there was another plane behind, a German Albatros fighter. It was preparing to open fire at point-blank range. I could clearly see the German pilot frantically trying to clear his guns, to this end.

"The Albatros must have been escorting the Gotha bomber. Now it was escorting yours truly. Well, with typical lightning decision of the kind just described, I upended the Camel into a loop and came down on his tail. You can do that pretty fast in a Camel. And before he could say Jack Robinson, or the Teutonic equivalent thereof, I had sent him into a spin. Whereupon he fell on the Gotha he was supposed to be protecting, and it went straight down as well. You may be interested to know it fell on a school. Fortunately it wasn't occupied at the time. My reward for this typical accident of war was a couple of kisses from a French general who had obviously had fish for dinner that day."

This went down fairly well, except with the correspondents, who, for some reason, were raising their eyes to the much-vaulted ceiling as if following the flight of an enervated bat.

But I wasn't playing to the gallery anyway. If Rackingham thought I was going to supply his paper with a lot of vile scandal and controversy, he had another think coming.

So, confidence rolling in again like the tide, I described two or three other incidents of the air war, employing that sly British stratagem of underemphasizing one's part in the heroic endeavor in such a way as to encourage the inference that one's role must necessarily have been a major one; this method being all the more effective because it induced in the listener a warm feeling of pride and satisfaction at the workings of his own insight. This in turn made him all the more impressed with the worthiness of the speaker, which in turn—

Anyway, thus encouraged (by myself), I ventured to comment on the chairman's speech, though in a thoroughly benevolent way. I certainly wasn't going to get mixed up in any controversy just to suit Rackingham.

Only, the more I talked, the more I realized I was against the chairman.

For one thing, I'd been quite impressed with some of the politicians I'd met, and his remarks about them rankled slightly.

"It's very commonly said," I said, remembering not to whine excessively, "as your school chairman has, uh, commonly said, that the difficulties of this war have invariably been caused by certain politicians in their treacherous interference with the military leadership. If the generals had been allowed to get on with it, without all this petty carping by the frocks, we'd really be getting somewhere, what?"

There was enthusiastic applause from everybody. "Hear! Hear!" the bishop said loudly. The headmaster pursed and unpursed his lips and nodded gravely.

"I guess this must be so," I said, also looking very grave and wise, "because so many of our leaders and representatives have said so. However, in all fairness, it should be pointed out that the generals *have* been allowed a free hand, for the past three years, and even though the newspapers have tried to show their gains as being significant, by the use of very small-scale maps and very large-scale arrows" – take *that*, Lord R. – "the fact is that their achievement on the Western Front amounts to a total gain of a couple of dozen miles of territory that for the most part is worse than useless."

This was stronger than I'd intended. I hurried on, making an effort to get back to the personal level again. "My own experience in the trenches, and observations from the air, seem to show that almost every time we make one of those magnificent advances – of five hundred feet – we invariably place ourselves in a worse position. Creating yet another bulge in the line, for example, so that instead of just being able to shoot at us from in front, the enemy can now take pot shots at us from three sides. I know of one general who tried to rectify a situation like that by ordering an attack on both sides of his particular bulge. He succeeded in getting his map nice and straight – at the cost of about half a division – but unfortunately this created a bulge farther along the line, so some other brass hat had to do a spot of map-straightening. It didn't occur to our general to pull *back* from the bulge, the way the Germans did to the Hindenburg Line. No, that would have meant a loss of four hundred feet of mud and rusty wire. Unthinkable, what?

"And these are the people," I said, carried away, "who should be left to get on with the war by themselves?"

At which point I noticed that the people behind me weren't applauding quite so enthusiastically as before. So I thought I'd better get back to some amusing anecdotes again. I wasn't sticking out *my* neck for anybody.

But I couldn't just leave things up in the air without justifying the tenor of my remarks with a supporting fact or two; so I mentioned the one and a half million men that Lloyd George was withholding from Haig. This created such a stir behind me, that for a moment I began to gibber a bit and lose my place. But the boys seemed to be enjoying it, and that steadied me; so I told them what the P.M. had told me: that at Haig's present rate of expenditure, only a third of those men would still be in one piece by the end of the year, which was why the P.M. was a trifle reluctant to sacrifice another million men for a theoretical net gain of another two miles of swamp.

Then I quoted from a War Office analysis of the Battle of Cambrai last November, which indicated that this remarkably successful tank attack on the Third Army front was the first fresh idea G.H.Q. had had since 1914; and that Haig had advised against it. The report showed that Haig had failed to exploit the breakthrough because he'd used up too many men at Passchendaele, "Which, incidentally, though described as a victory, was really yet another advance into an untenable position – possibly the worst yet."

This led so logically to the present situation that it would have seemed evasive and irresponsible not to have mentioned it, so I said that though in war as well as in algebra, everyone was entitled to his mistakes, the C-in-C seemed to have had more than his fair share. I understood that maintaining a strategic reserve was one of the basic principles of warfare, but in spite of his orders, which I detailed, Sir Douglas had made no effort to create a reserve force out of his available manpower, even though G.H.Q. was expecting – if not anticipating – a German attack sometime this spring.

"I know it's practically blasphemy to hint that Field Marshal Haig isn't perfect," I said, "and far be it from me to criticize him, but it does seem kind of obvious that if you're expecting hard times ahead, it's not very good management to commit all your savings to throwing wild parties.

"But I refuse to be too hard on the military," I said, leavening my remarks with just the right touch of bland humor. "We can't help it, you know. For the last hundred years we officers have been carefully educated – probably the way you boys are being educated here – to avoid using any initiative, imagination, or originality whatsoever."

There was a mass intake of breath at that, so I thought I'd better stick to the point more closely – I didn't want to offend the school. "We officers have been carefully educated, as I say, never to think for ourselves, but to learn only from the more inferior examples of military history, and rarely from the truly significant ones. To learn from the Sir John Frenches of this world, but never from the Napoleons. So you can hardly condemn people like Sir Douglas for running the war as if the Germans were merely a better-dressed version of the Fuzzy-Wuzzies.

"I've heard of a general at the Staff College at Camberley who is said to have spoken to three of the brighter officers there in the following terms: 'I'm told that you three have consistently shown signs of independent judgment, willingness to accept responsibility, unusual intelligence, and initiative.

"'Well, if you want to get on in this Army,' the general is reported to have said, 'you'd better pull yourselves together and learn to correct these deficiencies.'"

The boys cheered like mad. The Mayor of Chester and his wife seemed to be having a heated argument. In case anyone had taken offense at anything I'd said, I ended on a personal note, an amusing anecdote about how, as a subaltern, I had accidentally gotten a corps commander replaced when his superior officer misunderstood a perfectly innocent remark of mine. "Another example of the grasp of essentials, and the forthright, no-nonsense, down-to-earth simplicity of our military leadership," I said. And walked thankfully back to my seat and thumped down, beaming around as the thunderous applause rolled around the hall.

I had obviously made a considerable impression on the entire gathering, a really remarkable impression.

Flight from Fallow

It was about two o'clock as I circled the school to gain height.

After leaning out for a final wave, to which nobody responded, I banked away to follow the river's indecisive course through the indistinct countryside.

I'd gotten away just in time. The compass hadn't even settled down before the mist closed in below.

I'd topped up the tank on the way to Chester, so I'd plenty of fuel. Still, I hoped the mist wasn't too extensive. One hundred and seventy miles was a long way to navigate without reference to the ground, even for a faultless pilot like me.

The RE.8 continued to climb happily through the calm, cold air. At 8,000 feet, there was still a lot of cloud above, as well as mist below; so I decided to stay at that sunless altitude. After wiping the goggles, I settled down for some careful flying by map, timepiece, and compass, congratulating myself on getting away before Claud had a chance to get his own back.

Naturally I'd checked the aircraft very carefully before taking off. I wouldn't have put it past him to cut one of the control cables.

Though I will say this for Master Claud: he might be a surly, mean, vicious, treacherous, vindictive, whey-faced, bloodcurdling scoundrel of a schoolboy, but at least he wasn't a snitch. He'd obviously said nothing to his parents about the porridge. Or if he had, they'd been too preoccupied with other matters to mention it.

Not that it would have made much difference if he *had* told them. I had left under enough of a cloud as it was.

The first hint that all was not hearts and flowers after my speech, came when the mayor stalked out.

He hadn't even waited for the end of my amusing anecdote about General Farthing-Prebble. Without casting even a faintly apologetic glance toward the platform, he had risen and clanked out in his chains, the rigidity of his posture suggesting that he expected to be run through by a twenty-foot pike at any moment.

He was followed by his missus, who looked as if she didn't have a clue as to why she was also stalking out. I'd seen her nice old gray head nodding slowly toward her chest even before I'd got to all the dull facts and figures that I'd unwillingly recollected from Lord R.'s shredded notes.

I had felt a bit resentful about that – the mayor not having the courtesy to wait for the end of my amusing anecdote. However, the tumultuous applause from the schoolboys had made up for it a bit.

At least it had until the headmaster, who seemed to have dyed his face green since I last looked at him, had jumped up, head jutted forward like a buzzard, and glared at the boys as if attempting to memorize as many names in as short a time as possible. The applause had died away pretty rapidly then, to be replaced by an uncertain murmuring.

The M.P. hadn't been too pleased with my speech either. I could tell, because of the way he had stopped in front of me on his way out and treated me to a terribly inflamed sort of look, as if he would like to have lashed me between two horses going in opposite directions.

Captain Blankett's face had been a bit blotchy, too; and when I looked in increasing uncertainty at the rest of the people on the platform, they had all turned their backs or pretended to search under their seats for their brollies or smelling salts. Even Mr. Hewer, who was standing about indecisively, had avoided my eye.

When I started toward him with a friendly-dog sort of expression, he had recoiled as if I'd broken out in some sort of sordid rash.

This growing suspicion was confirmed when, a few minutes later, the headmaster, hearing that some newspapermen were waiting for me backstage, led me hurriedly out of the school through a side entrance, through the janitor's fetid quarters, and ushered me through the trees to his house, and there informed me that I had grossly abused his hospitality.

I gazed at him with a face on which nobility and bewilderment fought for a toe hold.

"I was only giving a few of my impressions, that's all," I said.

But he seemed incapable of saying anything, except that it would be best if I left as soon as possible, or he could not answer for some of the less restrained among the governors and members of the O.T.C.

"But what about my lunch?" I asked; whereupon a muscle in his cheek started to quiver so frightfully I thought I'd better do as he said. "Oh, very well, if that's the way you feel," I said with a toss of the head. "If that's all the thanks I get," I said.

This produced a thwarted sort of keening sound from between his clenched teeth. I thought for a moment he was going to bite me. I couldn't help backing away a foot or two, though I pretended I was just feeling behind me for the banisters.

There was even a fleck or two of foam on his lips, which would have made a bite rather dangerous, I thought.

As I squelched away from the house with my luggage, feeling very ill-done-to, Caelia came into sight, walking back through the trees with several other ladies. I waved dismally. She half raised her hand, then hurriedly lowered it, as if she'd caught herself in the act of making an improper gesture.

However, some of the boys still seemed well disposed toward me. A small crowd of them had assembled behind the pavilion by the time I got there.

As I made the line check around the plane, glancing a trifle worriedly at the mist that was already coiling round the goal posts at the far end of the field, one of the bigger boys, a handsome lad in a bumfreezer, said, "Well, *I* thought it was a jolly good speech, sir."

"'M'kew," I mumbled.

Several others murmured in what did not appear to be too hostile a fashion. When I asked if anyone would help me start up, there was quite a rush to the prop.

I showed the handsome lad how to suck in, climbed into the cockpit, and was about to call out 'Contact' when one of the boys said, "Here's the Axe, sir. I mean, Mr. Hewer. I think he wants to speak to you, sir."

Mr. Hewer was hurrying across the field, clutching his mortarboard. He slowed down as everybody turned to look at him. He strolled the last few yards, making an effort to look laconic.

He nodded, looking over the aircraft interestedly, though he had seen it before. "It's much bigger than it looks in the air," he said.

"M'm."

"What, um, sort of plane is it, Colonel?"

"Called an RE.8."

"I see. Does it go very fast?"

"Not very."

"I see." He looked along the fuselage, blinking. "Are you sure its back isn't broken?"

"No, it's only the way it looks."

"I see." He glanced at the boys and lowered his voice. "I, uh, I'm sorry if I . . ." He straightened his mortarboard nervously. "I must confess I was somewhat taken aback, you see. It wasn't quite what we expected."

"'S'all right," I mumbled.

"All the same, I think you're being treated very shabbily, and . . . anyway, I just wanted to say goodbye, and – good luck." He ran his finger around the red, white, and blue roundel on the side of the fuselage. "I should think you'll need it," he said.

A few minutes later, as I was swinging the Harry Tate around at the edge of the playing field with bursts of power, a figure appeared from the lane leading to the school and started to run toward the plane, waving his arms.

It was Claud. His face bright red with exertion, he was pelting across the grass as fast as he could manage, gesturing frantically.

But I'd had quite enough of Master Claud. I jammed the throttle to FULL. The engine bellowed, and the RE.8 slowly gathered speed, the wheels sending up dinky fountains of spray from the soaking grass. The tail rose, the rudder flicked from side to side, then steadied. The plane lifted off.

The green grass dropped away, and almost immediately began to turn grayish and indistinct. As I turned over the pavilion, I glanced back toward the lane and saw Claud standing there, staring up, his arm slowly falling to his side. But I wasn't even thinking about him. I was wondering what to make of that parting remark of Mr. Hewer's.

On and on the RE.8 droned, on a southward heading 'twixt cloud and mist. For about the fiftieth time since setting out, I peered over the side; but the earth was still obscured. I hoped it wasn't going to be like that all the way to Gosport.

I huddled down in the cockpit again, thankful for the warmth of the electrically heated sidcot, and drew another line on the map. Assuming there was as little drift as there seemed to be, Stratford-on-Avon must lie somewhere below.

Stratford, birthplace of Shakespeare. "Once more into your breeches, dear friends, once more," I intoned into the chilly, hissing wind. I reckoned I should be able to hit the coast opposite the Isle of Wight without too much course correction, though I wished now I'd phoned the airdrome before I left, to find out what the weather was like over Fort Grange. But, then, I never used the phone unless it was absolutely imperative.

Still, if it was misted in or anything, I could always put up at an inland airdrome. There was bound to be one that was clear. I still had three hours of fuel, so there was no problem there.

If I turned up late for work on Friday, why, then, I would just have to turn up late, that's all. After the ordeal at Fallow, Lord R. owed me an extra day off.

Another half hour or so drifted by. The mist below had now given way to continuous cloud. Though I still had about fifty miles to go, I decided to fly the rest of the way near the ground, if the ceiling wasn't too low.

I throttled back. The sway-backed beast grumbled into a glide.

As we sank onto the clouds, I buzzed the air-cooled engine, ostensibly to keep it dry and cozy in the wet air, but really to reassure myself occasionally – like every thirty seconds – that it was still functioning.

The altimeter unwound, the tin scoop vibrated, and the planes began to stream with moisture. Droplets of condensation dashed themselves into my face, so I had to keep wiping the goggles every few seconds.

As the 1,000-foot mark approached, we broke into the clear.

Dull green countryside stretched ahead: Salisbury Plain, scene of my dreaded infantry training. It didn't look as if the weather had improved much since 1916. The scene was as bleak-looking as ever. Only the occasional stone cottage relieved the almost featureless landscape. Any moment, I expected to see a band of ground-sheeted Tommies come route-marching out of the murk, all cursing dreadfully, the way my men used to.

It looked like Salisbury Plain, all right. But when I glanced back, a habit I'd developed over the front lines in case there were any unfriendly people in the vicinity, I saw the sea.

The sea? Behind me? But I'd been flying south, right down the middle of England.

I turned to the front and stared blankly through the whirling propeller for a moment. Then looked over my shoulder again.

But the sea was still there, gleaming dully in the miserable light, receding into a gray haze. I must have emerged from the cloud just as I was crossing the coast.

But I couldn't have. Unless there'd been a 200-m.p.h following wind, and that was France below. Which was hardly very likely.

I put about, still gaping down at the green fields and hedges. Could I have overshot the south coast, then made a 180-degree turn without realizing it? Nonsense. I'd followed a most careful heading. Besides, at the speed I'd been flying, about 90 m.p.h., and the time I'd spent in the air, I should have been many miles from the sea. *Any* sea.

I turned left along the coast, head sagging over the side as I searched for a coastal town that I might identify on the map. But nothing looked familiar, absolutely nothing.

The look of the shoreline was unfamiliar, too; rough pasture changing abruptly to yellowish rock and deserted, sandy beaches.

It was distinctly unsettling. I ought to have been flying over the land toward the sea. Instead I seemed to have been flying over the sea toward the land.

The more I thought about it – the sea being the wrong way around – the more the suspicion began to form that there was something wrong, somewhere.

I turned in the opposite direction, still flying along the coast. After a few minutes a promontory appeared, then a gray patch dead ahead. The grayness slowly turned into a large town or small city, with a river winding carelessly through it. Inland, purple hills blotched the horizon.

I throttled back and circled the town, comparing it with the map, still hoping to identify it as Weymouth or Bournemouth, or somewhere reasonably close to Portsmouth.

By the time I'd eliminated these possibilities, the RE.8 was down to 400 feet. As I headed out of the city again, I caught sight of a train chugging over a tiny stone bridge. Pushing up the goggles, I sideslipped to rooftop height and headed toward the bridge, flying along a short street of terraced houses.

As I opened up again, a couple of boys in knickerbockers who were playing soccer in the street, gaped up. The bridge hurried toward me. As I clattered past, I leaned out to read the sign bolted to it.

It was a rusty metal plate of the sort to be seen at most London, Midland & Scottish Railway stations, advertising such products as ladies' lace-up boots, Bagwash Trusses, and Lyle's Golden Syrup. This one was touting the virtues of MACNAMARA'S TAR.

I had to fly around again to read the rest. FOR THE RELIEF, it said, OF CATARRH, ASTHMA, CONSUMPTION, SCROFULA AND DEAFNESS. "MacNamara's, Marrowbone Lane, Dublin."

It was just as I'd suspected. I was in bloody Ireland.

Hopelessly Lost

It was dark by the time I came pattering through the puddles in a narrow lane on the outskirts of Dublin, sidcot flapping, map case vised under one arm, fur-lined leather boots spurting up fountains of brown spray.

I was hurrying along the lane because I was trying to catch up with a rag-and-bone cart. As soon as I'd hailed it half a mile back, the driver had put on speed, and was now hurtling along the lane at a mad, Irish pace. I had to break into a trot to catch up.

"I say," I called out. But that apparently was the wrong

expression, for the driver lashed his bedraggled nag all the harder. Perhaps I'd sounded English. I had to remember this was Ireland. I had better be more tactful.

"Hey, you, Paddy!" I bellowed, staggering alongside.

The driver cast me a fearful glance, but made no attempt to slow down.

"Which way to the nearest police station or Army post?" I shouted.

At this he went into a veritable frenzy of rein-wiggling and tremulous exhortations to his undersized horse, which also seemed to be casting apprehensive looks at me, as if it thought I was from the glue factory. Luckily it seemed incapable of hauling the rickety cart any faster.

"Listen," I said, panting. "I'm an intrepid birdman!"

The driver looked even more alarmed. "What?" he asked, his smallish, unshaven face working.

"An aviator. A flyer. A pilot. I've just come down over there–" I stopped to point toward the north. I had to run to catch up with him again. "I have to report to the authorities."

The little man's face went a terribly strange color. "Report what?" he squeaked. "I haven't done nothin', Misther, honest! Honest to God, Misther!"

"Darn," I said as I went through a particularly deep puddle, showering water into my boots. "I've been forced down," I shouted, getting a bit fed up with all the shenanigans. It wasn't easy, carrying on a conversation while pelting alongside a rag-and-bone cart in a dim lane in the pouring rain, wearing a heavy leather coat and carrying maps and gloves, and with an eight-day clock in my pocket, thumping against my thigh.

I hadn't had much luck back at the farm, either. I'd put down in a field nearby, only to find the farmhouse deserted and smelling of mildew.

By then it was getting too dark to try anywhere else, so I'd driven the airplane into the barn, to keep it out of the drizzle until morning; a rather pointless exercise, as the timbers had gone from the roof and it seemed to be raining even harder in the barn than it was outside.

So, after examining the cockpit as thoroughly as I thought I had done before leaving Fallow, and discovering the reason I was in Ireland, I stuffed as much as I could in the chest of drawers and locked it, and hurried off toward the city to get something to eat, as I'd had nothing since that solitary kipper at breakfast and some sticky porridge that I'd licked off my fingers.

But first I needed to protect the aircraft against moisture, tinkers, and other chance marauders. I tried to explain this to the rag-and-bone man.

"I need a guard for the aircraft, and a tarpaulin," I shouted. "Otherwise I'm going to have a wet cockpit."

The word was obviously unfamiliar to him.

"A wet whhat?" he said, stopping dead.

"My cockpit's going to get soaked," I panted. "And my engine. Can you give me a lift to the nearest police station?"

The rag-and-bone man went more rigid than ever. Whereas before he had tried to pretend I wasn't there, now he seemed unable to wrench his tiny, stricken eyes off me. What on earth was wrong with the fellow?

I gave up waiting for an invitation and heaved myself aboard his craft. The reins promptly dropped from his nerveless fingers, and his grimy Irish face almost fell apart with fright. I offered him the reins. He took them limply, still staring, petrified.

However, the horse started off again of its own accord. A couple of minutes later its hoofs were clopping over the cobbles of a city street.

Once again, as we lurched down a short avenue of terrace houses, I explained what it was all about. Gradually he recovered one or two of his wits.

"You're a flyer?" he asked.

"That's right."

"You've come down be accident, is it?"

"Yes."

"That's why you're wantin' to report to the aut'horities, is it?"

"You've got it," I said, flapping my coat to dislodge some of the rain water that had collected in the creases.

"Ah, I see, said the bloind man," the rag-and-bone man cried. "You're afther gettin' lost in your airplane, is that it?"

"That's it," I said.

"And why didn't you say so at forst, instead of all this sporadic talk about intrepid birds, and tarpaulins, and gettin' your thingamy wet, and I don't know what else. You just wanted a lift, is that it?"

I nodded wetly.

"Never let it be said," the little man said, suddenly joyful and bursting with self-confidence, "that Eamon Shanahan refused a helping hand to a brave English flyer, for whom he has nothin' but the warmest and kindliest of feelings!"

"Yes; well, listen, Eamon–"

"Listen, who?"

"Who, what?"

"What're you talkin' about? Me name's not Eamon, it's Tumothy McGuiness."

"But you just said Eamon Shanahan. You said you never refused a helping hand–"

"Well, it's his cart, you see, that you're privileged to be riding in. I just borrowed it for this one little trip, you understand."

I gave up, and looked around. We were now well into the wet-walled city, which seemed to have been evacuated. We had not met a soul on the road, and there was still nobody in sight. Perhaps they had seen Timothy coming.

He saw me looking curiously at a gutted factory. The waxing moon gazed through one of the window frames. "That's one of the buildings the Volunteers held for a week during the Easter Rising," Timothy said, "until they were shelled and machine-gunned into the next world by the English. Not," he added quickly, "that I'd one whit of sympathy for the misguided fellows, you understand."

"Course not."

"Sure and it was madness, thinking they could defy the grand, righteous, and overwhelming might of the glorious British Army."

"Madness," I said.

A few minutes later we passed the Parnell Monument. "Who's he?" I asked.

Timothy gave me a terribly stricken look.

The horse continued to plod onward, undirected, down Sackville Street, and turned along Eden Quay. Running along-side it was a river.

"That's the Liffey, is it?" I asked.

Timothy merely nodded, still looking a trifle miffed.

"Ah, ozone!" I cried, taking a deep, appreciative breath of salubrious sea odors: silt, salt, seaweed, crude oil, dead dogs, and other unmentionable flotsam.

"So you're a flyer, is it?" Tim said at length, as I sat there admiring a row of fine Georgian houses. "But you've a strange sort of dialect, sir, if you'll forgive me saying so."

"I guess so," I said. "You see, I come from–"

"Don't tell me!" he cried. "I pride myself on me ability to place a man within six miles of his place of borth, and I can place him within two miles if he comes from London, where I once lived for a good many heart-warming days; and sometimes, to be sure, within two streets." He thought for a moment. "You're from Newcastle," he said.

"Ottawa."

"There you are, you see," Timothy said triumphantly. "That's a suburb of Newcastle."

"It is not. It's in Canada."

"Canada? In America, you mean?"

"Well, sort of."

"You're from America!" Timothy cried in astonishment. "You're not an Englishman at all?"

"No."

"You're not one of that perfidious breed that's looted, plundered, and repressed the prostrate and recumbent body of downtrodden Ireland at all?"

"No."

"You're from America, the land of the free? Home of the Clan-na-Gael, Tammany, De Valera, and most of our Irish whisky?" A great snaggle-toothed smile bisected his little pinched face. "By all that's holy!" he cried. "Come and have a drink!"

It was only then I realized that, unbidden and unguided, the horse had dribbled to a halt outside a small, dingy pub in a side street off the Quay.

The interior of the pub was almost as sordid as the grimy façade and blistered doorway. Chocolate-colored wallpaper peeled from the walls, revealing some very unhygienic-looking fissures. Over our heads was a molded plaster ceiling, discolored by clouds of Irish shag.

The place reeked of stout and nanny goats, the latter odor seeming to emanate from the damp tweeds of a country gentleman who was lying on the floor below the bar, mumbling into a spittoon.

The rest of the clientele was composed of about five and thirty leprechauns in shawls and cloth caps, standing about in clumps, or sitting on benches with their backs to the wall and their porter supported on battle-scarred tables.

As soon as we came in, a hush descended, so that I had to continue my protests in self-conscious whispers. These were brushed aside elatedly by Timothy, who urged me to the bar and insisted on paying for the drinks until he discovered with a theatrical start of surprise that he'd come out without a blessed penny.

"I really ought to be getting on to the authorities," I whispered hoarsely. This increased the silence, if that were possible – and it were. Everybody was staring in a suspicious way at my military garb.

A couple of ladies were the first to break the tension. One had a huge, fat, whiskery face; the other looked as delicate as point lace.

"It's one of them dispatch riders," the first said.

"Oh, is that what he is, Maggie."

"One of them dispatch riders," the barrel-shaped one said, clasping a huge glass decisively.

"He's very big, isn't he?"

"A dispatch rider," the other said. "A very big dispatch rider."

Meanwhile, Timothy was explaining to the barmaid, at excessive length, that I was an aviator from America who had immigrated to Ireland by mistake.

As he did so, the atmosphere relaxed somewhat, and a low mumble of conversation started up, though everybody continued to rake me with the tines of their eyes, from my sodden flying helmet to my mud-spattered skirts. The barmaid, a girl of twenty-five or so, whose good looks were only slightly spoiled by a knobbly nose, leaned forward interestedly.

"My Uncle Seosamh Mag Fiadhchara lives in America," she said. "New York, it is. Have you ever met him?"

"Can't say I have," I said.

She pushed a gigantic glass toward me, and nodded at it encouragingly. Timothy was already drowning in his, or at least splashing about and gasping rather noisily in it.

I looked into the glass. It was filled with an ominous fluid that looked as if it had been drained from the Pontine Marshes.

"Drink up, drink up," Timothy shouted, going down for the third time. Somewhat doubtfully I took a sip. It tasted not unlike the laxative my mother used to pour into me as she held my greasy nose squeamishly between thumb and forefinger.

But it was obvious I'd be letting the side down if I didn't polish it off with some sort of style. So, putting my foot up with a flourish onto the bar rail, and quite forgetting my New Year resolution, I quaffed the lot in one go.

There was an approving murmur, followed by an upsurge of blarney. Another couple of huge, dimpled glasses appeared on the bar counter in front of us. As Timothy dived into his, a pretty woman in the far corner of the pub widened her eyes at me invitingly. She smiled, revealing two teeth. I shifted my gaze quickly to the stained-glass panel in the door beside her. It showed a pair of self-conscious honeymooners hanging around a municipal allotment. Or – was it Adam and Eve in the Garden?

When I'd finished the second pint, I said suddenly to the barmaid, "But I once met a Daniel McSwiney in New York."

"What?"

I repeated my sentence almost word for word.

"It's pronounced McSweeny," she said disapprovingly. "Not McSwine-ey."

The plump man next to me, who had been eating soda bread and prawns, turned and said, "So you're from America."

He introduced himself as B. Mulligan, and shook hands. He looked very stately and plump. "That's a rare Gothic-looking face you have," he said.

"'M'kew," I said, eying his soda bread hungrily.

"As a Customs and Excise agent, I should ask to see your import license for that face. You can't bring a fine, valuable face like that into the country without paying duty on it, you know. Or at the very least I should see your bill of ladling, you broth of a boy."

"I don't have a bill of ladling," I said, getting into the spirit of it, "but I have an invoice from Fortnum and Mason's for a glazed ham, if that's any good."

"It's your glazed ham," Mulligan said. "You should know whether it's any good or not."

I put my foot on the bar rail again, but then realized I was resting it on the country gentleman in the tweeds; so I removed it again and peeled off my fur-lined helmet and flapped it about a bit. Before I could stop him, Timothy had organized another two tubs. While I was paying, he hurried off though the crush, muttering something about *his* cockpit being wet now. He disappeared through the stained-glass door.

By then I was swashing with stout, Guinness, porter, poteen, aniline dye, or whatever it was in those whacking great glasses. I decided I'd had enough, and when the barmaid went farther along the counter to serve somebody else, I hunched over the glass, concealing it between myself and the counter, and the moment Mulligan looked away, tipped it surreptitiously toward the spittoon below. Unfortunately the stuff hissed spitefully down the dimpled cheeks of the glass and started spattering the gentleman in tweeds at my feet.

Instantly he scrambled to his feet and held out his hand, palm upward, and blinked at the ceiling, as if he'd been counting on a cloudless day. He then made unsteadily for the street door, muttering something about getting home before the cloudborst.

For a moment I thought it was his precipitate departure that had caused the hush. But then I became aware that a tense-looking man with a blue face had entered. He was looking at me very bleakly indeed.

I nodded. After a moment he came over. Mulligan made way for him with alacrity. Several others were also looking at the fellow with respect, but warily, as if they expected him to ask for a sizable loan in exchange for inadequate collateral.

"He's American, Charlie; it's all right," Mulligan said quickly. He steadied himself and went on carefully, "Allow me to 'traduce Charlie MacCurtains. And this . . ." He stopped, frowning, then stared into his glass as if hoping to see my name spelled out there in foam.

"Bart Bandy," I said. And to prove I was an American, I stuck out a horny hand and said, "Howdy."

MacCurtains ignored the hand – perhaps it was *too* horny – and picked up the whisky the barmaid had spontaneously poured for him. He continued to stare at me fixedly.

"He says he landed his airplane just outside town," she said, and gave MacCurtains the gist of Timothy's story, which I got quite interested in until I remembered it was my story she was recounting.

"Where exactly is this airplane?" MacCurtains asked in a low voice.

"Oh," I said, gesturing cautiously toward the magnetic pole. "Some field or other." I wasn't telling this mob a thing. They might go and rifle my drawers.

Which reminded me: I'd left my map case in Timothy's cart. I'd better not lose that or I'd have trouble getting back to Gosport.

"You'll be reporting to the Castle, I expect," the barmaid said to me.

"What castle?"

"The Castle. Dublin Castle, of course. Where the English are."

Mulligan blew out his cheeks and belched circumspectly. "I saw General Sir Hubert Perris arriving only yesterday," he said rotundly. "Driving from Dun Laoghaire with an escort of about seven hundred Royal Irish Constabulary."

"Bad cess to them," the barmaid said, looking at MacCurtains for approval.

I was about to claim acquaintance with Sir Hubert, and perhaps curry favor with the natives by slandering him a bit, when MacCurtains turned and slashed my sidcot to ribbons with the razors of his eyes.

"If you're from America," he said, "what are you doing in the British Army?"

"Oh, just fighting the war to end wars."

"We've been fighting our war for nine hundred years," MacCurtains said grimly.

"Is that right?" I said.

"Yes, that's right," he said sharply, and turned back to his drink.

However, after another snifther, he turned back again, and perhaps as much for the benefit of the others as for my enlightenment, he started on what was obviously his favorite subject.

"Ireland had already a distinct and separate identity," he said intensely, as several assorted refugees from an Irish farce drew closer to listen. "Until Henry the Eighth brutally suppressed us and took the title King of Ireland. But we've never knuckled under. There were Irish rebellions even in Elizabeth's time. And of course there was Cromwell. I suppose you've heard of him?"

"M'm. Vaguely."

He gave me a sharp look, but then smiled, somewhat sourly. "But, praise be," he went on, his voice rasping sarcastically, "we were finally given a Parliament of our own, in 1782."

"Jolly good."

"Then, just as we were becoming an independent country again, with a genuine culture of our own so that even the landowners were proud to be Irish, the English took it away from us again."

"That's hard luck."

"So there were rebellions in 1829, 1848, 1865, 1867–"

"You're well up in history, Mr. MacCurtains."

"He teaches in the school, Misther," somebody said soapily. "And a grand teacher he is, too, to be sure; isn't that right, lads?"

"Did you know that Gladstone tried to give us Home Rule as far back as 1886?" MacCurtains said.

"And we're still waiting for it," somebody else said.

"You'd have got it in 1914 if the war hadn't come along, wouldn't you?" I said, leaning over and placing my right elbow carefully in a puddle of porter.

"That was just another trick," MacCurtains said contemptuously. "They knew the Northern Protestants would never have stood for it. The Ulster Volunteers were already arming to attack us – with the support of the British Army, I might add. When we started to arm ourselves in self-defense, the English cracked down on us fast enough." He stared bitterly into his whisky. "What we've learned painfully over the years, Mister, is that the only way we'll ever get our independence is by fighting for it."

At this point, Timothy came blundering back into the parlor, chittering and grinning at somebody he'd met in the lavatory. His tiny, pinched face was flushed, and his little blue eyes were alight with jollity.

Until he saw MacCurtains.

He tried to dodge behind his pal, but MacCurtains had seen him. MacCurtains froze. A slack-jawed counterfeit of a smile rifted Timothy's face and he started to sidle toward the door, still grinning, obviously hoping his smirk would entrance MacCurtains long enough for himself to reach the door.

But he lost his nerve halfway there and made a dash for it.

He wasn't nearly fast enough. Flinging sycophants in all directions, MacCurtains rammed his way across the parlor. There was a swirling confusion of bodies and fists and a clamor of Irish-type ejaculations.

I stood on the bar rail for a better view, although I could already see clearly over the bobbing heads. MacCurtains was shaking Timothy like a pot of pepper.

"You left the cart outside? You stupid little man!" MacCurtains was hissing. He slammed Tim against the door. One of Tim's teeth fell out.

"I only dropped in for a minute, Charlie, honest to God," Tim squealed. "Out of hospitality – our guest–"

MacCurtains raised his fist. Tim curled up like a porcupine, yelping. A little old crone in a shawl picked up his tooth and offered it to him.

"Get it out of the way," MacCurtains hissed. "This minute!" He gave Tim another violent shove, and moved back. Tim scrabbled at the door and scuttled through, whimpering.

"'Tis bad luck to leave your toot' behind," the little old crone cried delightedly, "without utterin' the word *Bogsamorra* and stampin' your right foot three toims!" But Tim didn't seem too concerned about his toot'. He was already halfway across Dublin.

"Hey, wait!" I cried. "My map case!" And pushing and shoving through the crowd, I ran out after him.

The cart was already out of sight, but I heard it clopping somewhere off to the left. Once again I found myself pelting after that damn rag-and-bone cart. But I had to get those maps back or heaven knew where I'd end up next time I flew off: Sheep Haven, or Lough Swilly, or worse. I'd *really* have some explaining to do then.

As I skidded around the next corner, the centrifugal effect of the black liquid inside me carried me onward into the cobbled gutter, where I stood for a moment, foaming and swashing. There was nobody in sight (as usual); but twenty yards off to the left was a lane. He must have gone down there.

I reached it just in time to see the cart disappearing into a yard near the far end of the lane.

By the time I'd pranced around all the puddles that eyed the dim sky and had reached the end of the lane, the gates of the yard had been closed and bolted.

I was just about to start hollering and beating on the gates when I heard Charlie MacCurtains' voice coming from the yard. I was so surprised at his getting there ahead of me that my fists remained poised in the moonlight as if I were establishing the preparation for some wild Gypsy dance.

But then I realized that I must have gone right around the block and that this must be the rear of the pub.

"Bloody fool! Of all people to bring here!" Charlie was whispering hoarsely.

"But he's from America, Charlie."

"He's in the British Army, isn't he?"

Tim started to reply, but his words ended in a thump and a whimper. Then there was a hissing sound. Then a pregnant silence.

I skittered over to some garbage cans and hid behind them just in time. Bolts rasped, and MacCurtains stuck his head into the lane and looked up and down, his face hollow and eyeless in the moonlight.

A few seconds later, the gates were quietly bolted again. I sneaked back to listen.

Timothy whispered something.

"Shut up. He went running out to look for you."

"Oh, me God."

"You'll have to take the cart back to Eamon in the morning."

"What'll we do with the stuff, Charlie?"

"Leave it 'til I get back. I'm going to find out where he is. You stay here, you understand?"

There was silence. Then light gleamed, as the back door of the pub opened and closed.

I peered cautiously through a gap above the gate hinges. Tim was tying a feed bag to the horse, and upbraiding it. "It's all your fault," I heard him whisper to the animal. "If you hadn't stopped in front of the pub . . . yes, you might well shuffle your feet, you. . . . 'Tis the last time I ever take *you* out for the evening. . . ."

There was a jingling sound, then silence. In the distance a dog barked once. This left me in considerable suspense. It didn't seem natural for a dog to bark only once. I'd never known a dog to bark just once. Of course, it was possible that Irish dogs were different and had been trained to unsettle strangers by barking only once. But still. It was pretty unsettling.

Five minutes tiptoed by. I peered through the gap again, and was just about to chance it and climb over when Timothy reappeared. He was staring longingly at the pub door.

The horse shook its bag of oats and snuffled. Tim patted it nervously, looking around. He stared at the pub again and stood on tiptoe to try to gaze through the window. But he was too small to see over the ledge. He glanced around again, hesitated, then sneaked to the door and slipped inside.

Poor Tim would be in trouble again, for that. I was over the gate five seconds later.

The cart had been detached from the horse and pushed into the corner, near a coal chute. I went over and fumbled around the seat, searching for the map case. I was just starting to feel around under the seat when I saw it sticking out from beneath a pile of old clothes and sacking. I snatched it up thankfully. As I did so, the sacking flipped back. Several bars of yellow soap appeared. And the butt of a Lee-Enfield rifle.

"Aha," I said; then clapped a hand over my mouth to stifle any further exclamations.

I tossed aside the rest of the sacking. There were about two dozen rifles there, and two boxes marked W D.

I was poking around to see what else there was, when the pub door squealed. I ran noisily over the flagstones and flung myself at the gate.

Somebody shouted.

There seemed to be at least three of them. They were still fumbling with the bolt as I reached the end of the lane. I didn't bother going around the puddles this time. I turned left, away from the pub, and ran along the deserted street, heart thumping much harder than the exercise warranted. From the lane came shrill cries and shouted orders.

Five minutes later I thought I'd lost them, as I came panting up to what was obviously a main thoroughfare. Grafton Street. But even here there were only two persons in sight. I'd never come across such an empty city.

I hailed the men and started toward them. They were about fifty yards away. They stopped and looked back.

But when I shouted again, they turned and walked away. I started to trot. They started to trot. I ran, they ran, and hurtled down a side street and into a house and slammed the door.

Guilty consciences about something, I thought. A lot of people seemed to have guilty consciences in Ireland.

By then I'd lost all sense of direction. I went back to the main street, panting and sweating, and looking this way and that.

A car appeared at the end of the street and came spluttering toward me. I was just about to step out into the street and wave it down when Charlie MacCurtains and three other men appeared about a hundred yards away, at the intersection, as I learned later, of Grafton and Nassau streets. I recoiled into a shop doorway and watched.

They stopped in the middle of the intersection and held a hurried conference. After a minute they all marched off again with a purposeful air.

On the assumption that at least *they* knew where they were going, I followed, scampering from doorway to doorway. They were proceeding rapidly along a place called College Green. They reached Dame Street. Here they turned left and disappeared.

I got to the corner and peered around it cautiously. And there was Dublin Castle, gray and miserable in the moonlight.

It was very thoughtful of them, I thought, to have shown me the way to go home.

Picking Morosely at My Wings

"The colonel claims to have had an encounter with some I.R.B. men, sir," the duty officer said in a noncommittal tone. He was a slender, fresh-complexioned man with a careful accent and a typically untidy Army mustache. "I told him you'd retired for the night, sir, but he said he knew you and you wouldn't mind."

General Sir Hubert Perris and his wife were seated in front of an enormous marble fireplace in their cavernous living room on the first floor of the castle. The general was wearing trousers, shirt, and pullover, and had a blanket draped over his sloping shoulders, which made him look like a hastily constructed wigwam. His stockinged feet were thrust out over the tiles toward the fire, which was smoking chronically.

This may have accounted for the red-rimmed eyes of his wife, who was seated at the other side of the fireplace, twelve or fourteen feet away. She was busy knitting a jacket for her dog, an unpleasant-looking off-white beast with bow legs. It also had red-rimmed eyes. It hadn't stopped growling since the captain had ushered me into the general's lair.

"Damn you, I gave orders I wasn't to be disturbed!" Sir Hubert shouted. "I have a cold coming, after that blasted sea trip!"

"I'm very sorry, sir, but I thought you'd want to see him."

The general sighed exasperatedly from the depths of his blanket and muttered something about a blasted frigate. What with him and Bonzo both growling from either side of the fireplace, it sounded as if a dogfight was about to break out at any moment.

I thought it was about time I spoke up. After all, I'd been around for some minutes now and he hadn't even looked at me yet. I said heartily, "Well, this is a coincidence, Sir Hubert." I said, "Fancy meeting you here."

At this, the general started violently; and then grew terribly still.

"Though of course I shouldn't be too surprised to find you in Dublin Castle," I went on, "seeing as how you're in charge here, and . . . an Englishman's castle is his home . . . in this case," I said, faltering a bit as the boiled eyes slowly turned skyward.

As they reached my face I treated him to a nervous sort of wink that, combined with a friendly twitch of the old noddle and an encouraging sort of smile, had no placatory effect whatsoever. He continued to look at me as if I had just defecated on his front doorstep and then rung the bell to ask for paper.

I cleared my throat and looked away, still smiling brightly – only to meet the almost equally rigid gaze of his beanpole of a wife.

From her expression I thought I'd said something indescribably obscene. I hurriedly reviewed my last few words, but they seemed innocuous enough to me. Then I remembered that she hadn't heard my voice before. I guessed it was my whining drawl that was causing her to look at me in that half-paralyzed fashion; or possibly I had spoken too loud. Even my normal projection was one that a character actor might have envied, had he wished to be typecast as a hog caller for the rest of his life.

Meeting my eye, Lady Perris hurriedly looked away, patted her dog nervously, and resumed her knitting.

I glanced back at her husband. He was now staring incredulously at my tunic.

I suppose it was the state of the uniform as much as the sight of my insignia that was upsetting him so much. I always flew in my second-best uniform, and it was in rather a mess by now because of all the castor oil. Rotary engines tended to fling it around somewhat profligately. The egg stains, grease, blood, and Guinness didn't exactly help, either.

Moreover, the wings were a bit loose. It must have looked pretty silly, I guess, the way the cloth wings were flapping about like that on my chest. I'd been intending for some time to sew them on properly, before they flew away altogether; but somehow I'd never gotten around to it.

"What the hell's *he* doing here?" the general said at last, glaring at the captain, his face going all red and swelling up unhealthily.

The captain explained that I'd come scuttling into the castle half an hour ago under cover of some returning soldiers, complaining that some Irishmen were after me.

"All right, all right," the general interrupted. "Let him speak for himself. I know he can do that, all right." He glared at my red tabs, then shouted, "Go on, then, what're you waiting for? What's this about being chased by some Irish?"

"Well, it's like this, sir," I said, staring uneasily at the general's feet. They were far too close to the fire, in my opinion. His socks were beginning to smolder. Unless, of course, it was steam that was issuing from the instep. But I didn't think so, as the fumes rising from them had the definite odor of toasted sheep.

I wondered if I ought to tell him that his feet were on fire; but then I remembered the headmaster's loose button, and decided to keep quiet. After all, if Sir Hubert didn't mind having his extremities scorched in that fashion, it was no business of mine.

"Well, get on with it, man, get on with it!" Sir Hubert shouted.

"Well, it was like this, sir," I said. "I flew to Ireland by mistake this afternoon, you see. And–"

"You what?"

"Flew to Ireland by mistake, sir."

"You flew to Ireland by *mistake?*"

"Yes, sir."

"By mistake? To *Ireland?*"

"Yes, sir," I said, wondering if I could sit down uninvited. After all that running, my limbs were aching in every . . . limb.

They were also shaky with hunger. I'd had nothing to eat all day but a kipper.

The general meanwhile was staring at me bulbously. He opened his mouth to holler again, but then a thoughtful expression started to drift over his face, as if his brain was sending some sort of garbled signal. A deep frown settled somewhere above his sloping chin. He glanced at his feet, looked away, then quickly looked back as he caught sight of a yellowish toe. It was peeking coyly out of a rather disgusting-looking ruff of smoking wool.

He jerked his feet back abruptly and started to rub them, looking more irritable than ever.

"Go on, go on," he shouted.

"Anyway," I said, "I came into town on this rag-and-bone cart, you see, and–"

"A rag-and-*bone* cart?" he said incredulously. Even his wife looked up briefly at that, before going back to her clicking. "I thought you said you flew here!"

"Yes, sir, that was before the rag-and-bone cart, of course. I was running beside it most of the way–"

"You were running beside your airplane?"

"No, the rag-and-bone cart, sir. Running beside it and shouting. Anyway, I arrived at this pub."

"What pub?!"

"Well, I don't know the name of it, General, but, inside, it had a stained-glass window with a representation of Adam and Eve. Or possibly it was a honeymoon coup–"

"Shut up, Basil!" Sir Hubert interrupted, bellowing at the dog. It was still growling. I realized to my astonishment that it was the captain it was growling at, not me.

"All right, go on," Sir Hubert said, picking angrily at his charred hose. "You were in a common pub, is that it? Drinking, I suppose?"

"Well, I'd worked up quite a thirst, you see, with all that running and hollering, sir. Anyway, as I was saying, after all that riding around in a common pub, and having a drink in the rag and bone – Or, rather, no, I should say, after chatting in the pub with Adam and Eee . . . where was I?"

I seemed to have lost my train of thought. I shuffled about a bit among the cinders. I licked my thumb and fiddled with the wings, trying to stick them on.

I was just rounding up my thoughts again when I saw the captain looking down at the dog, which was slavering on his polished boots. The captain glanced quickly at the Perrises, then suddenly jerked his foot. He caught the dog on the jaw. There was a clopping sound as its teeth snapped together. The dog retreated, snarling furiously.

By then the captain was gazing upward, his lips pursed in soundless wonder at the beauty of the ceiling, which was covered with decorative stains and cobwebs.

"Stop that," Lady Perris said sharply. "Come here, Basil!" She flapped a hand at the dog. It continued to growl and dribble.

"Anyway," I said, knuckling my eyes, which were watering in the smoke, "to cut a long story short, I climbed over into the yard at the back and found these arms–"

"A yard? Now what the devil are you talking about? I thought you said you were in a pub?!"

"The yard at the back of the pub," I said, taking a deep breath of poisonous gases from the fireplace. "The one with Adam and Eve, or possibly a young married couple. By then, the rag-and-bone cart was also there."

"What in the name of thundering heaven are you blithering about?!" Sir Hubert said, his faded eyes almost boiling out of their sockets. "Who are these people Adam and Eve? They were riding around the yard in a rag-and-bone cart at the back of the pub, is that it?"

Before I could answer, there was another clopping sound, followed by a renewed snarling.

"I saw that!" Lady Perris cried, so loudly that we all twitched in unison. "Hubert, did you see that?!"

"What?"

"He kicked Basil! I distinctly saw him! I just knew he was going to do it, so I watched him, and he did!" She dropped her knitting and held out her arms. "Tum here, poor wittle doggie, come to mumsie, come on, poor wittle fing!" she cried, glaring hatefully at the captain, who was now staring down at the beads of canine spittle that gleamed on his boots. His face was brick-colored. "You brute! Don't try to deny it, I saw you!"

"I assure you, Madam—"

"Tum here to mum, poor wittle darling!" she said. The dog lurched over, smiling contentedly.

"Never mind that now!" Sir Hubert shouted, stamping his foot. Pieces of burned sock fell away, exposing several more toes.

Lady Perris was almost in tears. "But he did, Hubert!" she cried. "I saw him, I was watching!" She leaned over to pet the dog. Basil promptly fell over onto its side with a thump. It spread its legs, exposing a revoltingly pink belly. She stroked and tickled the beast agitatedly. Its pink tongue lolled out. And not only its pink tongue.

I looked away hurriedly.

"It was an accident, I assure you, Lady Perris," the captain said, his voice unsteady. "I was just shifting my position, you see—"

"It wasn't an accident! You did it on purpose! You're always doing it!"

Sir Hubert meanwhile was gazing morosely at Basil's pink parts from the depths of his blanket. He shouted in sudden rage, "I want to get to the bottom of this! You came to Ireland without authorization of any kind, is that it?"

"Well, yes. But–"

"You accepted a lift in a, a tinker's cart, is that it? You rode around some yard or other in a tinker's cart – a tinker, mind you! And you, an officer and a – a–" Apparently he couldn't bring himself to utter the next word. "After which you were tippling in a common Irish pub with some low people named Adam and Eve, and under these circumstances you thought you saw some arms – right?!"

I looked at him. He was obviously sitting far too close to the fire. His face looked as if it had been upholstered in Jersey cowhide.

"Yes," I said. "That's about it."

Sir Hubert flung aside his blanket and heaved himself up. It was several seconds before he was able to speak. "I don't like your manner or your way of talking, or anything about you, you revolting bloody colonial!" he shouted at the top of his voice. "I had quite enough of you last time we met! You come in here smelling of beer and wearing that disgraceful uniform – and, by God, I'm going to make some inquiries about that rank of yours, I can tell you! I don't believe for one second you're entitled to those badges! Colonel?! My God – bloody *Basil* there would make a better colonel than you! Now, get out! Get out, both of you, before I have you court-martialed, you – damned imposter!"

As we hurried along the drafty, ill-lighted corridor outside the C-in-C's quarters, the captain said thoughtfully, "I'm sorry for that beast, really."

"Sir Hubert?"

"The dog. I mean, my feelings about it. Kind of substitute, I suppose. Redirecting my pent-up aggression onto it, sort of thing."

"I guess that's what it is."

"Yes . . ." We clip-clopped along the corridor for a moment, in silence. Then: "All the same, I suppose we really ought to search this pub," the captain said. "Just in case the guns are still there."

He looked at me inquiringly.

"Somehow, I've a feeling I'll never be able to find that pub again."

"No?"

"No."

The captain's step seemed to lighten. "I take it you've no intention of looking further?" he asked. "You've reported it to the C-in-C, and you consider you've amply discharged your duty. Is that the situation, sir?"

"It is."

The captain nodded. "Well, I think that covers us both, then." We reached an intersection of corridors. He stopped and dug at the floor with his toe. "My name's McCarthy, by the way. I was born here."

"In the castle?"

"God forbid. No – Ireland."

"Ah," I said. We caught each other's eye, and smiled faintly.

"By the way," he said, "how on earth did you manage to fly to Ireland by mistake? I shouldn't have thought that was possible."

"It is, if some practical joker clamps a powerful magnet above your instrument panel," I said.

"Oh." The captain thought for a moment, then: "The compass?"

"Yes. It was about ninety degrees out."

"Well, well," McCarthy said. "Well, well. Still, it could have been worse."

"How?"

"It could have been ninety degrees the other way. You'd have ended up in Germany."

"M'm," I said thoughtfully. "Maybe that's what the little bastard had in mind."

"You seem to have made a lot of enemies," the captain said, sounding almost envious.

Me, Hedging

Early next morning Captain McCarthy borrowed a car and, followed by a solid-tired lorry filled with sleepy, grumbling soldiers, we set out to look for the deserted farm to the north of the city.

We had no difficulty in locating it, and the plane was unharmed, apart from an inch or two of water that was sloshing about in the front cockpit.

McCarthy detailed an unnecessary number of men to wheel the Harry Tate toward the open field. As they emerged from the barn, panting noisily to show how hard they were working, the sun came up out of the sea. It promptly disappeared again into the clouds.

"Do you have enough petrol to get back?" McCarthy asked.

"I'll refuel on the way," I said, wetting a forefinger and sticking it knowledgeably into the damp, chill air. The gesture might have been more effective if I'd remembered to take off my glove first.

We trudged alongside as the soldiers, clumsy in their great-coats, maneuvered the plane toward the sloping field beyond

the deserted farmhouse. The grass was deep and wet. Their
puttees were soon soaked through and through.

"I've never seen an airplane this close," McCarthy said.
"Doesn't look very safe."

A movement off to one side caught my eye. As I glanced
casually in that direction, a shadow drifted out of sight behind
a yew hedge, about a hundred yards away.

That was one reason I'd been glad of the escort, reasoning
that if Charlie MacCurtains had any intelligence at all at all,
he would question Tim as to exactly where he had picked me
up and would sleuth his way back to the airplane from there.
As I'd anticipated, he had put a watch on it, in case I was
foolish enough to return alone.

I caught McCarthy's eye. "Anything wrong?" he asked.

"Just have to pop over there for a pee," I said jauntily, and
walked the hundred yards or so to the hedge, where I proceeded to douse the Hibernian foliage.

"Careful," a voice whispered. "I'm damp enough as it is."

"Sorry."

"I've been here half the night, hoping to make your
acquaintance again."

"You shouldn't have bothered, really."

"But I wanted to. One doesn't often have the opportunity
to meet a Bandy every day."

"No, there's something in that."

"By the way, what did you tell the authorities?"

"Everything," I said.

There was a pause. Then the voice whispered thoughtfully
from behind the hedge, "It's a trap, is it? They're waiting to
collar the lot of us if we go near the pub again?"

I did up my sidcot and brushed at the skirts. The map
case fell from the pocket. I picked it up and stuck it under
my arm.

"But we haven't seen any sign of them yet," the voice whispered.

"Haven't you? That's strange."

"Incidentally," Michael Mansergh said, "how did you know it was me?"

I looked back at the Harry Tate. It was now just inside the field about 150 yards away. The soldiers were lounging around it, lighting cigarettes.

They were rather too close to the fuel tank for my liking. I was relieved when I saw McCarthy go over and wave them away from the four-bladed propeller.

"Your map case," I said to the hedge. "Your name's on it. I took it from the cart, thinking it was mine."

There was silence for a moment, then: "Yes, I left it there with the rest of the stuff. Careless of me."

Slowly another map case wiggled its way through the hedge.

"Will you swop, Bart?" Michael whispered.

"It'll save time if I keep yours. I see the course to northwest England is already nicely plotted."

"You're keeping my map case as evidence, are you?"

I didn't reply immediately. Overhead a skylark twittered, invisibly.

"I guess it was one of your Paddywhacks who claimed to have seen your Avro flop into the sea?" I said at length.

"Yes, he's a good lad. I suppose he'll have to desert, now."

"And I gather from your maps that you're using the Avro for flights between England and Ireland."

"Well, you see, it's getting too difficult to bring the stuff through the patrols on the Irish Sea. So I had to think of another way. That's the only reason I joined the Flying Corps," he added, "so I could help the cause with a spot of aerial gunrunning."

"It's treason."

"Well, we won't argue about that, Bart me love. Let's just say I was as patriotic as the next fellow, until after the Easter Rising."

I saw McCarthy looking in my direction, no doubt feeling pretty awed at the capacity of my bladder.

"Have you really told them everything, Bart?"

"I assure you," I said spitefully, "I've told the C-in-C, Ireland, every damn thing I know."

Which was true enough as far as it went. If I'd made no mention of Michael to General Perris, it was only because I hadn't discovered I had Michael's map case until five that morning.

So, in fact, nobody else knew about Michael. But I certainly wasn't going to tell him that. I was still thoroughly miffed at the way he'd fooled everybody.

I started toward the airplane.

"I have a gun trained on you, you know."

"You wouldn't get very far, with all those soldiers around."

"Don't bank on it, Bart."

But I kept going, more than half expecting a bullet to come whistling out of the hedge. I strolled away so stiffly I must have looked like an iron maiden on wheels. Perhaps that's what put him off.

I quite forgot to ask Michael if he had really been such a ham-fisted pilot or if he had handled the Avro so incompetently in order to make his carefully staged disappearance more plausible. In fact, I never did find out.

When I got back to the Harry Tate, I found that Captain McCarthy had pointed it up the hill. I suppose he thought it would be easier for the plane to take off that way – to give it a helping hand into the sky, as it were.

In the Mess Again

When I walked into the mess at Gosport that afternoon there was dead silence. This was mainly because there was nobody there. However, the bartender soon appeared, and I ordered a lime juice – straight.

A few minutes after one o'clock, the instructors, thumping their chests after the midday repast, came booting their way noisily into the mess and hurried dedicatedly in the direction of the booze, calling out their orders from a good twenty paces away in order to minimize the delay.

The ones at the front stopped abruptly when they saw me standing there smirking, with an elbow on the counter. The ones behind crashed into them. There was a swirl of confusion in the doorway.

"Good God–"

"–He's back."

"Who, who?" Captain Cole called out from the rear. Then his eyes widened.

"Afternoon," I said. "Trouble with the compass. Flew to Ireland by mistake. Escaped from some gunrunners. Had to come back via Lancashire to avoid the Welsh mountains. Nearly ran into some sort of tower at Blackpool. That's why I'm a bit late."

But they didn't seem to take it in at all. They remained bunched up at the door, staring at me fixedly. I might as well have read out the instructions from a seed packet, for all the interest they showed in my adventures.

"Come in, gentlemen," I said briskly. "No need to stand around so formally. Just forget I'm a colonel. Stand at ease, men. Oh, Potter, run out and fetch the commandant for me, will you? Want a word with him about the poor quality of the lime juice here. Not Rose's, you know. And do up your buttons, Cole, there's a good chap."

Nobody moved or did up their buttons. Captain Potter's face had a large hole excavated in it.

Fielding was also looking a trifle open-mouthed. He was the first to recover.

"Well, well," he said faintly. "The man of the hour."

He came forward, grinning strangely and looking me up and down in that superior way of his. "How did you manage to get away without being drawn and quartered, Herr Colonel?"

Thinking he was referring to the Irish, I said stiffly, "Slipped into the castle under cover of some returning soldiers, if you must know."

As if emerging from a six-day barrage, the others slowly moved into the room and stood in a defensive cluster at the far end of the bar. They reached feebly for their drinks.

"What castle?" someone asked. "What's he saying now?"

"Don't ask," someone else muttered.

"What are you gaping like that for?" I demanded. I glanced down at my uniform, but everything seemed to be in order, except for the wings, which were now nearly off altogether.

I looked at Treadwell. He turned away and leaned on the bar and stared into his Peasant's Bath Night Imperial Vodka.

"What kind of reception did you get at Fallow?" Fielding asked. "I mean, what did they do?"

"What d'you mean, what did they do? I gave my speech, they listened, they clapped, what else?"

"Clapped you in irons, you mean?"

I looked at him suspiciously, but he seemed to be quite serious for once.

"What's the matter with you all?" I snapped. "It was a great success."

I waited for the ribald comments. But they remained silent.

"The headmaster seemed a bit upset, that's all," I went on. "But one of the boys said it was a jolly good speech. Those were his exact words. 'A jolly good speech,' he said."

"What about the press?"

"Oh, well, they left a bit early, that's true," I admitted. Then, defensively: "But they probably had another engagement."

"Another engagement," Fielding said wonderingly. He felt behind him for the nearest armrest, and sat on it. "Haven't you seen the papers?"

"Eh? No. I've been flying."

"You certainly have. . . ."

Treadwell stirred. Everybody looked at him. He straightened, thought deeply for a moment, then moved across to the mess table and looked through an untidy heap of newspapers. He picked up one of them, shook it to make sure it was dead, then held it up with the main news page toward me.

It was Lord Rackingham's paper, I saw. I could read the headlines easily from twenty feet.

"'FURTHER SHORTAGE OF MEAT PREDICTED,'" I read out. Treadwell patiently tapped the adjoining columns with his forefinger.

HAIG DEFIES LLOYD GEORGE, IGNORES WAR COUNCIL, it said. Then: GROSS ARMY MISMANAGEMENT, AIR MINISTRY COLONEL ALLEGES. And, in still smaller letters: *A Violent Attack at Fallow.*

I was still staring at the headlines and starting to pick somewhat agitatedly at my wings again when the commandant came stumping in, followed by the adjutant.

When he saw me, his face seemed to swell up to twice its normal size. He looked around wildly; then, flinging captains in all directions, he seized a pair of fire tongs, or maybe it was a brass shovel – I didn't really have the time to find out – and started toward me, smoke and flames hissing from his nostrils.

He was prevented from attacking me mainly because the adjutant had him in a half nelson and was bleating into his ear, urging the commandant to think of his career. "He's not worth it, sir. Don't let him get you down at this late date," the adjutant whispered hoarsely as I hurriedly got behind the bar and started to serve drinks in all directions. "It's too much of a risk, sir," the adjutant went on. "They might not overlook it if you killed him. And think of your pension, sir. Think of your pension."

I didn't reach the Ministry until eight o'clock that evening. Normally dormant at that hour, the hotel was thronged with people, all hurrying about in a rigid sort of way, as if they'd been stricken with mass diarrhea.

If the atmosphere in the lobby was tense, it was nothing to the atmosphere of crisis evident in the upstairs corridors. Almost every office in the place blazed with light, and messengers were coming and going at an unprecedented rate.

For a ghastly few minutes I thought I was the cause of the crisis. I'd read the newspapers on the way up to town. They had all reported my speech in detail, some of them far from objectively. There was even a leading article in the *Globe* in which the word *treason* was used – twice. By the time the train had reached Paddington I could already see myself in a small cell at Aldershot, pleading temporary insanity to one of those frighteningly confident-looking British barristers – assuming I could find one who would represent me.

But really there was nothing to worry about, I kept telling myself as I stood hesitating outside Sir Aubrey Sprain's office. After all, had I not two of the most powerful politicians in England on my side?

I was still jittering there as the Chief of the Air Staff came along the corridor, talking urgently to a gray-haired sea dog with gold rings up to his elbows.

When the general saw me, he stopped as if he'd run into a pile of sandbags.

The worst of it was, he didn't say anything. It was the first time I'd met him in the Ministry without his baring his teeth and uttering at the very least a low growl.

But he didn't speak a word. His great eyebrows seemed to sprout a lot of extra hair, that's all. Otherwise he just looked at me.

And then he nodded, slowly and meaningfully – except I didn't know what he meant – and resumed his conversation with the admiral and continued on down the corridor.

It was the worst encounter with him yet.

When I finally plucked up courage to go in and see Sir Aubrey, I learned that the tension in the Hotel Cecil had nothing whatsoever to do with me. It was the news from the front. The German Army had started its big push early that morning, and although G.H.Q. was giving it out that there was nothing to worry about and that the enemy was suffering unbearable losses, it was already clear that he wasn't being contained. That in fact the British Army was in full retreat.

In Disgrace

Katherine and her father met me in the hall of their serene Georgian mansion that Sunday afternoon. Katherine embraced me warmly.

"It was silly of us to quarrel," she said, hiding her face against my chest. "I've been so unhappy. I knew it didn't mean anything, you having a couple of women in your bedroom."

At these words, Mr. Lewis' faint smile of welcome faded slightly. As Katherine and I walked through into the Long Room, he remained behind, staring fixedly through the fan-light above the front door.

There was quite a conflagration going on in the fireplace of the Long Room. Mrs. Lewis was sitting in front of it, sound asleep. Beside her lay a broken chair.

"Have you been fighting?" I whispered as Mr. Lewis followed us in.

"Hm? No, I was trying to glue the leg back on," he murmured. Then: "Did Katherine say you had two women in your bedroom?"

"Three, actually."

"It didn't mean anything," Katherine said loyally.

"It didn't?"

"Of course not," she said. "Even if they were undressed and everything."

"Undressed?"

"They weren't undressed," I said, avoiding Lewis' gaze but looking a portrait of Wellington straight in the eye. "Apart from you," I added.

"Well, they had their coats off."

"Just a minute," Lewis said. "I've missed a bit. Katherine was in your bedroom undressed? Where was this?"

"The Spartan. I was just saying good night, that's all," Katherine said.

"You always undress to say good night?" I asked.

"Course I don't. I told you, I just came along to say good night."

"Sounds pretty fishy to me," I said. "Getting undressed just to say good night. Well, I mean." I laughed cynically.

"Surely I'm supposed to say things like that?" Lewis said. "You're the one who's supposed to be looking discomfited."

"Well, I was," Katherine said hotly. She bent down and picked up the broken chair leg somewhat agitatedly, and twisted it in her hands.

"And where did the other two women come in?" Lewis asked.

"They came in from the bathroom and the cupboard, respectively," I said.

Lewis leaned his forehead against the marble mantelpiece to think about it. "Perhaps we'd better change the subject," he said at length, "before your mother wakes up."

"I just came up to say good night, that's all," Katherine said, a shade too convincingly for conviction. She started to poke the fire agitatedly.

"After all, you *are* getting married at the end of the month," Lewis said tactfully.

I thought it was very nice of him to be so understanding, but Katherine seemed incapable of dropping the subject.

"That was all there was," she cried, stamping her foot. "All I did was come along to say good night and get undress – get undressed and come along to say – oh, shut up!" she shouted, just as the poker caught fire.

Mr. Lewis looked at the end of his chair leg as it flamed and sputtered. He took a deep breath and gently removed it from Katherine's grasp and waved it about resignedly. The smoke of the burning varnish coiled and drifted in the fierce drafts. Mrs. Lewis, her face scarlet from the heat, woke up.

"What's that smell?" she demanded, looking at me accusingly. Then, seeing the smoking chair leg: "What on earth are you doing, William? That's not the way to mend a chair." She snatched it from him and looked crossly at the charred end. "Really, William. You're not much of a handyman, are you?"

she said, starting slightly as a bubble of varnish burst and hissed at her.

Nobody mentioned the speech until dinner was nearly over. As soon as Burgess had tottered out and closed the dining room door, however, Mrs. Lewis turned and spoke directly to me for the first time that evening.

"Well, you seem to have made a spectacle of yourself again, Bartholomew."

"I guess so, Mrs. Lewis."

"I consider it very poor taste on your part to have spoken so intemperately, especially on a subject you quite plainly knew something about."

"I didn't mean to. One thing just seemed to lead to another."

"Well, it has led to a good deal of unfavorable comment, I can tell you that. You have put me in a very difficult position, Bartholomew."

"'M sorry."

"The vicar is said to have preached a most disagreeable sermon this morning about your speech."

"Thank goodness you weren't there to hear it, Mrs. Lewis."

"Of course I was there. Are you accusing me of setting the country a bad example by failing to attend church service?"

"But . . . but I gathered you hadn't heard it. You said–"

"Of course I didn't hear it. The vicar's sermons are so tiresomely long I ceased to listen to them shortly before the relief of Mafeking. But several other persons heard it, including Cecily Talbot, who has given it as her opinion that you ought to be incarcerated in the Tower for your remarks."

"I wish I'd been there," Katherine said.

"In the Tower?"

"At Fallow. I wish I could have seen their faces."

"Did you see what the military correspondent of the *Post* said in yesterday's paper?" Lewis asked, pushing his prune stones around idly.

"I sure did."

"We met Repington once," Katherine said. "If I ever meet him again I'll claw his face to ribbons."

"Katherine."

"Well, I will," she said fiercely, and, ignoring a series of winces from my direction, proceeded to quote some of the celebrated Colonel Repington's more vicious remarks.

"Well, as long as the Minister's behind you," Lewis murmured.

"Yes . . ." I said.

He cast me one of those unexpectedly sharp glances of his.

"He's backing you up, of course?" he asked.

"Yes, of course. Though I haven't got in to see him yet, as a matter of fact."

"Oh?"

"I tried several times on Friday and Saturday, but he couldn't spare the time. And the P.M. hasn't spoken a word in Parliament yet, in spite of all the questions. Gee, I wish they'd start the ball rolling. I feel kind of up in the air at the moment."

Mr. Lewis lined up his prune stones in single file, then started pushing them around. There was an uneasy silence. Katherine stirred.

"I don't believe for one minute they'll betray you," she said.

She spoke so loyally that I jerked around in some alarm.

"Whatjamean?" I asked. "Rackingham and the P.M.? Why do you say that?"

"Nothing, nothing," she said quickly. "Just forget I spoke."

"Betray me? It's unthinkable."

"Of course it is, dear," she said vehemently and reached for my hand as if I were an invalid. Immediately, I began to feel like death painted on a wall. I started to gibber feebly.

"They wouldn't just not say anything at all," I faltered, "and leave me stuck out on a limbo. That's impossible."

"It *is* impossible, darling; you must believe that!"

"They promised."

"It's all right, Bart! Everything's all right!" she cried urgently. "There's nothing to worry about – nothing, do you hear?!"

"They promised faithfully . . ."

"Don't worry, Bartholomew! It's going to be *all right!* For heaven's sake, you must stop worrying about it!"

"I'm not worrying."

"Of *course* you're not – because there's nothing to worry about! You trust them, in spite of their– We all trust them, don't we, Papa?" Katherine cried urgently. "For God's sake, Bart," she implored, shaking me. "Everything is *going to be all right!*"

Katherine was getting her own back.

On Monday I tried and failed again to see Lord Rackingham, mainly because he didn't come in to work that day. As for the Prime Minister, he continued to parry questions about me in Parliament.

He was waiting for the right moment, I supposed. The enemy offensive was almost certainly occupying his mind to the exclusion of all else; except, of course, party politics. The Germans were rapidly approaching Amiens, which made the situation very serious indeed.

Still, I wished he would make at least a token gesture of support, instead of saying nothing at all. My position was getting more uncomfortable by the hour. At the Ministry, nobody would come near me. And outside the Ministry, on the Strand, one old lady tried to hit me with her brolly.

The fact that there was no general reserve available to the Fifth Army, which was taking the main weight of the attack, didn't help in the least. Instead of justifying my speech, it made things all the worse. Nobody seemed to care about what I'd said, only about the fact that I'd said it. One columnist even accused me of stabbing my commander-in-chief in the back at the most cowardly moment, when that gallant soldier was fighting with his back to the wall, failing to mention that I'd made the speech before the attack. The journalist also failed to explain how I was able to accomplish this feat. To have stabbed the C-in-C in the back when he had his back to the wall meant I'd have had to bore a large hole in the brickwork, surely?

But nobody else seemed to find his accusation unconvincing.

When I went into the Army and Navy Club that evening and was hissed at by several young officers, I thought it was about time the situation was clarified. I about-turned smartly and went straight to Bland House.

After a one-hour wait, I was finally shown into the Minister's study. He told me there was nothing to be done.

"Nothing to be done?" I said. "Nothing to be done?"

The P.M., he said, couldn't possibly carry out his plan to discredit Field Marshal Haig at such a critical juncture in the affairs of the nation, now, could he?

As for him, Rackingham, there was nothing he could do either.

"I've been – resigned," he muttered.

"Resigned to what?"

"Resigned, man! I've tendered my resignation. Last Saturday."

"You've . . . tendered your resignation . . .?"

"And," Rackingham added in an aggrieved sort of way, "it's been accepted."

The next morning I sat in my office listening to the plumbing. The pipes, the pipes are calling me, I thought.

The C.A.S. also called me. Sir Aubrey ushered me into his presence.

"Colonel Bandy, sir," he said.

"Who?"

"Colonel Bandy."

The Chief of the Air Staff leaned back at his desk and gazed at the civil servant in a puzzled way.

"Colonel Bandy? I know of no Colonel Bandy."

"Yes, sir, don't you remember, sir," I squeaked. "The military adviser, sir?"

The C.A.S. continued to look at Sir Aubrey in perplexity. But then his beetle brow began to crawl back into place again. "Oh, you mean that man along the corridor. The one in the, that spare room? But you're getting confused, Sprain. You've got it all wrong."

He turned and looked at me and gave a long, lingering, beatific smile.

"No, no, it's not *Colonel* Bandy," he said. "It's *Lieutenant* Bandy."

The smile transfigured his usually aggressive face, quite transformed it.

But then his face blackened again, and in a voice straight from Baffin Island he said, "Be so good as to stand at attention when I'm talking to you."

Sir Aubrey turned to leave. The general gestured sharply. "Stay where you are, Sprain." He looked back at me again. "All right. You may have been wondering why it's taken four or five days for some sort of action to be taken in your case, Bandy. Well, I can assure you we've been considering your case very carefully. Yes, we have not been idle. We have been thinking about you a great deal." He stared at me fixedly, obviously still thinking about me a great deal. "We've been thinking of a court-martial, as a matter of fact."

His voice grew still colder. "For gross breach of discipline and violation of official secrets, to start with."

I took a deep breath, and tried to release it as evenly as possible.

"Can you think of any reason why we shouldn't court-martial you, Bandy? Any extenuating circumstances?"

Sir Aubrey started to say something. The C.A.S. silenced him with a look.

"No, sir," I said.

"No. Just a jumped-up ass of a pilot, getting above himself. That's all it amounts to, isn't it?"

"I guess so, sir," I said, wishing he'd start ranting and raving a bit. The way he was talking wasn't like him at all.

"Yes. A miserable worm who thinks he has a right to put our leaders straight on a few points, just because he's earned a few bits of colored ribbon." He leaned forward. "From your lofty vantage point of age, wisdom, knowledge, and experience, you know better than anybody else how this war should be conducted, is that it?"

Sir Aubrey turned, and ignoring the general's glare, went out, closing the door softly behind him.

"Well?"

"You're going to court-martial me, then, are you, General?"

"Believe me, a great many people wanted to," he grated. "And any other time we would certainly have done so." With a sudden movement he seized a thick docket, opened it, and began to slash his way through it. He glared fierily at the pages. I half expected them to turn brown and start curling at the edges.

He took a deep breath and focused on me again.

"Tell me, Bandy," he said softly. "Next to a court-martial, what's the worst thing that could happen to you?"

"You're not – not thinking of making me your aide, are you, sir?"

It was amazing how long the C.A.S. could stare without blinking, just amazing. I was really impressed.

Finally I said, very craftily, "You're sending me to an active service squadron, sir?" Right then there was nothing I wanted more than to get back to the comfort and safety of the Western Front.

"You're getting warmer."

What could be warmer than war flying? I wondered.

"All right, I'll tell you," he said. He leaned back again. "We're sending you back to the trenches."

I stared at him uncomprehendingly.

"Ordinarily we'd have needed at least a court of inquiry to return you to the infantry," he said, "but it so happens there's a much simpler way out. A major at the War Office came up with the solution. You'll be glad to know it's solved all our problems."

"Yes . . .?"

"Yes. We're simply leaving you off the strength of the new Air Force," the C.A.S. said.

After a moment, he looked away.

I couldn't believe what I was hearing. It wasn't possible.

"You can't mean I'm being thrown out of the air entirely . . .?"

"You're already out, to all intents and purposes," he said in a tone that suggested the conversation was no longer worth continuing. He snapped the file shut and dropped it into a wire tray. "You may continue wearing your wings, but that's all," he said in a subdued tone. "You'll receive your instructions within the next few hours. Good day."

I stood in front of his desk for quite a long time, in a silence broken only by the scratching of his fountain pen as, looking not particularly triumphant, he signed his way steadily through a small stack of letters and memoranda.

PART TWO

Posing with the Forty Thieves

Amiens was in a state of chaos. The streets were jammed with traffic: armored cars, lorries (one with its tires missing), motor bikes, staff cars, tenders filled with bloodstained, bandaged officers, and ambulances so spattered with mud it was hard to believe they had ever been white.

Even the military policemen seemed to have given up and were standing around helplessly.

The sidewalks, such as they were, were just as crowded: men without officers, officers without men, N.C.O.s without officers or men. And refugees, pushing prams filled with clocks and pillows, fleeing through from towns that had not been under fire since 1914.

And a flight of German biplanes flying overhead, unhindered.

That was perhaps the most ominous sight of all, those two-seaters wheeling about up there in the yellow smoke. All the time I'd flown in France I'd never seen enemy aircraft on our side of the line, apart from the occasional hit-and-run balloon-raider. But there they were, four Halberstadts, taking their time about it as they laid their eggs into the messy nest. I could even make out their black crosses, a simplified design of cross, quite unfamiliar.

Near the town hall a small Whippet tank had struck the corner of a *marchand de légumes*, blocking a cobbled alley with carrots, turnips, and an infuriated greengrocer.

I reported to the town hall, but nobody seemed to know anything about my unit. Command seemed to have broken down completely. The entire front, an assistant provost marshal said, was in full retreat. He'd heard that the enemy was now only five miles from Fifth Army Headquarters at Villers-Bretonneux. Assuming Army H.Q. still existed, which seemed highly doubtful.

"What unit are you looking for?" the A.P.M. asked, his feet crunching over the broken glass in the echoing hall of the town hall. He had the burly presence of a Scotland Yard inspector and seemed the only calm man in the entire building.

"The 13th Bicycle Battalion."

"Bicycle Battalion? What's that?"

"I don't know. Some kind of mobile outfit. I presume they go around on bicycles."

He looked at me, then moved away to drive out a pack of Chinese coolies who were trying to shelter in the cloakroom. I couldn't blame him for looking suspicious. I'd been pretty taken aback myself when I'd read my orders.

The A.P.M. came back. "Come to think of it," he said, "I did see an unusual number of old bikes chained together outside the Hôtel du Rhin two or three days ago. Wondered what they were doing there. I thought they might belong to the Portuguese General Staff."

"I'll try there, then," I said glumly, and wrenched up my battered valises and staggered back into the turmoil. I hoped the battalion's equipment was reasonably modern and that I wouldn't be expected to ride a dandy horse, or a penny-farthing, or an 1887 ordinary. I couldn't quite see myself flying across country several feet up on one of those. As a matter of fact I couldn't see myself riding a bicycle at all. Though I'd learned to drive a motorcar at university, I'd only been on a bike once before, and on that occasion had gone straight over a bank and into the Ottawa River.

The Hôtel du Rhin was in almost as disordered a state as the town hall, though it had not yet come under fire. The lobby boiled with military personnel and war correspondents and smelled of unwashed bodies and mustard.

As I staggered in, several officers turned and glared at me out of inflamed eyes, as if the great retreat was all my fault. But then I realized they were merely suffering from the effects of poison gas.

I managed to elbow my way to the small reception desk. But the woman there merely shrugged when I inquired after Captain Craig, and continued shrugging hopelessly when I asked for a room.

An American correspondent looked at me curiously.

"Craig, did you say? Is that that good-looking Canadian in charge of about forty thieves on bicycles?"

"That could be him. Do you know where he is?"

"He crashed through here night before last on his way to the front."

I shoved my valises closer to the counter, away from all the boots. I didn't want anyone trampling on my bags, as they were filled with smoked hams, plum cake, cigarettes, and whisky.

The correspondent yelled across the lobby, "Hey, Stu! When did Ali Baba say he'd be back?"

He must have caught the reply, for he turned and said, "You might as well stay here, then. I'd let you bunk down in my room, but there's already four people in it, not counting me. If I were you I'd reserve some space in the cellar." He paused and looked closely at my Victorian Light Infantry badges. "You're a Canuck too? What're you doing in a British outfit?"

"I don't know," I said, certain now that I'd done the right thing in picking off my wings and ribbons. They would have been rather hard to explain.

"What's Craig like?" I asked.

"Looks like an assistant bank manager."

"Ah."

The correspondent gave me a malicious grin. "But you better start sorting through your steamy love letters, Lieutenant, before they send them home to your mother, along with the rest of your personal effects. Craig may look mild, but that's one ruthless hombre."

"Oh, dear."

"And he's in his element in this present foul-up. He can do just what he likes – and he's doing it."

"Who's that? Craig?" another correspondent asked.

"Yes. The lieutenant here's joining him."

"I wondered why he was looking so unhappy."

Nobody knew where Craig had cycled off to, so I cleared a space in the cellar and unrolled the sleeping bag I'd purchased in a hurry when I heard I was going to a mobile (?) unit. I spread it out on the straw and stood guard over the valises for the rest of the afternoon, until hunger finally drove me upstairs again.

Dinner was still being served, fortunately, though the few waiters who had not fled seemed to have their minds more on the distant gunfire than on the warm soup and almost equally warm veal.

When I came out of the dining room I saw the A.P. correspondent, Nathaniel Hilcheson ("Hell of a name to pronounce when you're drunk") sitting on the stairs talking to a dazed naval sublieutenant and two infantry officers. He waved me over, then continued to ask questions and listen sympathetically to the disjointed answers.

A bottle of Scotch was being passed around from mouth to mouth as the infantrymen described how the Germans had simply gone around their positions instead of attacking head on. The enemy had continued to infiltrate far to the rear, leaving pockets of resistance to their follow-up troops. "It worked damn well, too," a lieutenant said without bitterness. "Nobody likes being surrounded. Our unit held on – it was wonderful to be able to dish it out for a change, instead of being on the receiving end the way we've had to all these years – but a lot of people just ran."

"We ran, too," the captain said quietly.

"Only after the Jerries started shelling us from the rear," one of the young infantry officers said.

"What d'you think the situation is now?" Hilcheson asked.

"You tell us. All I know is we haven't had any direction from battalion, division, or army H.Q. for five days."

"They say the Germans have taken a quarter of a million prisoners."

"I wouldn't be surprised."

The naval officer, who was wearing a filthy bandage around his head, said haltingly, "I haven't had any orders either, since the twentieth. They used tanks against us. One of them ran over me."

Everybody looked him over carefully.

"Must have knocked me out. Don't really know what happened. When I came to, everyone else was dead, except for a few poor devils who . . . Anyway, I haven't seen a single member of my division since. Not one."

He stared at an oil painting that was hanging askew on the staircase wall. It was a pastoral idyll of peasant women working in a field. The sublieutenant got up and straightened the picture.

Captain Craig appeared at nine that night, introduced by the moan of a shell and a floor-heaving crash. He came walking sedately into the lobby followed by a flicker of flame and a vicious-looking sergeant who was carrying two machine guns.

Three uniformed correspondents and a heavy-hearted lieutenant converged on him.

"Did you get to the front?" Hilcheson asked.

"Front?" Craig turned to him with a smile. "There's no front."

He removed his tin hat and ran a hand through his damp, fair hair. The red line from the helmet stood out vividly against his pale forehead.

"Where did you go, then?"

"Oh, we just mucked about."

"How far are they now?"

"The Heathen Hun? Well, we narrowly avoided running into them the other side of Sailly-Laurette, didn't we, Sergeant?"

The sergeant grinned and dropped the machine-gun butts to the floor with a resounding thud.

A British correspondent, Rainsforth Semple, said tensely, "They're nearly at Sailly-Laurette?"

"A few hundred yards short."

"Good God Almighty."

The hotel lights flickered, brightened, then went out. The desk clerk lighted an oil lamp. The yellow flame half illuminated Craig's wry, handsome features. He didn't look the least dangerous to me.

"At this rate they'll be in Amiens in two days. We could easily lose the war," the correspondent said, with a tremor of excitement in his voice.

"Possibly. What's this?" Craig said as I passed over my papers. He held them closer to the oil lamp. "Ah. Reinforcements. That's splendid. How many men have you?"

"There's just me, Captain."

"Just you?"

"'Fraid so."

His sergeant looked me over disdainfully. "What the hell use are you?" he said. "We need a hundred men, not one lousy lieutenant."

The British correspondents looked shocked. They looked even more shocked when Craig used the sergeant's Christian name.

"Easy, Leo," he murmured.

"Well, what d'they think they're playing at?" the sergeant said. He was also a Canadian. I wondered if he, too, had been sent to this unit in disgrace.

Looking at those two, I wondered what I'd gotten myself into. I'd already heard a rumor that Craig had shot a major – an Allied major – for refusing to hand over several cases of new Lewis guns. Looking at him more closely I wasn't quite so ready, now, to dismiss the tales of his excesses. There was an assurance to his manner that suggested an irresistible force meeting an object that thought itself immovable. Nor did he seem so benign now, as he looked me over.

He murmured, "I suppose it's a waste of time wondering what it's all about. Still, I can always use another body."

He turned to leave, saying over his shoulder, "We'll be assembling in front of the hotel at 4 A.M., Mr. Bandy. Good night."

"Four? In the *morning?*"

He stopped and looked back inquiringly.

"But that's positively unnatural," I said. "I'm not used to rising before eight. Couldn't you make that, say, seven o'clock?"

Craig looked at his sergeant. His sergeant looked at me as if I'd suddenly started flouncing around in Pompadour heels and a stomacher embroidered in puke and popinjay. The correspondents began to edge away from me.

"Four A.M.," Craig said, and turned and went out, followed by his sergeant, who was now muttering ferociously into his whiskers.

At 4 A.M., after a scratch breakfast scrounged from one of the valises, I lurched semiconsciously out of the now deathly silent hotel.

I woke up pretty quickly, though, when, in the light of a lantern and a cold, bright moon, I saw the survivors of Craig's company. They were the most villainous-looking band I'd ever come across.

As Hilcheson had said, there were about forty of them, and every single one of them was unshaved, unpolished, and unhinged. They were festooned with flares, hand grenades, wire cutters, water bottles, Very pistols, machine guns, knives, and, in the case of the corporal, a German officer's sword, the blade covered with what I sincerely hoped was rust.

I turned to rush back into the cellar and burrow, whimpering, into the straw; but it was too late. They'd seen me. They hadn't exactly been chatty before. Now they fell utterly silent as they leaned on their bicycles – no penny-farthings among them, thank goodness – and stared with evil interest at my polished buttons and spotless British warm.

They looked as if they'd already been warned about me. Their silence was worse than the barrage that had kept me awake until two in the morning. They didn't even snigger.

The cynical silence went on and on, right up to the appearance of Captain Craig and his sergeant, the latter riding a sawed-off tandem bicycle that some mechanical genius had attached to a cart. Piled on the cart were trenching tools, haversacks, rations, and a positively frightening amount of ammunition.

Craig leaped off his bike and picked up a spare Lewis gun and strode up to me happily, saying, "Ah, you're coming, are you? Good."

But then he frowned, staring at my luggage. Beside the two valises I had a haversack, a small suitcase, and a sleeping bag. "What's this?" he said. "You can't take all this."

"It's valuable stuff."

"I dare say it is, but we have to travel light. A moment's thought would have told you that."

"Christ Almighty," the sergeant said.

I looked at him haughtily. "I don't approve of blasphemous language," I told him. One of the soldiers fell off his bicycle.

"You can put your haversack and bedroll in the cart, Bandy, and that's it. We've no room for anything else," Craig said. "Sorry. War is hell, I know."

Knowing from experience what the little luxuries meant at the front, I had ransacked Fortnum and Mason's and the best-stocked liquor store in the West End just before setting out. I had been intending to hand out the goodies forthwith, but now I decided that this was not the right time to offer them.

So I just said, "All right. I'll be back in two ticks."

The sergeant said something, and a rumble of laughter followed me into the hotel. I managed to wake Hilcheson and persuade him to look after the valises until I got back. If I didn't claim them within five days (the life span of the ham), he was to distribute the contents as he saw fit.

The forty thieves were already moving off when I came out again. They had left me a ladies' bike.

At least I think it was a bike. It was slouching against the wall of the hotel, a chipped, rusting, mud-spattered monster with two huge, pneumatic-tired wheels, handle bars that looked as if they'd been loaned by a battle-scarred buffalo, and a saddle that somebody had been gnawing at hungrily. The dreadful contraption was also suffering from curvature of the spine, and one of the pedals was missing.

However, there was no time for fastidiousness. The rest of the company had already disappeared into the silent but decidedly unholy night. Resting on the saddle was a Lewis gun with a strap clipped to it. I slung its not inconsiderable weight over my shoulder, climbed aboard, and pushed off manfully.

I had traveled sixty yards in the wrong direction before I had the thing more or less under control. Wobbling like mad, I turned on a reciprocal heading and pedaled after the rest of them furiously.

Just as I was catching up with the tail-end Charlie, the front wheel bumped into a section of the road from which somebody had borrowed several cobbles. As I went down, there was such a display of sparks that I half expected somebody to lean out of an upstairs window and holler angrily about the blackout.

I managed to catch up again about half a mile farther on. We headed due east along the Somme River, down which a wrinkled moon was floating.

For the first hour the *pavé* was deserted except for one alarming moment, when an armored car howled past at nearly twenty miles an hour. I didn't see it until it was almost on me. My bike went flying off the road. I was still trying to clutch at the non-existent brakes, fingers wiggling wildly in the moonlight, as it sailed into a field and fell neatly onto a cow pat.

So much for my new coat.

There was no fifty minutes travel and ten minutes rest with Captain Craig's lot. On and on we cycled into the ominous hush, squeaking and panting for mile after mile. It was no use trying to find out where we were going. Nobody would have let me past to reach Craig, even if I'd been capable of maneuvering up to him. So I continued to wobble along in the rear, trying not to think about anything other than the problem of correlating the erratic movements of the machine with the potholes that punctuated the road like Braille.

In a strange way, it was a relief to be at the front again, and not to have to do any thinking. The only thing I regretted was my winglessness. But I knew now, in spite of Katherine's stifled tears, that I had made the right decision, cutting the remaining stitches that attached them to my tunic. A pilot's badge would have made me even more conspicuous than I already seemed. Back in the hotel, one of the British correspondents, Mr. Rainsforth Semple, had been curious enough as it was, feeling sure he'd heard the name Bandy before.

Luckily he hadn't been reading his own newspaper recently, ever since he had had a fierce quarrel with his editor over expenses. The editor had, out of revenge, started mucking about with Mr. Semple's by-line, crediting his dispatches to the office boy or misspelling the correspondent's name as Rainsforth Simple, Rainsforth Dimple, Rainfall Pimple, or Rainwear Sample, or leaving it out altogether.

As for the wedding – but there was no point in worrying about that. Probably wasn't a very good idea getting married in wartime, anyway.

Just as I was starting to worry about it, I ran into the back of the rear half-dozen cyclists. The whole lot of us went down in a noisy heap of limbs and handle bars, and some very rude remarks were passed about the competence of a certain officer, who was alleged to be the sexually active offspring of a highly irregular union.

The head of Craig's wobbling column had halted at a bridge. Disentangling myself from a couple of broken spokes,

I wheeled forward to where the captain was talking to a cluster of tidy-looking American engineers.

"Welcome to the slaughter," Craig was saying to the Yanks as I limped up.

"Thanks. Are you going across, Captain?"

"Yes. Why?"

"We have orders to blow this bridge," the American lieutenant said. He had an intelligent, open face and a relaxed manner. He wore a British tin hat on the back of his head.

Craig looked at the bridge. "When?" he asked.

"Right now."

The other Yankees, about half a dozen of them, came closer, looking us over with friendly interest.

"Orders from whom?"

"One of your brass. A brigadier with two or three last names. We offered our services back in Amiens" – he pronounced it Ameans – "and he said to destroy this bridge here, just where the river turns north."

There was a flicker from the east, and several seconds later the thud of an explosion. The Americans looked up eagerly.

"My name's Bob Craig. What's yours?"

"Lin Halver."

"Lieutenant Bandy."

"Hello."

"If you blow this bridge, Lin, you'll cut off at least one field battery and what's left of a battalion of furious Scotsmen," Craig said, offering Halver a cigarette.

"Oh?"

"I was up here yesterday. The enemy is still about eight miles away."

The lieutenant tilted his helmet back still farther and looked at the bridge. "If that's true, they were goddamn stupid orders," he said.

"You'll get used to it."

"I better leave the charges in place, though, just in case. Where you headed, Captain? Captain?"

Craig was staring fixedly at the moon. He pointed to it abruptly. Everybody started to duck.

"'I observe,'" Craig intoned,

> "'Our sentimental friend the moon!
> Or possibly (fantastic, I confess)
> It may be Prester John's balloon
> Or an old battered lantern hung aloft
> To light poor travellers to their distress.'"

There was silence. Lieutenant Halver looked uncertainly in the direction of the moon, then back at Craig.

"I thought you'd know that poem," Craig said. "It's by a compatriot of yours, T. S. Eliot. My firm published it last year."

"Oh, I see," the lieutenant said, looking at the bridge as if wondering if he ought to blow it after all.

We went past Hamel as the moon (or battered lantern) faded. The sky was hinting heavily at dawn. Hamel was still burning after yesterday's bombardment.

It was impossible to thread our way through it, because of the rubble. Craig led the way across a couple of small farms. In one of them a small, pink piglet was running around anxiously. Someone had painted sergeants' stripes on its hide. This amused everybody except one member of our disheveled band.

We managed to get back onto the *pavé* a few hundred yards past Hamel. On the right side of the road, at the far end of a rough field, batteries of artillery were just discernible in the predawn grayness. A field kitchen flickered enticingly. Soldiers in khaki shirtsleeves and suspenders drifted about among the guns, and horses flapped their lips noisily.

Craig dropped back and jerked his thumb toward the camp. "There's a regular in charge of that mob, a real pukka sahib of the old school. He wouldn't let me use his field telephone."

"I thought all the regulars had been killed off."

"There's one left in the artillery."

We had traveled only a mile from Hamel when we were forced to leave the road again. It was blocked by an assortment of vehicles that had been caught in a bombardment whose accuracy suggested it had been directed from the air. Tenders, G.S. wagons, and other motorized vehicles, including a pair of white ambulances, were jammed along several hundred feet of roadway, smashed and overturned. Here and there in the wreckage, bodies sprawled.

As we wheeled past on the other side of the hedge that bordered the road, I caught a glimpse of a staff car that had apparently been blown off the road into the ditch on the far side, its radiator buried in the hedge. It didn't seem too badly damaged. I wondered why it had been abandoned so readily, until I wheeled back for a better look and saw the driver's head resting on the steering wheel. The rest of him was nowhere to be seen.

As we moved back onto the road again, the long-expected barrage started up. The sky flickered. Shells moaned in the distance and the ground vibrated faintly through the soles of our boots.

"Das ist der Donner und Blitzen," Corporal Warburton called out in a high-pitched, Teutonic sort of shriek.

The sun was just rising through the bands of smoke on the horizon when Craig led his forty thieves into a field not far short of Sailly Laurette. At the top end of the field was an extensive patch of woodland that was busy recovering from the bombardments of yesteryear.

Apparently the wood was our destination, for Craig called out, "String out just inside the wood, so we can cover the road." And to his sergeant: "Get the bikes out of sight on that cowpath."

The sergeant walked off, shouting.

"Looks like being a nice, sunny day," I said, over the noise of the distant barrage. My legs were trembling after pedaling that heap of scrap iron for at least fifteen solid miles. And I do mean solid.

Craig was gazing past the burning town. "The Scots are dug in about fifteen hundred yards in front of the town," he said. "I don't know if they'll be able to hold out. If not, we'll cover their retreat from here."

He showed me the position on a map, then nodded through the woods behind us. "The Somme winds past just behind the wood. I'll reconnoiter through there to make sure we can't be taken from that direction. I wonder, Bandy, if you'd mind letting the commander of the kilties know where we are."

I squinted toward the sun in the direction of the shellbursts, then nodded. "All right."

Taking the map, I went back to my bike. I was aching all over. My seat felt almost as tattered as the saddle it had been grinding against for three and a half hours. To make matters worse, I'd forgotten to fill my water bottle and I was dying of thirst.

I threw the water bottle and the rest of my gear, including my coat, into the wood and wheeled the bike back to the road.

As I reached it, a vast cloud of smoke and flame erupted from the south. The rumbling boom came half a minute later. An ammunition dump going up, probably destroyed on purpose.

The smoke billowed into the sky. As I watched, I caught sight of a pattern of tiny shapes glinting high above: a flight of Camels, or possibly Nieuports, going out on the dawn patrol.

I clambered dismally aboard the bike, winced, and got off again; and, with sudden decision, slung it into the ditch and set off in the wrong direction, away from the front.

A few minutes later I came to the wrecked convoy again. The flies were already busy in the warm, sunny air. I picked my way through the carnage to the staff car and looked it over.

For some reason it was called a Silver Ghost, though apart from the radiator shell and two whacking great headlights, it was black all over. Judging by the styling, it was several years old; but it seemed to have been well cared for – until a few hours ago, at any rate. The back was riddled with holes, the glass panel between the front and rear seats was shattered, and the left rear wheel was beyond repair.

The spare wheel, however, was unharmed.

The left front mudguard was also somewhat chewed up, but by some chance the thick pneumatic tire a couple of inches below it was untouched and still inflated.

I peered squeamishly into the bloodily occupied back seat, waving away the flies. I looked over the rest of the car. Plenty of fuel. The ignition was still on. There was a starting handle in a neat mahogany box on the left running board, but the nose of the car was jammed into the hedge, so it was impossible to insert the handle.

I removed my tunic and tried hauling the car backward, but it was far too big and heavy. While I was considering the situation, I dragged the bodies out of the rear cab and, muttering a prayer for forgiveness, tossed the driver's head into the ditch.

Then I thought of going around to the other side of the hedge; and sure enough, the radiator was just accessible. I stuck the starting handle into the hedge, and cranked. After only three tries the motor caught, and almost immediately settled down to a steady purring.

The hell with a ladies' bicycle. From now on I was riding in a Rolls-Royce.

It was nearly twelve before I got back to the field. By then the war had hotted up considerably. Enemy shells were chunnering overhead by the dozen and bursting in the rear. The smoke from the still burning ammunition dump drifted over the sky, turning the sun into a Jaffa orange. In the distance, low-flying planes were darting back and forth. A shaky line of walking wounded were making their way back along the road toward Hamel.

I came bouncing up the field in the staff car and jerked to a halt in a clearing inside the wood. Craig and several cyclists emerged from cover and gathered around. I opened the little black door and stepped out, smirking.

Craig walked slowly around the splendid if somewhat battered vehicle. He put his foot on the running board and bounced the car a couple of times, then peered into the impressive leather-and-walnut cab behind the front seats. I'd stopped at a stream on the way back to wash off most of the blood, and the interior was now quite presentable.

"Not bad at all," he murmured. "But where's the monocle? You can't turn up in a car like this without a monocle."

"I could wear a sneer, if that would do," I said.

Craig looked at me, and his brow lightened as if he had just arrived home after a long sojourn in the wilderness. "I trust you didn't kill the occupants, to obtain this magnificent vehicle?" he murmured.

"There were no protests," I said. "Incidentally, it travels surprisingly well over rough ground."

"So I saw." He grinned at his men. Then, briskly: "Did you get to the battalion commander?"

"Yes, sir. He has his post in an old pillbox. He was being shelled when I got there, so I didn't hang around too long."

"Very understandable. How are things up there?"

"Not too good. They've repulsed two attacks, but the adjutant doesn't think they can hold out much longer. They've managed to stop any infiltration; that's about all."

"He'll be withdrawing fairly soon, then?"

"Depends on how things go. But he only has a couple of hundred men left. Unwounded, that is. He's sending some of the wounded back now, as you can see."

There was a pause in the barrage. Then the pitch changed and shells began to fall along the road in front of us, sending up gouts of flame and yellowish-gray smoke. The walking wounded moved resignedly out of sight to crouch in the ditches.

As the shells were mostly missing the road, it meant they were beginning to fall perilously close to us. Craig waved everybody deeper into the woods.

"Better get your car out of the way, in case the Heinies get jealous," he said. "There's a cowpath back there. Warburton will show you where."

"Right. By the way," I said, "you can expect tanks fairly soon."

Craig looked up sharply. "Tanks? Enemy tanks?"

I nodded.

"How many?"

"Two, at least. The adj. pointed them out to me when I was up there."

I'd been able to see them quite clearly, maneuvering in open country about two miles farther east. "That was about a couple of hours ago," I said.

Craig chewed his lower lip. The men nearby glanced at each other, then away, pretending to look unconcerned.

"We can't do anything about tanks. I didn't even know the Germans had any."

"The Scots haven't anything to stop them with, either."

Craig nudged at a fallen tree with his boot. "Christ," he muttered. "We may have to let them through."

"We got grenades, Captain," the sergeant said.

"No good against tanks, I'm afraid," Craig said, walking up and down, head lowered. There was a flicker of flame deeper in the wood and a metallic bang like a big firecracker going off in a cookie tin. Shrapnel hissed. I moved hurriedly against a tree.

Craig continued to pace up and down without looking up. "There isn't a damn thing we can do about it," he said.

A few minutes later I went up to him again and said, "I was thinking about it on the way back. The ordnance we passed – what kind of guns do they have?"

"What? 18-pounders. Q.F.'s." He slowed down slightly. "Why?"

"If we had one of those up here . . ."

"That regular wouldn't lend us a lucifer to light our fag, let alone one of his precious guns," Craig said. But he had stopped pacing. He stared down at a ring of mushrooms that were pushing timidly out of the dank earth.

He nudged one of them with his toe. He straightened.

"Let's go," he said. To the sergeant: "Leo, you're in charge. You know what to do."

"Sure."

"Don't let the tanks know you're here if we're not back in time."

"Right," the sergeant said, watching me jealously as I hurried back to the car.

We drove down to the road, circumnavigating several new shell craters, turned right onto the road, and accelerated along it. A flight of aircraft droned overhead, but disappeared into the smoke before I could make out what kind they were.

"Have you been out here before, Bandy?" Craig asked as we purred heartlessly past some wounded.

"Yes."

"I thought you were a staff wallah."

"Heavens, what gave you that idea?"

"You have that impervious look."

"Ta ever so."

"What's your first name – Bart, is it? Who were you with, Bart?"

"Fifth Canadian Division, originally. As a matter of fact I'm practically back where I started with them, in 1916."

Craig glanced at my stiff profile. "Have you ever commanded a company or anything like that?" he asked.

"No."

After a moment, Craig murmured, "By the way, you mustn't mind my sergeant. He seems to think I'll do something silly, like falling into a duckpond, if he's not there to mother me."

"He does seem kind of protective."

"He needs someone to look up to, and I'm the only one in the company that's taller than him."

"I gather you were a publisher in civilian life," I said, glad to change the subject.

"Yes. I was O/C poetry," Craig said; and began to talk enthusiastically about modern poets, especially the war poets. He was reciting quite exuberantly by the time we came to the wrecked convoy.

A group of soldiers, plastered with field dressings, were staggering along the ditch. "How about a wee ride, sir?" one of them called out. He wasn't nearly so polite when I nudged past and turned into the field alongside the road.

We bounced along the field, skirting the wrecked vehicles, and got back onto the road a few hundred feet farther on. But it was crowded with retreating tommies. Many of them didn't even turn round when I honked the horn. They continued to hog the road, weaving about with exhaustion.

"Tanks!" I hollered, pointing back, hoping to panic them out of the way. "Tanks!"

"You're welcome, laddie," one of them said.

Ten minutes later, we'd covered only a few hundred yards and steam was wisping from the radiator of the car. There was no way past the soldiers, and the ditch at this point was too deep to cross.

Help, however, came in the form of three German Pfaltz scouts. They came howling down out of the smoke and opened up without warning. Explosive bullets flashed in the dirt. The Rolls shook violently as one of them burst on the roof, blowing a large hole in the right rear corner. The car filled with fumes.

The way ahead cleared like magic. I drove as fast as possible for a line of trees ahead, expecting the scouts to start chivvying us again at any moment. But they were either overwhelmed by their own audacity or were satisfied with the effects of one pass, for they flew east again and the roar of their engines faded.

"Pfaltz," I said.

"Same to you with knobs on."

"The planes. That's what they're called."

"You seem well up on aircraft recognition."

"M'yes," I said. "I guess I have a knack for it."

A couple of thousand yards from Hamel we turned off the road into the field where we'd seen the artillery.

They were no longer there.

The car puttered to a stop at the entrance to the field, steaming and hissing.

"Darn," I said.

Craig stared into the field, then stood up on the front seat, holding onto the huge windscreen. He looked around.

"There they are. Down the road."

I was busy plucking my sweaty breeches away from a pair of hot buttocks.

"Well, come on, man! What're you waiting for?"

I backed onto the road again. We caught up with the artillery as they were approaching the bend in the road where it led down into Hamel. The Rolls bounced wildly along the ditch, which was shallow here, and in that manner we managed to draw ahead of the column. We stopped near the entrance to the farm where the non-commissioned pig had been trotting around.

Leading the column was an impeccably attired major astride a white horse. He reigned in sharply. The horse-drawn field gun behind him almost went up his backside.

"What's the meaning of this?" he called out sharply. Then he saw Craig and glowered. "Oh. It's you again."

"Good afternoon, Major."

"I want no more trouble from you, Captain, d'you hear?"

"You're badly needed farther up, Major," Craig said. He climbed out and approached the major. The well-groomed white horse looked at him almost as suspiciously as its master.

"I dare say. Be so good as to get that car out of the way."

"Major, there's a couple of enemy tanks in this sector. We've nothing to stop them with."

"I can't help that. I've been ordered to pull back."

"If you could see your way to letting us have three of your guns, sir?"

"What? Don't be ridiculous."

"Two guns?"

"You heard me. Get on with it, Captain."

"One gun?" Craig asked. "A handful of shells? A mug of tea?"

The major's face turned a fiery red. "I won't tell you again, Captain!"

"But there's a couple of *tanks*, sir."

"What's your name?" the major asked quietly and ominously.

"T. S. Eliot."

"I'll give you one minute to get that car out of the way, Eliot. Then I'm telling my sergeant-major to move it for you. And I don't care how he does it."

His sergeant-major swaggered up, spread his legs apart, hooked his thumbs in his belt, and waited impassively. He looked capable of lifting the car off the road singlehanded.

The way Craig looked at the major, I was glad he'd left his Lewis gun in the car.

Craig gestured abruptly. I reversed the car into the farmyard. Slowly and laboriously, the long column started up again. The sergeant major grinned as he strode on, alongside the lead gun.

The 18-pounders with their attached limbers continued to creak past, each drawn by three pairs of horses. Toward the rear of the column there were a couple of tarpaulin-covered trucks with massive iron wheels and solid rubber tires. The rear one was filled with artillerymen. They were hunched over an ammo box.

"Playing cards," Craig said.

The last gun and limber had only one attendant, a small, bony-faced private who was nodding, half asleep, on the back of one of the horses.

Craig stepped into the road and put up his hand like a London bobby and, with the other, waved him into the farmyard.

The artilleryman reined in, his mouth dropping open, revealing an assortment of blackened stalactites.

"Hurry up, there," Craig said as loudly as he dared. "We haven't got all day." As the man continued to gape: "Come on, my lad, jump to it! Look lively now, 'less you want to get left behind!"

The lad jiggled the reins and, in a bewildered way, maneuvered his equipment off the road into the yard. The rest of the column groaned onward, tinglingly slow.

"Wharrisit?" the lad asked anxiously.

"Wharrisit, *sir!*" Craig bellowed. "And get down when you're talking to a hofficer!"

He scrambled down so fast his puttees caught in the harness and he fell on his face. As he scrambled up again, Craig looked him up and down and, no doubt drawing on memories of half the sergeant-majors in the Army, bellowed, "Yew horrible little man, yew – straighten up thar! Shoulders back, head up, chest in, stomach out, yew horrible little man, what are yew?!"

He then turned to me and saluted very smartly indeed. He even managed to clump his heels together.

"Is this the man, Major?" he called out.

Perched high up in the staff car, I gazed back at him blankly for a moment, then looked at the gaping artilleryman and said, "I'm not entirely sure, but . . . better shoot him anyway." I drew on a look of unutterable boredom. "Just to make sure, what?"

The artilleryman gulped, his eyes stretched wide open. "I 'aven't done nothing, sir, honest! Only–"

Craig brought his face close and said softly, "Yes? Only *what?*"

"It wasn't me, sir! I only done what the others done! They was running around loose, sir!"

"I'm sorry, lad," Craig said, taking out his Smith and Wesson a trifle regretfully. "You know what the regulations are."

"I won't do it again, sir, honest! It was only three chickens, sir! I only had a leg!"

"It was only three chickens, sir," Craig said to me. "He only had a leg."

"Three chaickens, three hendred thousand chaickens, it's precaisely the same," I said. "Shoot him."

"But, Colonel, I get a bit squeamish at the sight of people's blood pouring out of their poor, ravaged bodies in bucketfuls."

"Well, do it with your eyes shut, for heaven's sake," I said.

"But I might miss, and merely blow off his left tit, General."

"Get on with it, man," I said testily, "or I'll be late for my champers and caviar."

The poor wretch of an artilleryman sagged and actually wrung his hands. Craig led him aside and whispered behind his hand in such a theatrical manner I feared he was overdoing it, "We'll just go into the barn over there and I'll pretend to shoot you, lad. With any luck, the Field Marshal won't insist on seeing your poor, bloodstained corpse."

The artilleryman practically ran into the barn. Craig followed him inside. There was a pause, then a muffled shot. Craig reappeared, and as he secured the barn door with a length of splintered timber, whispered hoarsely through a crack to the effect that the artilleryman had better keep pretty quiet for at least half an hour. If the Commander-in-Chief out there in the staff car realized the artilleryman was still alive he would be very annoyed indeed, as he was a stickler for discipline and was known to be particularly hard on chicken stealers, even ones who'd only had one leg.

"We're going to have a job getting this gun back by ourselves," I said, giving the ammunition carrier a kick – but not too hard a kick.

"We'll manage," Craig said cheerfully. "You follow behind in the car. I'll ride on the limber and hold onto the draft hooks from the whiffletree to the front of the outer futchels."

"No need to be disgusting."

"Come on, help me point the damn thing in the right direction," Craig said grinning, "before that sod finds out one of his precious fieldpieces is missing."

We maneuvered the gun and limber onto the road again, not without some reluctance on the part of the horses – a tired, skinny bunch that didn't seem too happy about being pointed in the direction from which all the noise was coming. Craig climbed onto the box and, after confiding that he'd never handled horses in his life, shook the reins violently and gave an earsplitting yell.

The horses pressed forward against their harness and, urged on by Craig, broke reluctantly into a gallop. I watched for a moment, then hurried back to the car, cranked like mad, jumped in, and sped after him.

By the time I'd caught up he was a fair distance down the road and traveling at a pretty good lick for a novice. I was glad I wasn't riding with him, though, the way the equipment was rocking and swaying all over the road. Any moment I expected to see him overturn it into the ditch.

However, all went well for the next two or three thousand yards. When he met the retreating soldiers again, he made no effort to slow down but stormed straight through them. I held my breath, expecting to see several of them crushed to death by the sliding wheels or sideswiped by the gun barrel; but he missed them – mostly by inches. They scattered, hobbling frantically into the ditches, looking as if this was the last straw and as soon as they got back to safety they would be volunteering for a job that was a little more secure – like in a leaky submarine.

I smiled at them in a helpless, placatory sort of way as I luxuriated past; but they just looked all the more hateful, as if they thought I was sneering. I suppose they thought that was the best they could expect from the occupant of a staff car. I expect some of them would have spat at me if they'd had the saliva or the energy.

A few minutes later, as the gun and limber were coming up to a line of trees by the side of the road, I saw Craig hauling at the reins as if trying to strangle the horses. He was certainly wrenching at them with what seemed like unnecessary force.

I caught a glimpse of the front pair of horses. They were rearing and plunging frantically. The four-wheeled mass of metal behind them slewed dangerously over the road, first to one side, then the other.

The whole shebang finally rocked to a stop with the offside wheels near the edge of a two-foot drop into the ditch.

I climbed out and hurried forward to find out what on earth he was playing at, and found the front pair of horses thrashing about in a hole in the road, and the next pair, blowing and yellow-eyed, teetering at its ragged edge.

It seemed that a shell had landed in the road since we had passed that way half an hour before. Craig hadn't quite managed to stop before the lead horses skidded into it.

I made an effort to calm the horses before they dragged the gun into the hole with them.

"Never mind the horses; look for the bloody brake!" Craig shouted just as he found it himself, on the gun carriage. He seized the handle and revolved it, then kicked it tight with his foot. The horses continued to tremble and snort, obviously not in the least glad to be under new management.

"I suppose you know you nearly killed those soldiers back there," I said.

"I couldn't find the brake," Craig snapped. "Have you ever tried to stop two tons of metal at twenty miles an hour with just a pair of reins?"

"Let me think. . . . No, can't say I have."

"Well, then."

Craig stood and surveyed the situation irritably. It wasn't too promising. There was no way around the crump hole. It was possible to get into the field on one side, but a few yards farther on the undergrowth started. It was too dense to get through, so a detour was impossible.

We studied the hole. Craig snatched out a cigarette and lighted it with sharp, angry motions.

"Think we can drive through it?" he said at length, dragging a mouthful of smoke all the way down to his socks.

"Course not."

"We'll have to. We can't go round."

"Those horses will never pull the gun out once it's in."

Craig sucked again on his cigarette, staring viciously into the hole. "All right. We'll just have to fill it in, that's all."

"We'll have to what?"

"We either drive across it or fill it in. Unless you feel like lifting it across."

"What do we use for spades?"

"Shovels are part of the equipment, as you'd see if you'd open your eyes."

I looked and saw he was right. There was a GS shovel on each side of the carriage limber box.

But first we had to back the horses out of the crump hole, and that wasn't as easy as it sounded. The gun and limber kept jackknifing the moment they were put into reverse. The fact that one of the wheels was only inches from a deep part of the ditch on one side didn't help.

We struggled for several minutes with the horses. They were skinny, scabby, and ungroomed – obviously not too well cared for by the artillery people.

Just as we got them onto firm ground, the right wheel of the gun carriage started to slide into the ditch. If it had gone over, we might never have righted the carriage. There was only one way to avoid this, and that was to pull the horses forward again. So they ended up back in the hole.

"Looks as if we're doomed to spend the rest of the war in this bloody crater," Craig panted. Surprisingly enough, he had recovered his temper; his sense of humor seemed to improve the worse the situation became.

At last we got the horses back onto the road. "Scout around and see if you can find any debris to throw in," Craig said, and without waiting to recover his breath, seized a shovel and started to work like a maniac, digging out great clods of mangled grass and lumps of road and hurling them into the shell hole.

I stood for a moment watching some enemy aircraft in the distance. There seemed to be a whole *Staffel* of them. Pfaltz. They were diving and zooming at the ground about three miles to the east – shooting up some unfortunate troops, I guessed. There was no sign of any Allied aircraft. I grew quite tense, waiting for somebody to sneak up on them out of the sun and start picking them off, one by one . . .

"Come on, man," Craig wheezed. "Get a bloody move on or we'll be too late for all the fun."

Wrenching my eyes off the Pfaltz, I scuffled around, searching for material to fill the hole with. But there was little available, apart from a few rocks and dead branches. The undergrowth nearby was unsuitable for cutting.

After chucking in what I could, I grabbed the other shovel and joined Craig just as he was gasping out a song currently being sung at the front:

"Down in the sewer
Shoveling up manuwer,
Everybody's spade goes flippety-flippety flop.
Oh, it gives me great delight

To be shoveling up the shite –"

I joined in on the last line:

"I'm the leader of the gang, gorblimey!"

We grinned at each other, panting companionably.

After ten minutes we were both dank with sweat, streaked with dirt, and beginning to totter against each other. Then a platoon of Scottish warriors came straggling up, and Craig managed to persuade the few unwounded among them to lend a hand.

A sudden onslaught of 88 mm shells didn't exactly increase their enthusiasm for the task.

"Are you no the officer who passed us a while back and refused to gie us a lift?" a sergeant asked, ducking as a shell moaned overhead and whumped into the field behind us.

"Now, really," I panted, "do I look like the kind of fellow who'd do a thing like that?"

"That looks like your car doon the road, there."

"Couldn't've been me, Sarge. Only just arrived from Amiens, you know."

The sergeant continued to look at me suspiciously from time to time as I hurled lumps of muck into the shell hole.

Twenty minutes later, Craig decided that the hole was now shallow enough to risk driving the gun across. Reclamping the shovels and taking out a couple of the gun's drag ropes, I stumbled back to the car, attached the ropes to the frame under the front bumper, and lashed the other ends to the axles of the limber.

With Craig steadying the horses, I put the car into reverse, and slowly, but without too much difficulty, dragged the equipment backward. When we were about three hundred feet from the hole, Craig shouted and ran back to unhitch the ropes. He clambered onto the box, bending over as a shell landed perilously close. Shrapnel whizzed overhead. Our helpers departed in a hurry.

The shellburst had set fire to a patch of dry grass by the side of the road. As the smoke thickened, the horses began to rattle about fearfully in their harness.

"Well, here goes," Craig called out, and taking up the switch he had cut, he struck at the horses. They began to strain forward. Slowly the gun began to move. Craig lashed and shouted. The horses gathered speed, but they were only up to about ten m.p.h. by the time they reached the rough, shallow hole. Wild-eyed, mouths agape, they dipped down in pairs and floundered across. Then they were scrambling back onto the harder surface beyond.

As the four wheels behind them hit the soft earth and sank in, the horses reared back, jarring against each other, and began to swing wildly toward the ditch. The gun wheels hit the far side of the hole and bounced heavily. The horses were dragged to a complete stop. One of them fell to its knees, whinnying in fright. The wheels jammed against the edge and rose a few inches, not quite making it. I ran forward and hauled on the fallen horse, yelling. It thrashed back onto its feet just as the gun wheels started to slip back. I shouted again, hitting at every haunch in sight. The horses heaved, their necks distended. Inch by inch the wheels rose over the ridge of the shell hole. As they ground onto firmer ground, the carriage shot forward.

Craig reined in, twenty feet farther on, and the horses came to a stop, panting and trembling uncontrollably.

Then, by sheer bad luck, just as we were preparing to start off again an 88 struck the side of the road only a few yards ahead of the gun and knocked down three of the horses. In a second they had formed a screaming, bloody heap. Craig was blown backward off the limber. He went sprawling on his back in the road and lay still.

I ran to him, nerves fraying and parting at the sound of the horses as they continued to scream and thrash about in their harness. Another shell burst ahead with a deafening bang. Splintered branches rained onto the road. The smoke coiled away lazily.

To my relief, Craig was already stirring when I reached him. He pushed my hands aside and staggered to his feet, holding his head. He stared at the turmoil of horseflesh in front of him.

At least three of the horses were done for. I took out my revolver, walked close, and aiming carefully, finished them off; then, after a moment's hesitation, put a bullet into the fourth. It was bleeding from the neck.

I came back. Craig was leaning against one of the gun wheels.

"You all right?"

"Yes, I'm all right . . ."

He stumbled as the wheel moved. The surviving horses were plunging about in terror, hoofs skidding in the gore.

"You sure?"

"Yes, I'm sure! Let's get on! The tanks are probably there by now!"

I set about unhitching the two horses and backing them away from the mess. I was soon red with blood to the elbows. A handful of soldiers went past. They barely glanced at us.

We continued on with the two horses, both of us silent now. And once again we came to the wrecked convoy.

By then, the surviving horses could hardly move the equipment along the road, they were so spent with fright and fatigue. Craig halted them near the entrance to the field into which we had detoured earlier that morning. There was a fairly steep bank to negotiate. It was obvious the horses would never make it.

Nevertheless we tried to drive them up, shouting and whacking at the poor, trembling beasts; but it was useless. They were floundering and skidding even before they had taken the strain of the gun. One of them fell. It lay there, its sides heaving, its eyes desperate and imploring.

"They're finished, Bob. They couldn't drag up a box of iron rations."

Craig sat on the ground, his chest heaving painfully. He stared at the slope.

"I'll drive ahead and fetch some of the men," I suggested.

"There isn't time. What about pulling it up with the car?"

"I thought of that, but I don't know if the wheels will grip."

He looked at me and grinned painfully. "You and your bright ideas," he said. "If we had a gun up here, you said."

After a moment, he pushed himself up slowly, as if bearing half the Laurentian Shield on his back.

"Let's try, anyway," he said.

We unhitched the horses and set them loose into the field, then lashed the limber to the back of the car by the drag ropes, and with a good deal of difficulty maneuvered the gun and limber until they were at the best possible angle to the slope. I put the motor into low gear and drove onto the slope, and as soon as the ropes tautened, pressed gently on the accelerator and let up the clutch fully.

The rear wheels started to skid the moment they took the full weight of the gun and limber. In a minute they had gouged six-inch-deep tracks in the soft earth, but had not progressed up the slope by as much as a millimeter.

"All right," Craig said at last. "Let's try the pieces separately – as we should have done in the first place." He looked at his watch, his face white with strain. "Hell and damnation! We've been away nearly three hours."

As he said this, there was an outburst of firing from up ahead. The ground trembled. We looked toward the front, but strangely enough there was nothing to be seen below the smoky sky.

We separated the gun and limber easily enough. But the moment the car began to haul on the axles of the limber, the trail rose in the air, threatening to upend the contraption.

"You'll have to put your weight on it, hold it down!" I shouted from the car.

"Yes, yes! Keep going!"

He clung onto the trail as I started up again. The limber weighed nearly a ton, and he had quite a job holding it. If the car had slipped back, he would almost certainly have been crushed by the wheels.

I bet he was sorry he'd never learned to drive, so he could have had a cushy job like mine.

It occurred to us only after we'd dragged the limber to the top of the slope that it would have been much easier to have lashed the trail to the car instead of the axles. I suppose it was because we already had the axles roped. We'd been too lazy to go to the trouble of untying them and reversing the limber, I suppose.

Anyway, we managed to get it up the slope, then turned to the gun. It was a good deal heavier than the ammunition carrier, though, and the car wheels were soon doing their gouging act again.

We got the gun very nearly to the top of the slope. But then one of its wheels slid into a trough of sticky earth and jammed. The car wheels whined in the grass and the gun began to slip back. As the momentum increased, the car began to slide back as well.

Then, bewilderingly, there was a sudden rush of bodies, and Corporal Warburton and a party of men who had been sent by the sergeant to find out what was holding us up, ran up and flung themselves on the gun. With the car spraying them with muck and mire, they heaved against the wheels, and the gun slowly creaked to the top of the slope. Half an hour later we rolled back to the wood with the gun and limber bouncing about behind the Rolls, out of which nearly a dozen men were hanging, yelling and waving.

As it turned out, we had all of twenty minutes to spare before the tanks arrived.

Looting and Pillaging

By then, the last survivors of the Scottish battalion were moving back. Some of them were staggering over the torn ground only fifty feet from the wood, but hardly any of them seemed aware of our presence; or perhaps they just didn't care. They were so tired that whenever they fell they could hardly rise again.

Abandoned haversacks, tools, and even rifles soon littered the churned-up field in front of our positions.

By and by, one man, who seemed to have slightly more purpose to his movements, came up and stopped close to the wood and looked around, swaying drunkenly. Craig went over to him.

"It's all over," the second lieutenant said. "Tanks. They came behind them with bayonets."

"How many tanks?"

"Two."

"Did you stop them?"

"Don't be silly."

"How long have we got before they arrive?"

"A few minutes, if you're lucky . . . if that's the word." He looked up at the sky through bloodshot eyes. "Bloody Flying Corps. Buggering about all day; then, when we really needed them, they were home having their afternoon tea."

The lieutenant – he looked about seventeen – fumbled with his water bottle and drank from it shakily. A stray shell moaned overhead and burst in the wood with a hollow bark.

"The C.O. says it's up to you, now," he said. He hesitated, then turned unsteadily and walked off, carefully buttoning his holster though there was no pistol in it.

The sergeant, meanwhile, had hauled the gun into position just inside the wood, in a shallow clearing, with the barrel pointed in the general direction of the road. Craig pushed through the crowd of machine gunners that had gathered around to admire his trophy. Half an hour before, Craig had seemed on the point of collapse. Now, apart from a general pallor and dark patches under his eyes, he was once again his old, bustling self.

"Well, chaps," he said, leaning an elbow on the nearest shoulder, "does anyone happen to know how to operate one of these implements?"

He looked around inquiringly. Heads were shaken; voices muttered negatively.

"Nobody at all? Has anyone ever watched one of them being fired, then?"

The soldier he was leaning on, Private Thomas, who was looking sheepishly proud to be supporting his company commander's elbow, said in a Welsh singsong, "I watched once, Captain, but there were so many men mucking about with it, I couldn't make out what they were doing."

"How many men?"

"About ten, I think."

"Ten? Just to fire one gun?"

"They all seemed terr-ibly bus-sy, though," he said. He pointed to the two seats behind the gun shield. "Two of them were sitting in those little seats, if that's any help."

"Well, it's a start," Craig said cheerfully. "At least we know what the seats are for." Then: "I suppose basically all we have to do is find out how to load and fire it. That shouldn't be too difficult."

He studied all the little wheels and levers and pouches and things, and his face turned gloomy. I reached over and pulled tentatively at a lever. The breech screw and carrier swung out.

"There you are!" Craig cried, looking relieved. "Lieutenant Bandy has found out how to operate it already!"

"I suspect there's a few details to learn before we can fire it," I said doubtfully. "The shells will have to be fused for one thing, I should think."

"Fused? You mean we have to light a fuse? Ordnance has advanced a little beyond that stage, surely?"

I went over to the rear of the limber. It had been unhitched from the gun and pushed farther into the trees. I let down the sides of the ammunition box.

Twenty-four rounds were exposed in compartments, stacked in fours. I pulled one of them out by its canvas loop and nestled it in my arms like a baby, and studied it. A dozen others also gathered around to study it.

It was about two feet long, lacquered in ominous black and indented in the middle, where the cartridge joined the projectile. At the cartridge end was a brass clip with four arms, one of them painted red. At the pointed end was a cap with a tin band.

I indicated it. "This'll be the fuse, under the cap," I said. "You know – the mechanism that detonates the shell when it strikes. It'll obviously have to be set; they wouldn't carry live ammunition around, I shouldn't think."

I looked around. Nobody contradicted, so I reached for the tin band and tore it free. The cap fell off. Several of the men backed away hurriedly.

"Yes, there's the fuse scale," I said. I squinted at it. "It's set at safety – I guess. We'll have to find out how to activate it."

I studied it. There was a calibrated ring at the base. I tried to move it but it was too stiff.

"There must be some sort of key to fuse it," I said. "A ring with a handle, or something like that. Somebody see if they can find it."

Nobody moved. They all continued to stare at me with almost as much uncertainty as I was regarding the shell. Craig peered at me thoughtfully for a moment, then said briskly, "All right. We'll have three volunteers to start with: me, Warburton, Thomas. The rest of you take up your positions again along the edge of the wood. We don't have much time. Sergeant?"

The sergeant glowered at me, then started shouting angrily, driving the men away into the trees. I started to follow.

"Not you," Craig said impatiently. "You're one of the volunteers. Thomas, see if you can find the key Mr. Bandy described. Corporal Warburton . . ."

But he couldn't think of anything for Warburton to do. He glanced back at me. "I suppose we'll also have to find out how to sight the thing? I'm not very mechanically inclined, I'm afraid."

I laid the fused and primed shell carefully under the limber, where nobody was likely to trample on it, and then removed my tunic. My khaki shirt was soaked in blood and the sleeves were beginning to stiffen and crackle in a rather sickening way, so I tore them both off at the shoulder and threw them away. Thomas and Warburton watched somewhat blankly.

Bare-armed, I went back to the gun. After a moment I pointed to a telescope arrangement to the left of the open breech. "That'll be it, sir. There's the clinometer underneath."

"What's that?"

"It'll be to measure the inclination, like a spirit level. But I don't think we'll bother with that."

"What the hell did you mention it for, then?"

"Well, we may need it . . ." I said vaguely, trying to work out what all the various little wheels and handles were for. "If the gun isn't on an even keel, as it were."

But I really didn't have a clue as to what might happen if the gun wasn't on an even keel, as it were; and Craig didn't seem to be interested anyway. He had climbed into the left-hand seat of the gun and was peering through the telescope.

"Can't see a thing," he muttered.

"It might help," I whispered in his ear, "if you removed the lens cap."

Craig removed the lens cap, looking huffy. He peered again through the sighting telescope. "All I can see is bloody sky now," he muttered.

"Try that hand wheel in front of you."

He did so. "Hey," he exclaimed, "it raises and lowers the gun barrel! Say, it's all very simple, really, isn't it?"

But a moment later he drew back from the eyepiece, looking discontented again. "Except that it's all blurred," he said. "You have a look."

He got down. I took his place and looked through the sighting telescope and fiddled with it ineffectually.

"H'm. . . . It must be some kind of fixed focus," I said, trying to sound as if I knew what I was talking about.

I noticed the sighting point at the end of what I now know is called the rocking bar. I closed an eye and looked along it.

By pure chance the points at each end of the bar were perfectly aligned with the road to our left. I turned the elevating
wheel and raised the barrel slightly until the sights were on the
open field beyond.

"I have found the key!" Thomas called out eagerly. "It was
in this little pouch here!"

"Let's try the open sights," I said to Craig. "I don't suppose
everything's properly adjusted, but it would probably take a
week to do it by the book."

I looked around and located the trigger on the left of the
breech mechanism, and pointed it out. "There's a hole in it.
That's probably for a lanyard," I went on. "We'd better use
that so we can keep well clear of the gun when it fires, just in
case we put the shell in backwards or something."

"It'd be just my luck," Warburton said gloomily, "to get me
balls blown off at the first shot."

"Here's the key, *bach*," Thomas said, handing over a ring on
a short handle.

"Fine. Now see if you can find the lanyard – a rope with a
handle at one end and a hook or something at the other."

I climbed down. "The next problem," I said, starting to roll
up my sleeves with a commanding and purposeful air before I
remembered I didn't have any sleeves, "is what setting to fix
the fuse at."

"Here's something called an 'Indicator, Fuse'," Craig said,
pulling up a round plate from a case attached to the gun.

We studied it, heads together. The edge of its outer disk was
graduated in number from 2 to 22, and the inner one in figures
up to 6200.

"What's the range to that field on the other side of the road,
would you say?"

"Seven hundred feet?"

The outer wheel was graduated down to 600. But that was probably yards. I turned the scale back as far as it would go. Then looked at the number on the inner reader of the pointer. Except that there was no number, just a teeny arrow. The next figure up was 2. The arrow, therefore, probably stood for 0.

"Far as I can make out," I said, "the fuse should be set at zero."

"If it's set at zero, mightn't the shell explode immediately after you set it?" Craig asked.

"I sincerely hope not."

Craig bit his lip. So did several other soldiers who had started to collect around the gun again. "Are you sure," he asked, "that you know what you're doing?"

"No."

"In that case, *you* set the fuse while the rest of us retreat into the depths of the wood," Craig said.

However, he remained only a couple of feet away while I removed the clip from the percussion primer and wiggled the key down over the nose of the shell, onto the ring. I fitted it cautiously into a notch. I took a deep breath, and turned the ring to 0.

"Can you hear it fizzing?" Warburton called out from a safe distance.

After a moment Craig said, "All right. Let's try it."

I carried the shell over to the gun and pushed it gently into the breech, then seized the lever and swung the breech screw into position and locked it with a quarter turn of the breech-mechanism lever.

By then Thomas had found the firing lanyard; with commendable initiative he had already hooked it into the loop on the trigger.

I turned the safety catch down, gaining confidence with every action.

"Ready," I called out in a lordly sort of way.

"Just one small detail," Craig said, examining his fingernails.

"What's that?"

"It might help," he whispered in my ear, "if you removed the plug from the gun barrel."

I looked at him, then got down and walked around to the front of the gun and saw he was right. The barrel was still bunged up.

I hauled the plug out, trying not to notice Craig's nasty, grinning face.

A soldier came running up, his face red with excitement. "Sir, Sar'nt says he can hear the tanks coming!"

Craig stiffened, whirled, and stared out of the trees toward the road. There was nothing in sight.

"Where?"

"Over to the left, sir! He said he could hear them plain as anything! Over there, in front of that village – middle distance!"

"All right. Thank you," Craig said.

The soldier turned and hurried off through the trees. Craig turned back.

"Quick! Let's see if it works," he said. "Warburton! Get two or three more rounds from the ammunition thing!"

"I don't have to fuse them, do I, sir?"

"No, I'll do that," Craig said. He turned back to me. "Well, what're you waiting for? Test it! Fire it!"

"Too late," I said, and pointed.

The German tanks were just trundling into view from the far left, dipping slightly as they crossed a series of shallow crump holes. As we watched, one of them rose ponderously onto its hind legs and tore down several yards of smoldering hedge.

The tanks were squat and boxlike in appearance, with a shallow turret on top. From the front of each projected a gun of a decidedly lethal-looking caliber.

"Our gun's bigger than their gun, though," Warburton whispered.

As we watched, one of the tanks loosed off a burst of machine-gun fire; at no particular target, as far as we could make out.

Craig snatched a shell from Warburton and wrenched off the clip from the primer. I settled down on the left-hand seat and looked along the sights, then raised my head over the shield, trying to figure out where the first tank would cross the line of fire. I wished we'd had time to find out how to traverse the gun.

Otherwise our luck seemed to be improving. The tanks were traveling parallel to the road on the far side. They were headed straight toward where the 18-pounder was pointing.

I looked back at the tanks, surprised by how calm I was feeling, even though I knew we wouldn't stand much of a chance once I'd fired and given away our position.

Some distance behind the second tank came a line of German infantry. They didn't seem to be taking their victorious advance too seriously, judging by their easy pace. Perhaps the tanks had made them overconfident.

I looked along the open sights again, then back over the shield. The leading tank was starting to veer off now, farther away from the road, to avoid a particularly deep shell hole. I looked back along the sights and reached over to give the wheel in front of me another eighth of a turn, wishing I could traverse so as to take a pot shot at the tank right away instead of having to estimate the point at which it would cross the fore sight. But there was no time now to find out how to use the traversing gear.

All the same, the gun would have to be turned somehow. As soon as I fired, the tanks would certainly turn toward us to attack, and it wasn't very likely that they'd oblige us by traveling straight along the axis of the gun.

I remembered there was a handle at the end of the gun trail, above the sharp blade that was supposed to be dug into the earth to steady the gun against its recoil. Without taking my eye from the sight, I called out, "Thomas! Do you see that handle behind me, for lifting the gun?"

"Yess . . ."

"Be ready to lift it so as to turn the gun left or right as I call out."

"To point the gun, iss it?"

"You've got it. But keep clear until then."

I raised my head to glance quickly over the shield. The first tank was only twenty yards from the line of fire now, grumbling along at a miserably slow pace.

But the pest had altered direction again. He was closer to the road now, almost hidden by the hedge. I snatched at the elevating wheel and turned it until the sights were lined up once again in its path, and felt for the trigger.

I realized I would have to stay in the seat in order to fire at the right moment. I wasn't too happy about that. I had no idea how much the gun would jump when it fired. If it fired. I had intended standing well to one side and pulling the lanyard with my eyes shut, in case the gun blew up or fell over or something.

The brake! We hadn't set it. But Craig couldn't reach it now. I was in the way. The gun would probably roll back for miles when I fired. If I fired. The last thing Craig and his forty thieves saw would be the sight of me hurtling backward through the wood astride a smoking gun, yelling farewell as I thundered backward through the wood and into the Somme, to sink to the bottom, bubbling, with a 1¼-ton gun on top of me.

The tank was now only a few feet away. The desultory barrage had stopped some time ago. I could hear the tanks quite clearly, grumbling and straining.

Seeming to move inch by inch, the huge tank in the lead slowly appeared behind the point at the end of the rocking bar. I uttered a silent prayer, and fumbling aside the lanyard, seized the trigger and yanked at it.

The 18-pounder went off with a deafening bang, and the hydraulic buffer jumped. Smoke billowed around. My ears sang.

I couldn't see a thing for smoke. I fumbled around for the breech-mechanism lever and pulled at it. The screw swung open. The extractor clipped to the rim of the empty cartridge and hauled it out, and flung it down disdainfully.

I was looking around for another shell when I became aware of the cheering. I peered curiously over the shield again.

The first tank had stopped, and men were tottering out of it and scrambling for the cover of the nearest shell hole.

There was a messy-looking dent clearly discernible in the rear end of the tank body, with a neat hole in the middle of it.

It had not occurred to me for a second that I would actually hit the tank.

The most I'd hoped for was to give the occupants a bit of a scare when the shell landed nearby, and maybe, if I was lucky, confuse them long enough for me to pump one more shell at them before they were upon us.

I hadn't even been sure that the sights were parallel to the gun barrel. For all I knew, I could have been firing sideways, practically.

I felt a series of blows on the back. Craig was pounding me and leaping about in excitement.

"You hit it, you've bloody well hit it!" he was shouting, jumping and cavorting around, apparently unaware that he was cradling a fused shell under his arm.

"You devil!" he yelled. "You're a bloody artilleryman in disguise! You knew how to use this thing all along!"

"For God's sake, stick that shell in before you drop it on its nose," I said. "And stop shouting; I'm deaf enough as it is."

"Look, look! The other one's turning back! It's turning back!"

I peered over the shield, and was equally astonished to see the second tank turning away in the direction of Sailly-Laurette.

"Quick! Stuff the shell in!"

Pulling himself together, Craig scrambled over the trail and fumbled the shell into the breech and pushed it home with the flat of his hand. I slammed in the screw and locked it, then twisted around in the seat, expecting to see Thomas waiting behind the gun as arranged.

"Thomas–" He wasn't there. "Thomas! Where the hell is he?!"

He was prancing about with several other cyclists at the edge of the wood, watching the second tank as it slowly lumbered into the distance.

There was no sign of the enemy infantrymen who had been following behind it.

"Thomas! Oh, damn. Bob! Grab that handle! Swing that gun!"

"Lift that barge, tote that bale," Craig sang, somewhat inaccurately, as he ran to the rear of the gun. "Get a little drunk and you land in jay-ul!"

He seized the handle. "Which way, O Master?" he called out.

"In the direction of the other tank, where else?! Hurry! About two feet to your right!"

I looked along the sights, and banged my bloody nose on the breech lever as Craig heaved on the handle and swung the gun.

"Too far, too far! About half that!"

"Thomas! Give me a hand with this bloody thing!"

Thomas and one or two others ran up and joined Craig in heaving me about.

"Six inches to your right again! Another inch! That's it!"

They drove the spade into the ground. The result was I found myself sighting on a cloud about twenty miles away. I snatched for the elevating wheel, but the barrel refused to budge. It was already at the limit of its depression.

"You've stuck it in too far!" I shrilled.

"I beg your pardon?" I heard Warburton say, in maidenly disapproval.

"You have the tail too low! Put a rock under it or something! Hurry, hurry!"

The second tank would be out of sight in half a minute. I looked back. Craig and another man were hauling a fallen tree over to the gun. But they had to go around the limber. By the time they'd perched the blade on top of the log, the tank had passed the line of sight.

"Swing it another few inches to your right!"

They heaved the trail around another few inches and pushed the log under it again. The tank was just crossing the sights. I wasted a precious second hunting for the trigger.

There was another bang, and the gun jumped back and stopped with a jerk as the spade rolled off the log and bit into the ground. I was flung backward. I landed in a heap between the carriage wheels, banging my kneecap painfully in the process.

"Missed!" Craig shouted. "You've bloody well missed! I knew all along you were an imposter!"

I limped back onto the seat again and swung open the breech, coughing as the cordite swirled around. Craig came up with another shell, but it was too late. The tank had disappeared.

"Really, Bandy," Craig said sternly as I turned up the safety catch, scowling. "If you can't do better than *that* . . . well!"

"No," Craig said a few minutes later as we lolled in the wood waiting for the infantry assault that was bound to follow. "No, but it was a splendid effort. Damned good shooting."

I twitched my head slightly and smirked. Craig glanced over at the men nearest to him and winked.

"Even if the target was the size of a barn and only a couple of hundred yards away."

The men laughed and stirred in the undergrowth. They were lying along the edge of the wood and just inside it, every one of them with a brand-new Lewis gun at his elbow, and several drums of ammunition.

We were at the center of the line a few yards from the gun. We had decided to preserve it exclusively as an anti-tank weapon, as the range was too small to permit its use against infantry.

Craig lit a cigarette hurriedly. He was still keyed up and jittery with excitement. "And did you see the hordes of men that poured out afterwards? What on earth were they doing in there, holding a convention?"

"I only counted seventeen," the sergeant growled.

"Ah, you're just jealous, that's all, because I wouldn't let you fire it," Craig said, taking out a flask and holding it up. "Have a drink, you miserable supernumerary."

The sergeant drank morosely, hesitated, then passed the flask to me.

I hesitated, too. Then – what the heck? The rest of my New Year resolutions were all shot anyway.

"Are you sure you never fired a field gun before?" Craig asked.

"No, but I always was a crack shot," I said, spluttering as the spirits burned down my gullet.

"In that case, you should've hit the second tank, shouldn't you? Mind you, you only missed by a few feet, I'll grant you that. All the shrapnel rattling on that tin can must have thoroughly upset them, the way they turned tail so smartly. Anyway, we've stopped them; that's the main thing."

"Do you think it'll be back, Captain?" somebody asked.

Craig shrugged, hissing in lungfuls of smoke, and was about to say something when he became aware of the eerie silence that had fallen.

One or two of the cyclists stirred and raised their heads uneasily and looked toward the road. But there was no sign of activity.

After a moment, the sergeant picked up my Lewis gun and looked it over. He cleared his throat.

"You, uh, you want me to show you how to use this?" he asked, not looking at me. "You're gonna need it in a few minutes."

As he was obviously making an effort to be friendly, I asked him if he'd be good enough to show me. The sergeant brightened.

"Well, to begin with," he said, "we've took off the jackets and disconnected the self-inducing cooling devices. That's this part here. They don't really work, see, and just add extra weight, like. Right. Now, this is the magazine, see . . ."

I listened and nodded intelligently. I saw Craig looking at me fixedly. As he caught my eye he winked, guessing, I think, that I already knew something about the Lewis gun.

In fact, back in 1916 I had spent a lot of time practicing with the Lewis gun and had become quite proficient in its use. When I completed my training in the R.F.C. – how I came to transfer from the infantry to the Flying Corps is a story that Craig would probably have found highly instructive[*] – I had hoped to fly S.E.5s, as part of their armament was a free-moving

---

[*] See *Three Cheers for Me: The Bandy Papers, Vol. I.*

Lewis gun on a Foster mounting; though I had taken up Lewis gunnery not out of any particular desire to excel, but to get away from a friend of mine named Rupert Randle (I wonder what ever became of him?), who made me uneasy because he was always following me around and had a habit of placing his face only an inch from mine whenever he addressed me.

Anyway, it was to get away from Rupert that I had taken up Lewis-gun practice. Rupert had hated machine guns.

As the sergeant completed his demonstration, Craig blew a smoke ring and poked his finger through it.

"How did you come to get transferred out of your division, Bart?" he began.

I was saved from replying by a crackle of rifle fire. Craig stuck the cigarette in the corner of his mouth and picked up his Lewis gun, and peered out of the wood to see what the neighbors were up to.

A long, straggling line of gray-clad figures was just appearing from behind the hedge that bordered the road.

Craig shouted no heroic orders. In fact, nobody said anything, except for a quick swear word from the sergeant. Everybody seemed to know what to do. There was a hasty, nervous reaching for machine guns and an insertion of hips and shoulders into the shallow graves the men had scraped for themselves in the undergrowth at the edge of the wood; and then they lay still and watched, tense and bright-eyed, as the gray figures broke into a stumbling run across the field, yelling ferociously to scare us. They were wasting their time as far as I was concerned. I was already scared. My heart was thumping like a bilge pump on a sinking side-dragger.

It was the sight of all those sharp bayonets glinting in the smoky sun.

There was a rapid chatter of Hotchkiss machine guns. Bullets zipped and whiplashed overhead. My finger tightened on the trigger. But nobody had yet fired a shot, though some of the enemy were now only a hundred feet away.

Craig put the whistle between his lips, forgetting he was also gripping a cigarette. It fell inside his tunic in a shower of sparks. He beat his breast as if in the extremities of remorse. Simultaneously he blew the whistle.

Forty Lewis guns opened up at point-blank range.

Even by 1918, such concentrated fire power was unusual. When Craig signaled the cease fire, hardly more than a minute later, there were very few gray-clad figures left standing.

The surviving tank made no effort to support the attack. In fact, we never saw it again.

As soon as Craig had seen to his few casualties, he walked off into the wood. I started to follow, but the sergeant grabbed my arm.

"Leave him alone."

"What?"

"He has to be alone, after."

The sergeant, who was obviously much more sensitively aware than I'd suspected, lighted a cigarette. On an after-thought, he offered one to me.

I shook my head as I gazed reverently into the depths of the wood, quite misty-eyed at the thought of Craig with his spirit filled with poetry and aesthetic sensibility, his gracious, cultivated soul revolted at the slaughter of his fellow beings.

"He has to be alone, I suppose, to expiate this blasphemy against life," I murmured. "To wash away in poetic anguish the violation of his profoundest beliefs and ideals," I said, with a catch in my voice.

"Eh?" the sergeant said. "Hell, no. It's his bowels. He's as shit-scared as the rest of us."

There was a further assault before nightfall. This time they took us seriously and sent in about half a regiment, with flame throwers, grenades, trench mortars, and machine guns. We had eleven casualties, including four dead, and they cut our line in two at one point. But the closest they came was ten feet.

At dawn next day, the woods received a full-scale barrage, and the gun limber that nobody had thought of unloading blew up with a roar. This dug quite a crater in the once-moist earth, and would have killed quite a few of us if we'd still been there.

But, during the night, Craig had evacuated the wounded and placed them in and around the staff car, which, along with the bicycles, had been hidden several hundred yards westward, near a cowpath. He concealed the rest of his men along the bank of the Somme on the far side of the wood. Nobody got any sleep that night, and two of the cyclists were soaked when they slipped down into the river, but there were no further casualties in spite of a ferocious bombardment.

In a few hours the wood was devastated from end to end and left a blackened, stumpy ruin. As soon as the barrage lifted, we ran back through the embers and were in time to meet the next attack with bursts of Lewis-gun fire.

They kept on attacking until the paint and grease on the new guns was smoking and some of the attackers were heaped three deep along the black rim of the woods. Only one man got among us, a huge fellow, his face twisted with rage and anguish. He had bayoneted three men before Craig came charging up and emptied his revolver at him.

As soon as the fighting died down and the mass groaning arose from the field – a sound to sicken the blackest heart – Craig, white-faced and unapproachable again, signaled, and we withdrew westward, crouching, taking what cover was left, until we got to the car. The wounded were stuffed inside and on the roof, and exactly twenty-four hours after we had arrived, we pulled out again, with twelve men unscathed and seventeen wounded, two of whom died before we reached the casualty-clearing station at Hamel.

Back in Amiens the following night, Craig commandeered a fine house, not far from the Hôtel du Rhin, from which the owner had fled, and with the contents of my valise plus a little looting, threw a party that rivaled the worst excesses of a squadron mess for wild behavior and drunken debauchery. Attracted by the din, Hilcheson and a few others came over from the hotel bearing gifts of purest Scotch, and joined in. At midnight, Craig and his sergeant staggered out to the Rolls and came back fifty minutes later with nearly a dozen baggages, whose spirits were as elevated as their characters were debased. One of them, already inadequately underclothed, was dancing on a table with her skirts round her waist when the Assistant Provost Marshal I'd met three days before arrived with a posse of military police and French gendarmes and drove us out at the point of the bayonet (he arrested Corporal Warburton when he mistook one of the policemen for a strumpet and tried to carry him upstairs).

"Get out of town and don't come back," the A.P.M. said. Whereupon Craig went into an absurd crouch out there in the street on the greasy cobbles, his hand hovering over his holster, saying, "Smell when you say that, pardner." I suppose he meant to say 'smile,' but we were never to know, as he fell over a Whippet tank just then, and couldn't remember a thing when we left town at dawn the same day.

That was March 30. By then the German Army had fought to within a mile of Villers-Bretonneux. Fifth Army Headquarters, of course, had long since scattered into the hinterland and had still not resumed its former occupation of preparing inventories and handing out D.S.O.'s to its staff and suicide notes to its field commanders. So we continued to roam the countryside entirely without direction of any kind. As we also had no authority to order supplies, we were forced to improvise. We spent one rainy afternoon shooting off padlocks and helping ourselves from a row of stores huts near Cachy, I remember. With jerry cans of petrol rattling about on the roof of the staff car and the back seat loaded with blankets, bully beef, and seed cake, we fled in the direction of Moreuil, pursued by a staff sergeant who had the impertinence to fling several Mills bombs after us. His screams of rage as he stood there in the middle of his looted bailiwick, weeping loudly and pulling pins, were terrible to hear. So we all put our hands over our ears.

It went on like this for day after day in the chaos created by the great offensive. We weren't the only ones who were looting, of course. Requested by a bloodshot captain to find out why the enemy hadn't appeared to finish off his company on schedule, we probed forward into the smoke of battle – to find about half of Von der Marwitz's army staggering around a captured warehouse clutching armfuls of bottles. They were all laughing, quarreling, and falling out of windows, and more Heinies were hurrying up every minute to join in the festivities.

Craig watched them sympathetically for a few minutes. Then we quietly stole away.

Soon there were so few of us left that we could all be accommodated in the Silver Ghost. The last of the bicycles had long since been ditched, given away to refugees, or, in the case of the sergeant's Hercules, sold to a stray Chinese laborer for thirty francs.

"Hey, why don't we sell the staff car as well?" the sergeant said. "It would keep us in booze for nearly a week."

"Not on your nelly," I said. "I'm keeping it."

"You'll never get away with it," Leo said. "Sooner or later somebody's bound to ask what a lousy lieutenant is doing with a field marshal's car. Come on, let's sell it to the Chinese and give a dinner dance. There's this fantastic brothel in Amiens–"

"Nothing doing," I said. "I feel at home in a Rolls-Royce."

This was the day we finally received a coherent order: to join up with another company of the 13th Cyclist Battalion near Contigny.

Accordingly we headed south. But the roads were now so choked with Fourth Army reinforcements it was nearly dark by the time we got to Contigny. This may have been the reason we took the wrong turning out of town. Or possibly it was because of the large stone flagons of rum that Leo had lifted from an officer's mess the day before, of which I am ashamed to say I had my fair share.

At any rate, only twenty minutes later we found ourselves behind enemy lines.

Nobody could ever make out exactly how it happened. One moment we were thumping across open, scrubby country and wondering where everybody had vanished to, and the next we were passing a line of gray foot soldiers and traveling, along a dirt road between lines of trees, behind several very unfamiliar-looking vehicles.

I turned on the massive headlights of the staff car for a second, lighting up the rear of the truck ahead. Gothic lettering flashed into view, and the squinting face of a soldier in a decidedly Teutonic helmet.

He shouted at us. I switched off hurriedly. Before we could drop back and flee, another pair of trucks closed up behind, trapping us in the enemy convoy.

We waited rigidly for the inevitable alarums and excursions. But the convoy continued to lurch and rattle into the murk quite peaceably, and the German soldiers stumbling along both sides of the road continued to ignore us.

We had no option but to keep on going. There was no room to turn. Even though they were plainly exhausted, the soldiers alongside could hardly fail to remark our uniforms if we tried to pull out now.

"Now see what you've got us into," Craig said accusingly.

"Whatjamean?" I said.

"Shhh!"

"Whatjamean?" I whispered. "You're the one who said turn left at the pile of manure."

"Yes, but you turned right."

"Oh, yes, you're very good at making excuses."

"What the hell are we going to do?"

"I don't know. You're the boss."

"You got us into this; you get us out."

"I'm only the driver," I said, stubbornly hiccuping.

"You're only a silly bugger."

"Look," the sergeant said. "Will you two quit rowing and do something? We'll all be captured and have to spend the rest of the war in idle captivity if you don't do something. We'll end up in a P.O.W. camp with nothing to do except eat and drink and sleep and . . ." He stopped, looking a bit thoughtful.

"Now, now," Craig said. "Let's not have any disloyal thoughts."

"I haven't had no other kind since I joined the Army," Leo muttered.

I shifted up to second gear, then back down to bottom gear again. "Well," I mumbled, "how was I to know?"

The convoy continued to trundle onward through the darkness. A soldier called out to us plaintively. We thought it advisable not to answer.

"And you're a rotten driver, too," Craig said, to rile me. He knew perfectly well I was an excellent driver.

I sniffed, but otherwise maintained a dignified silence. The rum flagon gurgled from the back seat.

"Which direction are we going in?" Craig asked suddenly. "Does anyone have a compass?"

"I have," Private Crickwood said.

"What does it say?"

"I don't know. It's broke. Anyway," he went on, "how could it say anythink? Compasses can't talk. Who ever heard of a compass what was capable of saying anythink? That's ridiculous. Besides," he added, "it's broke."

"If the poor thing is broke then lend it some money," Private Bassett said. "Don't be so mean."

"Let's have another drink," Craig suggested. "It'll help us to think."

The flagon was passed around again. There was a thoughtful pause.

"We're going west," Private Bassett said suddenly.

"Don't be so pessimistic, Bassett," I said. "We'll manage somehow," I added bravely.

"No, I mean we're heading west. We must be, 'cause the sun sets in the west."

"There ain't no sun," Crickwood said.

"Yes, there is. I saw it only an hour ago."

"I saw it too," I said. "There was definitely a sun earlier on. I distinctly remember."

"That's all right, then," Craig said. "So long as we're going west it means we're heading in the right direction, because our side is in the west. That means that sooner or later we'll be on our side."

"We're already on our side," Bassett said sulkily. "If we weren't on our side we'd be on the enemy's."

"How can we be on the enemy's?" Crickwood said loudly.

"Shhh!" Craig said. "They'll hear us talking English if we . . . talk English."

"But he said he was the enemy, Captain," Crickwood complained. "I mean, what kind of a thing is that to say to your friends."

"All I said was we're already on our side," Bassett muttered.

"I'm not on my side," I said. "I'm sitting up." They all peered at me, as if doubting this. "I have to be," I went on. "Otherwise, how could I drive the car if I was on my side? That would be well-nigh impossible. I mean, I'd have to operate the clutch and brakes and so forth with my hands if I was on my side. I'd have to lie flat on the front seat and reach down and steer with my–"

"Oh, shut up," Warburton said.

"The point is," Craig said, "how are we going to extricate ourselves from this situation?"

"What situation?" Private Harris asked, waking up.

"Being in the middle of an enemy convoy, of course."

Private Harris stuck his head out the hole at the back of the car. His eyes widened. "Jeez," he said. "We're in the middle of an enemy convoy. How did that happen?"

"We've already been through all that," Craig said. "There's no point in rehashing it again, or indulging in recriminations," he went on in tones of noble forbearance. "So we won't mention Mr. Bandy's sheer, blind incompetence in getting us all into this fix."

We continued to bob up and down in the car like pistons, the flagon clicking continuously against various sets of teeth, until we came to a fork in the road. The vehicles ahead turned to the left. With lightning decision I kept on going.

I was just congratulating myself out loud at my quick thinking when somebody pointed out that the two vehicles behind were still following us.

Before we could stop him, Harris had stuck his head out the hole at the back and started shouting irritably at the trucks behind us. "You're supposed to go *that* way, you fools!" he hollered, pointing vigorously toward the other road. "No, not this way, that way! You should've turned off– Oh, the fools! They don't understand!"

"Maybe they can't hear you," the sergeant said heavily. "Maybe you should get out and tell them, and maybe show them the way."

Harris started to climb out. The sergeant seized him by the scruff of the neck and hauled him in again, glaring.

"It's all right, men," I said. "Leave it to me," I said, preparing for another lightning decision. We were approaching an opening in the hedge on the left.

It was the entrance to a field. As we drew abreast of it I hauled on the steering wheel, turning so sharply that the trucks behind had no chance to follow, even if they'd felt inclined, which apparently they didn't, for they kept on going. The sound of their motors slowly faded.

Craig and the others, however, weren't as appreciative of my efforts as they should have been. The sudden turn had flung them all into a flailing heap. They were even less appreciative as it became evident that there was no way out of the field.

The Rolls puttered moodily to a halt on the far side of the field. Everybody looked at me silently for a moment, then:

"Oh, for God's sake, Bandy," Craig said, and started to laugh.

I turned to him, opening my mouth to remonstrate haughtily, and stalled the car. As it convulsed and expired, his laughter increased. He began to thrash about as if taking part in a Punch and Judy show, clutching at the handle of the little front door of the car. It opened. He fell out.

The sergeant looked quite concerned for a moment. Then he, too, began to snuffle, growl, snigger, frown, and finally to guffaw; and the rest of them began to break down as well, and soon the car was rocking about wildly on its springs, with hoots, wheezes, shrieks, and gasps pouring out of every hole and tear and broken window. The sight of Craig lying in the grass kicking and groaning and holding his stomach sent the rest of us even deeper into convulsions. Soon we were flinging ourselves wildly around the interior, laughing uncontrollably, tears rolling down our cheeks, like madmen in agony, the sound of our hysterical laughter rising from the field in jangling waves, violating the still night air; until finally we could no longer even moan, but lay sprawled in and about the car gasping for air, looking for all the world as if we'd suffered a direct hit from Jove's howitzer.

By the time we got back to our own lines – about two miles in the opposite direction to the one in which we'd been traveling so optimistically – the cyclist company we were supposed to join up with had moved on again, and neither the town major at Contigny nor anyone else knew where they'd gone.

None of our party seemed too concerned about this. The gypsy life seemed to suit everybody, even though we could never be sure where we were going to sleep or where the next meal was coming from, or what we would be called upon to do next.

There were ominous signs, though, that order was gradually being restored at the front as the remnants of the Fifth Army, its commanding general dismissed, came under the control of a General Pétain. Nevertheless we stayed around Contigny for a few more days, helping what was left of a Lancashire division to fight off several heavy attacks on the town and later escorting German prisoners to a cage alongside the River Noye.

There were about ninety of the prisoners, a strange mixture of half-starved sixteen-year-olds and sunken-faced, gray-haired men. One of the latter told Craig that he had been on the

Russian front only seven weeks before. He didn't seem too unhappy about being taken prisoner.

By April 5, the line seemed to have stabilized itself about ten miles in front of Amiens. It was becoming clearer now that though the enemy had recaptured a prodigious amount of territory and had destroyed an entire Allied army, they had not achieved too much strategically. In fact, they may have done us a good turn, as there were persistent rumors that as a result of the German offensive, Field Marshal Haig was to come under the over-all command of the much-respected General Foch. From what I'd heard at the Ministry, Foch was one of the French generals who had finally come to his senses and abandoned the ruinous Spirit of the Offensive.

"Maybe the French will get somewhere," I said to Craig on our way back to Contigny from the prisoner-of-war camp. "The French have learned not to throw away men uselessly, you know. I admire the French. They're steady, loyal, sympathetic, and civilized," I said, just as we passed a column of French infantry and received an uproar of moans, hisses, sardonic applause, and catcalls, and some very rude French gestures, all of which seemed to suggest that the British weren't too popular with the Poilus just at the moment.

That evening, as we were ruining our teeth on some field rations beside the road, a French officer carrying a neat whip came striding up with a dozen men. He demanded to know who we were and what unit we were with. He had seen us pottering about the countryside for the past two or three days, he said, and he wanted to know why.

He was the coldest and most ruthless-looking fellow I'd ever seen in my life, with eyes like a couple of flints. He refused even to glance at our identity cards. He had seen us hobnobbing with the Boche only that morning, he said. He believed we were spies, and he was strongly inclined to shoot us at the first available dawn. What did we have to say about that?

It was only by the exercise of considerable charm and beautifully pronounced French that Craig persuaded him that we were on the side of Truth, Beauty, Logic, and *La Vie Parisienne.*

All the same, Craig looked very thoughtful when the officer finally marched off again, gripping his whip as if to prevent it from slashing at us of its own accord.

"I have the feeling," Craig murmured, fingering the grimy field dressing that covered a shrapnel wound on his neck, "that it's time to give up this happy, carefree life of ours and settle down like responsible citizens once more in the bosom of our battalion."

The rest of us were ahead of him. We were already packing.

It was amazing how quickly we were now able to locate the other cyclist company. They were camped alongside a railway track in the southern outskirts of Amiens, with their head-quarters located in a small signalman's hut.

As the staff car approached the camp, the company commander was hurriedly fetched. He and his second i/c were waiting for us at attention outside the hut as we rolled up. His right hand started toward his cap. It never got there.

"Craig? What the . . .?"

We climbed out stiffly, looking like London dustmen. The car radiator hissed placidly.

"Hello, Bartlett," Craig said, stretching. "Where on earth have you been?"

Captain Bartlett goggled. "Where have *I* been?" he asked.

"Well, if *you* don't know, Bartlett, I'm sure *I* don't," Craig said, lighting a cigarette.

Bartlett, a large, portly gentleman, looked on in an affronted manner as Warburton, who had broken his arm avoiding a

German bayonet, wiggled a cigarette casually at Craig. Craig lit it for him with the end of his own cigarette.

"Where's your company?" Bartlett asked.

"H'm?" Craig looked surprised. "Here they are."

"What're you talking about? There's only seven of you. And who's this?"

"Ah, that's Lieutenant Bandy. He's our reinforcement."

"How d'you do?" I said.

Bartlett looked at his second i/c, then: "Just what's going on, Craig?" he asked loudly. "I asked where the rest of your company was. And where are your bicycles?"

"We got saddle-sore, Bartlett, so we swopped them for this vehicle," Craig said, sitting on the running board of the car and scraping lumps of mud off his boots.

"You'd better get up and see the colonel," Bartlett said shortly. "He was furious when you failed to turn up at Contigny. Said he'd had quite enough of your independent ways."

"We were all supposed to be in Merville by tomorrow night," his second in command said.

"Oh, Christ, don't say we're on the Flanders front again," Leo said.

Bartlett looked him up and down. Admittedly Leo was in pretty poor shape: unshaven, filthy, wearing a greatcoat that looked as if it had been used by a burial party. He looked almost as bad as the rest of us.

"You'd better get into town and see the colonel right away," Bartlett said, and turned on his heel and went back into the hut. He'd probably have slammed the door if it had not been hanging by only one hinge.

Headquarters was established temporarily in a partially bombed house near the town hall. I went along with Craig and waited in the kitchen, where I hurriedly stuffed myself with bully-beef sandwiches and slices of jelly roll and mugs of steaming chicory.

After two hours I not only had indigestion but a conviction that Craig was being torn limb from limb in the colonel's office; and I was busy trying to guess what abject excuses Craig might be making to explain his long absence from the rest of the battalion so I could use the same excuses, when Craig came out grinning – with the colonel's arm around his shoulders.

The colonel had astonishingly long white hair, which nestled comfortably on his ears.

"Don't worry about the artillery fellows, my boy," he was saying. "We'll just tell 'em you've been severely reprimanded or flogged or something like that, what?"

He even gave me a pat on the back after Craig had introduced us. "Don't know who on earth you are, my boy," he said, "but welcome to the Battalion anyway. We must have a little talk sometime when you've, ah, when you've had a good bath, what? Ha, ha, ha, ha."

"Apparently the C.O. of that Scottish battalion put in a glowing report about us," Craig said as we stood at the bar of the Hôtel du Rhin a half hour later. "So the colonel had a rough idea what we were up to."

"In that case it's a wonder he hasn't already court-martialed and shot you, Craig."

"You mean because we borrowed all their food and petrol from the château? That's all been taken care of," Craig said airily, over the racket. The bar was crowded with administrative officers, including about half a dozen town majors who no longer had any towns to major. They kept looking at us. I suppose we did look pretty disreputable.

"I mean all the looting you've done," I said. "Not to mention the officer you shot, the rum you stole, the vehicle you pinched, the lies you told, the enemy you hobnobbed with, the government property you purloined, the transport you destroyed, the–"

"Oh, don't be such a nitpicker, Bandy. And it's your round."

"You're a brigand," I said, ordering another two gins.

"As for your accusation of looting, I was merely using up stores the Germans would have captured otherwise," Craig said. "Incidentally, I didn't see you exactly hanging back."

"If I'd hung back I'd have been blown to bits by all the Mills bombs that were being flung at you for looting."

"By the way," Craig said, swishing the inferior gin around his glass, "I've persuaded the colonel to give you a company of your own. He says he'll fix it as soon as your records turn up."

"He's remarkably accommodating. What is he, a relative?"

"Not bad. He's one of our authors. Military History, terribly obscure battles a specialty. I've promised to raise his royalties 5 per cent if he's nice to me."

"How much extra will that bring him?"

"About one pound seventeen and six," Craig said.

We both sniggered into our drinks.

"Matter of fact I'm quite happy as I am," I said. "I'm enjoying having no responsibilities other than to see you don't give wrong directions, especially past heaps of steaming dung."

"I gave the right direction," Craig said loudly. "You're the one who went the wrong way past the heap of steaming dung."

"Oh, sure, hindsight is easy," I said. "It's easy to be wise after the steaming dung."

"Excuse me," an elderly officer said, leaning over, "but are you two with one of those concert parties?" We gazed at him blankly. "You know, like the Fol de Rols or The Dumbbells?"

There was a thump as a bomb burst nearby. The array of liquor bottles behind the bar rattled and clinked, both of them. A hush fell on the boozing throng.

"Bloody Gothas again," somebody muttered, and hastily swallowed his drink and started out. Several others followed.

"I guess we'd better be getting back," I said.

"What? Leave the bar just when we've got room to move?"

So we stayed. This was a mistake, because a few minutes later a guffawing party of R.F.C. officers came tumbling into the bar. Or, no: it was the R.A.F. now. April Fool's Day had come and gone.

"Bandy!"

Oh, good God.

I turned, trying to disguise my face. A swaying captain stood at the bar gaping at me. It was Wordsworth. Absolutely unmistakable with that totally bald, shining pate above those youthful, haggard features.

"Well, I'll be damned! What're you doing here?"

"Drinking again, I'm afraid. Hello, Wordy."

Wordsworth, who had been the steadiest man in my old squadron, clung tightly to the bar counter staring at my coat, which was in an abominable state by now, stained with mud, blood, and ruin, and badly torn in places. Fortunately it concealed the part of my tunic where the wings should have been.

I hastily buttoned it up. It didn't take long. There was only one button.

"This is wonderful! But I thought you were at Gosport. Who are you with now?"

"I'm with Craig's lot," I said offhandedly, as if Wordsworth was bound to know all about Craig's lot.

There was a brief breathing spell while Wordsworth pulled himself upright and introduced the other members of his party: two flight commanders and a cynical-looking lieutenant.

"Well, this calls for a celebration. Do you know who this is?" Wordsworth cried.

"Bandy. You've just told us," the lieutenant said.

"No, I mean – this is *Bandy!*"

Everybody looked blankly at Wordsworth, including me.

"We'll have to close the bar, sir," the barman said.

Nobody paid any attention. Wordsworth was beginning to look annoyed. "Well, good God," he shouted, "everybody knows Bandy!"

"Yes, yes, Wordy," I said, humoring him. "But don't you think we ought to get out of here before we get struck all of a heap?"

With excellent timing another bomb burst nearby. The blackout curtain at the window sucked itself outward. Gin glasses clinked by themselves in a toast to the Gothas.

Wordsworth was staring in a puzzled way at Craig's wingless tunic. "I don't un – un'stand," he said. "What squadron are you with?"

"We're on the outskirts of Amiens," I said. "As a matter of fact, Wordy," I went on quickly, "you're just the man I wanted to see. I have this big car, you see, and I can't take it with me. When I move, I mean. We're moving tomorrow, you see, and we have to go back to riding bicycles and, well, the point is I've nowhere to leave the car, and I was wondering if I could leave it in one of your squadron hangars until I've an opportunity to pick it up later on, you see–"

"Bicycles?" Wordsworth said.

Craig was silent all the way back to the railway siding, but as we bedded down in the car beside the main line from Amiens to Paris, he said suddenly, "You were in the Royal Flying Corps, I gather."

"Uh, yes."

"What happened? Blot your copybook?"

"Yes."

Tactfully he said no more.

On the ninth, the great retreat began all over again, this time on the Second Army front. Come nightfall, the British had been driven back as far as Neuve Chapelle.

By the eleventh, half the territory that had been won in three and a half years' sacrifice had been lost. And once again there was chaos as the 13th Bicycles moved in.

We arrived at Béthune in thick fog, having had to push our bikes the last eight miles, for we were now crossing old battle-fields, from which most of the roads had long since disappeared.

On the morning of the twelfth, we moved up to support the 51st Highlanders, who had been holding a line along the River Lawe. But even that celebrated division couldn't cope with the new infiltration tactics, and were already being driven back when we arrived.

Meanwhile Craig had received about 120 reinforcements. Leo was now Company Sergeant-Major, Warburton was a sergeant, and Bassett a corporal. Apart from these and the other four survivors of the company, we had almost no experienced men. Accordingly, casualties were fierce. For the new men it was their first experience of the front, and they didn't like it at all. It was about a couple of years since this area had been fought over, but there were still so many human remains just under the surface they were reluctant to deepen the defensive works more than a few inches.

Nor did they appreciate the danger of gas, until Craig threatened to shoot the next man who tried to kill himself by wrenching off his respirator for a breath of fresh air.

We fought off two very determined onslaughts the first day, but had to pull back from the river the following morning, when encirclement threatened. Because of the gas, nobody had been able to eat or drink for twenty-four hours. We had no artillery support. It was pretty annoying to see the enemy guns being dragged though the mud within easy range and not be able to do anything about it.

The weather, as usual, had placed itself under Ludendorff's orders. The rain and mist were a great help to the attackers, while it kept the R.A.F. from giving any support whatsoever.

The battle went on for several days. Casualties were so bad that the wounded had to be left out in the drizzle on their stretchers because the clearing stations were packed. There were no further gas attacks, but the artillery fire grew steadily worse.

On the nineteenth, the Second Army pulled back from Passchendaele.

By that date we had personally retreated five miles. Of the 250 men of Craig's and Bartlett's companies who had set out from Amiens, only sixty-seven were left by the time the Germans reached Merville. The enemy had driven twenty miles in little over a week.

Then, silence. The same night, stinking and exhausted, we staggered back into reserve halfway between Merville and Béthune. The officers were billeted in a broken-down house in the middle of a mud field. I was the first to reach the bathtub. I had my first bath in a month. I lay in it for so long that Craig threatened to break down the door if I didn't give somebody else a chance.

I came out looking like a pink prune. I was just feeling my way into the nearest cot when a soldier clumped in with an urgent message for me to report to Battalion immediately.

Too tired even to snivel, I tottered back into the mud. But when I got to the farmhouse about a mile away, the colonel had gone to bed and the orderly room was shut. I couldn't face the journey back between the old shell holes and over the rotting duckboard, and went to sleep in a nearby henhouse, ruthlessly ignoring the protests of the field mice.

"Oh, yes, . . . Bandy, Bandy," the colonel said next morning. "You were supposed to report here last night, you know. That's not very good, is it, Bandy? Bless you."

I had just sneezed. I was catching a vile cold.

"Let me see, now, what was it all about? I wrote it down on a piece of paper. . . ." He started to sort through the piles of paper on the trestle table he was using as a desk. I sneezed again and blew open a book entitled *Terribly Obscure Battles*, Vol. II. The colonel peered at the book. "Yes, here it is on page 643. 'Bandy – Hesdin.' What does that mean? Oh, yes, I remember. You're to report to headquarters there, last night. Apparently they've been looking for you all over the place."

"Who has, sir?"

"The people at Hesdin, of course."

He peered at me through his hair. "The chap on the line said you were a pilot, is that right? What on earth are you doing on a bicycle, then? Oh, well, never mind; I think I'd rather not know. Anyway, there should be no difficulty about your going back to the Royal Flying Corps, or whatever it's called now."

"Going back . . .?"

"Yes, this place, Hesdin, is Royal Whatsaname Headquarters. It shouldn't be too complicated, I shouldn't think. Apparently you were never really transferred, you see. In fact, as far as I can make out, officially you've never actually been with us at all."

Deep in Conversation

"Glad to see you agaid, Colonel Treadwell."

"Look here, would you mind not dribbling snot onto my carpet! And where the devil have you been?"

"How do you mead?"

"We've been trying to track you down for weeks. Don't you ever report to anybody?"

"Most of the tide there was nobody to report to, sir."

"I want to know what you mean by wandering off like that into the bloody Army like a lost sheep. Just who d'you think you are, Bandy?"

"The Chief of Air Staff sent me."

"Rubbish. I put a stop to that the moment I heard about it. You're a pilot, not a trick bloody cyclist."

"I had my orders–"

"You had your balderdash. You never struck me as being subservient to orders, Bandy. You didn't even wait for that secretary fellow – Lewis – to do anything for you. You didn't wait for anybody. D'you think we spent several hundred pounds on your training just so you could go gallivanting 'round the countryside with a pack of suicidal cyclists? Oh, yes, I know all about that, and I don't think it's the least amusing! You could've been killed several times over – I ought to have you shot! Incidentally, where are your wings?"

"They cabe loose, sir."

"Get them back on right away. Not now, not now, you fool; put away that needle and thread. Good God, I'm beginning to have doubts already and you haven't even taken over the squadron yet."

"Taken over the . . . what?"

"I must be mad to've recommended you to the G.O.C., R.A.F.: Well, all I can say, Bandy, is you'd better not let me down. You'd bloody well better not let me down."

"Bart!"

"I didn't have a chance to tell you I was coming."

"Mother! Mother, look who's here!"

"It all happened so quickly."

"Ah, Bartholomew. You have turned up again."

"It's great to be home."

"What in the name of all things bright and beautiful have you done with your nose, Bartholomew? You look as if you've been using it as a pot scraper."

"I have a very bad cold, Mrs. Lewis."

"He's shivering, too. Burgess! Burgess! You're going straight to bed!"

"But I've only just got up, Miss."

"Not you, Burgess! Mr. Bandy, here."

"It's wonderful to be home. Gosh, I love this place. Your ancestral hobe. Such serene sybbetry, such inspiring simplicity apart from the bathroob with all those dreadful taps round the bathtub: *Shower*, *Douche*, *Wave*, *Pludge*, *Sprigkler*, and so ford. I love you all."

"He's delirious. Burgess, can we borrow your hot-water bottle? And put a fire in Mr. Bandy's room, will you."

"Certainly, Miss. And welcome home, Mr. Bandy."

"Thagk you very much."

"But what have you been doing to yourself, Bartholomew? You look positively *soiled*. I must say you have an extraordinary talent for deteriorating in remarkably short spans of time. Though, come to think of it, you have been going so steadily downhill ever since we first met you, that by rights you ought now to be distinctly subterranean."

"Don't keep him standing there in all the drafts, Mother. He has a temperature."

"Of course he has a temperature, otherwise he would be *totally* moribund. There is nothing in the least distinctive about his having a temperature. We *all* have temperatures – except the vicar, of course."

"How did you get back so soon, Bart?"

"I'm not sure, reely. I thigk I had to wait in Calais for three days. Luckily my fourteen days' special leave starts from when I land. Id seebs I'm back in the R.F.C., you see. I mean R.A.F."

"Oh, darling, I'm so happy for you. Daddy has been moving heaven and earth to do something about it. He–"

"Don't just stand there, Katherine, can't you see he's sniveling with cold? Take him up to bed. Which reminds me – the wedding will have to be prepared for all over again, not to mention the garden party on the fourth. It's highly inconsiderate of you, Bartholomew, to allow yourself to be postponed in this fashion. All these postings and transfers and demotions – it smacks, my dear Bartholomew, of *shiftiness*. I shall speak to the vicar about getting you married the moment you cease making that dreadful gurgling sound."

"Hello, Robert. Been out riding?"

"Yes. I had the gray. Rode over to see Binky and Chuff."

"And how are Binky and Chuff? Not to mention Iddles and Poopsy and Valikins?"

"How are you?"

"Not as pampered as yesterday."

"See you had quite a lively time at the front."

"How did you know that?"

"Kath said you were with a chap called Craig."

"Yes. That's all I told her, though. Except he deserves half a dozen medals."

"There's a bit in the *Guardian* about a Captain Craig. Reprinted from some New York newspaper. Take a look."

"Well, I'll be darned. Hilcheson. Good for him."

"Says Craig held up about half the German Army for twenty-four hours with only about forty men. I suppose that's the usual newspaper guff?"

"Seems to be fairly accurate, as a matter of fact. . . . Except it says here Craig used an abandoned field gun. Actually Craig stole it from a horse-artillery outfit. . . . Maybe it's just as well Hilcheson doesn't go into details. . . ."

"Read that bit. It says one of Craig's men went off on a bicycle and came back in a Rolls-Royce."

"So it does."

"Funny."

"What?"

"Soon as I read that bit I thought of you, Bart."

"Me?"

"Yes. Peculiar, isn't it? But I thought of you straight away. One of those irrational thought processes one has now and then."

"Robert? You're not by any chance accusing me of theft, are you? Of purloining government property? Of seeing to my own creature comforts in a time of self-sacrifice and acute national crisis? Of taking advantage of the military while they were busily engaged in putting their backs to the nearest wall, of–"

"So it *was* you."

"As a matter of fact I brought it back with me."

"You brought the car back with you."

"A friend kept it in a hangar for a couple of weeks or so until I could pick it up and drive it to Calais. That's why I took so long getting across, you see. I was talking a transport officer I knew into letting me drive it up the gangplank onto the cross-Channel steamer when he wasn't looking. It's in a London garage right now, being repaired and restored and painted a lovely dark-green color. You know, just in case some interfering busybody recognizes it some time in the future. Not that I've anything to worry about; my acquisition of it is a plain case of salvage, you know. The laws of salvage quite plainly apply here, and anyone who doesn't think so can go suck toffee apples."

"You came back with a Rolls-Royce."

"It's not a new one, of course."

"No? Good Lord, why didn't you return it right away and demand a new one?"

"It's a beauty, Robert. A 1908 Silver Ghost. Goes like a bullet on a good road – wouldn't do too badly at a fox hunt either. Raises the dust, terrifies girls, infuriates farmers–"

"My God."

"What?"

"You go off in utter disgrace with every man's hand against you, having caused practically a national scandal – and not only come riding back in sheer, decadent luxury, you're also promoted again. You're even given a squadron of your own. It's too much. All my life I've been polite to my superiors, circumspect, disciplined, dutiful, loyal, sociable–"

"You, sociable? To your horse; that's about all."

"–always been an all-round, selfless, dedicated officer, devoted to duty and – and what am I today? Still a flight commander after three years of total devotion to duty. And you come along and – they'll probably make you bloody *Sovereign* next!"

"What nonsense is that? You have to have royal blood to be King, and I don't have any. At least . . . I don't *think* I have. . . ."

"Good morning, Bart."

"Good morning, Mr. Lewis. Or – should I call you Father?"

"For God's sake, no."

"Good morning, Katherine."

"What's the matter with Robert?"

"I'll be all right in a minute. It's just the sight of that great, blank, horse-face there on the pillow – lying stinking there as smugly as if he thought he–"

"Ha, ha, ha, ha, ha, ha, ha."

"Ha, ha, ha, ha, ha, ha, ha."

"–as if he thought he was in complete control of everything that's happened to him."

"I don't know what you're all sniggering at. Everything that's happened to me I thoroughly deserve."

"I know."

"Well, at least he's not puffed up with his own importance any more. You should have seen him in his horrible colonel's uniform, Robert. It was gruesome."

"I did."

"Oh, yes, so you did. He was completely unbearable, wasn't he?"

"He still is."

"No, but he was *really* unbearable, Robert; it was unbelievable – strutting about looking like Genghis Khan's favorite nephew."

"Look at him now – he's actually enjoying being insulted."

"This is supposed to be my offended expression. If you're not careful I'll have a relapse."

"It would be an improvement."

"Talking about a relapse, Bart, Mr. Churchill wants to see you."

"Who? What? When? Why? Where?"

"Round at his house on Cromwell Road, at four-thirty on Thursday."

"Oh, heck, what have I done now?"

"I believe he told the Foreign Secretary that anyone who could replace the first cuckoo in spring as the main subject of interest in the correspondence columns of *The Times* might be worth meeting."

Mr. Churchill usually spent the morning at the Ministry of Munitions and his afternoons at the front. He arrived back at his house on Cromwell Road on time, but couldn't see me right away as he had one or two bigwigs to meet first.

In the meantime I entertained his three small children in the dining room: they kept peeking mischievously through the doorway and giggling at my face. Finally Mrs. Churchill shooed them away.

"You won't keep my husband too long, will you?" she said to me with a smile. "He's promised to mend some bricks at the back of the house before dinner."

However stormy his political life, his family life seemed to be happy enough, judging by the reception he'd got when he first appeared. I'd heard the children's excited chatter in the corridor and his wife's cheerful remonstrances, mixed with a fond rumbling sound.

When he finally came in I thought for a moment Mrs. Churchill had given up and brought in a real workman. He was dressed as he had flown from Verochocq, in shapeless overalls, and was still wearing his French tin hat. I very nearly directed him to the nearest broken brick.

He gave me a quick, searching glance before removing the light-blue helmet and gesturing with it toward a couple of seats near the window. The helmet had left a crease in his broad forehead.

So this was the man who'd mucked up the Dardanelles Campaign. "The more mediocre the talents of his opponents," Mr. Lewis had said about him, "the more deeply they distrust his impulsive genius." He didn't look much of a genius to me, though. Just another politician who'd used his connections to wiggle and wangle his way back into the cabinet – temporarily.

Still, I thought I'd put him at his ease. After all, I was not one to look down on a man even though his prospects were likely to be dim indeed once the martial chaos in which he thrived was ended. Nobody could accuse me of being a fair-weather friend.

So I gave him a friendly nod – but not *too* friendly, just in case he was in disgrace again and I hadn't heard about it.

"Honor to meet you, Mr. Churchill," I said coolly.

"Of course. So you're Bandy."

"Yes, sir."

"I thought you were a colonel?"

"That was only temporary, sir."

"I was a colonel two years ago, with the Scots Fusiliers at Plugstreet," he said in his slow rumble. "The officers were most displeased to have a politician flung into their midst without so much as a cry of warning. They were regulars, and were convinced that I would reorganize the battalion along the lines of an urban district council, and that no decisions would be made without a vote, or at the very least the formation of a subcommittee.

"On the day after my arrival at H.Q. (a farmhouse we shared with the French owners and a variety of livestock), when I called the officers together, hauteur and distrust were plainly inscribed on their faces. I said, 'Gentlemen: war is hereby declared upon the lice,' and followed this announcement with a dissertation on the social background, adolescence, and maturity of the louse, and its contributions to the art of war. I had culled this information the previous evening from a scholarly treatise entitled *The Bodybuilders: An Exordium on the Craft & Ambitions of the Common Louse, with Some Distasteful Side Glances at the Activities of the Pediculus Pubis* – or some such title; I'm

sure you're familiar with the work. The officers at first listened
in some uneasiness, but then began to laugh; and from then on
I had no further trouble in convincing them that I was not
entirely without martial initiative."

"I can imagine, sir."

"You've just returned from the front, I understand."

"Yes, sir."

"What is the situation there as you see it, Lieutenant?"

"A time, Mr. Churchill," I said portentously, "of tears, sweat,
and toil."

Churchill gazed at me fixedly for a moment. Then a
faraway look appeared in his eyes. "That's not bad," he murmured. "Tears, sweat, and toil. . . . But what about adding a bit
of blood?"

"Blood, toil, tears, and sweat?"

"Sweat, tears, blood, and toil?"

"Toil, blood, sweat, 'n' tears?"

"H'm." He thought for a moment. "Anyway, I must remember that. Might come in useful someday. You wouldn't mind
if I . . .?"

"Be my guest," I said expansively, stretching out my legs and
crossing my ankles. "Funnily enough, though, Winston," I
went on, "the morale of the men seems a lot better than it was
last year."

He scowled. Perhaps he didn't like having my boots sprawled
all over his polished floor. I sat up again and cleared my throat
to break the rather chilly silence.

"That is my impression too, but a Minister can never be
sure he's not being told what he wants to hear. I suppose it's
been difficult for you since you made that speech, Bandy. It
was, of course, an unforgivable thing to do."

"Yes, sir."

"Especially as you were merely simulating authority, while in actual fact you were occupying a position of no significance whatsoever. Isn't that so?"

"I guess so, sir."

"It was a ridiculous situation."

"Yes, sir."

"And the fact that a certain person put you up to it makes no difference."

"No, sir."

"You believed all that nonsense, Bandy?"

"I, uh . . . I thought I did."

"But you have now come to your senses?"

"No, sir. I mean – I thought I was talking common sense."

"If you knew anything about national affairs, you'd know that common sense is rarely used except in the direst emergency. Did you know that nearly a year ago I made a speech in secret session saying much the same thing?"

"Did you really, sir? No, I didn't know that."

"It made a profound impression, especially as I say so myself; and had no effect whatsoever."

"It makes you think, sir."

"We must both, mm, mm, Bandy, make more effort to learn from experience. Now tell me how Captain Craig stole the field gun and knocked out that tank. He said it was one of the new A7Vs. How fast did it travel? How good is this Russian Sokol it's armed with? And the crew – how many men? And for heaven's sake, man, stop trying to polish your boots on your trouser legs in that surreptitious manner. It's far too late to make an impression on me now."

Me, on My Honeymoon

We spent the first night of our honeymoon sitting up in the train to Scotland after a modest white wedding (Katherine's gown, my face) in a small country church, followed by a gay reception at the Lewises' ancestral home – and mine, now, too – where Milestone, who'd come over from his new squadron near Croydon to be my best man, became tight and unsentimental. The Lewises – Mr. Lewis had been granted a week's leave from the F.O. for the occasion – were charming, and even the groom contrived to look happy.

We had been invited by the Lewises' Scottish friends Sir Angus and Lady McIntock to spend our honeymoon at their place in Ayrshire, which was why we were sitting up all night, holding hands and coughing. Although the train windows seemed to be hermetically sealed, gritty smoke somehow managed to coil its way into our lungs.

McIntock was Lord Lieutenant of the County, I think it was called, and owned a large sandstone house on the Ayrshire coast. He was a large, genial man of sixty with unruly white hair and a kilt. His wife was a Highland lassie of about 220 pounds, also with unruly white hair, except that in her case she was growing bald on top. They were the most tactful of hosts, and after an enormous breakfast of pease brose, porridge, kippers, ham and eggs, Scottish rolls, strawberry jam, and more tea than could be poured into the gravity tank of a Sopwith Camel, they announced that the following days were entirely ours to do with as we pleased. They even, with straight faces and semi-incomprehensible dialect, gave us to understand (except that I *didn't* understand until it was too late) that we could go up to bed there and then at ten in the morning ("Tae sleep off the jurrney") if we so desired. But as I said, by the time I had it all

worked out it was too late, so we went for a walk instead.
Katherine was quite short with me for the first half mile or so.

She had changed a lot since I'd first met her; or perhaps I
had simply gotten to know her. She had been hard to get to
know well, but the weeks of companionship leading to our marriage had finally broken her down, revealing depths of levity
I had never suspected in her. Even the abruptness of her speech
had smoothed itself out. She had become almost self-assured.

We stood on a hilltop and admired the view. The sea glittered
in the distance and the air was balmy. We were not unhappy.

"Isn't it wonderful?"

"M'yes," I said, but thinking that it wasn't as wonderful as
Burma Park.

"Bart?"

"What, my love?"

"What are you thinking about?" she asked, squeezing
my arm.

"Oh . . ."

"You have almost an ecstatic look on your face."

"How can you tell?"

"You're thinking the same thing I'm thinking, aren't you?"
she said, blushing a little.

So she was thinking of Burma Park, too. "Yes," I said, and
squeezed her arm warmly. "It won't be long now," I murmured. In another week we would be going home.

"Oh, Bart," she said, breathing faster.

A half mile from the house she said, with a rush: "Have you
ever – you know – done it before?"

"Done what?"

"You know."

I glanced at her, but she was looking at her feet. "No," I said.

"Haven't you?"

"No."

As we neared the house ten minutes later she said, somewhat crossly, I thought, "Then, how will we know how to?"

"How to what?" I asked.

She looked up at the sky for a moment; then, "But of course," she said acidly, "I was forgetting: you've read all about it in *Pride and Prejudice*."

As we entered the house she said, "Well, I suppose I should be grateful it wasn't just the *Boy's Own Paper*, or we'd probably spend our wedding night over a tuck hamper saying, 'ouch,' 'yaroo,' and 'cave, you chaps.'"

"And 'leggo, you cad,'" I murmured.

Over luncheon Sir Angus insisted on talking about his own wedding night.

"Shush," Lady McIntock said.

"I will not shush, woman, for it is one of my treasured memories."

"Why?" I asked, interestedly. "Ouch," I added. Katherine had kicked me painfully in the shins.

"I beg your pardon, Lieutenant?"

"I said, 'Ouch,'" I said.

"Aye," Sir Angus said, nodding and drifting back forty years. "There we were, alone at last in the bedroom. It was a wee farm cottage up in the Isle of Skye. It had a terribly low ceiling, with great black beams."

Lady McIntock laughed heartily, then cut it off and frowned. "Shush, Angus," she said.

"So as I said, there we were, alone at last," Sir Angus went on reminiscently, "in our wee nightiegowns. And I clapped my hands the gether and I said, 'Well, Margaret,' I said, 'let's not be wasting any time.'"

"Shush," Lady McIntock said.

"So the next thing I knew, Margaret here said, 'Whee,' or something like that, and bounded into bed–"

"I was that nervous," Lady McIntock said.

"–but unfortunately she bounced so high she hit her head on one of the oaken beams and knocked herself silly. And," McIntock said, "I spent the rest of the night cycling round in a howling gale looking for a doctor."

"I still have the stitches," Lady McIntock said, inclining her head toward me. "Look, you can just see them if you search carefully."

"But it wasn't as bad, Katherine, as what happened to your mother and father. Shall I tell her, Margaret?"

"Look, Bart," Katherine said quickly, "isn't that a lovely tartan Sir Angus is wearing."

"This?" McIntock said, plucking at his kilt. "Yes, this is the Lamont tartan. An ancestor of ours once traced the Lamont line back as far as the twelfth century."

I looked suitably impressed; Katherine looked relieved.

Lady McIntock said, "With a gap in the line here and there, of course. Three hundred years here, a hundred there. But still."

"Yes," McIntock said imperturbably, "my ancestor was trying to prove we were descended from King Malcolm the Second, but he soon gave it up when he found that practically all our forebears were either sheepstealers busy being done in by hangmen or hangmen busy doing in sheepstealers. That explains why there's so many missing branches in the genealogical tree, you see. But I was talking about Mr. and Mrs. Lewises' wedding night. Like us, they couldn't wait to occupy the bedroom of their new house. And then afterward, feeling a bit peckish, they came galloping down the stairs for something to eat, riding piggyback, stark naked, with Mrs. Lewis shouting 'Yoicks,' 'Tallyho,' and similar expressions; and then all of a sudden all their friends and relatives, us included, jumped out from behind the curtains and the furniture shouting, 'Surprise, surprise!' It was indeed. Har har har."

Katherine didn't look at all amused.

"Well," McIntock said, putting his big red hands on the table and forcing himself up, "I'm off to have my nap. Why don't you two up and have a wee lie-down yourselves?"

Katherine was still looking down at her coffee cup.

"Well," I said.

"That's right," Lady McIntock said kindly. "You know where your room is, children."

As they went off down the corridor I heard Lady McIntock saying, "Yon's a peculiar chap, is he no, Angus? Does he not understand us, or is that his normal expression?"

There was silence for a minute or so in the dining room.

"Well," I said, stretching.

"Yes," Katherine said quickly. "I think I will, too. I'm feeling just a little bit tired."

"Oh," I said. "I was just going to suggest we stretch our legs. Go for a walk."

"Oh," she said.

"It's such a fine day."

"Yes," she said.

"But of course, if you–"

"No, no," she said.

After dinner we withdrew to the withdrawing room.

"Would you like to play the piano for us, Bartholomew?" Lady McIntock asked.

"Are you – are you sure we're not keeping you up or anything?" Katherine said quickly. "I mean–"

"I remember you saying, Katherine, that Bartholomew here was a fine pianist."

"Oh, I was just boasting," Katherine said. "You were asking what he was like, and that was the only thing I could think of in his favor."

McIntock laughed, as Katherine had meant him to. I think. She was saying curious things more and more of late. Mrs. Lewis had commented on this a few days before, intimating that the girl was coming too much under my influence; but I couldn't see that at all.

"Aye, play us something lively," McIntock said, slapping his Dundreary, or whatever that leather handbag was called that he wore in front of his kilt. "Something with a tune to it. None of this modern stuff, Wagner and Mendel, and the like. I've no time for it at all."

So I played them a medley of Scottish melodies, roving by means of a variety of florid *arpeggi* from the banks of Loch Lomond to the braes of bonny Doon. Ending with a triumphant flourish, I turned, smirking, to McIntock. He was nodding interestedly.

"Aye," he said. "Those'll be some of they Canadian square dances of yours, I expect." Lady McIntock was nodding, too; she'd fallen asleep.

"Canadian square dances?" I said.

Of course, I knew that I was not exactly a Paderewski or a Liszt or a Rubinstein or an Ian Smythe, but . . . Canadian square dances?

I suppose subconsciously the truth had been dawning on me for some time. The suspicion now fused into a flaring certainty. There exploded in me a blinding flash of revelation, a Moment of Truth so overwhelming as to make the matador's insight, just before the bull gores him, seem by comparison a mere idle thought or passing fancy. It had finally, irrevocably, unequivocally become clear: *I was not a very good pianist.*

"Well, that's it," I said, almost inaudibly. "That's it."

"That's what?" McIntock asked.

Deep inside me, of course, I'd always known. But I'd refused to face the fact, the truth that I was lacking in something:

co-ordination, imagination, technique, sensitivity, musical ability, knowledge of the keyboard – call it what you will, I was lacking in it.

I took a deep breath and closed the piano lid with an air of marked deliberation befitting the end of an era.

My air of marked deliberation, however, went unnoticed, so I had time to plumb the depths of the revelation. At the bottom was the fact that I'd never liked playing the piano.

Right from the start, when I'd had the hair at my temples tweaked for faltering over the introduction of a mediant triad into an F minor progression, or been rapped on the knuckles for stumbling over some clay-footed melody, I'd never really enjoyed playing. It was simply that the piano had become a nasty habit.

But I was free now. Free. And I announced to the company that I would never play the piano again.

The finality of my tones startled even me.

Katherine looked up slowly with an unreadable expression on her face.

"Do you–" she said; then stopped, overcome. "Do you," she began again, "do you really, truly mean it?"

"Absolutely," I said.

"Oh, Bart," she said, and again was unable to speak for a moment. Then: "But perhaps you shouldn't give up so easily."

"Why?" McIntock asked. "How long have you been trying?"

"Twenty years," I said.

I turned back to Katherine. "But," I said, "if you don't think I really ought to give it up, I–"

"Oh, no, no. You've made up your mind, I can see that," she said. She turned to McIntock. "Once he's made up his mind, *nothing* can budge him."

"M'well," I said, "I've given it up. Definitely."

Katherine clasped her hands together and bit her knuckles.

"I believe," I said, "I'll take up the oboe instead. Or perhaps the bagpipes."

After a long silence McIntock said, "Aye. Well . . ." He looked at his watch. "Nine o'clock. It's bedtime, I suppose."

Katherine sat up straight. McIntock gave her an encouraging smile, then turned and shook his wife. "Wake up, Margaret," he said. "It's time for bed, is it not? It's after nine o'clock."

But Lady McIntock seemed to be taken off guard. "What are you talking about, Archie?" she said sleepily. "You know we never go to bed before ten."

"Aye. That's right," McIntock said, somewhat heavily.

Katherine slumped back again, squinting.

There was a silence. Lady McIntock seemed to be concentrating hard.

"But surely it's past nine o'clock," she said at length, brightly. "Are you sure your watch is right, Angus?"

McIntock brightened. So did Katherine. "By Jupiter, you're right," he exclaimed. "It's stopped." Then he looked at his watch. "Aye, so it has," he added.

Katherine started to yawn daintily.

"No, my watch says nine o'clock too," I said. I listened to it. Yes, it was ticking. "Yes, it's ticking," I said.

Katherine's mouth slowly closed, and a slight film spread over Lady McIntock's eyes. They all looked at me in a strange fashion. I was forced to point to the mantle clock in self-defense, which clearly registered two minutes past nine.

Katherine looked away. Then I saw her stiffen, so I followed her eyes to a grandfather clock in the corner. *It* clearly registered twenty minutes past ten. Katherine was just about to say something when the grandfather clock started to rattle alarmingly; then chimes announcing the three-quarter hour were heard; then there was a breathless pause and the clock struck nineteen times in rapid succession, then hesitated, then struck twice more. Then it settled back into an irregular ticking.

There was a brief silence.

"It's broken," McIntock said.

We all nodded.

There was another silence.

"Do you care for cards?" Lady McIntock asked me.

"That's a good idea," Katherine said. "Give him a pack of cards. He could play patience."

"Aye," McIntock said.

About nine-thirty Lady McIntock heaved herself up. "Well, I don't know about you young people," she said, "but I'm feeling terrible tired, so I'm off to my bed."

We all got to our feet. Katherine said, "Yes, and I'd better have a bath." Then she stopped, and went on a little defensively, "I always have a bath beforehand." We all nodded. "I mean, every night, regardless of what–" then stopped again and hurried out of the room.

"Well, Bartholomew, would you care for a nightcap?" McIntock asked me with revived joviality.

"No, I – I've never worn one," I said. For some reason I was suddenly feeling nervous.

"I'm talking about a wee dram," McIntock said.

"Oh," I said with an enlightened expression, and laughed heartily. So did McIntock. "A what?" I asked blankly.

McIntock's eyes glazed. "A drink, man," he said. "A drink."

"Oh," I said. "Oh. Yes. Och aye." I laughed again. "A wee dram. Of course. Yes, I – yes, I'll, I'd like a wee dram."

When McIntock said a wee dram he meant a wee dram. He poured about half an inch of Scotch into two huge tumblers; that is, a quarter inch in each. We drank and nodded at each other. There was another of those frequent pauses with which the evening had been strewn. McIntock seemed to be waiting for something.

At last he said, "I must say you're – you're one of the most patient fellows I've ever come across." He squinted at me. "When you consider the circumstances," he began, then halted, looking lost. Then: "Are you sure – are you *quite* sure you wouldn't like a nice game of chess? You know, to while away the time?"

I hesitated. I didn't really feel like playing chess at the moment, but he had been so pleasant I thought it was the least I could do in return if he really wanted to play at this late hour. "Well," I said, "if you'd really like a game, I–"

McIntock almost dropped his whisky glass. "Great thundering McGubbins, man!" he shouted. Then he sighed and helped himself to another wee dram, except that this time he filled the tumbler about half full.

Finally we went upstairs. I was about to barge into the bedroom; then hesitated, and knocked.

"Who is it?" Katherine said from within.

"It's me," I said.

"Who?"

"Bandy," I said.

"Bandy?"

"Yes," I said. "Don't you remember?"

"Oh," she said in a muffled voice. "You mean *Lieutenant* Bandy?"

"That's right," I said through the door. What on earth was wrong with the girl?

"What do you want?" she asked.

I didn't quite know how to answer this. I was beginning to feel somewhat foolish, lurking about in the hall talking through a closed door. "Can I come in?" I asked.

There was no answer; so I took a firm grasp of the door-knob and pulled.

"It's locked," I said in surprise. "Why have you locked it?" There was no answer. "Katherine?" I said.

Katherine pulled the door inward, and without a word went back to combing her hair at the dressing table. The door hadn't been locked at all. I'd become so used to doors that opened outward, and . . . well, the Nissen hut doors opened outward, and so did the doors of the Spartan Hotel.

Our room was frilly with lace, flowery pelmet, ornamental fireplace, patterned antimacassar, and fussy lamp, and had a tiny adjoining room, presumably for the ladies because it contained only a dresser, chair, and a large mirror for powdering the nose, and so on; and it was this little room that Katherine went back to. She was wearing a blue silk nightgown that trailed around her ankles and the awful quilted dressing gown I'd seen her in at Burma Park. She didn't say anything, so I shuffled around the bedroom for a while, picking things up and putting them down. Then I gazed out the windows. Then I realized the curtains were drawn, so I pulled them back, which enabled me to gaze out the window. But not being able to see anything, it being quite dark outside, I took up my towel and my little toilet bag and went to the door.

"I'm going to the bathroom," I said.

There was no answer, so I went and had a bath, brushed my teeth and cut my toenails, and when I got back Katherine was reading in bed. I wandered about the room for a bit, tidying my clothes and so on. Finally I got into bed.

Katherine went on reading. I sat there for a while, having a little stretch. It was a huge bed, and there was a considerable acreage between us.

After some time I got up on my hands and knees and crawled across to Katherine and leaned over to look at the book. "What are you reading?" I inquired.

She showed me the cover, then went back to her reading. It was *Quentin Durward*.

"Oh, yes," I said. "Walter Scott."

Five minutes later I said, "Is it any good?"

"It's not bad when you get into it."

A couple of minutes later I said, "I see."

Katherine had been sitting bolt upright, very stiffly. She now lay back on the pillows. This outlined her bosom. It pouted very prettily against the silk nightdress.

"Well," I said, feeling short of breath. "It must be getting late."

"It's only half-past ten," she said. "I forgot to tell you: I always read until dawn. Then I like to go for a long walk."

"Mm," I said.

She turned a page. I took a deep breath, drawing it in as unobtrusively as possible, and put my arm round her shoulders.

"It's been a long day," I remarked conversationally.

There was another of those damned pauses; then she put the book aside and looked at me. She had long since lost any self-consciousness about her slight strabismus; I'd told her so often it made her look all the more desirable. It did now. My face was fiery.

"Yes," she said. "It's been a damned long day." And laughed a bit shrilly.

I started to put my other arm around her. She was apparently wearing nothing beneath the blue silk, and as my fingertips brushed her stomach she twitched and hid her face against me. "Put the light out," she whispered. Her breath tickled my neck, and I started twitching too.

The frilly lamp was on her side of the bed. I didn't want to kneel up and lean over because my pajamas were noticeably bunched, so I got up and walked around the bed, sideways.

With the light out, the room was pitch dark, and walking back to my side of the bed I smashed my toe against the bedpost.

"What's the matter?"

"I hit my toe."

It was all the more painful because it was the same toe I'd broken when I kicked that rock in France. However, the throbbing soon died down, and I groped my way back, but all that hopping around had set my compass spinning, and I went in the wrong direction. There was a tremendous clatter as I fell over some fire irons.

"What on earth's the matter now?" Katherine asked in a despairing tone of voice, and switched on the lamp again to find me in the fireplace about twenty feet away. Fortunately the fire wasn't lit, but one of my hands was black with soot and I had to go back to the bathroom to wash it. I met McIntock in the corridor. He stopped and looked at my hand.

"I expect," he said, "you were trying to get away up the chimney. Is that it?"

"Of course not," I said coldly. "I was on my way to bed but walked into the fireplace instead, that's all."

"Aye," McIntock said.

When I got back, the lamp was still on and Katherine was all covered up in bed, pretending to be asleep. I switched off the lamp once more, being careful to take my bearings properly this time, and I managed to navigate back to bed successfully.

There was silence for some time. Katherine didn't stir.

I reached over inch by inch, my heart pounding.

It certainly was a large bed. I couldn't locate her at all. I moved over three or four feet and reached out again, but even though my arm was stretched to its limit I still wasn't making contact. I felt around. I was damned if I could find her.

After a moment I whispered hoarsely, "Where on earth *are* you?"

She didn't answer. I expect the poor girl was suddenly a mass of nerves, and, making allowances for this, I moved over another foot or two and whispered tenderly, "Where the hell are you, Kath?" But again drew a blank. My hand was swishing over the sheets, searching for her. "I can't find you," I complained. Really, this was a bit much. There *was* such a thing as excessive modesty. I moved again, a trifle impatiently, and fell out of bed.

Feeling myself fall, I naturally tried to grasp for some support, and in so doing grabbed the tasseled cloth covering the bedside table, and the next moment there was a shocking din as the table, the tasseled cloth, the frilly lamp, two or three ornaments, and I crashed to the wooden floor. I got a splinter in my behind. The door to the little powder room was flung open and Katherine appeared, outlined against the light.

"I fell out of bed," I explained.

She leaned against the wall for support.

I got up and trod on some glass from the shattered lamp.

When Katherine had pulled herself together, she said, "You'll have to ask McIntock for some first aid for that foot."

I knocked at McIntock's door. He emerged, blinking, to find me smiling ingratiatingly, balanced on one leg in my pajamas, which now had blood as well as soot on them.

"Sorry to disturb you," I whinnied, "but would you happen to have anything that might be helpful in stopping the flow of blood?"

McIntock looked terribly concerned. "You rotten beast," he said. "Oh, the puir wee girl," and started to rush along the corridor.

"Come back," I said. "It's not Katherine; it's me."

"Great thundering McGubbins," he said. "It's the first time I ever heard of–"

"I trod on some glass," I said.

There was quite a long silence.

"I fell out of bed, you see," I went on, but then dried up, possibly because of his expression.

Lady McIntock came out "What's up?" she asked.

"Nothing yet," McIntock said. "It seems Bartholomew has fallen out of bed now, and cut his foot on the lamp. I did not dare ask him what the lamp was doing on the floor, of course."

"No," Lady McIntock said. She stared at me balanced on one leg and smiling fatuously, looked as if she was going to say something, but apparently decided against it and fetched the first-aid kit instead, and fixed up my foot there in the hall.

When I got back to the bedroom once again, Katherine had just finished clearing up the mess and was talking to herself. She soon stopped, however, and switched off the light in the adjoining room and we got into bed once more. I gave a grunt and got up again.

"*Now* what's the matter?" she said.

"Oh, it's nothing."

She got up and switched on the powder-room light again. "What *is* it?" she said, shaking me. "Come on, tell me. Out with it; it's something *else* now, isn't it? Tell me, tell me!" She sounded just a trifle hysterical and was shaking me so hard my answer was a tremolo.

"I have a splinter," I quavered.

A couple of minutes later there was a knock at the door and McIntock and his wife came in with a bottle of iodine for my foot and found me lying face down on the bed, and Katherine holding a large safety pin poised over my right buttock.

The McIntocks stood transfixed for a moment, then slowly began to back out, obviously fearing that they'd interrupted some dreadful perversion culled from the pages of the Marquis de Sade's *La Philosophie dans le boudoir*, or *Les Crimes de l'amour*.

"It's all right," Katherine said, almost inaudibly. "It's only a splinter."

"Aye," McIntock said.

"We forgot to put iodine on his foot," Lady McIntock faltered.

They gathered around. By this time I wouldn't have cared if they'd brought in the butler, half a dozen upstairs maids, and a poacher or two. I just shut my eyes and tried to think of other things. They took turns trying to pry the splinter out. Lady McIntock won.

Finally we were alone once more, and in the light of the powder room – by this time Katherine didn't dare switch it off – we snuggled up, our two faces jammed together like workmen's braziers. I was rather inept, I'm afraid, for though I knew the technique in theory, in practice it didn't seem to be quite so simple. Still, Katherine appeared to be happy enough at the end of it, and I was reminded of what Queen Victoria was supposed to have said to Albert: "Do you mean to say," she was supposed to have said, imagining, I suppose, that supreme bliss was somehow a royal prerogative, "Do you mean to say that the common people enjoy this just as much?"

I mentioned this to Katherine, but she was not amused.

Catching Up

It was a glorious June morning in May. The sunlight, aged and mellowed in sherry-saturated casks, was slanting through the high Georgian windows of the Long Room at Burma Park. I was sitting at a Sheraton table near one of the windows in my sole surviving uniform, diligently licking my thumb and turning over the pages of a stack of newspapers and glossy magazines.

I was trying to catch up on a month's news but was continually being interrupted – by my own euphoria. I couldn't help pausing every few minutes, glowing with health and optimism, to contemplate my sheer good fortune in still being alive and kicking.

A dozen times in that wild month at the front I ought to have gone to my reward, or at the very least earned a sleeveful of wound stripes. But I'd come out of it with nothing worse than a mild dose of influenza. It made me wonder if Somebody Up There wasn't saving me for a rainy day.

If I'd known any operatic arias I'd have burst into one of them forthwith. But all I knew was Gilbert and Sullivan's "When You're Lying Awake with a Dismal Headache," so I contented myself by getting up and going for a short walk around the table and then sitting down again with an ululation of pure pleasure.

However, it was bad luck to dwell too much on one's good fortune. To distract myself I picked up a copy of last month's *Punch* for a good laugh at one of its very amusing cartoons.

DISILLUSIONED, the first one announced, under a full-page drawing of a tall, thin man in a beard who was pointing accusingly at another chap in a beard. This second chap was holding a paper on which were the words NO CONSCRIPTION IN IRELAND.

I chuckled heartily, then read the caption:

> UNCLE SAM (to Nationalist Leader): "See here, if you
> mean to disgrace Ireland in the eyes of all decent nations,
> you get no more sympathy from me."

Still chuckling and twitching my head in an appreciative
way, I turned the page. After a minute or so I turned back to
peer at the cartoon again.

I knew that the recent extension of conscription to Ireland
had caused quite a stir in that country, and some Irish nationalists in the British Parliament were vociferously opposing it,
but I couldn't quite see what the joke was. Unless it was the
idea of Uncle Sam frowning at Ireland's lack of patriotism. Yes,
maybe that was it: the idea of the United States, always sympathetic to Irish independence, pretending to condemn Ireland
for protesting against being further exploited. Maybe that was
the joke.

For further enlightenment I turned to the *Essence of
Parliament* section, where a Mr. William O'Brien was describ-
ing the Conscription Bill as ". . . a declaration of war upon
Ireland," and a Mr. Devlin, ". . . not to be outdone, said his
beloved country would never allow such a *stamina* to be
inflicted upon her brow.

"Nevertheless, leave to bring in the Bill was accorded on a
division by 299 to 80."

I didn't know anything about it, but I must say I was a bit
astonished at all this. An awful lot of Irishmen had volunteered
for and been killed in the British forces. The Irish could hardly
be expected to take kindly to being forced to join up at this late
date, especially after such recent incidents as the treatment of
the I.R.B. leader Tom Ashe, who had died of cold and starva-
tion in Mountjoy Prison.

This made me think of those guns Michael had been bringing in. I wondered what he was doing now, and whether he had
summoned up the nerve to resume his aerial smuggling. He
probably had, as soon as it became evident that the authorities
were not taking any action against him.

I suppose I still felt a bit guilty about that affair. But, after
all, why should I pursue the matter when the Commander-in-
Chief in Ireland had refused to? No, darn it; nobody could say
I hadn't tried.

Abandoning *Punch*, I turned to a back issue of the *Daily Mail*
but hastily abandoned it as well when I came across a two-
week-old report of a speech in the Queen's Hall by an admiral
who couldn't understand why the author of the recent Fallow
address hadn't been hung up by his thumbs for his outrageous
meddling, or keelhauled under a dreadnought encrusted with
exceptionally sharp barnacles.

"If a twenty-four year old aviator – 'this Clausewitz of the
Air Ministry' – who was said to have gained his staff appointment by political toadyism rather than by any talent for
administration, was permitted to condemn his own superiors
in such gross and treasonous terms, then we would have
nobody but ourselves to blame when others followed his
example, the admiral said.

"'Allow him to get away with such vicious pronunciamen-
tos and we can soon expect to hear of dustmen advising the
town clerk on how to conduct civic affairs, munition workers
showing company accountants how to add up their figures,
and perhaps even stokers second class calling the bridge to
complain about the course laid down by the flag officer,' the
admiral said, to enthusiastic applause."

I wasn't too upset by this belated broadside. I knew the
admiral had fired it as much for personal as patriotic reasons.
He was one of Lord R.'s Air Ministry advisers, whose attempt

to purchase ten thousand Japanese hand-warmers for the Air Force had been vetoed by Lord R. in one of his more lucid moments. The admiral had blamed me for the loss of his commission on the deal, for I'd been the one who had to tell him. I had made matters worse by arguing against another proposal of his, that the terms *port* and *starboard* be adopted by the R.A.F. Although in this case he had succeeded in imposing his nautical terminology on the Air Force, he had strongly resented my opposition and had avenged himself by referring to me as Colonel Water Closet and by directing streams of people with diarrhea to my office.

Deciding I'd had enough news for the time being, I got up for a luxurious stretch, then started toward the piano for a spot of practice, which I badly needed, as I had not tickled the ivories for several weeks now. But then I turned away again, assuming that the piano was locked – it always seemed to be locked whenever I visited Burma Park – and stood on my hands instead. Not even the knowledge that my new family were rank imposters could chill the feeling of well-being that suffused me.

Mr. Lewis had been so eager to give us the bad news that he had met us at Euston Station.

All the way down in the train I'd been anticipating a joyful homecoming to Burma Park, that simple, inspiring house, reeking of grand old English tradition, where I felt I belonged.

The first thing Mr. Lewis said was that he had been sacked.

"What happened?" we asked, appalled.

Lewis looked at me sadly. "You remember those papers under the carpet in my office?"

"Yes?"

"Well . . . when I had that week's leave of absence – you know, for your wedding?"

"Yes, go on," Katherine said, gripping his arm.

"Well . . . they decided to have my office redecorated while I was away. Sort of a surprise. And they found the papers. . . ." He looked down, and pushed a dusty crust of bread around the station platform with his foot. "You see," he said, his face still averted and his voice apologetic, "for years I'd been getting various requests for information and, you know, action, and, well . . . I just didn't know what to do with half of them, you see."

"So you just shoved them under the mat," I said flatly.

"Yes," Mr. Lewis said, hanging his head.

A train hooted and spun its wheels excitedly. "There were 412 of them," he added inconsequently, "dating back to the Boer War."

In the taxi on the way to the Savoy for a late dinner, Katherine began making those queer sounds of hers which by now I knew signified mirth.

"Well," she said. "You've always wanted to devote all your time to ferns, haven't you, Daddy?"

"M'm," he said, looking at me sheepishly.

A moment later he added, "Of course it will make a difference. We have an independent income, but it will mean giving up Burma Park, of course."

"Oh. Oh, well, never mind," Katherine said, kissing him.

I sat up, staring at them. "Give up Burma Park?" I asked faintly. I expected them to laugh, but their faces remained serious. "Give up Burma Park?" I repeated incredulously.

"Have you – have you both gone mad?" I said. "Your ancestral home? You can't do it. Think of tradition!"

"Tradition?" Lewis asked, as if he'd never heard the word before.

"What ancestral home?" Katherine asked.

"Why – Burma Park, of course." They looked at me blankly. "It's been in your family since Time Immemorial," I said. "You can't just get up and go as if it were just a – just a–"

"What are you talking about?"

"You've got it all wrong, Bart."

"You can't give up the investment of tradition just like that. Where would the stately homes of England be if everyone thought like that?"

"Thought like what?" Lewis asked. "We've only been there since the Boxer Rebellion."

"You've what?" I said, my head whirling, my heart sinking, my bowels constricted, and my stomach in knots.

"I don't know what you're talking about," Katherine said. "We haven't any investment in Burma Park."

"We just rent it," she said.

I was still so upset at dinner that I could only eat five or six courses.

"We won't have to leave right away, of course," Mr. Lewis said cheerfully.

"Where will you live?"

"We'll move to town, as soon as we're able to repossess our Kensington house. The Friends of Borneo Society is occupying it at the moment."

"But where will I land my plane?" I demanded, casting them large numbers of outraged glances. "How big is your property in Kensington?"

"About two acres."

"There you are, you see! How d'you expect me to land my plane on two acres?" I said, ignoring the fact that even if their city property had been extensive, the London County Council would hardly have approved of a flying machine dodging about among the lamp standards, church steeples, the Albert Memorial, et cetera.

Perhaps I sounded just a trifle unreasonable; but though I'd been staying at The Park only since 1917, I found it hard to adjust to the idea of living anywhere else. I'd come to think of that Georgian mansion as a haven from the madness of military life, the only harbor I had to tie up in. For a time I'd even had an uneasy suspicion, now entirely dissipated, that my engagement to Katherine had been a sort of harbor dues.

However, I'd finally faced up to the situation. "I guess," I admitted, "that I have to go out onto the High Seas of Life *sometime* or other."

"That's the spirit," Mr. Lewis said. "And don't worry. There'll be plenty of room for you in the Kensington house. There's a very nice attic there. I'm sure that with a bit of scrubbing and repair work . . ."

Mr. Lewis was worried, though, about the effect the move might have on his wife, whose activities were distinctly agrarian. She so much enjoyed scattering her calling cards around the county, terrorizing the peasantry, pottering about her arbors and rose garden, and bewildering the soil with strange vegetables, that Mr. Lewis wondered how she would adjust to city life.

However, she loyally insisted that she had long since exhausted the possibilities of the pastoral scene, and was looking forward to invading the drawing rooms of the capital from an advance base instead of having to satisfy herself with the occasional sporadic raid.

So who was I, I thought, as I grunted my way across the carpet on my hands, to continue moping and looking ill-done-to, especially as nobody was paying any attention anyway?

I managed to travel a good thirty feet on my hands before falling over – just as a pair of sensible shoes appeared in the doorway of the Long Room.

Looking up, I met Mrs. Auchinflint's expressionless gaze. She had arrived earlier that morning to help Mrs. Lewis with the preparations for the garden party. She didn't look the least surprised to find me sprawled on my back on the gold Balkan Tabriz.

Neither, of course, did Katherine, who followed her into the room a moment later.

"All set for Gosport, Bart?" she asked. She was wearing a new, dove-gray dress and white gloves, and carried a car rug over her arm.

"Yes," I said, scrambling up and giving her an enthusiastic kiss on the lips, not in the least concerned with what Mrs. Auchinflint might think of this shamelessly open display of affection. Every day, I loved Katherine more, for her humor and her growing delight in life. (It seemed typical of me that I should experience the symptoms of love mainly after I'd gotten married: the stalling sensation when I smelled her, the tingling experience when I touched her, and the almost mystical feeling that the sight of her slender nakedness inspired – mystical, that is, until the old blood started boiling and frothing in the old veins.)

"What's the car rug for?" I asked, panting more than ever after the osculatory submersion.

"It's to hide the bloodstains," Katherine said.

"Oh, good idea."

Though she couldn't have known that we were referring to the car's upholstery, Mrs. Auchinflint's expression remained as unsurprised as ever. I wondered what *would* startle her? A cancan by the Bishop of London? The entry of a band of Laplanders playing "The Blue Danube" on reindeer bones?

"I'll tell Papa we're off, then," Katherine said, smiling sweetly and swaying her hips as she made her way to the library at the far end of the room.

Even Katherine's walk had become joyful since her discovery that the female waist had a use other than that of simply separating the rib cage from the hipbone.

As she went out, a constrained silence descended. Mrs. Auchinflint went over to the table and started to leaf through an *Illustrated London News*. I picked up my cap and fiddled with it. I'd have fiddled with my stick as well, only I'd lost it during that hurried trip to the front.

"Have you heard from Mr. Rodominov since you got back?" she asked abruptly.

"No, I haven't."

"He hasn't called me since . . . since that time."

"I thought you insisted it was all over and done with between you."

"He could at least have called me."

She looked closely at a page of glossy text, her thin shoulders hunched. "He's left his place in Balham, and he's not with the hotel any more. I don't know where he is."

I nodded and looked down at my brown shoes. Though still frowned on in conservative quarters, slacks and shoes could now be worn officially.

"I wish I were dead," Mrs. Auchinflint said, tidying her hair.

"Don't say that," I murmured, standing on one shoe and rubbing the other against the back of my slacks to remove an incriminating fingerprint.

"I think I'll cut my throat."

"Well . . . well, remember to keep your chin down when you do it, Mrs. Auchinflint," I said in a helpful sort of tone.

"My chin?"

"Yes. If you put your head back when you cut your throat, as so many people do, you'll only cut the tendons, you see. That's a mistake a lot of people make."

"Indeed?"

"I used to be a medical student, you see; that's how I happen to know. So remember to keep your chin down when you do it."

"You're wonderfully helpful, Mr. Bandy."

"Don't mention it, Mrs. Auchinflint."

"But I want to mention it. It's really heart-warming to have friends like you."

"'M'kew," I said.

Well, at least she'd got the sharp, sarcastic look back in her brown eyes.

There was the sound of quarreling in the distance. Mr. and Mrs. Lewis were just entering from the far end of the room, followed by a grinning Katherine. "Nonsense, William," Mrs. Lewis was saying. "If the wine is sour, all we need to do is add a little sugar, surely? We're certainly not contributing the Saint-Julien to the garden party."

"Vinegar punch," Mr. Lewis murmured. "Oh, well."

"I'll put an extra gallon of alcohol in it," she said, sailing across the yellow carpet, her stays creaking in a nautical way, "and give it to the pilots. I understand they'll drink anything."

Since abandoning her Bulrush Period, Mrs. Lewis had turned on the vine that cowered in her greenhouse, with the intention of producing her own wine and selling it to those of her neighbors who hadn't yet tasted her mead. She had already purchased a large vat, into which, come summer, she proposed driving the servants in their bare feet for a spot of grape crushing – assuming she was still here by summer, and also assuming that the servants hadn't volunteered for minesweeping by then.

"About the side shows," she went on. "I still have the coconuts left over from the Hospital Fête, so that takes care of the coconut shy. Handley is coming over this afternoon to glue them down."

"I've laid out the croquet pitch, by the way," Mrs. Auchinflint said, looking at me as if she'd prefer to have laid me out instead.

"Ah, splendid, Edith," Mrs. Lewis boomed. She turned her severe look on Katherine. "Have you found the mallets yet, child?"

"I think the gardener was using them to knock in the tent pegs," Katherine said.

"Well, as long as we know where they are," Mrs. Lewis said. She caught sight of me, started, then frowned. "Of course," she thundered, "I don't suppose anyone will come after Bartholomew's very ill-advised speech."

"They'll come, all right," Lewis said, opening the piano, which apparently hadn't been locked at all. "If only for all the black-market food they know you'll somehow acquire." He laid a hesitant hand on the piano keys and timidly essayed a dominant seventh.

"I sincerely hope so. I must say that excellent suggestion of Katherine's should raise the event above the merely memorable," Mrs. Lewis said. "We simply cannot allow our garden party to be outdone by Lady Smollett's, who, as you remember, brought her Stained Glass campaign to the heights of Roman drama with a splendidly vulgar bonfire – a display of ostentation that was remembered and discussed throughout the County for many minutes afterwards."

"I don't think Lady Smollett actually *intended* to burn down the east wing," Mr. Lewis murmured.

He saw me approaching the piano eagerly. He closed the piano lid and sat on it, looking terribly thoughtful.

"Nevertheless, it was a most climactic coup," Mrs. Lewis thundered. "And I shall expect Bartholomew to at least emulate it with his display of intrepid birdmanship."

That was the reason Katherine and I were going to Gosport: to persuade them to lend me an airplane for a brief aerial display at the garden party on Saturday.

Beside a Brook, Babbling

It was about fifty miles to Gosport as the crow flies. Taking the English highways into account, we had planned on a five-hour journey.

Accordingly, the car was crowded with honeymoon-type luggage, including swimming wear, a picnic basket, warm champagne, a throw rug, a ground sheet, Liquorice Allsorts, sketching materials, a four-volume history of North America that Katherine was loyally trying to interest herself in, and umbrellas, raincoats, and a bailing bucket, in case the weather did one of its quick-change acts.

But the sun continued to beam on the expedition, and Katherine's ribboned bonnet fluttered gaily in the warm currents that eddied around the high, double windscreen of our splendid vehicle. We must have looked very posh indeed as we purred along the winding highways of Berkshire and Hampshire. The garage in London had done a beautiful job of restoration while we were on our honeymoon: repairing the shell holes, replacing a front mudguard, adding a spare wheel, levering on three new tires, painting the body a glowing green, and submitting a bill that I hoped to pay off by eating and drinking as little as possible for the next five and a half months.

What with a French painting, a Russian samovar, and a Green Ghost, as Katherine called it, I was quite the man of property these days.

At one o'clock we picnicked in thoroughly *cliché* style on a mossy bank beside a babbling brook at the edge of a Hampshire forest of beech and hawthorn.

Unfortunately the idyll was somewhat spoiled by my latest bad habit, of regarding the countryside tactically rather than aesthetically. After that feverish month in France I could no longer look at a rustic bridge without imagining it being blown. I couldn't even admire a clump of azaleas any more, without seeing shells bursting among them, sending the shreds of their glorious blossoms fluttering through the martial air.

I felt particularly uneasy with the site Katherine had chosen for the picnic. It seemed to me we were most disadvantageously placed in the event of an attack, with no protection whatsoever from either tanks or aircraft. Nor did I like the way our rear was unsecured. Any moment I expected gas shells to come plopping onto the picnic linen, and enfilading fire to start lashing overhead.

Also, I'd have been a lot happier if there'd been some barbed wire around.

I grew so tense, in fact, that when Katherine trod on a dry twig I very nearly flung myself into the babbling brook. I was halfway down the bank before I pulled myself together and pretended I was merely down there to rinse my shoes.

"What on earth's the matter with you, darling?" Katherine said as she set out the Patum Peperium, The Gentleman's Relish. "You're looking quite wild-eyed."

"Oh, it's nothing. Don't you think we ought to move further into the wood, Katherine?"

"What do you have in mind?" Katherine asked in what seemed an unnecessarily abandoned fashion.

"We're in danger of having our flanks exposed."

"That's a danger?"

"Let's get going, shall we?"

"My goodness, Bart. There's no holding you back since you've experienced the joys of connubial bliss."

"Eh? I mean, our rear could be too exposed."

"Yes, I suppose there are a few mosquitoes around. You're giving me little enough sleep as it is, without my spending the remainder of the night scratching my exposed rear."

"Katherine."

"I'm getting terribly vulgar, aren't I?" Katherine said contentedly. "It's ever since I met you. No, but I think we'd better be getting on, darling. They're expecting us at four, and we've still twenty miles to go."

They were indeed expecting us. As we hummed to a halt outside the squadron mess at Fort Grange, almost every one of the instructors emerged and gathered around. Some students also stopped to watch, and even a few mechanics were peering around various corners.

"What in God's name is he now?" somebody said despairingly. "A general?"

In fact I still had the lieutenant's insignia on my regimental tunic. The new, sky-blue uniform with the major's rings had not yet come from the tailor's.

As I helped Katherine down from the running board, Treadwell came up and kissed her hand.

"Mrs. Bandy," he said gravely.

I started and looked around, thinking my mother had turned up. I hadn't gotten used to hearing Katherine's new name yet.

"Welcome to Gosport."

"Thank you very much, Mr. Treadwell," Katherine said.

I saw Fielding staring in a desperate sort of way at my two cloth pips. As soon as Katherine had been introduced to everybody he burst out, "Look here, Bandy, I wish you'd make up your mind what you are! First you're a captain, then a colonel, and now you're a bloody – sorry, Mrs. Bandy – now you're a blinking lieutenant – but in a whacking great staff car! Damn it, man, it's too much!"

"That's the way it goes," I said, looking around warily for the commandant.

"What d'you mean, that's the way it goes? It doesn't go that way for anyone but you!

"We never know what the devil to expect of this husband of yours," he said to Katherine in an aggrieved tone. "I mean, dash it all. And what's this about you being sent back to the infantry?"

"Actually it wasn't the infantry, it was a bicycle battalion," I said. "That's where I got the car, you see."

Fielding's eyes glazed over. He turned and thudded his forehead against the wall of the mess.

But I wasn't looking at him. The commandant, accompanied by the adjutant, was approaching over the cinders, swinging his stick in rather a businesslike fashion.

I backed away and felt behind me for the superstructure of the car, ready to jump inside and slam the door in case he became violent.

But he merely stopped a half dozen paces away and regarded me fixedly for a moment. There was rather a tense silence as his eyes slowly shifted to the pips on my sleeve.

Then, showing practically every one of his largish teeth, he smiled. He smiled very contentedly indeed, and even rose up and down on his toes a couple of times and took several appreciative breaths of salubrious sea air.

Then he turned to the adjutant, who was also looking relieved. "You know, Colin," the commandant said, "the world's not such a harsh and unjust place, really."

"No, sir, it isn't. In fact there's a lot to be said for it sometimes."

"There is indeed," the commandant said, and stamped on the cinders gently with his heel, causing his spurs to jingle in a merry way.

He looked so full of the joys of spring I thought it better not to mention that I was taking over the command of a squadron in another four days.

He remained in such an affable mood, in fact, that as the instructors were preparing to take off on the year's first bathing party to Haying Island, he suggested that Katherine might like to go along as well. Or, rather, he hinted that, though carrying civilians was forbidden, he would be far too busy with all the blasted paperwork the Air Ministry was sending him to notice if one of the aircraft was carrying an extra passenger, and even if he did notice he would be bound, he said, to assume it was merely a favored student.

I was surprised and rather impressed by this flexible and very kind gesture. As for Katherine, she was ecstatic. She flung her arms around the commandant's neck and kissed him, to his considerable embarrassment and pleasure, and said that she had wanted to fly ever since 1915, when the R.F.C.'s elementary training machines had first started crash-landing at Burma Park. She asked the commandant if she could go somewhere to put on her bathing suit under her dress so she could go swimming as well, and wondered excitedly if she could borrow a flying helmet and goggles – she didn't in the least care if her hair got disarranged; and she affirmed that the commandant wasn't an old grouch at all, as everybody had said, but a dear old gentleman–

"Grouch? Who said I was a grouch?" the commandant snarled, glaring around ferociously.

Katherine was still smiling all over her face as I buzzed the 504 onto the runway. She showed only the slightest trace of apprehension as the tail lifted and the ground fell down.

We made a gentle, climbing turn over the Member's Bridge, and circled Portsmouth a couple of times in the sunlit air, before banking away toward Hayling Island.

A month later she was still writing letters about the landing on the hard, flat island sand, and the larking and splashing about, and horseplay and laughter; and especially about the return journey with the other aircraft all dancing along in formation: Avros, Camels, and a Brifit; flying at an exhilarating ten feet over the sea; and then zooming and diving on Southsea Pier from several different directions, at ten-second intervals.

As we passed over the pier I shouted to her and pointed down. But she couldn't hear. I was trying to tell her that I could hardly believe it was only four months since Michael Mansergh and I had battled for control of this very same Avro over that very same pavilion. Even the two elderly citizens fishing from the end of the pier seemed to be the same ones who had watched us hurtling straight down on them that day. They looked just as petrified now (if it was them), as the nine aircraft thundered overhead and wheeled inland, where they darted at the common like well-drilled swallows and then skidded away across the harbor mouth.

I was so busy thinking about it all that I made a decidedly poor landing at Fort Grange. Luckily Katherine thought that landings always made you feel as if your spine was sticking out of your bonnet.

The postprandial celebration in the mess that evening was just as joyous. By then, Katherine's unexpectedly irreverent humor had so captivated the pilots I could hardly get near her, they were clustered around so densely. Even the commandant was there, nodding in almost a benign manner.

"You haven't told the old boy you're on your way up again, I gather," Treadwell said as we stood with our backs to the bar, surveying the mob.

"No, and for heaven's sake don't tell him, at least not until after the garden party. Or he'll take the plane back." The commandant had agreed to supply a Camel for the festivities, on condition that I brought it back in one piece.

"I don't think I'll ever tell him," Treadwell said. "Let him retain some illusions, at least."

Potter came up, red-faced and sweating. "Illusions about what?" he asked.

"About you, Potter," Treadwell said. "The commandant thinks you're a wonderful fellow."

Potter nodded and looked at me complacently. "So you're back where you started, eh?" he said. "Never mind, old boy, they'll probably give you back your pip, if the war lasts that long." He laughed to show it was just a joke.

Treadwell looked at Potter as if he'd trod in something, then turned to me. "By the way," he said, "did you see the *Gazette* this morning?"

"No?"

"That chap – Craig, is it?"

I gripped his arm. "What about him?" I asked fearfully. "He's not – he's not . . .?"

"Yes," Treadwell said. "He's been awarded the V.C."

Katherine and I were staying the night in a Portsmouth hotel. The telephone rang at a very awkward moment, as we were experimenting with two stiff-backed chairs and a regimental tie.

"Don't go," Katherine gasped, clinging on still tighter.

"I couldn't – without spraining myself!"

"We mustn't risk that!"

"Let's not answer it."

"It must be important, though. It's one o'clock in the morning."

"Maybe we can sort of heave-ho . . ."

We synchronized an octopuslike movement closer to the telephone. "Heave-ho, me hearties," Katherine gasped, and dissolved into giggles.

It was her father. I heard him say that somebody connected with Home Office wanted to see me next morning at eleven, in London.

"What's it about, Pa?" Katherine panted.

"Seems awfully windy on this line," Mr. Lewis said tinnily. Then: "It's, um, a security matter."

"Oh, gosh," I said, subsiding rapidly, thinking about Ireland.

I *knew* I ought to have pursued that little matter of Michael smuggling guns in a stolen airplane. I just *knew* it.

Wearing a Hunted Look

I wasn't the only one who was having difficulty finding the right address in London that Thursday morning. As I was standing outside a boarded-up shop in a side street off Charing Cross Road, peering at a scrap of paper on which I'd scrawled the directions Mr. Lewis had given me, a plump, sandy-haired man in pince-nez and a black raincoat buttoned up to his Adam's apple approached and asked hesitantly if I knew where the Tabernacle of the Many-Colored Coat was situated. He was the new pastor, he said, from Blackburn, and he'd been looking for the past twenty minutes for the tabernacle, which he understood was in temporary quarters in an old building hereabouts. Somewhere near Charing Cross Road, he said.

I had to admit that I was a stranger here myself, and that in fact I didn't even know where Charing Cross Road was any more.

However, I finally located my destination in a dingy building a few feet away, but I didn't feel the least glad about it as I made my way through the Victorian arched entrance and up two flights of stairs that smelled of marsh gas, mice, and old, stiff mops.

The nerve center of the operation was a small, cluttered room, the floor covered with loose brown lino that tapped mysteriously every time somebody walked across it. There were no windows, but an excess of doors, one of which led to a loft filled with cooing and fluttering noises. The elderly lady who had been working in the outer office on a *fin de siècle* typewriter, and who had introduced herself as Miss Ada Crump, settled me in a stiff chair beside a row of wooden filing cabinets and then disappeared into the loft.

"I'll be with you in two ticks," the chief of the section called out. He had a distinctive sort of figure, being as high and narrow as a drainpipe with a bulge in it: his pot belly, which was exerting a relentless pressure against his primrose waistcoat. Below his strangely ridged bald pate was a sly, equally bony face.

He was busy telling off one of his minions. "Got lost, Mr. Chillington-Blain?" he was saying. "Again? My dear boy, I'm perfectly well aware it's not too easy for a stranger to find his way to this address. That, after all, is the whole point of the exercise. But in case it's escaped your attention, you've been working for us for several weeks now. How can you keep getting lost, Mr. Chillington-Blain? Mr. Herd doesn't get lost.

Miss Crump doesn't lose her way. *I* don't misplace myself. So how is it that *you* keep leading yourself astray?"

"Well, I'm not used to this part of town," whinnied the Honorable Hyphenated (for it was he). "I only know Mayfair and parts of Belgravia."

Boney sighed heavily and shook his head. "I don't know," he said, "why they ever thought an assistant censor would be useful in this line of business. . . . They'll be sending me a botanist, next." He looked disgustedly at the sulky young man. "You're not exactly God's gift to Intelligence, are you? Look at that business in Horse Guards Parade the other day."

"Well, how was I to know he was one of ours?"

"If you could even trail a suspect, that would be something. But no. You start off with a suspicious alien in Hampton Court and end up following an Irish navvy in Lambeth."

"I got confused by the Underground."

"Tchk," Boney said, taking out a large pocket watch and holding it at arm's length to get it into focus. "Yes, well, it's high time we opened for business, don't you think, Mr. Chillington-Blain? The other shopkeepers down there will be getting suspicious if we don't open for business now and then."

"Do I have to serve again, A.1.? I've been serving all month."

"Well, Mr. Herd's busy with his banana," Boney – or A.1. – said; somewhat obscurely, I thought.

"What about Miss Crump?"

"You know very well she has her communications duties," Boney said.

"It's not fair," Chillington-Blain muttered. "Don't see why we need the shop, anyway."

"It's our cover, Mr. Chillington-Blain," Boney explained patiently.

"Yes, but a fish and chip shop? It doesn't seem, well, *dignified*, somehow."

A placid-looking man in an untidy brown suit wandered in at this point, and immediately Boney's remark became slightly less obscure, for he was gripping a banana.

"Certain amount of truth in that, A.1.," the newcomer said. "A spy wearing an apron and serving fish and chips – projects the wrong sort of picture, somehow."

"And another thing," Chillington-Blain said, heartened by this support, "it takes too long getting down there – having to go out into the street and then in again. Why can't we use the secret passage?"

"Because it's blocked with sacks of potatoes, of course," Boney said with a long-suffering look.

"All moldy, by the way," Mr. Herd confided to his chief.

Miss Crump came clattering down from the loft, bearing a piece of cigarette paper like a miniature flag of truce. "Here," she said, offering it to Boney.

"You know very well I'm trying to give up smoking, Miss Crump," Boney said offendedly. "It's not fair to tease me this way."

"It's a message, A.1.," she said. "Just came in by carrier pigeon."

Boney drew an enormous magnifying glass from a drawer and studied the message closely. "Hello, hello, hello," he said. "It's in Russian."

"I didn't know you knew Russian, Chief," Herd said.

"I don't, but all the letters are backwards. Everyone knows the Russians write their letters backwards."

"Surely you're thinking of the Chinese?"

"Not at all," Boney said. "I *never* think of the Chinese – that's Montgomery's department. Anyway," he added, "*they* write their letters from the bottom up. Or am I thinking of the Hebrews?"

Miss Crump reached over and rather rudely reversed the cigarette paper. Boney looked at her with an injured air, then studied the message again through the magnifying glass.

"Well, I couldn't read it properly," he muttered. "Looks as if it's been written with a sharp clothes peg dipped in dried boot polish. . . . Hello, hello, hello. It says we can expect the tour of inspection any time now. Damn, we'll have to sweep the floor."

"The Minister'll probably arrive with a large retinue of toadies and lickspittles," Herd said, nudging aside a mousetrap baited with smoked salmon.

"What about Major Bandy?" Miss Crump asked, jerking her head toward me. I'd been too fascinated to utter a word so far.

"Eh? That's not a major, Miss Crump. Surely you've learned your Army ranks by now."

"I *am* a major, actually," I said. "It's just that my new blue uniform hasn't come yet."

This obviously made perfect sense to Boney. "Ah," he said. "But what's he doing here, Miss Crump?"

"Nothing. He's just sitting there."

"I mean, *why* is he here?" Boney said, sighing heavily in order to get his own back on Miss Crump.

"You asked to see him. S.10."

"S.10. . . . Ah, yes. . . ."

"Haven't I seen you before?" Mr. Chillington-Blain asked.

"Yes," I said. "At Lord Rackingham's. And the Lewises'."

"Oh, yes. I thought I'd seen you before somewhere. I have such a frightful memory for faces, don't you know."

"And names," Herd said.

"And places," Boney said. "Oh, and before you go," he went on pointedly, "to serve your country – nip out and make us all a cup of tea, will you?"

Chillington-Blain went out, slamming the door.

"Well, to business," Boney said, rubbing his hands together briskly. "Miss Crump, bring us the file, will you, there's a dear."

"What file?"

"The appropriate file, of course. The one about which we have called in . . . this chap here."

Miss Crump brought the file and went out again. Mr. Herd sat in the corner and fiddled with his banana. Boney looked through the file, nodding his head wisely as he came to a particularly significant bit.

"I, uh, I guess I should have told you about it before," I said.

"You should, rather," Boney said in gentle reproach.

"I did tell the C-in-C, Ireland, though."

"Eh? What did you tell *him* for?"

"Well, I thought it was the right thing to do. It wasn't my fault if he didn't follow the rag-and-bone cart up."

"Rag-and-bone cart? What would he want to follow a rag-and-bone cart for?"

"Follow it up. To the pub and everything." Then, when Boney continued to look blank: "The one with Adam and Eve. You know."

"Adam and Eve?"

"Well, whoever they were. Maybe they weren't; I couldn't swear to it."

Boney looked at Herd; but Herd was now making notes with a pencil, using his kneecap as an *escritoire*.

Boney started to say something. There was a knock at one of the doors. Miss Crump returned, looking uneasily at the door that had been knocked on.

Boney's eyes were wide. "Do you think it's the Minister?" he whispered.

"We've nothing to be scared of," Herd said, looking up. "We haven't done anything."

"For years," Miss Crump said.

The knock was repeated. Boney sat frozen.

"Look, if we don't let him in to make his inspection," Miss Crump said, "we'll be in trouble. They might post us somewhere useful."

"He's said to be a stickler for tidiness," Boney said. "Personally I don't hold with spit and polish and all that nonsense, and if he expects it, well . . . it's results that count," he added, and looked more worried than ever.

Mr. Herd finally opened the appropriate door. The minister who had accosted me in the street walked in, fiddling nervously with the top button of his black raincoat.

"I'm awfully sorry," he said. "I've been completely lost for the last half hour."

"Are you the Minister, sir?" Herd asked doubtfully after looking up and down the corridor outside.

"Yes, I am. . . . I've come to see our little operation in . . . operation, as it were. I haven't come to the right place, have I, by any chance?"

"Well," Mr. Herd began.

"Just one minute, Mr. Herd, if you please," Boney said firmly. "First we must make quite sure this is the right person. We don't want to get involved in one of those absurd cases of mistaken identity that were so enjoyable in the farce comedies of yesteryear. Now, sir, would you be good enough to tell us exactly who you are?"

"My name's Trevor, if that's what you mean?"

"You're quite sure, are you, sir?"

"Yes. It says so in my birth certificate. Wilfred Roehampton Trevor."

Miss Crump examined the cigarette paper again, frowning.

"And you are the Minister, are you, Minister?"

"Yes. . . . But I don't quite . . ."

"We have to be very careful, you see," Boney said with an espionage-type wink. "We can't afford to make mistakes in our business, eh?"

"I suppose not," the minister said, looking around dazedly. "It's not exactly what I expected. What about the pews . . .?"

"Of course. Do take a pew," Boney said, hurrying to supply the minister with a chair. I tried to catch his eye, but he was busy fluttering around the visitor. "You're by yourself, are you, Minister?"

"Yes. Why?"

"Oh, just that we expected you to arrive with a large pack of toadies and lick – an extensive retinue of officials," Boney said. He clapped his hands together jovially. The minister started, and his glasses slipped off his nose. "Well, now: may I, on behalf of my staff, welcome you to S.M.I.T.(n)," he said, just as Chillington-Blain came in with four cups of tea, and looked annoyed when he saw he had another guest.

"I . . . what?"

Boney clapped his hands together again. "Perhaps I should start by introducing my staff, Minister. This is Miss Ada Crump. Miss Crump is our communications director, is that not so, Miss Crump?"

"If you mean I have to clean up after the pigeons, yes."

Boney chuckled, to cover up what he plainly considered a case of extreme disloyalty. "Such a sense of humor," he said. "Don't know how we'd get on without her.

"But we could soon find out," he said to her in an undertone, as the minister recoiled from the sight of something nasty on top of a filing cabinet. It was either a false beard or a dead rat; it was hard to tell which.

"Next," Boney went on, "there's our Mr. Chillington-Blain. Possibly the name is familiar to you, sir. His father is Admiral Sir Chillington-Blain, K.C.B.O."

"*V.*O.," Chillington-Blain said, glaring.

"And this is Major Bandy. Or Lieutenant Bandy, whichever it is," Boney said. "But he's not with us, of course."

The minister looked at my vacant expression and nodded uneasily.

"And last but not least there's Mr. Roger Herd. Mr. Herd is our Chief Cypher and gadgets wallah. Show him what you're working on at the moment, Mr. Herd, if you please."

Mr. Herd showed the minister his banana. The minister gazed at it warily, licking his lips – though the banana didn't look particularly appetizing to me.

"It's a gun," Mr. Herd said.

"That banana is a gun?"

"Or to put that banana another way, that gun is a banana," Boney said archly. "Be so good as to demonstrate, Mr. Herd."

Roger aimed the banana at the ceiling. There was a bang. Plaster rained down on Boney's pate.

"Very clever, Herd," Boney said coldly.

"Well, you said to demonstrate."

"I didn't mean fire the banana, man! I meant show him the mechanism! Really, Herd. It hasn't occurred to you, I suppose," he went on, pointing at the hole in the ceiling, "that somebody might have been seated at a desk immediately above that hole – or bending over to tie his shoelace? You don't think, Herd. You just don't think."

I tugged at Boney's sleeve. He brushed my hand away.

"And to complete the introductions, Minister," he said, "there's me. I'm A.1."

"I'm glad to hear it," the minister said. "It's more than I am."

"Well, now, sir, what can we show you? Perhaps you'd care to start by looking at our operations."

"He's not looking at *my* operation," Miss Crump whispered to Mr. Herd.

"Is there anything in particular you'd like to see?" Boney asked.

"Well, if I may, I'd like to see your organ," the minister said, looking around confusedly.

"Well, I . . ." Boney smirked modestly. Then: "I beg your pardon?"

The minister looked at him uncertainly. Boney went stiffly to the nearest filing cabinet. I lifted a forefinger to raise a point. Boney ignored it.

"Perhaps we could start by showing you files of cases we've been involved in," he said rather coldly. "I think you'll find these interesting. Matter of fact, some of them make pretty sickening reading." He opened the top drawer. It was empty. "Hello, hello, hello," he said. "Someone has taken them. Still, we've plenty more."

"Listen, A.1.," I said, tugging at him again. "This gentle-man—"

"I just don't understand," the gentleman was saying. "What has all this to do with the tabernacle?"

"Tabernacle?"

"Yes. . . ." The minister gestured around wanly. "What has it to do with the tabernacle?"

"Nothing that I can think of," Boney said, still looking a bit stiff.

"Why a tabernacle?" Herd asked, interested.

"What?"

"I said, why a tabernacle, Minister, rather than say a Moon Worshippers' League, or a Society of Snake Charmers?"

"What?" The minister laid a trembling bunch of fingers on his brow. "I . . . I wonder if you could show me where you hold the service," he said. "Perhaps that will . . ." His words faltered as if he were afraid where they would lead to.

His fears were not ill-founded. "The service?" Boney asked.

"He means in the shop," Chillington-Blain said.

"Oh, yes, of course. We were just going to start the service before you arrived, Minister."

"Yes, I was rather late," the minister said, thinking he was being reproved. "But better late than–"

"Hurry up, then, and start the service," Boney said to Chillington-Blain.

"But surely *I* should," the minister faltered.

"*You* want to serve, Minister?"

"Well, after all . . ."

"Well, all right, if you wish," Boney said doubtfully, handing the minister a greasy apron.

The minister looked at it stupidly. "What's this?" he asked.

"Well, we don't want you getting spattered with fat, do we, sir?"

"Spattered with fat?"

Ada Crump came to the rescue. "The minister may not know about the shop," she said.

"Oh? Haven't you been told about the shop, sir?"

"I don't seem to have been told about anything."

"It's our cover, you see."

"Except it doesn't cover anything," Chillington-Blain said.

Boney looked annoyed. "That's just a temporary situation, sir, because the secret passage is blocked with moldy potatoes."

The minister looked around wildly and began to back toward the door.

"Well, now," Boney said, clapping his hands together noisily and rubbing them. "Is there anything in particular you'd–"

"No!" the minister said quickly. "I've seen enough." He turned and hurried out. There was a crash. He came limping back into the room, followed by a mop and two or three cleaning buckets, which rolled about the room helplessly.

"That's our cleaning cupboard," Boney said. "I didn't think you'd be interested in that, sir."

The minister was now scrabbling at another door. When he saw that it gave onto a flight of wooden stairs spattered with pigeon droppings, he closed the door again. "Oh, God," he said.

"Perhaps I should explain," I said, possibly a shade tardily, but I'd been so enthralled. "I don't think this gentleman is from your ministry at all. I believe this gentleman is really from some nearby tabernacle. In fact I know he is, because I've met him before."

There was silence. Everybody looked at me.

"The Tabernacle of the Many-Colored Goat," I added.

"Many-Colored *Goat?*"

"Or, Coat, is it?"

Boney gave me a look. After a moment he took the minister's unresisting arm and propelled him gently but firmly into the corridor.

"Out the front door, turn left, first right, then first right again," he said. "And don't breathe a word of what you've seen or heard, is that understood?"

"Now," he went on, very coldly, turning to me. "Let's get down to business, Lieutenant, or whatever you are. I understand you're acquainted with this fellow whatshisname. . . ." He looked at the file. "Rodominov."

"Rodominov? Michael, you mean."

"Who?"

"Rodominov?"

"That's what I just said, isn't it? I can't give you any details, of course, but he's suspected of obtaining secret information from the War Office."

"Who is?"

"Rodominov, of course."

WEARING A HUNTED LOOK

"He's suspected of *what?*"

Boney raised his eyes to the hole in the ceiling as if to implore whoever was up there to save him from yet another lummox. "He is sus-pec-ted," he said, breaking it down like a much put-upon kindergarten teacher, "of obtaining highly confident-shal information."

"*Rodominov* is? How?"

"Through the wife of one of the officers there." He flipped through the file again. "A Major Auchinflint."

I gaped at Boney.

"I can't tell you what the information is, as I said," Boney went on, "but–"

"Armed intervention in Russia?"

"What's that? How did you know that?"

"I . . . just happened to hear about it at the . . . the War Office. . . ."

"I see."

"But what on earth would Rodominov want with that information?"

"What d'you think he'd want with it," Boney said sharply. "For the Bolsheviks, of course."

"The Bolsheviks? But he hates them."

"I don't know anything about that. All I know is he works for them." He looked at me. "Weren't you aware," he asked, "that Rodominov is a Bolshevik agent?"

At the Garden Party

By May 4, the day of the garden party, the sky was still cloud-less and a glorious sun burned down on Berkshire's brilliant greens. The morale of the civilian population shot up like the mercury. Even the darkest pessimists (two little old ladies over at Pye Cottage), who only a week before had been whispering that perhaps the Allies might not win the war after all, were now acknowledging that Ludendorff mightn't really have achieved very much in spite of, or perhaps because of, his superb planning in the field.

"We British may be lazy, stubborn, hidebound, arrogant, and hypocritical," Mrs. Lewis thundered, "but, by George! at least we're not *efficient*."

Everybody pretended they had never doubted for an instant that the might of Great Britain would ultimately prevail, or that she would continue to run the rest of the world in a gentle-manly fashion, under the exclusive patronage of God (who was obviously long overdue for a knighthood for His services to the British Empire), with a token gesture of support from the United States, which was still, after all, a basically decent member of the family, even if it had kicked over the traces back there in 1876, or whenever it was. (The fact that the Americans had revolted over the question of *tea* was seen as evidence that their sense of values was basically sound and British.)

At two o'clock that feverish afternoon, the first guests started to arrive on foot and in ponies and traps, horses, carriages, horseless carriages, and taxicabs, to be greeted by a splendidly gaudy scene of pennants fluttering and striped canvas bellying on the sward in front of the white Georgian mansion. Whatever she might say, Mrs. Lewis' organization was exceedingly good when it came to frivolity: orange, mauve, light-blue, and red-and-yellow-striped tents blazed on the grass in artful disarray, and everything functioned: booths and side shows, food booths, lemonade stalls for the children, a Gypsy fortuneteller's caravan, a champagne tent for the toffs and a beer tent for the lower classes. There was even a band from a local motorworks, cleverly disposed on the front steps so as to prevent the gentry from entering the house and pinching the silver.

As soon as the crowd reached a density to justify their labors, the brass band struck up a marching tune, "Major Bogey" (he hadn't yet been promoted). The sound echoed and re-echoed off the walls and rolled jauntily across the vast lawn.

I was feeling as cheerful and optimistic as everybody else that glorious sunny Saturday afternoon. A few hours before, I'd received a letter from Craig. I'd already read it three times.

> Dear Major Bandy (General Bandy? Corporal?): I trust this will find you at that pukka address in Berkshire, before you are fed once more into the martial mincing machine, to emerge, no doubt, as a sausage of an entirely different composition.
>
> Where will you go next, I wonder. The Navy? As a matter of fact I can quite easily visualise you as a ship's officer, pacing up and down the crow's nest, calling out, "Hoist that petard" and "Belay that bollard," as the ship slowly sails into the jetty, and you step ashore through the wreckage to claim the salvage money.
>
> Finding out about you was like a piece of criminal detective work. When you came back that morning from H.Q. and said it looked as if the Air Force was taking you back, and then you hastened off, sneezing, to Hesdin, I didn't think much more about it, though we were all sorry to see you go. Until I got word about the V.C.

It was immediately obvious why I'd been awarded it. G.H.Q. had been looking around for a hero, to demonstrate to the home front that the Army was still batting, even though the wickets were down and the club house was on fire; and had decided to make an example of me. Nevertheless I wanted to talk to you about it, and sort of apologise for the fact that I was being singled-out for this award when it rightly belonged to everyone in the Company, not least to you. So I telephoned R.A.F. headquarters, but they said you were on leave. I did learn, though, from a young officer there, that you were being given command of a squadron when you returned to France.

That was all he knew, but it certainly made us all think. So the first opportunity I got, I went to see that chap Wordsworth we met in the bar that evening, the one who'd been looking at you in such a puzzled way. I had a hell of a job finding his squadron. In fact it took several days, and I arrived just too late. He had been shot down only the day before. (Don't worry, they said he made a good landing, though behind enemy lines.) They invited me to stay for dinner in the mess, and there I learned that you had been one of the big Hun-getters of '17.

This was a considerable surprise to me, as you can imagine, but there was worse to come, when a young lad who'd just arrived from Blighty said suddenly, "I read about a Bandy in England – but he was a colonel at the Air Ministry. Couldn't have been him, could it?"

"No," I said. "Utterly impossible. No, there's not the slightest chance it's the same man." "This colonel got himself involved in an awful scandal," the young lieutenant said. "That's him," I said. "That's Bandy, all right." And believe it or not – it was.

Finally I looked up Nat Hilcheson to see if he could get hold of a report of your speech. I'm afraid I was rather disappointed in it, my dear Bart. Because of the unusual coverage it had apparently received (were there political overtones?), I'd come to expect an oration of epic proportions. What I read sounded more like the 'So are they all, all honorable men' speech from Julius Caesar, as it might have been rendered by Charley's Aunt. Nor did I hear myself cheering at your wild swings at D. Haig. From what I know of him he's a man of unfortunately small eloquence but a competent general who has relied too heavily on some atrociously bad advisors. And just who could replace him?

Still, I suppose you genuinely believed all that tosh, and it must have required a good deal of courage (though we all know you have plenty of that) to go against the civvies' hero-worship of the generals, and it explained an awful lot about you that had puzzled us all, particularly your expression of injured guilt.

Anyway, it all makes me feel a lot better about the award, and I shall now wear it with only a slightly stricken conscience. After all, I understand you already have your fair share of medals. I have managed to convince myself that you are sufficiently satisfied with your reinstatement as a pilot, special leave, promotion, flying pay and the somewhat bemused admiration and affection of your former comrade in the Bicycle Battalion.

Incidentally, Leo (who will never be the same again, after learning that we'd been harbouring a refugee brasshat) pointed out to me soon after you joined us that you had perforations in your collar which suggested you'd once worn tabs; but I pooh-poohed the idea, saying it was probably just the moths that had been at you. That's all, my very dear Bart. Maybe if I'm spared (this war looks like going on until 1930), I'll drop in at your squadron one of these days for one of our brilliant exchanges of utter nonsense. In the meantime,

Vale!

Bob Craig

"I'd no idea it was to be as elaborate as this," I said to Treadwell as we gazed around at the brilliant tents and throngs of people. "Isn't it wonderful?"

"Don't get too carried away with your aerial display, Bart," he said. "We don't want you cracking up."

I looked at him misty-eyed, thinking what a grand friend he was, to be so concerned about my safety, until he added, "I'm not having my plane smashed to pieces. It's got a brand-new Bentley engine, and it's just been rerigged."

The runway for the aerial display had been marked out with red flags three hundred yards in front of the house. To protect it from souvenir hunters, the Sopwith Camel that Treadwell had flown over the previous evening had been hidden in the stables at the back of the house.

This was perhaps just as well, as Claud had turned up. I'd caught a glimpse of him with his mother a few minutes previously, dressed in a navy blazer, white shirt, and a necktie in those dreaded school colors of his.

Well, at least his father wasn't here; that was something.

A croquet lawn had also been laid out, a group of morris dancers laid on, and a maypole erected, before somebody realized it was in the middle of the runway.

People continued to stream into The Park from all points of the compass; or, to be precise, from one point of the compass, 262 magnetic, along a tree-lined avenue, this being the only direction from which The Park could be approached.

By three pip emma the grounds were littered with fox hunters, vicars, absentee landowners, merry widows, and other ladies and gentlemen, and pilots. Several of the instructors from Gosport had come by train with their wives or girlfriends. Robert, too, had brought a small contingent from his Home Defence squadron.

The moment his lot arrived, they made straight for a twitter of nurses who were at one of the side shows, looking daintily helpless as they rolled pennies down little wooden chutes and cleaned out the stall of all the best prizes.

"Where do we buy tickets?" a worried-looking lady kept asking.

"There're no tickets," Mr. Lewis explained.

"But what's the garden party for? I mean, it must be *for* something. Charity, is it?"

"It was supposed to be a postwedding celebration," Mr. Lewis said, "but in the circumstances, Bartholomew being rather *persona non grata* at the moment, we thought it best just to, to celebrate spring and . . . being alive," he ended lamely.

"But we can't just *enjoy* ourselves," the lady said anxiously as a platoon of boys and girls in velvet and lace infiltrated past, licking and sucking noisily at free Mintoes, pear drops, aniseed lumps, sherbet, and licorice sticks, jelly babies, and striped brandy balls.

To complete my delight in the occasion, my new R.A.F. mess uniform had arrived, and I was wearing it, even though I wasn't in a mess. It was of a distinctly distinctive cut, with a gorgeous flying badge in gold embroidery, which set off the medal ribbons very becomingly, and had tons of gold braid on the cap, and yards of gold lace rings on each sleeve. And it was a brilliant, blinding sky blue.

When the Lewises had first caught sight of it they had slowly backed into the nearest alcove as one man, shielding their eyes and emitting faint cries of wonderment at the sheer splendor of it all. They hadn't been able to speak coherently for some time, but I could tell they were terrifically impressed; though when they recovered they had asked whether I was jockeying for position as understudy in a touring version of *Maid of the Mountains* or was I merely promoting the recent cinema success *Memories That Haunt?*

But of course they were just making sure I didn't get a swelled head, that's all.

So I strolled around the grounds to give everybody an equal opportunity to admire the new design. As I emerged from a crowd of farmers and their wives and daughters, nodding at them regally, a group of Air Force officers and pretty girls turned around.

"Good – *God!*"

Milestone was among them, gaping in paralyzed homage. He was standing between Katherine and his latest catch, a capable-looking girl in a flowery dress and freckles.

The rest of them gathered around, goggling. "You were right, Kath," Jolley said. "He *has* turned up as a Siamese admiral."

"It's the new R.A.F. uniform," I said.

"If I have to wear that, I'm transferring right back to the War Graves Commission," Captain Cole said. "It's absolutely . . ." He stopped, swallowing convulsively.

"It is, isn't it?" I said proudly, flicking a speck of dust off my gold rings.

Everybody laughed as Milestone slowly felt his way out of the circle and, leaning heavily on his girlfriend, weaved blindly toward the nearest champagne tent.

Katherine smiled at me and took my arm. She was looking pretty fashionable herself. She was wearing a white frock with blue spots, and an old cartwheel hat of her mother's to which she had added an orange ribbon salvaged from a recent live-stock contest.

The shortness of the frock, almost up to her knees, had already drawn a few clucks from some of the older ladies, and slavering stares from some of the more mature schoolboys.

As for me, I took one look and very nearly suggested we nip upstairs for a quick nibble.

This new sex-consciousness of mine was very disturbing, though. Ever since that blasted honeymoon I hadn't been able to take my mind off it, as if something was compelling me to make up in a few days for what I had been denied during a decade of puberty.

Mrs. Cary noticed the change straight away.

"Marriage seems to have done something for you," she said, half listening to the band and lazily twirling a parasol over her gleaming blonde head. "There's a positively inspired light in your eye. The left one, I think."

"It's because you're such an inspiring sight, Angela, my dear," I said in a smooth voice and ogling her mammaries.

She looked at me coolly from under the parasol. "Yes, you have changed," she murmured, but in that distant way women use when they've lost interest in you.

"By the way," she added with a distinctly malicious smile, "have you met General Pusey? Marmaduke, darling?"

A major-general, who had been waving his stick at the band in time to the music but not very accurately, came up and smiled soppily at her. He had a G.H.Q. sort of mustache that almost completely concealed his lips. His voice was thin, presumably on account of being strained through all those nicotine strands.

"Bartholomew, this is General Pusey. General Pusey, Colonel – no, Major, now, isn't it? – Major Bartholomew Bandy."

Pusey tapped the top of his boots with his stick and nodded toward me without taking his eyes off Mrs. Cary. She slipped her arm through his and pressed his arm against her exciting left breast (the other was just as exciting, of course) and glanced at me triumphantly as if to say, "See what you've missed, you fool?"

"*Bandy?*"

I started and looked at the general.

"Bandy, did you say?"

"Yes, sir, how d'you do, sir?" I whined, folding myself slightly at the waist in an effort to look smaller than him and pasting a groveling smile into place.

It didn't do a bit of good. His face turned as chilly as a witch's tit. After a baleful moment he turned his back, tightening his grip on Mrs. Cary's forearm, and drew her away. "Delightful music, isn't it, my dear," he said loudly. "I have a particular fondness of the tuba, don't you know. Oompah, oompah, what? Ha, ha."

He chuckled richly. Mrs. Cary's laugh tinkled back.

I glared at his departing back. "Oompah, oompah yourself," I said, but not too loudly.

Turning, I saw Claud grinning at me.

I'd had the impression he'd been working his way toward me for the past twenty minutes. As I caught his eye, he stopped smiling and looked down at the driveway. He shuffled his feet in the gravel.

When he glanced up again, red-faced, he looked almost timid. Timid? Claud?

"It's a jolly good garden party, isn't it, sir?" he said.

"Yes," I replied, reaching defensively for my pistol before remembering I wasn't wearing it.

"That's a ripping uniform, sir," he went on.

"Ta."

"We're on hols just now because of the flu epidemic," he said. "Matron was the first to get it."

"That's nice," I said warily.

"The mater took me to see *Chu-Chin-Chow* last night."

"It's still on, is it?"

"Yes, sir. It's a jolly good musical comedy, isn't it? I really enjoyed the part where they tortured that chap." He hesitated; then: "I'm looking forward to your aerial display, sir, very much."

I looked at him, wondering if I ought to cancel the display right away, before the wings fell off. Claud twisted about a bit and looked sideways at a flower bed. I wondered if he was thinking of peeing on it.

"I'm sorry I did that," he mumbled.

"What?"

"Stuck the magnet in your plane. . . . I thought . . ." His words faded, then strengthened again. "I thought you were just another . . . you know. Hot-air merchant . . . ."

I looked at him carefully, considered kicking his teeth out, then said, "It's all right. No harm done."

"Is it really? Is it really all right, sir?"

"Sure."

He stuck out his hand, not too hopefully. He flushed scarlet when I shook it.

I patted him on the back. "Come and watch the morris dancers," I said.

The morris dancers were prancing about sadly by the croquet lawn: six glum-looking chaps in Robin Hood outfits and white puttees, accompanied by an accordion and a fiddle. I thought they were all suffering from bad colds, but then saw that the hankies they were clutching were part of their act.

There was enthusiastic applause from a group of frock-coated gentlemen and their ladies, as the dancers completed some dull but intricate footwork. Treadwell was watching from the far side. I studied his face appreciatively. He was staring at the rustic capering with such an incredulous expression that I started to snuffle and snort, and had to move away when some of the ladies turned and frowned.

Not the least put out by Pusey's snub, I continued to stroll contentedly through the grounds, stopping to chat now and then to whomever was prepared to overlook my recent conduct. Claud followed closely, acting as if I were some feudal squire to whom he had been indentured for life.

I didn't really understand what had caused his change of attitude; unless it was because I finally had a uniform that fitted. Maybe that was it.

"I say, shall we have our fortunes told?" he suggested as we passed the Gypsy caravan. Several ladies were queuing up outside it, giggling and gossiping.

"I'd rather not know," I said. "It's bound to be upsetting."

"What'll we do, then, sir?"

"Why don't you play with *them?*" I suggested, as a crowd of children pelted past, yelling and kicking each other.

"They're *bugs*," Claud said. "*I'm* nearly thirteen."

"Oh, sorry. Let's go have some champagne, then."

In the champagne tent a pair of young ladies were peeking hungrily under the damp cloth at the sandwiches, pies, and other goodies heaped on the trestle table. As she leaned over, one of them exhibited a very pretty bosom. She caught my frozen stare and straightened, tittering at her companion; and thereafter cast me several coy glances that soon had my nostrils dilated something adulterous.

Her breasts had been gleaming slightly with perspiration. As was my brow. At this rate I'd never be able to hold out in France. Good Lord, I was turning into a satyr.

I hurriedly gulped another glass of champers. Nearby, a farmer with a rough, red face was holding his glass as if afraid it would break in his hands.

"So this be bubbly, be it, sir?" he said.

"I guess so."

"Very noice, very noice indeed. Though personally oi'd raather 'ave a point of the old moild."

"Yes, it does seem kind of weak. Let's have another and see if that helps."

"Grand oidea, sir. After all, it be free. And at least 'tis better than my woif's tonic that she takes regular for her kidneys. You're from Somerset, oi take it, sir?"

"Canada. This be a Canadian accent, it be," oi said; then made a face. I really must get out of this habit of adopting other people's accents.

"Ar. Oi've heard of it. Very cold it is, oi hear," he said. He nodded several times, gravely. Then: "The North West Mounted Police."

"Oh?"

"Ar. Chasing people all over the countrysoid on snowshoes they do, before foinally getting their man. Isn't that roight, sir?"

"Yes. Mind you, it gets pretty hot in summer where I come from. The temperature goes up to a hundred."

"Is that roight, sir?" The farmer stared into his glass for a moment, considering this. "But wouldn't that melt all the oice and snow, then?"

"Uh, yes, it would, that's true."

The farmer frowned, obviously unable to reconcile my words with his mental imagery.

"Ar. Well, there you are, sir," he said, as if something had been settled, possibly the fact that I was an unmitigated liar.

Claud tugged at my sleeve. "Let's try some of the sideshows," he said impatiently.

On our way out I nearly collided with Major Auchinflint. He stiffened at the sight of my uniform, threw a magnificent salute, then flushed. "Oh, it's you," he said.

"Yes. Grand day, isn't it, Major?"

"Have you seen my wife?" he asked, glancing into the tent.

"I saw her watching the croquet players about half an hour ago."

He stared haggardly at a chocolate wrapper on the bright green grass. I wondered if he knew.

Then I was sure, when he looked up with glaring, red-rimmed eyes and said thickly, "Have you seen that Russian?"

"Rodominov, you mean?"

"Yes, Master Rodominov."

"No. . . . I don't think he's been invited."

"He's a friend of yours, isn't he?"

Auchinflint looked so fiendish I had an impulse to deny ever having met Rodominov. Luckily he didn't wait for an answer. "Did you know about him?" he asked, staring at me fixedly.

Not knowing whether he was referring to the prince's affair with Mrs. Auchinflint or his activities as a Bolshevik sympathizer, I gazed sincerely over Auchinflint's beaky head and said, "Um, know about him?"

"Don't play around with me, Bandy," he said, his voice trembling. "I'm damn sure you know. Just like everybody else. Angela Cary has seen to that. About their . . . their assignations." His voice was shaking uncontrollably. Claud, who was still mooning about, shuffled closer, his head cocked.

"You don't want to believe everything you hear, Major," I murmured, looking around embarrassedly.

"I believe my wife."

"You do?"

"She admitted it herself. Yesterday. She told me everything."

Good Lord, I thought. Mrs. Auchinflint seemed to have a compulsion to spill the beans.

But what iron self-control the woman had. She'd been around Burma Park all morning, but not by a word or change of expression had she hinted that her affairs had reached a crisis.

"Well, she'll pay for it, I can assure you," Auchinflint said violently. "I told her last night why Rodominov was making up to her. That all he'd ever wanted was the – some information, War Office information. Which she gave him, incidentally. *Which she gave him.*

"I told her he was nothing but a dirty little spy. And she was nothing but an accomplice. Oh, yes, I told her. I said, did she think he was merely interested in her? A scrawny, wrinkled bitch like her? I told her Rodominov had just been *pimping.*"

Other people besides Claud were beginning to edge closer. "Steady on," I murmured.

But Auchinflint didn't seem to care that he was creating a scene. "She just kept on saying over and over that he loved her," he said, his prominent ostrichlike beak slashing the air to ribbons. He laughed harshly. "Her? A good ten years older than him? Don't make me laugh, I told her."

"Let's go inside for a drink," I said, touching his arm.

He shook his arm violently, glaring redly at a guy rope, his eyes moving up and down it feverishly from the peg to the tent fringe, then down to the peg again, as if his eye had caught on it like a motorcar wheel in a tram track.

I could visualize the scene quite vividly. The major, mercilessly underscoring the fact that his wife had been used, and Mrs. Auchinflint, with bright red spots on her cheeks and wide, stricken eyes in a thin, ascetic face, trying to convince herself out loud that it was love that had brought Rodominov to her.

Or had Rodominov shown too much interest in the confidential papers that, according to Boney, Auchinflint had been in the habit of bringing home from the War House? Had she, as a result, suspected the true state of affairs? Had she been trying to goad me that time, after the fox hunt, into snitching on her in an attempt to resolve an intolerable situation? Or had I been reading too many novels?

Without waiting for me to finish thinking, Auchinflint fixed me with a quivering look. "You have some part in this, I'm sure," he said.

"Me?" I said, widening my eyes.

"I don't like you, Bandy," he said. "I didn't like you the moment I clapped eyes on you. And I still don't like you."

Gad, I thought. I'd never have known.

"And don't think because you've managed to weasel your way into the Lewis family you'll be any more acceptable in our crowd. Don't think that for a moment."

"That's a relief," I said.

Well, I'd been restrained and civilized while he was mauling somebody else's reputation, but it was different now he was turning on me.

He flushed an even deeper red and clutched his breeches, his knuckles whitening. He brought his sharp nose dangerously close. "Don't think I don't see through you, Bandy. You have no sense of decency or honor whatsoever. You're a *bounder*, sir."

I thought this was the worst word in his vocabulary of abuse. But no: there was worse to come.

"You're not a gentleman," he said. "And you never will be."

Before I had a chance to tell him my seconds would see him in the morning (while I was in bed), he whirled and marched off through a small crowd of eavesdroppers – fan-fluttering ladies, starry-eyed little girls, and Sunday-bested tenants – who were all looking thrilled to bits with this jolly good argument that Mrs. Lewis had laid on as part of the entertainment.

I slunk off, trying to pretend I didn't care in the least that I wasn't a gentleman. Everybody looked away, as if I'd been caught at a Royal Command Performance with snot on my face. Even Claud had abandoned his role of body servant and had disappeared into the canvas countryside.

I started muttering to myself in *au pied de l'escalier* style as soon as I was clear of the crowd. I heard myself delivering such rejoinders as, "Look who's talking," and "Same to you with knobs on," and similar skillful ripostes. Soon I was thoroughly horsewhipping him around Mrs. Lewis' rose garden, with shrill cries of "Take that, you cad!" Finally I cornered him in the forecourt of Buckingham Palace and ran him through with a mace. Or was it a halberd?

Anyway, whatever I was running him though with, there was a lovely lot of blood.

All the same, it was rather undermining to be snubbed and told off twice in one hour. When I met Katherine a few minutes later she said right away, "What's the matter?"

"Oh . . . Auchinflint seems to be blaming me for his wife's affairs, or something."

I'd told her all about Rodominov on Thursday as soon as I'd felt my way home from S.M.I.T.(n).

"Never mind, darling," she said, squeezing my arm. "N.C.I."

She was right. Nobody was going to grind me down. "All the same," I muttered, as "Land of Hope and Glory" banged and echoed off the dazzling white walls of the house so that it sounded as if three motor-works bands were oompahing simultaneously, "who does he think he is? Him and his kind in their first-class compartments – looking at the rest of us as if we belonged in steerage, or the bilge. When I think of all those eager kids just out of school they've thrown away, and the cotton-mill workers and underpaid clerks – all the posterity they've killed off in the name of posterity, without having the slightest understanding of what they've done – or even how they've done it . . ."

"What on earth are you talking about, sweetie pie? What's that got to do with his wife's love affairs?"

I mumbled something, then caught her eye, and couldn't help smiling.

Soon my face started to dissolve into splinters and porridge.

"No," Katherine said quickly. "We can't leave the garden party. Besides, you're giving your display in an hour."

"Gosh, is it nearly four already?" I said, taking a deep breath and looking blindly into the sky. "Yes, so it is. Well, guess I'd better start warming it up."

"I told you, darling, we–"

"I mean, running up the engine."

"Oh, Bart. I do love you, though."

"Me, too."

"I know – let's have our palms read."

I looked doubtfully at the Gypsy caravan. A girl, flushed and bright-eyed, was just emerging from the caravan. There was nobody waiting.

"Come on. It'll be fun."

We lowered our heads and fumbled our way into the caravan, blinking self-consciously in the semidarkness. All the windows were covered except for a small opening at the back.

The Gypsy was seated at a fancy table, gazing morosely at her crystal ball as if she'd finally read her own fortune and it wasn't as promising as she'd hoped.

However, she brightened as the two new customers stumbled in, banging their knees. She was a lumpy soul in a blackout curtain and a scarlet silk robe, her head wrapped in a yellow cloth covered in cabalistic signs of some sort. Scores of bangles jangled at her cork-colored wrists, and two rings that looked suspiciously like brass curtain runners hung from her shell-like ears. Her large, brown face was not unattractive, as far as one could make out in the gloom.

"Cross me palm with silver," she screeched.

I waited for Katherine to pay up, but she had no money. Reluctantly I handed over a half crown, which the Gypsy promptly seized and bit with an unpleasant crunching sound.

"Thank you, kind sir," she cackled, picking a flake of enamel off her tongue with one hand and depositing the coin in some noxious recess of her person with the other.

As soon as we'd settled ourselves in the chairs facing her, she grabbed Katherine's hand, uncoiled it as if searching for more silver, and peered closely at the tram lines. "You name," she hollered, "is . . . let me see . . ."

"Katherine," Katherine said helpfully.

"Don't tell me. You name is – Katherine!"

"That's right," Katherine said, digging her nails into my wrist.

"You are . . . twenty-three. Your mother was over forty when she gave birth to you," the Gypsy went on in her awful voice. She was also breathing rather noisily in the stifling and not particularly salubrious air of the caravan. "You were alone most of your childhood. . . . You loved a young man who was killed in the war. You are now," the Gypsy said, glancing distastefully at me, "as happy as can be expected, me pretty."

"Everyone knows all that stuff," Katherine said, twitching as the Gypsy ran her finger along one of the lines in her palm.

"You will meet a tall, dark, handsome stranger," the Gypsy said.

"She already has," I said with a smirk.

"Oh, then you should have brought him along, my dear," the Gypsy cackled. "I could have read *his* palm, as well."

She paused to dab the perspiration from her temple with a foul-looking bandanna.

"Will I have any children?" Katherine asked, trying to keep her face straight.

"Let me see, my pretty, let me see. Yes, I see fourteen or fifteen of them in several colors. You're either going to be a schoolteacher, or your husband doesn't know how to restrain himself, the dirty swine. You will soon be going on a long journey – to Basingstoke. Let me see, what else. . . . Yes, you have a mole on your hip in the shape of a mouse. . . . You will live to be a hundred and three if you don't meet your maker before then. . . . Your lucky number is 17,458, and your favorite color is false-teeth pink. But beware, my dear. Beware of–"

"The bull?" I suggested.

"Beware of a greengrocer with cauliflower ears and several teeth missing. He will have much to answer for–"

"Sounds as if he already has," Katherine said. "Is that all I get for my half crown?"

"*My* half crown," I said.

The Gypsy looked offended; but then brightened as she turned her attention to the crystal ball. "As for the lovely gentleman," she shrilled, "he is from a land across the sea. He is from . . . Turkey."

"Turkey?"

"He is a Kurd. I see him very plainly in my crystal ball–"

"You can tell by the outraged expression on his fez?" Katherine asked.

At which the stupid Gypsy cackled excessively. "I see he has recently made a long journey," she said at length. "He is in a flying machine. . . . I see him flying away from a reform school. . . ."

"Not bad," I said. "Fallow."

"And you are flying to – Portsmouth. But wait. . . . No, you must concentrate, dearie, I can't quite make out . . . yes. You are going the wrong way. I see you swooping down to . . . an emerald island. . . ."

Katherine and I looked at each other.

"Now you are riding in a rag-and-bone cart. . . . I see you now talking to a man – a military man with rows of out-of-date ribbons and bulging eyes. . . . You are speaking. . . . You are saying there are guns as well as rags and bones in the cart. . . . But strangely, nothing is happening. . . . It is very strange, but nothing else is happening. . . ."

Katherine felt for my hand. "Michael?" she said.

Michael folded back his headdress and sighed. There was a pink streak from his right temple, where the sweat had run.

He cleared his throat several times. "Me poor ould t'roat is achin' loik an infantryman's foot," he said in a dreadful, stage accent. "Hello, Katherine me darling. You're looking more beautiful than ever. Old horse-face there seems to be good for you, for some inexplicable reason."

"Michael. . . . What in God's name are you doing here?"

"I had to find out why there was never any action taken against us," Michael said. "Every time I've flown since, I've wondered if I was going into some elaborate trap. It's hard on the nerves, Bart. I just had to find out what was happening."

He brought out an Army pistol from the folds of his dress and pointed it at me. "I thought you'd never come to have your fortune told," he said.

That's Me at the End

When we came out of the caravan twenty minutes later, we saw Robert Lewis and Treadwell talking nearby to a couple of Army officers. Or, rather, the four of them were interrupting a profound silence now and then with a smile or remark or other brief response such as, "Ha," "Hm," "Quite," or "Rather." The infantry officers were obviously as little disposed to social banter as the two pilots.

As if Katherine and I were out on a field trip and had had our attention drawn to some intriguing aspect of nature, we both stopped at the same time, to contemplate the hesitant quartet: Robert, staring into a pint glass of beer, swishing it around gently; Treadwell, slightly bent over, gazing at his brilliantly polished boots, lips pursed; the Army captain, nodding at something Robert had said twenty minutes ago, looking through half-closed eyes at the blue sky; the slender second lieutenant, hardly out of school but already looking mature and resigned. All standing in that motionless, accepting way of the experienced warrior, all remarkably alike in their simplicity and honesty, as well as their reticence.

I looked at those four men, fighting the war unreservedly, because there was nothing else to do, and thought about them, and about all the other privates and sergeants and subalterns, putting up with the misery and suffering without complaint, doing what they did not because they hated the enemy but so as not to let themselves or their families down. And I was suddenly overwhelmed with feelings of love and sadness, and something like shame when I thought of myself strutting and smirking through the conflict like some tedious Shakespearian porter or gravedigger.

However, there was no point in adding self-condemnation to
my other vices. One could only try to do better. I took a deep
breath and Katherine's arm, and sauntered up to the four officers, looking insouciant, as if I were as good as them any day.

Treadwell treated us to one of his dark, disgusted looks, as
if we'd just announced our intention to take up morris dancing.

I wondered what he'd have said if he'd known that Michael
Mansergh was alive and kicking, and only ten feet away, dressed
up as a bangled, burnt-corked, Romany soothsayer.

"You'll be careful not to overrev the engine, won't you?"
he said.

"All right," I said, possibly sounding a trifle subdued.

Treadwell looked at me anxiously. Robert, meanwhile, was
studying his sister from under his eyebrows.

"Anything wrong?" he asked abruptly.

"No . . . no," she said. Katherine adored her brother and
normally confided in him. But she knew he had conventional
ideas about duty and loyalty and stuff, so she had told him
nothing about Michael. "No," she repeated. "Just that Bart
nearly had his fortune told."

"Yes, that would turn anyone pale."

Katherine and I continued on, whispering conspiratorially.
Michael had told us little about his recent activities, except
that he had crashed the Avro a week or so ago in the Welsh
foothills and was now looking around for alternative transport.

"If you take another plane, this time I will tell all," I'd said.
"I mean it, Michael."

"It's all right, me boyo. The airplane was beginning to
attract too much attention anyway. I had a party of Royal Irish
Constabulary snooping round my landing field in County
Meath only a few days ago. Luckily they didn't find anything
incriminating, except Charlie MacCurtains' underwear."

"Don't think I approve of all this," Katherine said. "I think it's awful."

Michael tried to take her hand, but she drew it away. "Try and see it from our point of view as well," he said quietly. "The last thing I want to do is shoot, but if we don't gain our freedom soon, we never will."

"England's misfortune is Ireland's opportunity," Katherine said cuttingly.

"Whatever happens," Michael said in his fancy dress and burnt-cork face, putting away his revolver, "remember that I love you both."

Katherine and I continued on to the refreshment tent, both of us suddenly feeling hungry. But everything had been gobbled up. There wasn't a sausage left.

We looked doubtfully at the punch in its five-gallon earthenware jar. Katherine picked out one of the bright-red slices of orange and nibbled at it.

"Well, at least there's plenty of punch left," I said.

"Mother will be forcing it on us for the next four months."

"So long as it's finished by the time I get back on leave."

"Oh, Bart. I don't know what I'll do without you. Don't look at me like that. You make me feel all collywobbly."

"Katherine. I just want to say . . ."

"What?" she asked guardedly, as if expecting an insult.

"I love you more and more every day."

"You certainly do," she said.

We looked at each other. Her face slowly relaxed.

"All right," she said shakily. "Come on."

The brass band was slaking its thirst around the beer stand as we approached the front steps. We tiptoed through the gleaming brass instruments and hurried inside.

Milestone was just reeling downstairs, holding onto the

freckled lass in the long, flowery dress. He turned an accusing eye approximately in my direction.

"Listen, Bandy," he said. "Listen. You'n . . . you'n no condition to fly, you drunken birdman. Look at you, weaving about like that, dishguised as El Gorblimez, the Bolivian dictator." He hiccuped and passed a drunken tongue over his dry lips. A stern expression marched onto his face. He straightened and said in tones of command, "Better let me take up the plane for you. Right?! Right. That's settled, then." He put out his foot to march off to the airplane, and fell down the last three steps.

"Can you manage?" Katherine asked the girl.

"Oh, yes. I'm used to bringing my brothers home," she said. Kneeling, she let Milestone slump over her shoulder, then secured him in fireman's-lift fashion and headed confidently for the door.

"Useful girl, that," I said as we scuttled guiltily along the upstairs corridor to our room.

"Half the county saw us sneaking inside," Katherine whispered, her face flushed, her hand trembling in mine. "Well, I don't care."

"Shhh."

"Well, I don't."

"No, I mean, shhh," I whispered, indicating the room next to ours.

The door was open a few inches. From inside came the murmur of voices. As we halted, the murmuring ceased; then started up again.

"He's quite prepared to go on as if nothing has happened. I couldn't bear that."

"Hoots, is impossible. My country is in chaos."

"I don't care, so long as I'm with you. Rody, take me with you."

Katherine and I looked at each other.

"You don't understand. Is impossible. Already there is civil war. There is fighting."

"I don't care."

Katherine pushed open the door. Mrs. Auchinflint and Rodominov sprang apart. She looked a wreck, with ravaged face and hair hanging over her eyes. Rodominov was flushed, his eyes unnaturally bright. He was clutching a handkerchief. Spots of blood showed between two of his fingers.

I had a feeling that he hadn't much further to go.

"You must be mad," Katherine whispered. "Don't you know they're looking for you, Rody? What're you doing here, anyway?"

"I had urgent message from Edit'," Rodominov said. "She said was wery important."

"I didn't," Mrs. Auchinflint said distractedly. "I told you I didn't."

"I have to go now, Edit'. I have passage on a sheep. Is going to Italye."

"Don't tell us, for heaven's sake!" Katherine exclaimed. "We don't want to know."

"I trust you."

"You fool!"

Mrs. Auchinflint turned away to tidy her hair at the dressing-table mirror. When she turned to face us again, she looked as if they had merely been discussing the weather.

"I suppose it is ridiculous, thinking you really wanted me," she said. "I mean, look at me." She laughed.

Rodominov shrugged. "You want to get away. I understand," he muttered, looking around feverishly. "But if Allies inwade Russia . . . is already half destroyed by war. There will be looting, rape, for years, years. There will be famine, cold you have never dreamed, disease. You will be lucky to have blanket for your bed, roof over head. You will not be too comfortable."

"What about you? You've been used to luxury all your life."

"I have not been comfortable since friend of mine from university went mad in Peter Paul fortress, because it was so silent."

As if to illustrate, we all fell utterly silent and motionless. The ticking of the clock sounded unnaturally loud. Unnaturally, because there was no clock.

The sound had come from the corridor outside: the tap of light feet on the polished boards.

The sound stopped. Somebody knocked urgently next door.

Katherine looked at me uncertainly, then peered into the corridor. She went out and closed the door behind her.

"You won't take me?" Mrs. Auchinflint asked calmly.

"No."

"I never really meant anything, did I? It was just . . . getting what you wanted."

Rodominov shrugged, looking away.

"If you could just say you – felt something for me. . . ."

"Is true. Was like frozen pipes bursting. I was swept away in flood. You are passionate woman, Edit'. Was frightening."

Mrs. Auchinflint drew herself up, and very nearly smirked.

The door opened.

"Bart! Quick!"

I went out, followed by the other two. Claud was standing out there in the corridor in his dreaded school tie. His face was flushed and excited.

"Bart, he says he overheard Auchinflint! He's bringing up some soldiers to arrest Rody!"

"It's true, sir! I heard him talking to another officer! He's had them ready all afternoon. It's not a jape, sir, honest! That Russian chap you were talking about before, that's who they're after!"

Mrs. Auchinflint could think pretty quickly when she had to. "That message," she said, turning to Rodominov. "How did you get it?"

"Was left for me at tobacconist shop. Wery, wery important, you said."

"Rody, I didn't even know where you were."

They stared at each other.

"My husband sent it, I suppose," Mrs. Auchinflint said flatly. "To trap you."

Claud was jumping up and down. "He went to meet the soldiers, sir!"

"Where?"

"Down at the road! Where you come in to The Park!"

Rodominov shrugged into his cloak. He looked quite calm now, almost indifferent.

"That's the only way out," Mrs. Auchinflint said. "You'll have to go through the woods."

"Is not enough time. I would not get to sheep before eleven o'clock," Rodominov muttered. He looked at me. "I can fly out in your airplane?"

"Certainly not! Damn it all, man, you're a spy; I'm not helping a spy. And neither are you, Katherine, whether he's a friend or not. I have *some* patriotism left, damn it all! Besides," I added, "it's a single-seater."

"Goodbye," Rodominov said. He looked fixedly at Mrs. Auchinflint for a moment, then turned and strode rapidly down the corridor, his ridiculous cloak rising and billowing in the slipstream.

As I went out to the stables a few minutes later, after changing into my flying tunic, Katherine said, "We can't just – abandon him."

"Good Lord, Katherine, we've got to draw the line some-where," I exclaimed. I sounded terribly pompous. But, damn it all, one had to draw the line somewhere.

"It seems so awful. . . ."

"I'm definitely not helping," I said. "I'm determined from now on to keep out of trouble, and that's all there is to it."

There was a reverberating bellow from the corner of the house, off to the left. We were just in time to see Treadwell's red and white scout plane disappearing around the corner of the house, followed by a yelling pack of children.

"Hey!" I shouted. Stuffing my flying gear under my arm, I started to sprint after it.

"It's all right," Robert called out. "Treadwell's just warming it up for you, Bart."

I skidded to a stop beside him. "But where's he taking it?"

"Just taxiing it out to the west side of the field. Thought you might run it into a wall or something."

"Why doesn't he just take it up as well?" I said angrily.

"He thought of it, actually, but then remembered this was supposed to be your occasion."

"Him and his precious plane!"

I trotted after the Camel, muttering ferociously as I hauled on my flying helmet. Bloody Treadwell. And bloody Rodominov as well. The whole show was going to be ruined on account of that blasted Bolshevik. I mean, who was going to take any interest in a flying display when a maddened major came storming up to the house at the head of a squad of counterintelligence agents to arrest a foreign spy in a billow-ing black cloak? I'd a good mind to cancel the whole affair.

"Good luck," Mr. Lewis called out as I padded peevishly past him and a group of nobs. He waved. I glared back, muttering.

Crowds of people were streaming up to the red flags along the south side of The Park. I pushed through. "What's the matter, Major – late for your plane?" a pilot shouted. There was a wheezing guffaw and a lingering snigger.

I came panting and scowling up to the plane just as Treadwell was turning it to face down the runway. The roar of the rotary engine expired in a phutting sound, like a damp firecracker. Children were milling around, being shrieked at by their mothers as they came perilously close to the propeller, now that it was stationary.

"There you are," Treadwell said as he climbed out. "All ready to go. Don't forget to throttle back to 1,250 revs as soon as you're up. It's a brand-new Bentley. And go easy on the fine adjustment–"

"Oh, shut up about your lousy engine – or I'll rev it flat out all the way!"

"What's the matter with you?"

"Well! I'm perfectly capable of taxiing my own plane!"

"It's not your plane, it's mine."

I was hopping on one foot and driving the other into the sidcot trousers. There was a tearing sound. "Now see what you've done!" I shouted.

"Listen, old bean, you'd better calm down, or you'll strain the controls."

"Bloody hell! Look at my sidcot!"

A lady nearby said, "There are children present, young man. There's no need to use that language."

"Well," I muttered, red-faced, pouting, and sweating as I forced my way into the rest of the suit and rammed the goggles over the helmet.

"What's going on over there?" said a portly gentleman in cream flannels. He was standing on tiptoe, peering over the heads of the crowd. "I say, are we having a military tattoo as well?"

Other heads began to turn. There was a rising murmur as soldiers, with rifles at the slope, came into sight from behind the trees on the west side of The Park.

At the head of them, a revolver clenched in his fist, strode Auchinflint. A junior officer in full battle order was marching self-consciously alongside him.

Finding a party of armed men even more interesting than a gleaming red and white fighter plane, the children began to run, shrieking happily, as more and more soldiers appeared marching impeccably in fours. As we watched, the young officer beside Auchinflint called out a command, his voice incongruously shrill, and the men broke into a quick march that imparted a highly dramatic air to the proceedings.

More and more men appeared from the trees. Twenty-four, twenty-eight, thirty-two – what in God's name was Auchinflint thinking about? Forty, forty-four, forty-eight! Did he expect Rodominov to fight a pitched battle or something?

"What's that all about?" Treadwell asked.

"Stupid – *bastard!*"

Treadwell looked at me, startled.

Auchinflint had brought up sixty-four men! It was typical, typical! Attack head on. To move around the flank, that was sneaky and ungentlemanly. Send one man to reinforce a company and several dozen to move a piano. March in about two platoons of infantry to deal with one unarmed Russian prince instead of leaving the job to two Special Branch men and an inconspicuous warrant.

I suppose he wanted to create a stir. To show the rest of us that heroism wasn't confined to the front, that the staff could put on just as good a show when they wanted. Or he was proving something to his wife, perhaps.

I scrambled into the cockpit. "Switch off, suck in!" I shouted.

Treadwell turned and regarded me gravely.

"Go on, go on," I yelled. "*Swing*, you bugger!"

He looked off into the distance at the soldiers, who had now come to a resounding halt at the front door of the house. He shrugged and walked to the front of the plane.

"Switches off, petrol on."

"Yes, yes, switches off, petrol on!"

He hauled back on the propeller. "Contact."

"Contact!"

Treadwell swung and then ran for it, out of the way of the plane – there were no chocks against the wheels. The engine caught on the first swing.

A party of gentlemen were crossing the runway about a hundred yards away, strolling laconically in the direction of the house, pretending not to be the least interested in the sudden appearance at a garden party of two officers with revolvers in their hands, and sixty-four armed men. I opened the fine adjustment, pushed forward the throttle in the same quadrant. The engine bellowed and the plane jumped forward. The tail came up, rudder flicking. The leisurely gentlemen stopped, and frowned disapprovingly at the sight of the gaudy scout hurtling over the grass. It gradually dawned on them that it was heading straight for them. They started to trot, looking ruffled. Then, deciding that perhaps life should occasionally take priority over dignity, they ran, and flung themselves to safety between two flags, just as the Camel blasted past and jumped into the air.

I climbed on full throttle, so steeply the controls were mushy. The engine had twice the power of the one I'd been used to at the front. The scout went up like a lift.

It was at nearly 2,000 feet as it passed over the wood pasture beyond the house. I was making a climbing turn. I continued to bank, holding the mansion steady between the tips of the left planes, throttling back now, but only slightly. I was in a hurry to get around again and see what was happening.

As the front of the house wheeled slowly into view again, an extraordinary scene presented itself. The impeccable military formation had broken up. Men in khaki were running about, gesticulating wildly, trying to break through the crowd that was clamoring around them.

Then I saw the gaudy figure galloping across the grass toward the runway flags – a flailing figure in red and yellow, dressed like a woman but proceeding in distinctly male fashion, with great loping strides. For a moment I thought Rodominov's espionage activities had gone to his head and he was trying to escape in a dementedly inappropriate disguise. As if he didn't already look suspicious enough in that black cloak of his.

But then I realized it wasn't Rodominov who was running for his life. It was Michael. He must have thought the soldiers had come for him.

And they were, now. The moment he'd made a break for it they must have jumped to the conclusion that he was their quarry. As I banked over the narrow avenue that led into The Park, twenty or thirty of the soldiers were streaming away from the swirling, excited crowd and charging through the tents after Michael.

I banked vertically and hauled back on the stick, and straightened out. The middle of The Park whirled into view. I put the wing over and dived straight toward the greenhouse. The greenhouse revolved rapidly, glinting and flashing in the sun. The Pitot rose to 170. The wings shook, the wires screamed. As the greenhouse grew large, I pulled back the stick and shot over it at the fantastic speed of 200 m.p.h. The Vickers guns and Aldis had been removed from the fuselage of the plane, but for some reason not the ring sight. I had an unusually clear view, over the howling engine, of a brilliant yellow, red, and black figure tripping and flailing over its skirt as it headed desperately for the cover of the trees. It grew rapidly larger in the ring sight.

Suddenly aware of the aircraft diving toward him, Michael staggered to a halt, gaping. He half ducked as the Camel howled overhead, still descending.

Soldiers now appeared in the ring sight. The red wheels of the Camel spun toward the ground. The grass was a rushing blur. The soldiers flung themselves in all directions. One of them fell over a guy rope. A tent collapsed. I jerked back the stick as the refreshment tent flung itself onto the scout. The house appeared, then jerked out of sight. Blue sky. Puffs of cumulus. A sharp horizon, upside down. Trees. Grass. A red flag. The field again. Soldiers, picking themselves up. Auchinflint, pointing his pistol at the fleeing Irishman.

He heard the Camel, still going at nearly full throttle. He saw it skimming the grass, headed straight toward him. He dived under a lemonade table. It heaved as his back struck it.

A frantic zoom. The plane almost cleared the maypole that nobody had yet danced around. They were dancing around it now, though, soldiers and scampering gentlemen. There was a barely discernible tug at the aircraft. As I soared over the rose garden I twisted around just in time to see the maypole slowly falling onto the biggest tent on the lawn, the red and yellow one. Gay streamers from the maypole fluttered from the Camel's wheel struts.

As I banked over the avenue again and dived back toward the field, a phaeton with yellow wheels came swaying out from behind the house, driven by a frantic-looking black horse and a Transylvanian sort of figure in a flapping cloak, looking like Count Dracula caught in the sunlight. Guests scattered as the phaeton skidded off the gravel and rose on one wheel, veering toward one of the sideshow tents. It failed to right itself in time, disappeared, then reappeared, wrapped in striped canvas.

I think I saw the whites of the horse's eyes as I screamed past, going in the opposite direction.

The beating of the rotary bounced back alarmingly loud from the front of the house. Then it stopped so abruptly I thought the motor had quit.

The next time I came around, the place was in such a shambles it was impossible to distinguish the military from the civilians, they were all so mixed and tangled up together in collapsed tents and overturned beer barrels and big glass lemonade tanks, the lot decorated with gay maypole bunting. The brass band was in full flight, presumably headed back for the peace and quiet of the motor-works. One of the morris dancers was waving his hanky like a flag of truce. As I banked toward the greenhouse again I caught a final glimpse of Michael. He was now just inside the wood, wrenching at his skirts, which seemed to have become entangled in a briar patch. He turned his blotched brown face upward as I thundered overhead.

I skidded to port in a steep sideslip, to where Rodominov was also having his difficulties, wrenching and flailing at the striped canvas that was flapping wildly behind the bouncing phaeton. He continued to gallop toward the road, and his sheep to Italye.

After throwing one or two halfhearted stunts, sort of to justify my presence in the air, I curved in for a graceful landing, buzzing the engine over the trees, leveling, sinking, holding off, then dropped daintily onto wheels and tail skid. The Camel rolled to a stop halfway down the runway. The engine fell silent. I climbed out, and looking really concerned, hurried over toward the seething tangle of ropes and limbs and bright-red faces and jumping, gleeful children, and staring pilots, and broken glass, and disgracefully swearing gentry, and ladies looking in dismay at their best dresses, and Auchinflint standing there without his cap or revolver, dripping with lemonade.

"I say," I said. "I say. I do hope the flying display didn't *upset* anybody."

There was utter silence. Even the children stopped clutching at each other and dancing about, and turned to look at me.

Mr. and Mrs. Lewis and Katherine pushed slowly through the disheveled crowd, looking around wonderingly. Auchinflint continued to stare down soddenly, seemingly incapable of uttering a word. Nearby, a flap of canvas heaved and the tousled head of a small private soldier appeared. He looked around, then slowly drew back under the canvas again.

Mrs. Lewis looked at me with her long, lined, haughty face. I braced myself.

For a moment the tense silence continued. Then she said, "Not at all, Bartholomew, not at all. It was an excellent display, excellent. Quite memorable, in fact; and definitely calculated to put Lady Smollett's garden party in the shade. Quite in the shade."

A side show groaned faintly and subsided in a heap around several little sticks, on which the coconuts were still jauntily perched.

End of Volume II of
The Bandy Papers.

Volume III will soon be available in this series under the title *It's Me Again*

OTHER TITLES FROM
DOUGLAS GIBSON BOOKS

PUBLISHED BY McCLELLAND & STEWART LTD.

THREE CHEERS FOR ME: The Journals of Bartholomew Bandy, Volume One *by* Donald Jack
The classic comic novel about the First World War where our bumbling hero graduates from the trenches and somehow becomes an air ace. "Funny? Very." *New York Times*
Fiction/Humour, 5½ × 8½, 330 pages, trade paperback

A PETER GZOWSKI READER *by* Peter Gzowski
The man who affected the reading habits of millions of Canadians gives us the work of a lifetime in this selection of his best writing, much of it never before published in book form.
Anthology/Essays, 6 × 9, 320 pages, hardcover

HATESHIP, FRIENDSHIP, COURTSHIP, LOVESHIP, MARRIAGE *by* Alice Munro
A new collection of nine stories by Alice Munro at her remarkable best. Simply unforgettable. Literature at its best by the writer Cynthia Ozick called "our Chekhov." *Fiction, 6 × 9, 320 pages, hardcover*

LIVES OF MOTHERS AND DAUGHTERS: Growing Up With Alice Munro *by* Sheila Munro
Part biography of her famous mother, part family memoir (with snapshots), part autobiography, this affectionate memoir will fascinate all of Alice Munro's legions of admirers.
Biography/Memoir, 6 × 9, 60 snapshots, 240 pages, hardcover

RAVEN'S END: A novel of the Canadian Rockies *by* Ben Gadd
This astonishing book, snapped up by publishers around the world, is like a *Watership Down* set among a flock of ravens managing to survive in the Rockies. "A real classic." Andy Russell
Fiction, 6 × 9, map, 5 drawings, 336 pages, hardcover

A PASSION FOR NARRATIVE: A Guide for Writing Fiction
by Jack Hodgins
"One excellent path from original to marketable manuscript. . . . It would take a beginning writer years to work her way through all the goodies Hodgins offers." *Globe and Mail*

> *Non-fiction/Writing guide, 5¼ × 8½, 216 pages,*
> *updated with a new Afterword, trade paperback*

AT THE COTTAGE: A Fearless Look at Canada's Summer Obsession
by Charles Gordon *illustrated by* Graham Pilsworth
This perennial best-selling book of gentle humour is "a delightful reminder of why none of us addicted to cottage life will ever give it up."
 Hamilton Spectator

> *Humour, 6 × 9, 224 pages, illustrations, trade paperback*

THE GRIM PIG *by* Charles Gordon
The world of news is laid bare in this "very wicked, subversive book . . . it reveals more than most readers should know about how newspapers – or at least some newspapers – are still created. This is exceedingly clever satire, with a real bite." *Ottawa Citizen*

> *Fiction, 6x9, 256 pages, hardcover*

NEXT-YEAR COUNTRY: Voices of Prairie People *by* Barry Broadfoot
"There's something mesmerizing about these authentic Canadian voices." *Globe and Mail* "A good book, a joy to read." *Books in Canada*

> *Oral history, 5⅜ × 8¾, 400 pages, trade paperback*

WELCOME TO FLANDERS FIELDS: The First Canadian Battle of the Great War – Ypres, 1915 *by* Daniel G. Dancocks
"A magnificent chronicle of a terrible battle . . . Daniel Dancocks is spellbinding throughout." *Globe and Mail*

> *Military/History, 4¼ × 7, 304 pages, photos, maps, paperback*

ACROSS THE BRIDGE: Stories *by* Mavis Gallant
These eleven stories, set mostly in Montreal or in Paris, were described as "Vintage Gallant – urbane, witty, absorbing." *Winnipeg Free Press*
"We come away from it both thoughtful and enriched." *Globe and Mail*

> *Fiction, 6 × 9, 208 pages, trade paperback*

OVER FORTY IN BROKEN HILL: Unusual Encounters in the Australian Outback *by* Jack Hodgins
"Australia described with wit, wonder and affection by a bemused visitor with Canadian sensibilities." *Canadian Press* "Damned fine writing."
Books in Canada

Travel, 5½ × 8½, 216 pages, trade paperback

DANCING ON THE SHORE: A Celebration of Life at Annapolis Basin *by* Harold Horwood, *Foreword by* Farley Mowat
"A Canadian *Walden*" *Windsor Star* that "will reward, provoke, challenge and enchant its readers." *Books in Canada*

Nature/Ecology, 5⅛ × 8¼, 224 pages, 16 wood engravings, trade paperback

HUGH MACLENNAN'S BEST: An anthology
selected by Douglas Gibson
This selection from all of the works of the witty essayist and famous novelist is "wonderful . . . It's refreshing to discover again MacLennan's formative influence on our national character." *Edmonton Journal*

Anthology, 6 × 9, 352 pages, trade paperback

JAKE AND THE KID: *by* W.O. Mitchell
W.O.'s most popular characters spring from the pages of this classic, which won the Stephen Leacock Award for Humour.

Fiction, 5½ × 8½, 211 pages, trade paperback

THE BLACK BONSPIEL OF WILLIE MACCRIMMON *by* W.O. Mitchell
illustrated by Wesley W. Bates
A devil of a good tale about curling – W.O.Mitchell's most successful comic play now appears as a story, fully illustrated, for the first time, and it is "a true Canadian classic." *Western Report*

Fiction, 4⅝ × 7½, 144 pages with 10 wood engravings, hardcover

FOR ART'S SAKE *by* W.O. Mitchell
"*For Art's Sake* shows the familiar Mitchell brand of subtle humour in this tale of an aging artist who takes matters into his own hands in bringing pictures to the people." *Calgary Sun*

Fiction, 6 × 9, 240 pages, hardcover

LADYBUG, LADYBUG . . . by W.O. Mitchell
"Mitchell slowly and subtly threads together the elements of this richly
detailed and wonderful tale . . . the outcome is spectacular . . . *Ladybug,
Ladybug* is certainly among the great ones!" *Windsor Star*
Fiction, 4¼ × 7, 288 pages, paperback

ROSES ARE DIFFICULT HERE *by* W.O.Mitchell
"Mitchell's newest novel is a classic, capturing the richness of the
small town, and delving into moments that really count in the lives
of its people . . ." *Windsor Star*
Fiction, 5½ × 8½, 328 pages, trade paperback

WHO HAS SEEN THE WIND *by* W.O. Mitchell
First published in 1947 this wise and funny novel of a boy growing up on
the prairie has sold over 750,000 copies in Canada, and established itself
as a timeless popular favourite. Complete text edition.
Fiction, 5½ × 8½, 384 pages, trade paperback

THE ASTOUNDING LONG-LOST LETTERS OF DICKENS OF THE
MOUNTED *edited by* Eric Nicol
The "letters"from Charles Dickens's son, a Mountie from 1874 to 1886, are
"a glorious hoax . . . so cleverly crafted, so subtly hilarious." *Vancouver Sun*
Fiction, 4¼ × 7, 296 pages, paperback

PADDLE TO THE AMAZON: The Ultimate 12,000-Mile Canoe Adventure
by Don Starkell *edited by* Charles Wilkins
From Winnipeg to the mouth of the Amazon by canoe! "This real-life
adventure book . . . must be ranked among the classics of the literature
of survival." *Montreal Gazette* "Fantastic." *Bill Mason*
Adventure, 6 × 9, 320 pages, maps, photos, trade paperback

THE HONORARY PATRON: A novel *by* Jack Hodgins
The Governor General's Award-winner's thoughtful and satisfying third
novel of a celebrity's return home to Vancouver Island mixes comedy and
wisdom "and it's magic." *Ottawa Citizen*
Fiction, 4¼ × 7, 336 pages, paperback

INNOCENT CITIES: A novel *by* Jack Hodgins
Victorian in time and place, this delightful new novel by the author of *The
Invention of the World* proves once again that "as a writer, Hodgins is
unique among his Canadian contemporaries." *Globe and Mail*
Fiction, 5⅜ × 8⅜, 416 pages, trade paperback

THE CUNNING MAN: A novel *by* Robertson Davies
This "sparkling history of the erudite and amusing Dr. Hullah who knows
the souls of his patients as well as he knows their bodies" *London Free Press*
is "wise, humane and constantly entertaining." *The New York Times*
Fiction, 6 × 9, 480 pages, hardcover

PADDLE TO THE ARCTIC *by* Don Starkell
The author of *Paddle to the Amazon* "has produced another remarkable
book" *Quill & Quire*. His 5,000-kilometre trek across the Arctic by kayak
or dragging a sled is a "fabulous adventure story." *Halifax Daily News*
Adventure, 6 × 9, 320 pages, maps, photos, trade paperback

THE MACKEN CHARM: A novel *by* Jack Hodgins
When the rowdy Mackens gather for a family funeral on Vancouver
Island in the 1950s, the result is "fine, funny, sad and readable, a great
yarn, the kind only an expert storyteller can produce." *Ottawa Citizen*
Fiction, 5⅜ × 8⅜, 320 pages, trade paperback

SELECTED STORIES *by* Alice Munro
"The collection of the year," said *Kirkus Reviews* of these 28 superb
stories representing Alice Munro's best. "The whole volume makes one
believe anew in fiction's power to transfigure." *Washington Post*
Fiction, 6¼ × 9¼, 560 pages, hardcover

THE MERRY HEART: Selections 1980-1995 *by* Robertson Davies
"A marvellous array of Davies' speeches and reviews, interspersed with
bits of his personal diaries." *Hamilton Spectator* "It's a happy thing that
the voice from the attic is still being heard." *Montreal Gazette*
Non-fiction, 6 × 9, 400 pages, hardcover

THE SELECTED STORIES OF MAVIS GALLANT *by* Mavis Gallant
"A volume to hold and to treasure" said the *Globe and Mail* of the 52 marvellous stories selected from Mavis Gallant's life's work. "It should be in
every reader's library." *Fiction, 6⅛ × 9¼ , 900 pages, trade paperback*

HITLER VERSUS ME: The Return of Bartholomew Bandy *by* Donald Jack
Bandy ("a national treasure" according to a Saskatoon reviewer) is back
in the RCAF, fighting Nazis and superior officers, and trying to keep his
age and his toupee as secret as the plans for D-Day.
Fiction/Humour, 6 × 9 , 360 pages, hardcover

TEN LOST YEARS: Memories of Canadians Who Survived the Depression *by* Barry Broadfoot
Filled with unforgettable true stories, this uplifting classic of oral history, first published in 1973, is "a moving chronicle of human tragedy and moral triumph during the hardest of times." *Time*
  Non-fiction, 5⅞ × 9, 442 pages, 24 pages of photographs, trade paperback

THE CANADA TRIP *by* Charles Gordon
Charles Gordon and his wife drove from Ottawa to St. John's to Victoria and back. The result is "a very human, warm, funny book" (*Victoria Times Colonist*) that will set you planning your own trip.
  Travel/Humour, 6 × 9, 364 pages, 22 maps, trade paperback

THE ICE MASTER: A Novel of the Arctic *by* James Houston
Part sea-story (involving a mutiny and a hurricane), part Arctic saga that tells of Inuit and Yankee whalers in the North in 1876, this rousing historical novel is "a straight-away adventure." *Winnipeg Free Press*
  Fiction, 6 × 9, 368 pages, 40 drawings, trade paperback

AN EVENING WITH W.O. MITCHELL *by* W.O. Mitchell
"A collection of 31 of Mitchell's favourite stories . . . which he regularly performed with ebullience and dramatic flair to delighted audiences across the country." *Toronto Star* "An excellent performance." *Saskatoon StarPhoenix*
  Anthology, 6 × 9, 320 pages, 30 photographs, trade paperback

HAPPY ALCHEMY: Writings on the Theatre and Other Lively Arts *by* Robertson Davies
"Far more personal than anything published under Davies's name, and all the more enjoyable for it" (*Edmonton Sun*), this collection shows the full range of his wit and wisdom.
  Non-fiction, 6 × 9, 400 pages, hardcover

THE LOVE OF A GOOD WOMAN: Stories *by* Alice Munro
"Her stories *feel* like novels," writes Robert MacNeil. The power of love – and of sex – is the theme of these eight marvellous new stories by the writer who has been described by the *Washington Post* as "our Chekhov."
  Fiction, 6 × 9, 352 pages, hardcover

ZIGZAG: A Life on the Move *by* James Houston
This "remarkable account" (*Books in Canada*) ranges from the Arctic to
New York and beyond and tells of Presidents, hunters, glass factory gaffers,
leopards, walrus, movies, bestselling books and 10,000-year-old meatballs.
Memoir/Travel, 6 × 9, 288 pages, drawings, trade paperback

BROKEN GROUND: A novel *by* Jack Hodgins
It's 1922 and the shadow of the First World War hangs over a struggling
Soldier's Settlement on Vancouver Island. This powerful novel with its
flashbacks to the trenches is "a richly, deeply human book – a joy to read."
W.J. Keith *Fiction, 5⅜ × 8⅜, 368 pages, trade paperback*

RED BLOOD: One (Mostly) White Guy's Encounter With the Native World
by Robert Hunter
The founder of Greenpeace looks back on a wild, hell-raising career.
"Hunter acts. He does things. . . . In all his adventures humour is a com-
panion, but he can also write angry political commentary." *Globe and Mail*
Non-fiction, 6 × 9, 280 pages, trade paperback

FOR YOUR EYE ALONE: Letters 1976-1995 *by* Robertson Davies
These lively letters, selected and edited by Judith Skelton Grant, show us
the private Davies at the height of his fame, writing family notes and
slicing up erring reviewers. "An unmitigated delight." *London Free Press*
Belles lettres, 6 × 9, 400 pages, facsimile letters, notes, index, trade paperback

W.O. MITCHELL COUNTRY: Portrayed *by* Courtney Milne, Text
by W.O. Mitchell
A beautiful book for all seasons, showing prairie, foothills, and mountain
landscapes. "Milne's photographs are as dramatic, as full of colour and
as moving as Mitchell's best writing." *National Post*
Art/Photography, 10½ × 11½, 240 pages, 200 colour photographs, hardcover

HIDEAWAY: Life on the Queen Charlotte Islands *by* James Houston
This gentle book is a song of praise to the rainforest magic of Haida
Gwaii, its history, its people, and the little green cottage the author loves.
"James Houston finally writes about his own backyard." *National Post*
Memoir/Travel, 6 × 9, 272 pages, 40 b&w illustrations, map, trade paperback

HOW I SPENT MY SUMMER HOLIDAYS *by* W.O.Mitchell
A novel that rivals *Who has seen the Wind.* "Astonishing . . . Mitchell
turns the pastoral myth of prairie boyhood inside out." *Toronto Star*
Fiction, 5½ × 8½, 276 pages, trade paperback

THE LIFE OF A RIVER *by* Andy Russell
This story-filled history of the Oldman River area in the foothills shows
"a sensitivity towards the earth . . . that is universally applicable"
Whig-Standard (Kingston)
History/Ecology, 6 × 9, 192 pages, trade paperback

SINCE DAISY CREEK *by* W.O. Mitchell
Being mauled by a grizzly has changed Professor Colin Dobbs's life; it
teaches him many lessons – about teaching, divorce, the law, and the love
between parent and child. "An irreverent, touching, life-affirming novel."
Books in Canada   *Fiction, 5½ × 8½, 336 pages, trade paperback*

THE VANISHING POINT *by* W.O. Mitchell
Carlyle Sinclair is a white teacher on a reserve full of memorable characters (including Archie Nicotine), who comes to understand the different
world he inhabits. This 1973 novel, mixing harsh reality and high
comedy, is "a superb book about Indians." *Saturday Night*
Fiction, 5½ × 8½, 398 pages, trade paperback

CONFESSIONS OF AN IGLOO DWELLER *by* James Houston
The famous novelist and superb storyteller who brought Inuit art to the
outside world recounts his Arctic adventures between 1948 and 1962.
"Sheer entertainment, as fascinating as it is charming." *Kirkus Reviews*
Autobiography, 6 × 9, 320 pages, maps, drawings, trade paperback